The Five-Pound Murders
An April Showers Murder Mystery

S C Southcoat

7

Books by S C Southcoat

Invitation to a Murder

The Five-Pound Murders

Written by Steven as Steven Turner-Bone

Friends and Enemies

The Enemy Within

Farewell to a friend

In need of a Friend

The Firebird Inheritance

ISBN: 9781838147822

Printed by Book Printing UK
Remus House, Coltsfoot Drive, Peterborough, PE2 9BF

Acknowledgements

To the people I owe so much and without whom, I could not have published this book.

My wife Sue: for her help, understanding and patience, while I created this work.

Also

I would like to give a big special thank you to Victoria Groves for proofreading this book for me and Sandra Hood for painting the scene through the window on the book cover.

Dedicated to my Mother,
Margaret Southcoat.

Author's Note

Driffield is a small market town in rural East Yorkshire. It is a friendly town with a feel of the 1950s about it, a town where shopkeepers know their customers by name. It is a place to meet friends and chat over coffee. A town where the pace of life is just that little bit slower than other bigger towns and cities in Yorkshire.

I have set my April Showers stories in the 1950s. At a time of great change in Britain, when the country was recovering following World War II. However, the financial recovery would take a long time to arrive. In the meantime, more than ever, Europe was politically and militarily divided. Britain and its allies found it had new enemies to guard against in the east.

In the midst of these changes, April Showers is a feisty young woman in a new age. Ahead of her time, she is determined to do things her own way in a post-war world where most women are still simply expected to marry and have children. Only April has aspirations of her own and the will to see them through to the end.

Chapter One   1

Chapter Two   22

Chapter Three   40

Chapter Four   53

Chapter Five   72

Chapter Six   92

Chapter Seven   114

Chapter Eight   134

Chapter Nine   154

Chapter Ten   172

Chapter Eleven   194

Chapter Twelve   211

Chapter Thirteen   233

Chapter Fourteen   241

Chapter Fifteen   255

Chapter Sixteen   270

Chapter Seventeen   290

Chapter Eighteen   309

Chapter Nineteen   328

Chapter Twenty   352

Chapter One

You know what it is like. One day starts much like any other. My story starts on one of those ordinary days. One where you least expect anything unusual to happen.

Should I be doing this? I asked myself whilst I sat in the lounge of the Bell Hotel in Driffield. I hadn't seen or heard anything from Holly for weeks. Whilst waiting for her to arrive, I couldn't shed my doubt about whether we were still friends or not. You see, when I telephoned her, she had been cagey about agreeing to meet me, making me think something had come between us. If she didn't turn up, I'd know for sure. I knew the lack of contact with Holly was as much my fault as it was hers. Picking up the telephone and arranging a date should have been easy, but somehow, I always found an excuse not to do it until two days ago. But now, the anguish I was feeling, whilst waiting for my friend to turn up, was making my stomach cramp. As I rubbed my itchy palms up and down the arms of my soft leather armchair, the comforting aroma of warm beeswax rose from the polished hide. I looked at my wristwatch; it was after eleven o'clock. She was late, even by Holly's easy-going standards. I wondered if she had changed her mind about coming. My self-doubt took advantage of me as I watched a couple sitting on the far side of the lounge. They looked as though they were enjoying each other's company. In fact, they looked as though they were blissfully happy together. He wore the uniform of an RAF officer. He was probably from the airfield just outside of town. She was long-legged, slim and blonde, in an elegant dress and high heels.

Fifteen minutes late, Holly breezed into the lounge, paused for a moment, spotted me and, with a beaming smile, swept across the floor full of confidence with her arms open wide in greeting. I was on my feet in a second, all doubts about our wounded friendship dashed and forgotten.

'Hello, sis,' said Holly, using the term of endearment I'd chosen for us both when we first met in London. 'I'm sorry, I should have called you sooner, but it's taken me ages to settle into the school routine and I put in so many out-of-school hours, it's unreal, but I love it. How have things been for you since our last adventure?'

'A bit of an anti-climax, really. At first, I received a lot of newspaper attention for discovering who had murdered Aunty Violet and then again when people heard about the size of the inheritance she had left to me. But as you would expect, there's been no publicity about the other business that Rex and I were involved in. That was all hushed up. But, I did have my holiday in Spain. Then shortly after I came home, I stopped living with my parents and got a place of my own. It devastated mummy when I left, but I still go to see her two or three times a week. She worries about me, though I think Daddy is glad of the peace. Work has returned to the normal routine of detective work, the only difference being, thanks to auntie's inheritance, I no longer have any money worries.'

I waved a hand at a passing waiter and informed him we were ready for our table in the restaurant. After checking the table was ready, he escorted us to our seats. As Holly and I became reacquainted, we continued our conversation whilst perusing the menu.

'It's been so long since I saw you last. What it is like being a drama teacher as opposed to a famous film star?'

'The teaching is great fun. I even think we have a couple of budding film or stage stars in the making. As for being a film star, well, as far as that goes, being a teacher is a whole lot less stressful. I don't have any lines to learn. The lines I need to know I can keep in my hand. It's a regular wage. The children are too young to be familiar with my films, so they don't care about my past career. I'm happier. Best of all, during the school summer holidays, I have time to spend with my parents in Norfolk.'

'What about Rex?' I asked before I could stop myself. I looked away, not wanting to look her in the eye, dreading the answer.

'Oh, Rex. He's a different story,' said Holly matter of factually. 'I told him I don't want to see him anymore. It's not that I dislike Rex. It's just that his life is just too complicated for me. I want a regular 9-to-5 guy who I can rely on. Not someone who has a job where he gets mysterious phone calls in the middle of the night and then disappears for days on end. And then, when he returns, can't say where he's been or what he's been doing. Also, I think the main reason he enjoyed being with me was that I was once famous and in the movies. But the main reason why I dumped him was because he kept asking about you.'

'Me! Why me?' I asked, astonished by her response. But before Holly could answer me, we were interrupted. The waiter returned, order pad at the ready. I sighed, frustrated at the interruption of our conversation.

'I'll have the Melon Glacé followed by the Dover Sole.'

'And I'll have the same,' said Holly.

'Wine, Ladies?'

'Just a half carafe of the house white,' I replied.

'I can't drink wine when I've got to go back to school this afternoon,' Holly whispered across the table. I made a show of turning in my seat to look around the restaurant.

'Well, I can't see any schoolchildren, and I don't believe many teachers come here for lunch, so I think you'll be safe with just one glass of wine.'

'What would I do without you, sis?' sniggered Holly.
I smiled across the table at my friend and then reached out, taking her hand in mine.

'We are so alike. In another life, we could have been proper sisters. I've missed you. I know, at half term, we'll go on holiday together. Now that I've been to Spain, I've got the urge to visit more places,' I said excitedly.

'As long as it was during the school holidays. And, I insist on paying my way. I will not have you paying for me just because you are filthy rich.'

'I'm not filthy rich,' I exclaimed, embarrassed by her statement. 'I just have the money left to me by Aunty Violet and the income from a few investments she made.'

Over our meal, Holly and I bounced ideas around about where we would like to go for our holiday. One half-carafe of white wine turned into two.

'Oh, my gosh; look at the time. I'm going to be late for work; I've got to get the bus back to school,' declared Holly, looking at her watch.

'It's Okay; I'll drive you; my car is just around the corner.'

'Excuse me, Miss, but aren't you Holly Starbrightly, the film star? My younger sister goes to your school. May I have your autograph, please?' It was a teenage waitress who'd been watching the two of us from the corner of the dining room.

Holly beamed a smile at the girl.

'I used to be Holly Starbrightly. Now I'm just Miss Wood, but I'll sign your autograph book for you.' Holly scribbled her stage name in the girl's book.

'Oh, thank you, Miss Starbrightly. Wait until my friends see this.' The waitress took her autograph book and slipped it into her apron pocket. 'Are you ready to order dessert, Miss Starbrightly?'

'No, thank you. We have to be going,' answered Holly. The waitress stepped away from our table, looking a little disappointed, and then went to attend to a new customer. Holly looked at me, 'I wonder if she'll ever forgive me for turning down her offer of a dessert?'

I laughed. 'She'll get over it when her friends see your autograph and make a fuss over it. You're right; it is time to get back to work. I'll pay for this; you can pay next time we have lunch together.'

'Thanks, April.'

I called the waiter over and handed him a five-pound note. 'Keep the change; we are in a rush.'

Holly and I dashed out of the hotel, found my car and five minutes later, just as the school bell was ringing, I dropped Holly off at the gates of Driffield Academy for Girls.

*****

Back in the hotel restaurant, the waiter took the five-pound note to the till to cash it in. The manager, having seen the five-pound note from across the dining room, followed the waiter. While the waiter gathered up the change, the hotel manager removed the five-pound note from the till and looked at it. Holding it up to the light, he turned it over and over in his hands, examining both sides of the banknote. The waiter looked on puzzled.

'Who gave you this?' asked the manager.

'The detective, Miss Showers, sir, but she and her companion have left. She said I could keep the change.'

*****

When I returned to my detective agency on Exchange Street, the hotel manager, Mr Parador, was in my office, waiting for me. As I entered, the hotel manager stood up. I noted his serious expression and that he hadn't greeted me as warmly as I had expected, considering I'd known him for several years.

'Martin, what brings you here? We had a wonderful lunch today; you must thank the chef for me.' I hung my coat on the back of the door and went round to my desk.

'Now, what can I do for you? I guess this is a business call and not pleasure?'

I watched Mr Parador remove a five-pound note from the inside of his jacket pocket and then slide it across my desk toward me.

'This is the five-pound note with which you paid for lunch.'

'Is there a problem?' I asked.

'This banknote is a forgery. It's the third one to turn up at my hotel this month. I'm sorry, April, I'm going to have to report this to the police, and give them your name. If you had been anyone else, I would have brought a police officer with me. May I ask where you got it from?'

I was stunned by Martin's accusation.

'I'm not sure. It may have come from a client or as change after buying some new clothes. Martin, I'm so sorry. I had no idea the five-pound note was a forgery. I've had the notes in my purse for a few days. Holly and I were having a girls' catch-up lunch. That's why I used it today. Let me exchange it for one-pound notes whilst I try to remember where I got that one from.'

'No. I must hand it to the police. The police are trying to discover who is distributing them.'

'Yes, I suppose you do. But I still have some one-pound notes to pay my bill. I take it you've no problem with those?'

'Not that I'm aware of. The problem is April. If a customer received a forged fiver from my hotel, it would destroy the hotel's reputation. I'd go out of business. No one would want to stay there. Find the person responsible for these forgeries for me. Have them arrested! Save my hotel!'

'You have my word on it, Martin. I will get right on to it.'

'Thank you. I'm sorry, April, but I still have to go back to the hotel to telephone the police and report the forged five-pound note you gave me. No doubt you'll be hearing from them.'

I followed Martin Parador out of my office and said goodbye. Then made my way to the East Yorkshire Savings Bank. My father is the manager of the Driffield branch. In his office, I explained what had happened at the hotel and asked him what he knew about the forged five-pound notes circulating in Driffield.

'Forgeries have been turning up around town for days. The police told me not to breathe a word of it to anyone except my staff. I have instructed the bank staff to make a note of everyone who tries depositing a forged five-pound note at the bank. Then when they cash up, I look for reoccurring names to see if it's the same person depositing them. Once I've checked the list, I pass the list on to the police. Unfortunately, I haven't found the same name cropping twice yet.'

'Daddy, you could have told me about the counterfeit notes. I am your daughter and a private detective. I could have started looking for this person ages ago.'

'I couldn't, April. I have to do what the police tell me to do. It's what my regional manager agreed with the Chief Constable. Counterfeiting is a very serious matter. It's not just some random criminal making a few pounds to pay the bills or buy a new car. These people make millions of pounds worth of banknotes. If the counterfeit money got mixed with our legitimate currency, it could ruin this country's economy. No one could trust the value of the pound in their wallet. All the banks would go bust, and the economy of the country would be ruined.'

'Yes, I suppose you're right. I have two more fivers in my purse; will you have a look at them for me, please?'

Father examined the banknotes.

'These two look fine to me. The ink on the forgeries is not quite the right colour, and the paper is not as good as the real ones.' He handed back the money.

'I have to find out who's doing this, Daddy. There is no need for me to mention the bank. It was Martin from the Bell Hotel who asked me to find the person responsible.'

'I don't know, April. Maybe you should leave this case to the police. The gang behind these forgeries will be a very ruthless lot and extremely dangerous.'

'Not on your life. I promised Martin I would investigate this, and I'm going to.'

With the echo of the warning from my father still ringing in my ears, I returned to my office on Exchange Street. As I opened the front door, Jennifer, the freelance typist from the office across the hall to my room, rushed out to greet me.

'Two policemen are waiting for you in your office. I told them you were out, and that I didn't know when you would be back, but they insisted on staying. They wouldn't tell me what they wanted,' said Jennifer in a low voice.

'I know what they want. Leave it to me.'

'Has there been a murder?' asked Jennifer, wide-eyed with curiosity.

'No. Let me talk to these two first. Then, when they are gone, I'll tell you what I know.'

Jennifer looked on as I took a deep breath and entered my office, closing the door behind me.

I confidently marched across the floor to sit behind my desk before offering a greeting to the police officers already seated in front of my desk. The elder of the two men was probably in his early forties and dressed in a smart, navy-blue, two-piece suit, crisp white shirt and maroon coloured tie. The other man wore a grey tweed jacket over a white shirt and striped tie, he also wore charcoal-coloured trousers which required pressing.

'Good afternoon, Gentlemen. I believe I know why you are here. My name is April Showers, Private Detective, and you are?'

The elder of the two pulled his warrant card out from the inside of his jacket. 'I'm Inspector Longstreet and this is Sergeant Rivers. We would like to know where you obtained the forged five-pound note that you tried to use at the Bell Hotel when you paid for lunch for yourself and a friend Miss Holly Wood, better known to some by her stage name of Holly Starbrightly? We will also be speaking to Miss Wood later today.' The sergeant, notebook and pencil in hand, wrote everything that was being said.

'Let me make it clear from the start, Inspector. Holly has nothing to do with forged five-pound notes. We were just two friends who hadn't seen each other for a while and were meeting for lunch. You have no right to involve her in this. I did not know that the five-pound note was a forgery, and I cannot remember exactly where I got it. I run a business; money exchanges hands. Do you know where every pound note and coin in your pocket has come from? Though I assure you, Inspector, I intend to conduct my own investigation into the forgeries.'

'This is police work, Miss Showers. It's not a job for private citizens to get involved with. Drop this case, Miss Showers. If you don't and you get in my way, I will arrest you for passing forged banknotes and interfering in police business. It's only because the hotel manager is not pressing charges against you that I'm not taking you down the station right now.'

'You have no evidence that I'm involved in the forgery business, Inspector. You've come here hoping to intimidate me and keep me away from investigating this crime, simply because I have exposed the ineptitude of the Driffield police before, and you don't like it.'

'Just remember this, Miss Showers. It is a crime to withhold evidence from the police, so anything you discover relating to this crime has to be handed over to me immediately or you will be arrested. Do I make myself clear?'

Inspector Longstreet got to his feet and headed for the door. His partner, taken by surprise at the speed of his Inspector's departure, hastily closed his notebook and followed him out of my office.

'Goodbye, Inspector,' I called to the back of the Inspector's head.

With the slamming of the front door to 23a Exchange Street, Jennifer stuck her head around my office door.

'Is it safe to come in yet?' she asked.

I took a deep breath and let it out slowly. There was no way I was going to deter her.

'Yes, come in.'

Jennifer rushed in and occupied the vacated seat in front of my desk, eager to hear about what the police had wanted with me.

'Is this a juicy bit of news, or is it just the police telling you to back off?'

I smiled at my friend and office mate.

'A bit of both, really. I paid for lunch with a forged five-pound note.'

'You didn't?'

'Yes. But I didn't spot that it was a forgery.'

'However, when I got back here, the hotel manager was waiting for me.'

'What did he say?'

'He wasn't happy. I apologised and said it was a mistake, and that I didn't know the fiver was a forgery, but he said he was going to report it to the police. I felt so bad about the whole thing. I ended up promising Martin that I would find out who was responsible for the forgeries. Later, when I went to speak to my father about the forged money, he said he knew all about them. Only, he'd been told to keep quiet about them by the police, until they had investigated where they were coming from.'

'Have you told Patsy and Annabelle about the fivers yet?' asked Jennifer.

'No, not yet. That was the next thing I was going to do.'

'This sounds like we need an office meeting. I'll make the tea and get the biscuits. You fetch Patsy and Annabelle. I'll be in your office in five minutes.'

I knew there was no way to get out of this impromptu get-together with my other office mates, so I went upstairs to inform Patsy and Annabelle of the meeting. Five minutes later, back in my room with a teapot, cups and a plate of biscuits scattered across my desk. I told my story all over again.

'Well, I know the Germans got up to that sort of thing during the war. Do you think they are still doing it?' suggested Patsy.

'I don't think so, Patsy. But it's one line of enquiry,' I reassured her.

'How can you tell the real fivers from the forged ones?' asked Annabelle.

'I'm not sure. It's something to do with the quality of the paper and the colour of the ink.' I explained.

'I don't see many five-pound notes,' offered Jennifer. 'All my clients pay by cheque or directly into my bank.'

'Mine pay me by cheque,' said Annabelle.

'I only get cash,' said Patsy. 'Usually a ten-bob note or silver.'

'What are you going to do about those two police officers?' asked Jennifer.

'Ignore them,' I responded glibly.

I looked at my watch. 'There is not much I can do with what's left of this afternoon. I'm going home to get a good night's sleep, so I'll be ready for a fresh start in the morning.'

Normally, at weekends, I sleep late, skip breakfast, and then go out with a friend for an early lunch, after which we like to do a bit of window shopping in Hull or Beverley. But, this Saturday, I was awake at my more normal time for a workday. The forged five-pound note and the visit from that obnoxious police Inspector playing on my mind. Lying in bed, staring at the ceiling, I knew I'd never settle back to sleep again until I figured out where the forged fivers were coming from and who it was who had given me one in my change. Thinking about it as I lay snuggled up in bed, I concluded the forgery couldn't have come from the bank or my grocery shopping. It must have been given to me in my change when I bought something expensive. That limited it to only a few shops. I had recently purchased a couple of new outfits from a good retailer in Driffield. The only other place was the draper's shop, where I had selected some very nice material and requested it made into new curtains for my house. I would start with those two shops and then work my way along Middle Street and then Market Place, asking the shopkeepers of the higher branded shops if anyone had bought goods with forged five-pound notes.

I started with the shop selling ladies' fashions. Mrs Hemmings is the proprietor. A stylish and business-like woman who had helped me to choose two outfits to start my wardrobe of smart, professional, but fashionable clothes to wear for work. She recognised me as soon as I entered her shop.

'Miss Showers, how nice to see you again! Are you ready for a couple more outfits?' She held out her hand for me to shake.

'Good morning, Mrs Hemmings, no, actually, I'm here on business. I have a rather delicate question to ask you. Have you at anytime come across a forged five-pound note when you have cashed up at the end of the day or unwittingly taken one to the bank?'

'Really, Miss Showers, How could you suggest such a thing? I run a respectable shop. I'm quite sure I could spot a forged five-pound note a mile away. The clientele that frequent my shop wouldn't dream of associating with the sort of people who are in that kind of criminal activity. I'm surprised you even considered my shop as a place that would deal with people like that.'

'I didn't mean to insult you, Mrs Hemmings, but I had to ask. You see, there is someone in town passing high-quality, forged five-pound notes and using them to buy goods. They gave me one, and I didn't realise that it was a forgery until I tried to spend it.'

'Good gracious, I hope you didn't pay for your new outfits with counterfeit money!' Mrs Hemming rushed to her till and opened the draw to examine her banknotes.

'Mrs Hemmings, if you had deposited a forged fiver at the bank over the past few days, the bank manager would have told you. Has he done so?'

'No, of course not; I would have told you if he had.' She wasn't convinced and continued to examine the paper money in her till.

Just then, a new customer entered the shop. Mrs Hemmings' demeanour changed to her more convivial character.

'If that is all, Miss Showers?' 'Good day to you, madam; how may I be of service?' Mrs Hemmings left me to give her full attention to her new customer. It was as if I no longer existed. So I left to try the next shop.

Mrs Blocking ran the draper's shop. A small, thin lady with long fingers. I noticed them when she had shown me some fabrics to choose from for my new curtains. Her fingers seemed to crawl across the material like a five-legged spider as she straightened and smoothed the fabrics on the display table. Her nimble fingers then gathered up the edge of the curtain material to show me the different headings I could choose from. This time, when I entered the shop, two other women were already inside browsing through bolts of floral cloth.

'I'm sorry, Miss Showers, your curtains won't be ready for a few more days,' said Mrs Blocking.

'Yes, I know, Mrs Blocking. May I ask a question about some material?' I led her to the side of the shop furthest from her other customers and, in a hushed voice, asked. 'I'm here in an official capacity. Have you received any forged five-pound notes from any of your customers?' Mrs Blocking stepped away from me with a shocked expression etched on her face.

'What are you saying? What are you accusing me of?' she retorted, somewhat louder than I had expected. The other two customers stopped talking and turned to give us the full benefit of their attention.

'I'm not accusing you of anything. I was simply asking if anyone had tried to pay for some material with a forged five-pound note.'

An audible gasp and then mutterings came from the ladies on the far side of the shop. They glared at me for a moment and then, to disguise their nosiness, turned back to the fabrics on the shelf, but did not continue chatting with each other.

'You're talking utter nonsense. Why would I pass on forged five-pound notes? You must be mad.'

'I'm not accusing you of anything, Mrs Blocking. I'm simply asking you if anyone has tried to pay for curtains or fabric with a forged five-pound note.'

'No, they haven't. I don't know why you should think such a thing about me. I run a respectable shop.'

'I'm not saying you don't. It's just that forged five-pound notes have been turning up in Driffield recently, and I'm trying to find out which shops the crooks have targeted to discover if there is a clue or pattern in the spending pattern of the perpetrators.'

'Well, why didn't you say so right from the start?'

'Please, forgive me, Mrs Blocking. I should have made a better job of explaining myself.' We were once again under the scrutiny of the lady bystanders.

'No, Miss Showers, to the best of my knowledge, I have not received any of your forged five-pound notes.'

I let out an exasperated sigh. 'They are not my forgeries, Mrs Blocking. Thank you; good day.'

I left the shop, looking back over my shoulder as I closed the door. The lady bystanders were at the counter with Mrs Blocking, their heads locked together, deep in conversation. I looked up and down Middle Street, wondering where to go next and uncertain if I would get an honest answer from any of the storekeepers. That was when I caught sight of the BP sign hanging at the entrance to the garage and car showrooms. The garage looked like a good place to try next. It would regularly receive five-pound notes when customers paid for vehicle repairs or bought spare parts for their cars.

Crossing the garage forecourt, I spotted a man in dirty overalls filling a car with petrol. The driver remained seated behind the steering wheel, waiting for the pump attendant to finish.

'Are you the owner of the garage?' I asked the man dispensing petrol.

'No, love. You need Mike Bentley; he's inside.' He indicated with his thumb to the car showrooms.

'Thank you.'

Through the large window of the car showrooms, four smart, highly polished cars faced the glass, all their chrome gleaming in the sunshine. More but older-looking cars were lined-up behind the ones on show at the front. Just to one side of the four smart cars, a man sat at a desk writing in a large book. As I entered the showroom, he looked up, spotted me, and closed the book. Ignoring the cars, I made straight for his desk. He immediately got up, the practised smile of a salesman printed on his face.

'Good morning, Miss, are you looking for a car? I'm sure I'll be able to find something that will suit you. Is it just for you, or do you need a family car?'

This time, I tried a different approach. Retrieving a business card from my handbag, I handed it to him as I introduced myself.

'My name is April Showers. I'm a private detective. Are you able to spare me a few moments? I would like to have a word with you?'

'That depends; what's it about?'

'I'm sure you know that forged five-pound notes are circulating in Driffield. The Bell Hotel has hired me to discover who is distributing them. My first job is to discover how many other businesses in Driffield have suffered at the hands of the forger.'

'Thank goodness for that. I thought you were going to say you had been hired by my wife.' He gave a nervous laugh. 'In answer to your question, yes, I've had a few come my way. The forgeries have always come to us from over-the-counter sales for spares. My lads are wise to the forgeries and bring me all five-pound notes to check when a customer hands one over. My bank manager showed me how to tell the difference between a real one and a forgery. I've told my lads to get the name and address of anyone using one of these duds so I can inform the police; for what good it's doing. The notes still keep coming in. Whenever I can, I get my customers to pay by cheque if they want to pay a large bill, but there are plenty of old farmers around here that don't trust cheques and banks. They like to keep their cash at home hidden under the floorboards or in their mattresses.'

'Do you have a list of customers who have given you a forged five-pound note?' I asked.

'Not here, love. I send one of the lads round to the police station each time I get given a dodgy fiver. Then, my lad will give the police the name or a description of the customer. It's the police who keep the list of names; ask them.'

'Unfortunately, the police are not in the habit of sharing information with people like me. But, thank you all the same. I'll leave you my card. If you get any more dodgy fivers, please save a copy of the person's name and address for me. That way, we may be able to help each other put a stop to these forgeries.'

'I'll look forward to it, Miss Showers. If only to get to see your pretty little face once again.' Happy that I seemed to have won him over, I moved on.

I tried a couple of other places but had no luck. It seemed to me as though whoever was passing the forgeries was limiting the places they were using them to businesses that regularly handled large sums of cash.

Chapter Two

With large numbers of military personnel stationed just outside Driffield and at bases in the surrounding area, the market town of Driffield was always busy, especially on Friday and Saturday nights, when many servicemen liked to use their weekend passes to escape the confines of the military camps. One of the new enterprises which had sprung up in Driffield was The Golden Shot indoor archery range.

Saturday
Robert Hood curiously browsed through the equipment on sale in the shop at the archery range while he waited for the instructor to arrive. As Robert whiled away the time, he noted the seven others who waited with him, suspecting they were also new students. Robert introduced himself to the closest person first, soon learning the names of all the other students. There was Doctor Pfeil, a local G.P. Terrance Nock, a road sweeper. Jack Frisket, a printer. Andy Stringer, an electrician. Fred Button, a plumber. Danny Gold, an RAF sergeant and Charlie Bowyer, an RAF corporal.

As the archery instructor came through to the shop, he collected a clipboard from the reception desk and introduced himself as Mr Bodkin.

'Please come this way, Gentlemen. I will show you the archery range and your equipment.'

The Golden Shot was in a converted warehouse close to the centre of town. The warehouse's long and wide-open interior was ideal for archery no matter what the weather was doing outside. Inside and along the far wall of the shooting range stood a row of evenly spaced targets. Each one stood resolutely defiant, daring a student to shoot at it.

'That's right, Mr Hood, draw the bowstring back with three fingers until it touches the tip of your nose, and you can kiss the bowstring with your lips. Aim along the arrow and then - release.'

The arrow whistled through the air, thudding into the target twenty yards away, finding the blue ring.

'Very good, Mr Hood, you scored a six; that was an excellent first attempt. You must take after your namesake. Only next time, keep your right elbow up a little higher before you release the arrow. Try again in your own time,' said the instructor.

'Namesake? Who is ya talking about?' Mr Hood's Texan accent gave away his nationality to all the other students.

'Robin Hood, Mr Hood. An English outlaw who robbed from the rich and gave what he stole to the poor.'

Mr Hood looked a little bewildered at the instructor's revelation about Robin Hood.

'Not in the states, he wouldn't have. The man sounds like a fool. Our outlaws keep all the loot for themselves.'

A titter of amusement rippled through the students.

'Yes, well, that's as may be, Mr Hood. I think we'll forget about English folklore for now and continue with the lesson.'

Mr Hood set his second arrow on the bow. Taking his time, he took a deep breath, then drew back the bowstring. His left hand, which was holding the bow, trembled under the strain of the increased tension from the stretched bowstring. The unleashed power of the bow as it bent fought against the muscles in his left arm. The slender bowstring bit into the fingers of his right hand as he tried to hold the bow steady whilst aiming. With so much to think about, holding the bow steady, keeping his right elbow up and aiming the arrow, he held his breath. Mr Hood's aim wavered over the gold-coloured centre of the target as his face turned red. He released his arrow, letting out a gasp of breath. The second arrow flew and struck the target a couple of inches closer to the centre ring than his first arrow. He smiled, pleased with his achievement and the cheers he received from the other students. However, the effort had brought sweat to his forehead and upper lip. The amount of effort he had had to use in achieving the improved score had been more than he had expected.

'Well done, Mr Hood. Carry on and shoot the rest of your arrows whilst I watch the next student.'

Robert did as instructed, only now, with everyone's expectations of him raised, he found it hard to coordinate everything he had been told. Kissing the bowstring while aiming the arrow, standing in the right position with his elbow at the correct height, his left arm having to be straight as he strained to keep the bow level without shaking and the bowstring biting into the fingers on his right hand. Each arrow he shot drifted a little further from the centre and towards the black and the white outer rings on the target. Archery was harder than he had expected.

'Now it's your turn, Doctor Pfeil,' said the Instructor. Robert took a seat and watched as the doctor stepped up to the shooting line for his one-to-one tuition. Listening carefully to the instructor, the doctor took up position and loaded his arrow on the bow, drew back the string, and loosed the arrow. It missed the target entirely, thudding into a safety curtain running the width of the wall behind his target. Robert didn't feel so bad now, seeing how the doctor had missed the target completely.

'It doesn't matter, Doctor; that happens to most people when they first shoot. All you have to do is adjust the point at which you are aiming a little and you will hit the target.' The doctor, red-faced, set his second arrow on the bow, took aim; and fired again. This time the arrow landed in the blue, scoring a five.

'Very good, doctor; carry on whilst I move onto Mr Frisket.' The instructor repeated his pattern of tuition with Mr Frisket, his first two arrows landing one in the white outer circle and one in the black circle. At least I got two in the target, he thought; and thanked the instructor before carrying on shooting the rest of his arrows.

The archery instructor took all eight of his new students through the basics of the sport, after which he suggested they all retire to the club bar for a drink and a rest before the next part of their lesson.

As all the students ended the first part of their lesson, they placed their practice bows on their stands. One student followed Robert.

'You're very good, Mr Hood. Have you done any archery before?' asked Mr Nock.

'Thank you. No, I haven't. I guess it was just a lucky start. Let's wait and see how well I get on with the next part of our lesson. But from what I saw, you looked like you knew what you were doing.' His American accent, clear and unchecked in the hollow space of the archery range.

'That's kind of you to say so,' said Mr Nock.

'May I buy you a drink, Mr Hood?' The request came from a different student.

'Yes, why not? And it's Robert.'

'Great, what'll you have? I'm Jack Frisket by the way.' Jack led Robert away from Mr Nock, who looked on, stunned and a little hurt at the audacity of his new acquaintance being whisked away from him and not being invited to join Jack and Robert. Two other men from the group hung back a little, heads together, whispering.

'What'll you have?' asked Jack as they reached the bar.

'A pint, please,' said Robert. Jack ordered two pints of beer from the barmaid.

'You like our English beer?' asked Jack, surprised. 'I thought you Americans only drank neat whisky.'

'Only in the movies, though we prefer our beer chilled, unlike you Limey's.'

Jack and Robert, drinks in hand, joined the rest of the trainee archers to listen to what their instructor, Mr Bodkin, had to say about the first part of their lesson.

'You all did very well, Gentlemen. Hopefully, when we return to the range, you will have relaxed a little. Just remember what I taught you in part one of your lesson. The next part will be a bit more fun. When we return, divide into teams of two. On your targets, you will find balloons. The winning team will be the one that bursts all their balloons first. Drink up as soon as we are all ready, we'll return to the range.' The students, eager to return to the archery range, finish their drinks.

Jack turned to Robert. 'Now we are pals, we can make our own team?'

'Sure, glad too. We'll show the rest of them how it is done.'

When they got back to the shooting range, they found each target had balloons attached to it. A small balloon in the centre and three larger ones randomly scattered across the face of the target.

As Robert and Jack collected their bows and arrows, Jack asked, 'fancy a wager for who can hit the most balloons? How about sixpence per balloon?'

'Yes; why not? But, why not make it a shilling per balloon? Let's say a shilling for those around the target and half a crown for the one in the centre?' suggested Robert.

'You're on,' replied Jack eagerly.

'Okay, Gentlemen,' announced the instructor. 'When I blow my whistle, you may start. Each partner in the team will take his turn to shoot until you have shot all six of your arrows. The team that bursts the most balloons wins. Good Luck!'

Mr Bodkin blew his whistle, and the competition began.

Jack shot first but missed his balloon. Robert stepped up to the line and loosed his first arrow, taking out the centre balloon with a loud bang that stopped all the trainee archers as they looked around to see who had scored the first hit.

'That's two and six you owe me,' cried Robert triumphantly.

Jack took his turn, missing the next balloon by a whisker. However, Robert hit the balloon dead centre with his next arrow. 'That's number two; you've got some catching up to do,' he laughed and prepared his next arrow.

'You sure you're not related to Robin Hood?' asked Jack.

The competition between them continued until Robert had burst all the balloons on the target. It also worked out that they were the first team to finish. While they waited for the other teams to catch up, Jack paid Robert his winnings.

'Well done.'

'Thanks. Honestly, it was just luck. I work well under pressure,' said Robert.

'What line of work are you in?' asked Jack.

'I'm an accountant. My firm designs roads, bridges, houses that sort of thing. How about you?'

'I own the printing business next door. I print everything from business cards to small magazines, but it's advertising posters that make up the bulk of my work. You know the kind of stuff, leaflets, shop window posters, flyers,' said Jack 'If your firm needs any printing done, just let me know, and I'll give you mates rates.'

'Thanks, I'll let my boss know,' said Robert.

Their conversation was interrupted when the instructor blew his whistle and drew his students around him. He singled out and congratulated the winning team and then went on to say that the students were free to continue practising for the next hour, after which he would be in the shop to help them with any advice on purchasing archery equipment. Rather than carrying on shooting, Jack and Robert followed the instructor to the shop to investigate what sort of equipment a beginner in the sport should buy and, after buying a bow and some other equipment, returned to the range to try them out. After another round of betting on who could get the highest score with six arrows, Robert finished the hour lesson with more winnings taken from Jack.

'Are you lucky with cards as well?' asked Jack.

'I like a game or two, but nothing too big,' replied Robert.

'There's a card game in the back room of the Black Bull pub in Leconfield on Tuesday night. Fancy trying your luck?'

'Yes, why not? I've got to give you a chance to win your money back.'

'Great, I'll see you there. The Black Bull is easy to find; it's on the corner of High Street and Arram Road.'

*****

Later that day, while sitting in the living room of his two-up, two-down terraced house, Terrance Nock stared at the wall where a piece of wallpaper had peeled away in the corner. One more irritation to add to his pent-up anger and resentment. He clenched and unclenched his fists, his mind battling with the loss of another friend.

Robert Hood had been taken from him just as he'd plucked up the courage to speak to him. Terrance sighed. 'If only I could only get my hands on that Jack Frisket!' He mumbled to himself as he slammed his fist down on the arm of the chair.

Terrance's memories tumbled back to his school days when all his troubles started.

It was just the same back then; he thought. He stared forlornly into the fire grate.

Everyone hated me; just because my dad didn't have a good job and because my clothes smelt a bit. It wasn't my fault my mum was always ill.

His thoughts jumped forward to his archery lesson.

I could have made that American my friend. He wouldn't have cared about my job or my past. But Jack bloody Frisket barged in and stole him away from me. What did I do wrong? I did what it said in that magazine. I made the first move by complimenting Robert on his archery skill. But it didn't work, did it? It's always the same; every time I try to make a new friend, someone or something spoils it for me. I hate Robert

Hood. I hate Jack Frisket. If only I could afford to buy some modern archery gear, I'd be able to impress them all. Then, they'd notice me and want to be my friend.

Terrance Nock turned around in his chair to look in shame at his bow and quiver propped up in the corner of the room. He'd bought them second-hand from a market trader to save hiring a set each time he went to the archery club. Terrance toyed with the idea of giving up on archery and selling his archery equipment.

I don't need friends. They're more trouble than they're worth. They only cause me pain.

He'd just about made up his mind to quit archer when doubt set in and had second thoughts.

If I'm serious about making new friends, I'll have to try again.

He looked at his photograph on the wall. It was of a young man in an officer's uniform, strong, proud and confident looking, a complete contrast to what he felt now. Then he surveyed his room. It was a mishmash of various bits of furniture and ornaments. Most of it was his parents' cast-offs or stuff he had bought in junk shops. Some pieces had been rescued after homeowners on his rounds had thrown them out.

His thoughts drifted back to his days before the war and to his job in the engineering works as a designer; he'd loved that job, but he'd struggled to make friends there as well. Then the war had come. The engineering works had taken a direct hit one night during an air raid and never reopened. So he'd joined the Royal Artillery as the war hotted up. Terrance smiled as he remembered receiving his field commission to second lieutenant. His bravery, in continuing to fight and then take charge, had saved the battle when his artillery battery had come under intense enemy fire and his officer had been killed. Under his command, his battery had held its ground and made the defining difference between winning and losing in the defence of the small town where they were stationed. The Germans had stolen Keith, Michael, and George from him when his battery took a direct hit. He'd been the only survivor, and it had taken him a long time to recover from his physical injuries. The glory he received following his promotion soon passed when his superiors realised his nerves were in tatters and any loud noise turned him into a trembling mess. The metal ones never healed and the army let him go, signing him off as medically unfit for duty.

Returning to an engineering job hadn't worked out; it was too noisy and would bring on his headaches. After many varied failed jobs, he'd started work for the council as a street cleaner. He liked it. He was his own boss when walking the streets, emptying litter bins, and keeping the streets clear of old newspapers, dog mess and discarded cigarette ends. The only trouble was no one saw him, and no one spoke to him. It was as though he and his dustbin on wheels were invisible.

Getting up from his armchair, he stood in front of the fireplace and looked into the wall mirror which hung above the mantelpiece.

'I do my best to keep myself clean and not smell,' he told his reflection just before sniffing at his armpit to make sure. From the corner of his eye, he caught sight of his only photo of his ex-wife. It stood at the end of the mantelpiece.

'I showed you, didn't I? I showed you what happens to people who leave me,' the venom in his voice was clear for anyone to hear, had there been anyone else in the room. He picked up the photo frame and studied it for a moment.

'I'm not going to speak to you for a week. That'll teach you,' he told the photograph before turning the photo frame to face the wall. Smoothing down his hair before leaving the mirror, he turned and went through to the kitchen to fill the kettle.

'I'll have a nice cuppa and read of my book before I make tea,' he told the empty room. 'Toast and honey tonight, I think.'

*****

'You coming into town for a pint tonight, Danny?' asked Charlie, as they walked back to the RAF station on the outskirts of Driffield after their archery lesson.

'Don't know mate. It's a bit of a trek there and back, and the beer is cheaper in the NCO's mess. Anyway, I'm short on cash. Most of what I earn goes straight to my misses and the kids. You know, if it weren't for the RAF paying for these archery lessons, I couldn't afford to do it.'

'What, even on a sergeant's pay?' exclaimed Charlie.

'Yes. The kids are growing up quickly. They always seem to need new shoes or new clothes. I tell ya. It was a brilliant idea you had about starting an airbase archery team and then talking Flying Officer Blenheim into asking the C.O. to pay for our lessons. Did he go for the idea straight away?'

'More or less, I was in his office when I saw his school trophies. I mentioned them to him and he told me how he'd been the county under sixteen champion. That's when I got the idea of starting an RAF Driffield archery team. I thought about it for a bit and then went back to him with the idea and asked if he'd teach me and a few lads what to do. He said he would ask the Commanding Officer if it would be Okay. The next day when I went to see him again, he said he'd got permission to go ahead with the archery team. It was a stroke of luck that Driffield had an archery club. F.O. Blenheim said he didn't have time to teach us the basics, but he'd got the C.O. to agree to us going to the archery club in town to learn and he would run the team on the airfield.'

'Brilliant,' said Charlie. 'It also gets us out of doing duties on the base and it gives us free time in town for our other social pursuits, with no one from the base to check on us.'

*****

Andy Stringer, the plumber, shouted through to the lounge from the kitchen. 'Fred! I'm finished in here. You can come in and do the wiring when you're ready. I'm going upstairs to the bathroom. I want to finish off the plumbing in there.' As Andy pulled his head out from the space under the sink where he had been connecting the hot and cold water pipes to the sink taps, Fred was standing in the doorway to the kitchen, watching him.

Another week and we'll have this house finished. How much do you think we'll be able to sell it for? asked Fred.

Andy remained sitting on the floor, resting his back against a kitchen unit whilst the ache in his back eased. 'I'm not sure until I do the final invoices for materials, but I reckon we'll be able to sell this house for about a grand, maybe twelve hundred quid; enough to make a nice profit so we can put a deposit down on the next one. Something bigger. The bigger the house, the greater the profit we'll make. With a bit of luck, it won't be long before we can go into the house renovation business full-time.'

'So long as I can still go to the archery range at the weekend. I need that time to help me relax,' replied Fred.

'No, don't worry, Fred. If everything works out as I've planned, you'll be able to buy your own house with its own archery range before very long,' said Andy.

'That would be great, but it's back to work on that housing estate on Monday,' said Fred.

'Don't complain, Fred. Just remember this. The more stuff we can nick from that council housing estate job to use here, the more profit we'll make when we sell this place.'

*****

'Doctor Pfeil! How may I help you?' asked the doctor as he answered the telephone. He picked up his pen, ready to make a note of what the caller was saying.

'Hello Doctor, it is Otto Schroder. My wife, Greta, is having difficulty breathing. Her asthma is much worse now. I'd like you to come out to see her. I am very worried.'

'Very well, Mr Schroder, I will come to see you immediately. Remind me of your address. Thank you. Keep your wife calm and get her to use her inhaler for now. I will bring an oxygen tank with me. If this attack does not ease after she has had some oxygen, she will have to go to the hospital,' warned Dr Pfeil. He put down the receiver and gathered together everything he needed to deal with Mrs Schroder's asthma.

'Hello doctor, please, come in. Greta is in bed. Let me carry the oxygen cylinder for you.' Otto Schroder led the doctor up the stairs to the larger bedroom of his two-bedroom terraced house. Greta lay in bed gasping for breath, her face pale and sweaty. Her husband stood the oxygen cylinder up next to the bedside table holding the mask and tube ready for when the doctor would ask for it.

Doctor Pfeil lifted Greta's hand and felt for her pulse, then removed a stethoscope from his bag and listened to her chest. Turning on the valve of the white cylinder, he took the mask from Otto and placed it over Greta's face, watching how she responded to the gas. Gradually, Greta's fight for breath eased and returned to a more normal rate. Without saying a word to the woman in the bed, Dr Pfeil placed Greta's hand on the mask as an indicator for her to hold it in place herself. Getting up from sitting on the edge of the bed, Doctor Pfeil indicated for Otto to leave the room ahead of him. Once on the landing, and in a low voice, the doctor spoke to Otto.

'Your wife's condition is quite serious, but not life-threatening, yet, but it soon will be if you don't get out of this damp house and find somewhere better to live.'

'I can't afford anywhere better, Doctor. We are Germans; jobs are not easy to get in England when you are German. Working at the tannery was the only work I could get. My wages are barely enough to pay for what we have now. I keep trying to find different work; just a few shillings a week more would make such a difference. Then we could get a better place to live than this. I've applied for a job with a printer; I hope to hear from him any day now.' An image of Jack Frisket from the archery club immediately flashed across the doctor's mind. 'Though, if we could, we would prefer to go back to Germany, but you know how things are there,' continued Otto.

*****

Kevin Bodkin locked the doors to the archery range and set off home, tired and worried. His archery range was in a converted warehouse off Eastgate North in Driffield and had been his dream to own. Kevin and his wife lived not far away on Bridge Street. As he reached his front door, he sighed, releasing the tension of the day. Inserting his key in the Yale lock, he pushed the door open. The aroma of home cooking greeted him; it smelt good. He considered himself a lucky man; Susan was an excellent cook, able to create tasty meals from the most meagre of provisions and never complained. As Kevin hung up his coat, Susan appeared at the kitchen door.

'Had a good day; would you like a cup of tea?' she asked, before popping back into the kitchen without waiting for an answer.

Her cheerful voice rang through to Kevin. 'Tea will be ready in a minute.'

Kevin kicked off his shoes, wiggled his toes and slipped his feet into his slippers.

'Come on, slowcoach, it's on the table,' called Susan.

Kevin's heavy heart lifted a little as he entered the kitchen and saw his dinner waiting for him.

'There's chocolate pudding and custard when you've finished that.'

Susan sat down and waited for Kevin to join her. She let him eat his mince, mushroom and onion in gravy with mashed potatoes and carrots, in peace. Then, as she cleared away their plates and put them in the sink, she asked, 'how did it go at work?'

She turned her back to him to remove the pudding from the steamer and turn the gas up under the custard pan.

'Slow,' confessed Kevin. 'Weekends seem to be picking up. It's just midweek when it goes slack. More sales in the shop would help a lot. The income I get from membership fees and renting out equipment only just covers the cost of the building. If you weren't working, we'd have nothing to live on.'

'Then there's nothing to worry about, is there?' responded Susan. 'The archery range will pay its way one day soon. You just need to be patient. One day, you'll own a string of archery ranges all around the country; just you wait and see.'

'I was actually thinking of closing the range on Mondays, Tuesdays and Wednesdays and getting a part-time job. I've applied for a job at Jack Frisket's printers, the one next door to the archery range. It would ease my money worries until the archery range gets busier.'

'Well, that's up to you, but I'm sure business will pick up soon. Have you thought about holding an archery competition? You could charge everyone five-bob to enter and the winner would get a five-pound voucher to spend in the shop. If you advertise the competition well before the event, it will encourage people to come to the range to practice more often in the hope it will help them win a prize.'

'That's not a bad idea. I'll give it a go,' said Kevin. 'What would I do without you?'

Chapter Three

Tuesday Night

Robert Hood found the red-brick pub on the High Street in Leconfield. Its wooden, painted sign above the door depicted an enormous black bull with a ring through its nose and a man in a white coat holding on to the bull's halter. Robert entered the pub; the air was thick with cigarette smoke, the smell of stale beer and raised male voices, which lulled as the stranger entered. Everyone's eyes were on him as they wondered who the stranger might be. Even though the bar was crowded, Robert spotted Jack easily, as he was wearing the same jacket that he'd worn at the archery range. He was speaking to another man.

'Hi.' Robert interrupted their conversation.

'Robert, great, you've made it.' 'Excuse us, Bill, I have business matters to talk over with Robert.' 'Let's get you a drink and I'll give Lenard the nod that we are here for the card game. He'll take us into his back room to meet the others,' said Jack.

'Lenard! A pint of your best bitter for my mate, if you please,' Jack asked the landlord as they approached the bar counter.

Lenard eyed Robert suspiciously, unsure of the stranger, wondering if he could be trusted. Lenard had already been warned by the police about after-hours drinkers in his pub. If they got to hear about the card games, he would lose his licence for sure. In return, Robert eyed Lenard with the same suspicion, wondering if this card game was a set-up. A means to fleece him of all his money. To be on the safe side, Robert had only brought twenty pounds with him, which was all he was prepared to risk. Jack started the conversation by talking about their archery lessons, telling Robert how he'd always fancied having a go at the sport, but never had the time or the money before.

'I come from Leeds, but I was sent to RAF Driffield to do my National Service. After my National service. I stayed here. I liked the area and the people. So I bought the printing business next to the archery club,' answered Jack to Robert's question about his print works.

'What's your line of work?' asked Jack.

'I'm an accountant in a small firm of accountants.'

'Too bad,' said Jack. 'I had you pegged as an oilman.'

'No such luck. I've never done anything exciting. I even missed the war in Korea because I was an accountant. The Army stationed me in Washington when I got called up. So you could say being an accountant did me a favour and may have even saved my life.'

A flash of something about what Robert had just said pricked the back of Jack's mind, but he couldn't expand it. He put it aside, eager to get to the game. They finished their drinks. Jack signalled for the landlord to come over.

'We've come for the business meeting,' said Jack. The landlord cast an eye over Robert. 'It's alright, Lenard, I'll vouch for him.' Lenard gave Robert a piercing look.

Robert picked up the unwelcome vibe from the landlord.

'I don't know, Jack. Maybe some other time.'

'It's okay Robert, Lenard has to be careful because he doesn't know you. The Military Police come in here from time to time looking for airmen out without a pass, and to ensure the ones that do have one don't get into any bother with the locals. You know what it's like, you must have done your National Service back in the states. When you get off base for the first time in weeks, the first thing you do is head to the nearest pub with your mates for a drink and meet the local girls. Most of the national service guys are too young and stupid to go look for a pub further away.'

Lenard came out from behind the bar, removing a key from his pocket. Jack and Robert followed him as he led them through a door marked Private, then into what looked like the landlord's living room. They continued to another door that the landlord opened for them. From the single illuminated light bulb, Robert saw a round table in the centre of the room. The bright light hung from the ceiling over a baize-covered table, which was surrounded by eight chairs, five of which were occupied. The rest of the room contained odd bits of furniture pushed into the room's corners. Boxes marked - Johnnie Walker Black Label - lined the entire length of one wall. The landlord allowed them to pass inside and then closed the door.

'Now then lads, this is Robert; he's a mate,' said Jack as he marched confidently towards the table. 'He likes a little bet now and then and would like to join us for a game of cards.'

As Robert sat down, Jack introduced him to each of the other card players.

'This is Stan, Bob, Pete, Colin and Danny Gold, you know, from the archery club.'

'Hi!' said Robert as each card player introduced himself. He gave a smile and a nod of recognition to Danny. Whilst introductions were still being made, the landlord returned with two bottles of Scotch and a tray of glasses. Unfortunately, it wasn't the good stuff lining the wall just a few feet away. As the evening progressed, Robert settled into the game, even winning a few hands, so that by eleven o'clock when the pub closed, he'd won nearly ten pounds. The other players seemed nonplussed by their losses. For Robert, the only problem was his winnings were all in coins, half-crowns, two bobs, and shillings. The coins made quite a bulky handful.

'Here, I'll do you a favour,' said Jack. He pulled out his wallet and removed a five-pound note. 'I'll swap this fiver for some of your change. I'm always running out of silver back at the print shop.'

Happy to exchange some of the coins for the banknote, Robert agreed. Just as Robert and Jack were leaving the pub, Jack asked, 'fancy another game next week?'

'Yes, I'd like that.'

Saturday

Robert didn't see Jack again until they met for their next archery lesson. The lesson went well for both of them. However, this time, Jack didn't offer any bets on who would get the highest score. Just before the lesson ended, Jack reminded Robert about the Tuesday night card game at the Bull.

'You still coming to our business meeting?' Jack asked cryptically, in case anyone else was listening.

'Yes, I'll meet you there like last time.'

'Great, I'll see you on Tuesday. Sorry, I must dash. I have a new customer who wants some printing done in a hurry.'

Tuesday evening

Robert arrived at the Black Bull pub, bought himself a pint, and sat in a window seat to wait for Jack to arrive. He didn't have long to wait before Jack strolled through the door and sallied up to the bar. He ordered a pint before turning to view who else was in the pub. Spotting Robert, he signalled to him, asking if he wanted a drink by pretending to drink from a glass. Robert shook his head and held up his half-finished drink. When Jack joined Robert with his own drink, they made small talk for a short while until the landlord came over.

'The meeting is about to start,' grunted the landlord.
Jack nodded, and both he and Robert got to their feet. With the landlord leading the way, they all went to the back room where the same five men Robert had met last week were waiting for them. As before, the landlord, after showing them into the

backroom, left and then returned with two bottles of scotch and a tray full of glasses before the game started.

After the first couple of hands, the size of the pot grew rapidly. Robert prepared for the sting. He was going to be forced out of the game by the size bet increases. He'd lose all his stake in the game or be forced to borrow money to stay in the game. But, to his surprise, the next person around the table announced, 'Call,' and laid his cards on the table. He had a pair of queens and a pair of aces. All the other players gave up and threw their cards into the centre of the table. But not Robert, he was holding four eights. As the other players waited for him to fold or show his hand. Robert drained his glass, looked around the table at the expectant faces, and then laid his cards on the table.

'Well, look at that,' said Jack. 'You're a dark horse; I thought you were bluffing. There must be a hundred pounds in that pot.'

Robert scooped up his winnings, unable to hide the delight written across his face.

'Well, that cleaned me out said one of the other men.'

'Yes, I've got to call it a night as well,' said another.

'Me too,' said a third. 'I wasn't expecting the pot to grow that quickly.'

'Right lads, next week we come prepared. Robert here seems to be having a streak of luck. We'll have to watch and learn from him,' said the dealer.

The circle of players broke up with some friendly banter and everyone vowed to meet up the following week. Robert filled his pockets with one-pound notes, fivers, and more than one handful of silver coins. Before leaving the pub, Jack took Robert to a table in the empty bar.

'I can change some of the silver for fivers if you like?'

Robert agreed and exchanged twenty pounds' worth of silver and twenty pounds of one-pound notes for five-pound notes. Robert's eyes opened wide as Jack pulled out a large roll of five-pound notes wrapped in an elastic band from his trouser pocket.

'You came prepared for a big game,' exclaimed Robert in a hushed voice.

Jack gave a wry smile. 'I'm ever hopeful of a big win and for that, you need a lot of cash. There's no point in playing cards if you're going to chicken out when the pot gets serious.'

'You mean the pots get bigger than tonight's?' asked Robert.

'Sometimes. The other players all have their own businesses. They're wealthy men and can afford their losses. However, when times are good, we sometimes play for big stakes.' As Robert sorted his coins into neat piles, ready for counting and exchanging for five-pound notes, Jack gave Robert a tip.

'By the way, I wouldn't go putting all that money in the bank, not unless you want to end up paying half of it to the tax man. Save it for our next game,' said Jack.

'Um, thanks, I hadn't thought of that,' said Robert.

'Good. I guess I'll see you at the archery club on Saturday.'

46

'Yes, sure thing,' said Robert. The friends parted company. With his pockets bulging with money, Robert drove home. 'They must think I got off the boat yesterday,' said Robert, gloating over his win. 'If they think they can draw me into a big bet and take me for everything I've got, they're sadly mistaken.'

Wednesday morning

Whilst Robert Hood sat at his desk in the GCHQ Scarborough office, his phone rang. The loudness of the voice on the other end of the line instinctively made him remove the receiver from his ear. The message was short, terse, and abrupt.

'Come to my office immediately!' was all the voice said.

Robert didn't need to ask who it was; he knew the sound of the Colonel's voice. He returned the papers he was working on to their file and then locked them in his desk drawer. Standing up, he straightened his tie and adjusted his jacket before leaving his desk. He quickly cast an eye over the other people working in his hut. They all kept their heads down, but he knew they couldn't have failed to hear the Colonel's angry voice over the telephone. Putting on a brave face, he marched from the hut to cross to the main building.

Entering the Colonel's outer office, his secretary, Miss Thornwick, without looking up, pointed to a chair. Robert sat without comment. He knew better than to ask Sergeant Thornwick why the Colonel had summoned him; he was in trouble. The minutes passed like hours; perspiration broke out on his upper lip as he wondered what he'd done wrong. If a bad report went back to his boss at Langley, he could be returned to the states and disciplined. Worse still, he could even find himself with a desk job any rookie could do until he'd kissed enough arse to earn a second chance at fieldwork. The hammering of the Sergeant's typewriter thundered in his ears like some kind of medieval torture until finally, the buzzer on the Sergeant's phone sounded. She stopped typing and looked across her desk at him, but Robert knew what it meant and he was already getting to his feet before Sergeant Thornwick said a word. The typist restarted her work. Robert knocked on the Colonel's door.

Colonel Bempton took off his glasses, dropping them on a file in front of him as Robert entered his office. The Colonel, his face red and full of thunder, remained seated. Robert shut the office door and stood at attention in front of the Colonel's desk.

'Your gambling sessions at the Black Bull Public House are over. If you go near that pub again, you'll find yourself up on charges and on the next aeroplane home! Do I make myself clear? Get out!' roared the Colonel, spittle flying from his lips.

Robert's back stiffened as he looked directly ahead. 'Yes, Sir. Thank you, Sir.' Dismissed, Robert about-faced military-style, and left the office, pausing for a second to catch his breath once the Colonel's door was closed. The secretary didn't look up but kept on typing. As he stepped outside the main building, he sucked in a breath of cool air, now came the real challenge, returning to his hut and desk to face his colleagues, each one would know from the grapevine that he'd just had a metaphorical caning from the headmaster. However,

Robert wanted to know how word of his gambling had reached the Colonel.

Thursday

Robert took the morning off work and went to his bank in Driffield to deposit his winnings from the card game. Now the Colonel knew about him playing cards, there seemed little point in hiding the fact he had the money. As he handed over the notes to the bank teller, she put the five-pound notes to one side before adding up the rest of the cash. She made a note of the amount on a slip of paper before adding up the fivers, making a second note of their total amount.

'Would you mind just waiting a moment, please, Mr Hood? There is something I need to check with the manager?' The teller put up a closed sign and pulled down the shutter on her section on the counter. A couple of minutes later, Robert was approached by the branch manager.

'Good morning, Mr Hood; will you follow me, please? There is a small matter I would like to discuss with you about your deposit.' Confused by the unusual request, Robert followed the manager to his office, wondering if the bank manager's sudden interest in him had anything to do with work. Once in the manager's office, Robert was directed to take a seat at the manager's desk.

'I'm afraid, Mr Hood. I have to ask you from whom did you get these five-pound notes? You see, most of them are forgeries.' The manager waited for a reply.

Robert stared at the manager, unable to believe what he was hearing. If the Colonel found out the money he'd won in the card games was dodgy, he'd not only be out of a job, he'd probably end up in jail.

'I don't know. I can't remember.' He stammered. He paused to think, then went on to say. 'I've been saving five-pound notes for months. Any number of people or shops could have given one of them to me.'

'You must have been buying some expensive things to get this many five-pound notes in your change, Mr Hood. However, your account doesn't reflect that kind of financial activity.'

'Well, er, it all started with a win on the horses. With the winnings, I bought an antique vase which turned out to be worth more than I bought it for, so I sold it and bought something else, and so it went on. Buying and selling. All the transactions were in cash.'

'I see, so you have receipts for the items you bought and sold?'

'Sorry, no. The people to whom I sold the items kept the receipts that went with the antiques to prove their provenance. You know what antique dealers are like about fake antiques.'

'Yes, Mr Hood, I do, and I also know what the police think about people who circulate forged money. You are lying to me, Mr Hood. Stay here until the police arrive. You can tell them your story.' The bank manager reached for the phone.

'No, wait. You don't understand.' Robert pulled out his CIA identification card and showed it to the bank manager. 'I'm working with the British Secret Service. We are in a joint operation investigating the source of the forged banknotes. My job is to discover if your bank is involved in the dispersal of counterfeit money. You have passed my test. Clearly, you are not involved. However, I must ask you to keep up your vigilant checking for forged fivers whilst I search for the people responsible.'

The bank manager, surprised by Robert's security services I.D. revelation, readily agreed.

'Oh, yes, Mr Hood. I didn't realise you were part of the secret service. I will do whatever I can to help you, of course.'

'Thank you, I will stay in touch. If someone else tries to deposit a large amount of forged banknotes, contact me first, on this number.' He scribbled his name and telephone number on a page from his notebook and handed it to the bank manager.

After leaving the bank, barely able to contain his anger, Robert went straight round to Jack's printing works. The shop door at the front of the premises had a closed sign in its window. Robert looked at his watch, it was still mid-morning, so why was the shop closed? It was too early to shut for lunch. He tried the door and, finding it unlocked, entered the shop. Slamming his hand down on the bell sitting on the counter, it rang loudly, but no one came to see him. He rang it again repeatedly and called out.

'Hello, shop! Jack, are you there?' Silence. Robert waited a moment before he noticed it. The silence. It was too quiet. There should be sounds coming from the workshop at the back of the premises. Lifting the counter hatch, Robert went through to the rear to look for Jack Frisket. The work area was still, none of the machinery was running, and Jack was nowhere in sight.

'Jack! It's Robert; where are you?' As Robert made his way to the delivery door at the rear of the premises to see if Jack was out back, he almost tripped over Jack lying on the floor. Jack was lying partly hidden behind a bench, blood oozing from a hole in the side of his head. As Robert knelt to check Jack for signs of life, he felt a heavy blow to the base of his neck, before all went silent and black.

Chapter Four

Friday

At the security services, GCHQ Signals Intercept Station near Scarborough, Rex Barker, the station's resident MI5 agent, waited in the Colonel's outer office. Rex had been office bound for the past few weeks and was bored. Having been called to the Colonel's office, he hoped it would be good news, a new assignment. He looked at Miss Thornwick, curious to know more about the indomitable woman. Unlike the rest of the staff who worked within the GCHQ listening station, she insisted on wearing her army uniform to work, whereas everyone else, including the commanding officer, dressed in civilian clothes. The rumour around the station was that she had worked for the colonel during the war when uniform wearing was mandatory and that she remained in uniform in memory of a loved one lost on the beaches of Normandy on D-day. The only relaxation in formality she allowed in her office was the Busy-Lizzy potted plant on top of one of the filing cabinets.

Rex listened to the frenetic clickety-click of the typewriter keys as Miss Thornwick hammered out a letter or report for the Colonel. The only pause in the clatter came at the end of every line of typing when the carriage slammed back to its start position or the paper was changed for a fresh sheet before she started again. Finally, the buzzer sounded on the secretary's telephone and without raising her head to look at him; she instructed Rex to go through to the Colonel.

'Captain Barker, take a seat.' The Colonel's greeting was friendly though business-like. Before Rex had even got the chance to become seated, the Colonel began his explanation of why Rex had been summoned.

'I have a job for you, Captain. The East Germans have sent another agent to our neck of the woods.' Colonel Bempton slid a slim file across his desk towards Rex. 'I'd hoped we might have put them off the idea of spying on us after our last run-in with them, but it seems like they are here again. The man to whom I'd given this case originally is dead, but what makes it worse, he was an American on loan to us. He'd been seconded to our department from the Central Intelligence Agency as part of an exchange scheme. Now that he's dead, the Americans want to send their own people over to find the people who killed him, but the Home Secretary has put a stop to that, for now. He has persuaded the CIA Head of Operations in Europe to leave it to us to find the person or persons responsible for Robert Hood's murder. I've just got off the telephone with the head of British Intelligence. He has ordered me not to let the Americans run this murder investigation or we'll have gun battles in the streets. The Americans have to understand this is not the Wild West or Chicago, Barker. We will find out who is responsible for the death of the American agent in our own way. The trouble is, if Hood was murdered by this new East German agent, he must know we are looking for him, so he will have gone to ground for the time being. Hopefully, that will give us enough time to flush him out quietly. However, I don't want to risk any of our people going after him directly. He'll be looking for that kind of move. I want to come at him from a different angle. Do you think that lady detective friend of yours is up to the job of finding him?'

'I don't know, sir. It's a bit out of her league; she wouldn't know where to look. She may even end up getting herself killed.'

'No Captain, I didn't mean that I wanted you to toss her into the lion's den all on her own. I want you to remain at her side to assist her. So you can step in and take over when she finds the new agent. Thing is, Captain, she mustn't know she is after a foreign spy. Hood's death has to look like a straightforward murder over money.'

'Then, how is she to learn about who we are after, sir?'

'The dead CIA agent will be found with his neck broken in his own home. Miss Thornwick will act as the grieving widow and the person who has called the police. She will tell the police about a supposed intruder and hearing voices. She'll claim her husband was murdered by the intruder. Then, the following morning, Miss Thornwick will telephone Miss Showers and employ her to investigate her husband's death. She'll tell Miss Showers the police don't believe her husband was murdered, which they won't. I'll make sure of that with a phone call to the Chief Constable.

However, when Miss Showers turns up at the house, Miss Thornwick will have planted additional evidence just for her to see. It will link Robert Hood to the printing works in Driffield. Miss Thornwick will tell a slightly different version of the story about her husband's death to Miss Showers from the one she told the police in order to accommodate the new evidence and encourage Miss Showers to take the case. When Miss Showers starts her investigation and speaks to the police, they will verify the murder complaint by Mrs Hood. Then, as Miss Showers investigates the murder, you will stick close to her. Show interest in what she is doing, offer her your assistance, take her out for a meal, win her over; do whatever you have to do to get her to take the lead on this case and keep you involved until we know for sure who killed Robert Hood. However, there is also one more thing you need to know. When Robert Hood was found inside the print works, alongside him was the body of another man who'd had his head bashed in. He was the owner of the print works. His body is on ice for now. Just before Miss Showers visits the print works, we will replace his body for Miss Showers to find. I want to know why Robert Hood was interested in this man. I want to know who was killed first and who killed the second victim. Meanwhile, I'll get another, more official investigation going from here. If the East Germans are involved in these murders, I want them watching us and not Miss Showers. With a bit of luck, we may catch the East Germans with their trousers down.'

'Who did find the bodies, Colonel?'

'A local bobby on his late-night rounds. He saw a light on in the print works. He tried the door to the shop and found it unlocked, so went in to investigate. As soon as Robert Hood's identity was discovered, I was contacted. I telephoned the Chief Constable, explained the situation and got the constable suspended and sent to some out-of the-way-place where he'll stay until the investigation is complete. As an incentive for him to keep his mouth shut about who he had found, he'll get a promotion and transferred to a different town.'

'What will be the local police's involvement with the investigation?'

'They will find Robert Hood at home at the bottom of the stairs, indicating that he had suffered a fall.'

'I see. May I suggest that I take a temporary leave of absence so I can give Miss Showers my full attention?'

'Good idea, Captain, but don't forget to keep me informed of her progress.'

'Right, thank you, Colonel. I'll get on to it straight away.' Rex tucked the file the Colonel had given him under his arm, ready to return to his desk.

'On your way out, ask Miss Thornwick to pop in, will you?'

'Yes, Colonel.'

The Colonel's secretary took the seat offered to her opposite her boss.

'Miss Thornwick, I have a special request to make of you. You know about the death of Robert Hood, the CIA Agent. Well, with your permission, and if you are willing, I'm hoping that you will agree to help me by posing as Mrs Hood in an undercover operation. It is to entice April Showers into helping us with our investigation into Mr Hood's murder. The thing is, I don't want Miss Showers to know about our involvement in this case.'

Rex dropped the Robert Hood file into his briefcase, picked up his overcoat and headed out to the car park. It was a half an hour's drive from Scarborough to his and his parent's home in Wetwang.

Monday
'Hello, is this Miss Showers the private detective?'

'Yes, how may I help you?'

'My name is Mrs Hood. My husband died last night. The police told me he had fallen downstairs; however, I suspect he was murdered. I would like to hire you to investigate his death. Would you come to our house, please? There are some things you need to see.'

'I'm very sorry to hear of your loss, Mrs Hood, but if your husband was murdered, surely it is the police you should be talking to, not me.'

'Please, Miss Showers. I've tried to explain my suspicions to the police, but they keep saying my husband simply fell down the stairs during the night and broke his neck when he landed on the floor. They say there is no evidence of an intruder, so unless I pushed him down the stairs, he must have missed his footing in the dark and fell. Miss Showers, my husband was not that clumsy. When you see the evidence the police have ignored you will understand why I think it was murder. Will you come out to the house and just look at the evidence for yourself? Then, if you tell me it was an accident, I will let the matter drop.'

I looked at my watch. 'Very well, Mrs Hood, I will be with you in about twenty minutes. But if I don't consider the evidence good enough, I will not take the case. What is your address?'

As agreed, I pulled up outside 30 Church Lane, Little Driffield, twenty minutes later. The black and white house was opposite the village duck-pond and had one of those old-fashioned-looking front doors made in two halves, top and bottom. The house, many years ago, would have had a thatched roof, but now had a tiled one. I spotted the closed curtains at all the windows even though the sun was shining, a sign that there had been a death in the family. As I approached the front door, it opened and a middle-aged woman stepped forward to greet me.

'Miss Showers, I presume,' the woman held out her hand, waiting for me to respond like-wise.'

'And you must be Mrs Hood. Please accept my condolences.' I shook Mrs Hood's hand over the threshold to the house before Mrs Hood stepped back to allow me to enter. There was no hall. The front door opened directly into the first room, which was Spartanly furnished with just a couple of straight-backed chairs up against one wall. Above them was a row of wooden pegs on which to hang coats. A quiver full of arrows hung from one peg. A man-sized raincoat from another. Propped up against a chair was a wooden longbow. As Mrs Hood closed the front door, I noticed that next to it stood an umbrella stand with two black umbrellas in it. Against the wall on the left was a stout brown wooden cupboard. Close by, a pair of wellington boots lay scattered in the corner as though they'd just been kicked off the wearer's feet and an old worn Persian carpet covered the central part of the tiled floor.

'Come through to the lounge; the kettle has just boiled, I'll make some tea,' Mrs Hood turned on her heel passing through another door that led deeper into the house. The lounge wasn't furnished much better than the first room. It contained a leather sofa and matching armchairs, only one of which was close to the fireplace, which was unlit. A bureau stood against the far wall and, though it was closed, papers lay heaped on top of it. Next to the bureau, but sat on the windowsill, was a black telephone. American football trophies occupied one end of the mantelpiece. The other end of the mantelpiece was empty.

'Take a seat. I won't be a moment.' Mrs Hood indicated I sit on the sofa in front of which was a coffee table. Whilst Mrs Hood was preparing the tea in the kitchen, I cast an eye around the room, noticing there were no photographs of children or family to be seen. In fact, the house didn't give off any sense that a family lived in it at all. It felt temporary, as though the occupants had no intention of staying. Mrs Hood returned with a tray loaded with a teapot, cups, plates and a Victoria sponge cake. I thought it odd that having been brought here to talk about the possible murder of the woman's husband; I was being entertained with a cup of tea and cake. As Mrs Hood poured the tea, I asked my first question.

'Your distress at the sudden loss of your husband is very understandable, Mrs Hood, but what is it that makes you think your husband was murdered?'

Mrs Hood set down the teapot and then paused to think for a moment.

'Last night, I heard voices coming from downstairs. Robert was talking to someone.'

'When was this, Mrs Hood?'

'I'm not sure. It was dark. Robert must have gotten up. I awoke when I heard the voices.'

'Did you recognise the voice of the person your husband was talking to?'

'No. All I can say for sure is that it was a man's voice.'

'Do you know what they were talking about?'

'No. I couldn't hear them clearly enough. They must have been walking about.'

'Were they arguing over something?'

'Yes, now you come to mention it. I believe they may have been.'

'And did you mention that to the police?'

'I can't remember; I suppose I must have done.'

'What did the police say to that?'

'They said that there was no sign of anyone else being in the house; no sign of a struggle, no upset furniture, so I must have dreamt it.'

'Didn't you find it strange that they dismissed what you had to say so flippantly in the light of your husband's death?'

'You have to understand, my mind was a muddle. I was still in shock after finding Robert dead.

'Yes, I understand. What was it that made you get out of bed?'

'The voices stopped, and then I heard a thud. After which, I heard a door slam. I called out to Robert, but he didn't answer me. That's when I got out of bed to see what he was doing. When I got to the top of the stairs, I saw him crumpled up at the foot of the stairs.'

'So he may have fallen down the stairs?'

'No. The lights were on. He could see clearly, and he would have called out had he fallen down the stairs. He didn't call out and there was no sound of him falling down the stairs.'

'I see. But if you said your husband was downstairs talking or arguing with someone, how could he have fallen down the stairs?'

'That's what I've been trying to tell you. He didn't fall down the stairs; he was murdered by the intruder.'

'You mentioned on the telephone that you have evidence that points to your husband being murdered?'

'Yes.' Mrs Hood stood up and crossed to the bureau. Opening the front of it, she removed a beige envelope and brought it back to the sofa. 'I found this in his desk. I showed it to the police, but they said they'd had no reports of money being stolen, so it must belong to my husband.' She handed it to me. Inside, I found a wad of brand new five-pound notes; one hundred pounds worth.

'Did Mr Hood usually keep this much cash in his bureau?'

'No. If he had a large sum of money to pay anyone, he would give them a cheque.'

I offered the envelope containing the cash back to Mrs Hood.

'No, keep it,' she said. 'It will act as a down payment on what I will owe you for starting the investigation.'

'Thank you.' It crossed my mind that some of the fivers could be forged. I'd get Daddy to check them. I put the envelope with cash into my handbag, a visit to my father being my next port of call after leaving Mrs Hood. 'Have you found anything else that seems unusual for your husband to have in his possession since the police have left?'

'No, but there's the black footprint on the kitchen floor. I've tried washing it off, but I can't shift it.'

'You mean it's not a muddy footprint?'

'That's right, follow me, I'll show you.' Mrs Hood arose and headed towards the kitchen. 'It's not paint either. I don't know what it is,' she continued.

Just inside the backdoor, Mrs Hood pointed to a faint, black boot print on the tiled floor.

'Have you mentioned this to the police?'

'Yes, I telephoned them when I realised that it couldn't have been Robert who had made it. They said that as soon as someone was free, they would send an officer round to look at it.'

I bent down and rubbed at the impression on the floor with my finger. It made no difference to the stay on the tile, but my fingertip became black. When I tried to clean the black stain off my finger with my handkerchief, it wouldn't come off. All it did was stain the white cloth, black. I showed my finger to Mrs Hood.

'You can wash your hands over there.' She pointed at the kitchen sink. A new thought occurred to me. This could be an ink stain. I put the handkerchief in my handbag for later investigation.

Whilst I washed my hands, I continued to question Mrs Hood. 'What did your husband do for a living, Mrs Hood?'

'He was an executive at a firm of accountants in Scarborough; Clayton, Irvin and Allerston.'

'Could the money have come from them?'

'Oh no, I told them about the hundred pounds in the envelope when I informed them about Robert's death.'

'That must have been very distressing for you. What did they say?'

'There wasn't a lot they could say except to offer their condolences. But they said the money must be Robert's, as he had no access to cash within the firm. They asked me when and where the funeral would be so they could send flowers.'

'To which funeral directors has your husband's body been taken?'

'Lovall and Makepeace, the funeral directors, in town.'

'I don't understand; why wasn't an autopsy arranged by the police? That would be the usual procedure.'

'I'm sorry, I don't know why. Maybe it was because a doctor came out with the ambulance and diagnosed the cause of death.'

'You never mentioned that a doctor had already seen your husband's body?'

'Didn't I, oh dear? It must have slipped my mind.' Mrs Hood moved away from the footprint and returned to the living room. I followed her. Once again seated on the sofa, I took a sip of tea.

'Had there been any changes to your husband's routine lately? Some different activity he was involved with, or someone new he was meeting?'

'He made a new friend when he began archery lessons in Driffield. Thinking about it, it was about the same time he'd started gambling again. I suppose the one hundred pounds may have been his winnings, and he was keeping it to one side to play cards with. You know what I mean. So he didn't have to take his gambling money out of our bank account.'

'Didn't he tell you about winning at cards?'

'No, he never mentioned it. I didn't like his gambling, but he was good at it.'

'Would he normally do things you didn't like, Mrs Hood?'

'I'm not sure what you mean. He enjoyed playing cards. Maybe he wanted to surprise me with a large win so we could go on a holiday, a cruise perhaps.'

Her answer seemed weak, but I knew from the little things my father had said in the past that some married couples kept their personal finances separate and secret from their spouses.

'Do you have an address for the archery club?' I asked. Mrs Hood crossed to the bureau and retrieved a leaflet which advertised the club. 'What about his gambling? Do you know where he went to play cards?'

'I'm not sure; I think he said something about a pub in Leconfield, but I know it was always a Tuesday night.'

'Leconfield is not a big place; it should be easy enough to find which pub he was using.'

'So you will take the case, Miss Showers?'

'Yes, Mrs Hood, I will. As you say, there are too many unanswered questions surrounding your husband's death.'

'Thank you, Miss Showers, I feel so much better now someone is taking my concerns seriously.'

'However, I still have to ask you a few more routine questions. Did your husband have any enemies that you know of?'

'No, not that I am aware of.'

'Have you noticed if anything has been stolen or removed from your house?'

'No. Nothing.'

'What about your finances? Do you or your husband owe money to anyone?'

'No, Miss Showers. We have always been very careful with our money.'

'What about your husband's gambling? Isn't that a little risky?'

'My husband's bank balance is quite healthy, Miss Showers. Would you like to see a bank statement?'

'Yes, please. Having an insight into your husband's finances may help determine where the one hundred pounds came from.'

'Oh, I see. Well, er, let me see. Where did he keep his bank statements?'

Mrs Hood went back to the bureau to look for a file of bank statements.

'I'm sorry, Miss Showers. I don't seem to be able to find them. When I do, I'll bring them to you at your office.'

For the first time, Mrs Hood had become flustered. Despite the recent passing of her husband and throughout my interview, she had remained calm, until now.

'It doesn't matter, Mrs Hood, later will do. I have one last question. Forgive me but, do you think your husband could have been having an affair?'

'Oh, no, Miss Showers, of that I am very sure.' Once again, she gave the appearance of a woman back in control of her situation.

'Thank you, Mrs Hood. I wish more of my clients were as sure of their spouse's fidelity as you are. That should be enough information to begin my investigation. I will telephone you if there is anything that I have forgotten to ask.' I closed my notebook, sliding my pencil into its spine. Just before leaving, I shook hands with Mrs Hood, they were cold and clammy. As soon as Mrs Hood closed the front door, I took out my handkerchief and wiped my hands clean before getting in my car. Spotting the black stain on my handkerchief reminded me I needed to find out what it was.

Back in my office, I put the handkerchief to one side and rummaged through my handbag for my nail varnish remover. A couple of drops of the solvent on the handkerchief loosened the stain and made it spread. Telling this was an ink stain. Next, I went through my notebook, putting down on a separate piece of paper a timeline of events as described to me by Mrs Hood. Below it, I listed the varying points of evidence she had presented to me. So much of what she had said made little sense. There seemed to be no motive for the murder; only Mrs Hood's suspicions.

Nothing was taken from the house.

Where had the one hundred pounds really come from? It seemed to belong to Mr Hood, even if Mrs Hood was unsure of where her husband had got it from.

Why weren't the police interested in it with so many forged fivers in circulation? The wad of five-pound notes had to be a clue. Daddy would tell me if they were forgeries or not.

The boot print in the kitchen wasn't mud or paint, as one would normally expect. It was an ink stain. I'd recognised it as soon as I saw it on my handkerchief after I tried to clean the stain off my finger. I pondered over the boot print for a moment. Why was there just a single ink impression on the kitchen floor and why was it still wet enough to transfer to my finger, if it had been there for a couple of days? Also, why wasn't there more ink on the kitchen floor? Could whoever had made the ink stain on the floor have taken their boots off when they noticed the stain? But in that case, why didn't they clean it up?

As I continued with my list, I added, must contact the police to ask them for the names of the investigating officers and the pathologist who went to investigate the sudden death of Mr Hood.

I made a note to visit the Golden Shot Archery Range. Asking questions at an archery club was going to be different from my usual interview locations. I knew very little about archery, so interviewing the other archers and watching them shoot would prove interesting. I would also have to visit Mr Hood's place of work. He must have had a friend or two there who could provide more background detail on Mr Hood's activities. Happy with the notes I'd made so far, it was time for me to go home and show the money to Daddy.

'Where did you get these from?' asked Daddy.

'They're from a new client. She said her husband died under suspicious circumstances, and she wants me to investigate his death. She said she found the money in his bureau but has no idea where the money has come from. When I saw it was all in five-pound notes, I thought it best to speak to you about them before I did anything else.'

Mr Showers put his glasses on and examined the first few five-pound notes in the wad, then quickly flicked through the rest.

'April, they are all forgeries. Have you informed the police that you have them?'

'No, I haven't. However, according to my client, the police have seen the money, but didn't take it.'

'Do you know if the police have examined the notes? Are they aware that they are forgeries?'

'I don't know. She didn't say.'

'The thing is, these forgeries are different to the one you brought to me at the bank. These are printed on the correct paper and use the right type of ink. But they are still forgeries because there are printing errors on them. We could have two gangs forging money, or these notes could be the forgers' latest attempt at perfecting their technique. It's the mistakes the forgers make in the design of their banknotes that lets them down; look I'll show you.' Daddy turned one of the five-pound notes over to the side with Britannia's face on. You see here, in the corners. The top left and bottom right-hand rim of the watermark should be rounded not pointed like the other two corners of the design?'

'Yes.'

'On these banknotes, they all have pointed watermark corners. It's the one thing that makes these notes easy to identify as forgeries, but you would have to know this to spot it. You must hand them in at the police station and tell them where you got the money from. Your client may be a link to the forger. What is her name?'

'Mrs Hood.' At the mention of the name, Daddy dropped the notes in his lap and sat up straight in his armchair, removed his glasses and looked at me using his serious face.

'What's the matter?'

'A Mr Hood was in my office a short while ago. He'd tried to deposit a forged five-pound note into his account. However, the teller at the desk spotted it and told me about it, but it wasn't one of these. It was of the same type you had been given. I called Mr Hood into my office intending to report him to the police, only he showed me his identity card and said he was working with the police investigating the forgeries. I had no reason to doubt him. His credentials looked real, but thinking about it now, I suppose his credentials could have been forgeries as well.'

'That's interesting. I had two unpleasant police officers interview me over the forged five-pound note I tried to use. Though neither one of them said his name was Hood.'

'First thing tomorrow, hand the forgeries in at the police station. You must let them deal with it. Forging banknotes usually involves dangerous, professional criminals; you could be putting yourself in serious danger if you continue investigating this case.'

I felt my heart miss a beat and my blood run cold at the thought of dealing with hardened criminals with no scruples about using violence and murder to get what they want. I remembered how close I came to being killed in my last big case. Daddy handed back the wad of money. 'Yes, Daddy, I will go first thing tomorrow.'

Mummy arrived and set down a tray piled high with fruit scones, butter, clotted cream and jam between Daddy and me. 'I made a batch of scones for the Woman's Institute tomorrow evening but decided my daughter was more deserving,' she informed us both. 'I'll be back with the tea in a moment; it's all made.'

Mummy's cooking was one of those things I missed now that I was fending for myself. We spent an hour eating, drinking and talking about how my business was doing and if I was taking care of myself properly. With Daddy's warning about hardened criminals fresh in my mind, I drove home, wishing I still lived with my parents.

Chapter Five

Saturday

After a disturbed night dreaming about Mr Hood's death, forged five-pound notes, desperate criminals lurking in dark alleys waiting to pounce on me and those horrid police officers hovering behind me gleefully waiting to lock me up, I was somewhat bleary-eyed when I finally awoke. Looking at the alarm clock, it read eight o'clock. What was I doing awake at this time on a Saturday morning? Then I remembered. Reluctantly, I got up and went downstairs for breakfast. However, Daddy was right. I had to hand the money to the police and tell them I had found more forged fivers. At least that was one up to me; the police should have taken the banknotes away to be checked. With a knot in my stomach the size of a football over my police visit, I only drank half of my tea and nibbled at my toast. I wasn't going to rush to get there.

I'd just placed my teacup and plate on the kitchen surface next to the sink when the telephone rang.

'Driffield 3726.'

'Good morning, April. It's Rex. As it's a beautiful day, I thought you might like to go for a drive?'

'You've got a nerve. Holly told me about you dumping her, and now you phone me as innocently as you please, expecting me to drop everything I'm doing to jump in your car. You're insufferable.'

'April, wait. It wasn't like that. We broke up weeks ago. Please, let me explain. Meet me for coffee in the lounge at the Bell Hotel in half an hour. Give me a chance to explain my side of the story.'

I didn't know what to say at first and just held the telephone to my ear, wondering if I should do as he asked or just slam the receiver down and ignore him.

'Please, April.'

Finally, I relented. 'Okay, I'll see you in half an hour.' I put the receiver down with an idea in mind. If Rex was keen to see me again, I reckoned it shouldn't take much to convince him to accompany me to the police station and give me a bit of moral support.

After arriving at the Bell Hotel, I made straight for the lounge and paused in the doorway. Rex was already seated with a tray of coffee and two cups in front of him.

Hmm, you're keen, I thought. Unbuttoning my jacket, I made my way across to him. He stood up as I approached, indicating to the seat next to him. I chose the seat opposite instead.

'It's been a long time since we shared a coffee; how are you?' he asked as I settled in my seat.

'Oh, you know, fine; and you?' I asked indifferently.

'Yes, I'm good; keeping busy.' He filled my coffee cup and handed it to me. 'I took the liberty of ordering some crumpets, just in case you'd missed breakfast.'

'What made you think I missed breakfast?'

'Just guessing, you arrived quicker than I expected,' he said with a smirk.

I narrowed my eyes as I looked at him, thinking what a conceited, smug, smart aleck he was. 'As it happens, I was already up and preparing to come into town. I have some business to do relating to a couple of cases I'm working on.'

'Working on a weekend; these cases must be important. Anything I can help with?'

'Not really. The police are already involved with one case of my cases, and I'm helping them to solve it. The other case I have doubts about. I've been hired by a woman who thinks her husband has been murdered. However, it'll probably amount to her having nothing more than an overactive imagination.' I was interrupted when the waiter arrived with a tray loaded with crumpets, butter, and jam.

'Help yourself,' said Rex. 'There's enough here to feed an army.'

Putting my coffee on the small table at my elbow, I took two crumpets, and put them on a plate; I loaded them with soft, creamy butter and a dollop of strawberry jam, then sat back, eating hungrily.

'What makes you think his wife is overreacting?' asked Rex.

I wiped away a spot of jam from my chin, before answering. The jam was threatening to drop into my lap.

'His wife found him at the bottom of the stairs with a broken neck. There was no sign of a break-in and as far as I could tell, no obvious motive for his death other than an accident in the dark. Mrs Hood says that she heard her husband talking to someone in the middle of the night, but she saw no one. The only real clue I have about any criminal activity is one hundred pounds in forged five-pound notes. Mrs Hood said she found the money in her husband's bureau, but she doesn't know where it came from. Mrs Hood suggested I should keep them as payment for taking the case. Only, I haven't told her that I've had the banknotes checked and that one hundred pounds is funny money. I'm leaving the police to interview Mrs Hood about the forgeries. I'm already aware that forged five-pound notes are circulating around Driffield. I was given one and unwittingly tried to pay my lunch bill here with it. What I have to discover is where they are coming from. Mr Parador, the hotel manager, has asked to look into it.'

'Do you have any clues as to where they are coming from?'

'No, not yet. According to my father, there doesn't seem to be a lot of them in circulation, thank goodness, but they have cropped up in Beverley once or twice. However, Driffield seems to be the distribution centre. More forgeries have been found here than anywhere else. The strange thing is; if you wanted to get rid of a lot of forged money, surely you would do it in a big city, not a small market town.'

'So, what's your next move?' asked Rex.

'Well, after I've handed in the forged one hundred pounds. I was planning on visiting the local archery club; it seems Mr Hood was a member there.' I started on the second crumpet, tasting the warm, melted butter which had soaked deep into the confection. There is something deliciously comforting about warm buttery crumpets in the morning.

'Great, I'll come with you,' said Rex. I left his suggestion hanging in the air until I had finished my coffee.

'Do you know anything about archery?' I asked, changing the subject.

'Not really, do you?'

'You amaze me. Here's poor little me thinking you know everything about everything. Well, I suppose there has to be a first for everyone.' I stood up and adjusted my jacket, ready to leave. 'Come on, you can walk me to the police station.'

'But my car is in the car park and you did say you wanted to go to the archery club as well?'

'Very well, if you insist.' I wasn't going to admit it to him, but I did like the thrill of being in his sporty, two-seat Jaguar.

At the police station, I asked the constable at the enquiry desk if I may speak to Inspector Longstreet.

'He's not on duty this weekend, Miss. Can I give him a message for you?' responded the constable.

'Is Sergeant Rivers available?' The constable checked the duty rota once again. 'Yes, Miss, would you like to see him?'

'I think that's the general idea, Constable,' interjected Rex impatiently. I turned and gave him an irked look that inferred to stand back and leave this to me.

'If you wouldn't mind, Constable, I have some information about a case he is working on.'

'What name should I give him, Miss?' I didn't answer but gave him one of my business cards instead.

'Very well, Miss Showers, I'll see if he can spare you a moment.' The constable picked up the telephone and dialled a number.

'There's a Miss Showers at the front desk to see you; something about a case you are working on.'

The constable put the phone down. 'He'll be right with you, Miss. Would you like to take a seat over there?' He indicated to a row of tatty, wooden chairs lined up against the wall. Moments later, Sergeant Rivers came through a door behind the enquiry desk. He was wearing the same clothes he'd had on the day he'd come to interview me, only now they were liberally covered in what looked like biscuit crumbs with drips of tea dampening his tie.

'Good morning, Miss Showers, come to confess all, have we?' The smile left his face when he caught the expression on Rex's face. The sergeant muttered something quietly to the desk officer, who shrugged his shoulders as they both stared at the man at my side.

With Rex at my shoulder, I stood before the enquiry desk.

Sergeant Rivers cleared his throat. 'Begging your pardon, Miss Showers, just a little light police humour. I understand you have some fresh evidence to show me?'

I slapped the envelope full of forged five-pound notes on the counter. 'Mrs Hood gave me these. She said that they belonged to her husband and that the police told her to keep them. My father is a bank manager, and I've had him look at them. Did you know all these five-pound notes are forgeries, Sergeant?'

'No, I didn't. Who is Mrs Hood?'

'So, it wasn't you who went to investigate the sudden death at Little Driffield the day before yesterday?'

'No. I've heard about it, of course, but it's not my case. So, this Mrs Hood and her husband are the forgers, well done, Miss Showers.'

I sighed in disbelief. 'No Sergeant, well, at least not Mrs Hood, or she wouldn't have given this money to me, would she?'

'Yes, I see what you mean. I'll inform Inspector Longstreet on Monday morning. I suspect we will go out and interview Mrs Hood.'

'As a matter of interest, what are the names of the pathologist and the two officers who went to Mrs Hood's house to investigate Mr Hood's sudden death?'

'That would be Constables Bill Flowers and Ben Potts. The pathologist was a chap called Doctor Weed. He was the one who reported it was an accidental death, with no suspicious circumstances. So, Bill and Ben left it at that.'

'Thank you, Sergeant. You've been very helpful.' Pleased that the encounter with the police had gone better than I had hoped, no doubt because of having Rex with me as a witness. We left the police station.

'Right then, that's job one done. To the archer club, Madam?' said Rex as he held his car door open for me.

'Thank you, Jeeves.' Once we were both in the car, I turned to Rex. 'Thanks for backing me up in there. I suspect Sergeant Rivers wouldn't have been as helpful had I been on my own.'

'You are very welcome, Madam, glad to have been of service.' He made a joke of tugging at his forelock. Rex can be endearing at times.

'Where is the archery club?' he asked.

'It's on East Gate North, according to the leaflet Mrs Hood gave me.'

A couple of minutes later, as we drove into East Gate North. We soon spotted a sign on the wall of a house, Golden Shot Archery Range. It had a big golden arrow painted on it, pointing down a lane alongside the house.

'We've found it,' declared Rex, as he rapidly slowed the car to enter the lane. I grabbed hold of the leather door strap to prevent myself from falling against Rex as the car responded to his sharp turn of the wheel. In the narrow lane, the sound of the car's powerful engine echoed off the walls, making it sound much louder. I imagined the growl of some mythical beast from the pit.

A turn to the right at the end brought us to the building housing the archery range. Attached above a door, a sign read, The Golden Shot Archery Range. It was the only thing that looked new about the place. I gave the front of the building a quick once over before getting out of the car. To the left, there above the building's double doors, I could still see the old warehouse name beneath the thin paint obscuring it. I looked at Rex, 'looks like a bit of dump, I wonder what made Mr Hood come to this place?'

'Come on, let's get this over with, then we can go for lunch; my treat.'

Once inside, my opinions about the place changed. The shop/reception area inside the front door was clean, bright, and smart. The walls and ceiling were freshly painted and a new tiled carpet covered the floor. Archery equipment hung from the walls or stood on display stands and shelf units with racks of different styles of bows lining one wall. The man behind the counter greeted us with a welcoming smile.

'Good morning Sir, Madam; how may I be of service?'

'Good morning.' I fished a business card out of my handbag and handed it over. 'We are here to ask about a chap by the name of Robert Hood. I believe he was a member of your archery club?'

'Regrettably, I cannot help you, Mrs Showers. I am not at liberty to divulge information about our members.'

'It's *Miss* Showers and Mr Hood is dead, possibly murdered according to his wife, so he's no longer a member of your club. It's only a matter of time before the police make the same connection between this place and Mr Hood, as I have done, so by talking to me first, you may save yourself having the police pestering you and your membership.' I picked up a leaflet from the counter and read the name on the bottom, asking the man, 'are you Mr Bodkin, the owner?'

'Yes, and I'm also the archery instructor.'

'Good, you'll know who I'm talking about then.' Mr Bodkin's face changed through an array of expressions as he processed the information I just confronted him with. Rex stepped up to the counter, placing both his hands on the surface as he stared at the perplexed proprietor. Somewhat intimidated by Rex's stare and posture, Mr Bodkin wilted.

'Come with me. We can talk through here,' he instructed. He led us from the shop through to the archery range, where, on the far lane, one person was shooting at a target. From the range, he took us through to the bar where a young woman was polishing glasses.

'Would you mind looking after the shop for a bit, whilst I talk to these two, please Angie?' Angie put down the cloth and the glass she'd been polishing. 'Sure Mr Bodkin.'

'Can I get you both a drink?' asked the owner.

'Not for me, thank you,' I responded as I took a seat at a table. Rex simply shook his head before joining me. Mr Bodkin seated himself on the far side of the table.

'What happened to Mr Hood?' he asked.

'I regret to have to inform you that, yesterday, Mr Hood was found dead at home, his neck was broken.'

'Then why are you here? This has nothing to do with the archery club.'

'Foul play is suspected, Mr Bodkin. So I'm investigating Mr Hood's recent activities.'

The archery club owner looked from me to Rex and back again. 'If Mr Hood had really died under suspicious circumstances, it would be the police interviewing me, not you. What do you want?'

'The police will be here when they get around to it. Make no mistake about that,' interjected Rex.

I resumed my questioning. 'Mr Bodkin, Mrs Hood has hired me to investigate her husband's death. She is the one who pointed out his recent membership to your archery club.'

'I still don't see what Mr Hood's death has to do with me or the archery club?' insisted Mr Bodkin.

'There may be no connection at all, but at around the same time, according to Mrs Hood, Robert Hood started gambling. Do your members bet on archery matches?'

'Not to my knowledge. They're all amateurs; they're a long way from being completion ready,' insisted the club owner.

'Not even a little wager between themselves?' interjected Rex.

'How would I know?' snarled Mr Bodkin. 'I teach them archery. All I can add is that a bit of friendly competition between the students is a good way of improving their skills. If they are having bets between themselves, I know nothing about it.'

'So, Mr Hood made some friends in the short time he was here. Who are they?'

'I don't know,' blustered Mr Bodkin.

'You're trying to tell me you don't know the names of your students? That, you don't see them speaking to each other? And, you don't notice them congregating in groups to talk or share a drink here in the bar? You're not very observant for an archery instructor, are you, Mr Bodkin?' I said, pressing the floundering club owner a little harder.

'What I meant was that I don't socialise with them once they have finished their initial training. But some students do strike-up acquaintances; it's only natural. However, I know nothing about what they get up to away from the club.'

'I see. Very well, Mr Bodkin, who did Mr Hood form an acquaintance with?'

'I'm not sure, he chatted freely with all the students from his group, you know what Yanks are like, but I suppose the main one would be Jack Frisket.'

'Robert Hood was an American?' I couldn't hide my surprise.

'Yes, by the sound of him. I didn't ask him directly. I just made a joke of his name, you know, Robin Hood – Robert Hood. Only, he didn't get it at first. I had to explain to him who Robin Hood was.'

I suddenly remembered the American football trophies on the mantelpiece at his home.

'Thank you, Mr Bodkin. Just one last thing, I would like the names and addresses of all the students in Mr Hood's group, just in case he was socialising with one or two of the other students.'

'You can't; it's private.'

'Would you like me to come back with the police so all your students can see that something dodgy is going on here, or would you prefer to keep my investigation private and discreet?' Just at that moment, Angie popped into the bar.

'Your next group of students have arrived, Mr Bodkin.' I looked Mr Bodkin in the eye and gave him a pleasing smile.

'Right you are, Angie. I'm on my way. Miss Showers needs some assistance. Would you mind dealing with it for me, please?' He got up without saying another word and left me sitting at the table.

'I think you've upset him,' said Rex.

'Never mind, he'll get over it.'

Rex and I followed Angie back to the shop section of the Golden Shot club and waited for Mr Bodkin to take his new students through to the archery range.

'How can I help you?' asked Angie.

'I'd like the names and addresses of all the students in Mr Hood's archery group.' Angie paused, unsure if she should do as I had asked. 'It's alright; Mr Bodkin instructed you to help me. I'm investigating one of your ex-students. I'm sure Mr Bodkin will tell you all about him later on, I've no doubt.'

Armed with my new list of names and addresses, Rex and I left the Golden Shot. Rex opened the car door for me, so I stepped in to be cosseted by the soft leather of the passenger seat as I settled in. His car was far better than mine, but there was something special about my little green Morris Minor. Even though I could afford a better car, it had been with me from the start of my career as a private detective, and I felt as though we belonged together.

'May I see the list?' asked Rex before we set off.

'What now?'

'Why not?' He waited a moment for me to hand it over but when I didn't. He shrugged his shoulders, then looked at his watch.

'I'll take you to lunch. I know where there's a new Italian restaurant that's just opened.' He started the car and without another word about the list of archery club members, we drove out of the lane and headed into town. The drive only took a couple of minutes, but it was long enough for me to suspect that Rex was up to something. It wasn't him asking to see the list that made me suspicious, it was the way he gave in too easily.

As we stepped through the door of the restaurant, the bar was to the left. It was decorated with vine leaves, plastic bunches of grapes, small Italian flags, and raffia-wrapped bottles of Chianti. Italian stringed music played in the background. A waiter in a long white apron rushed forward, Signore, Signorina, welcome, welcome. A table for two, yes? Come this way, I have the perfect table for you. We were led to a table next to the restaurant window. The waiter pulled my chair away from the table so I could be seated. Just before I pulled my chair closer to the table, the waiter snatched my napkin from the table and, with a flourish of the hand, laid it across my lap. Once Rex and I were seated, the waiter introduced himself.

'My name is Giuseppe; whata would you like to drink? No, wait, I have something special for you. An Italian wine so perfect it will go with anything you would like to eat. You permit, Signore?'

'Yes,' said Rex.

'I bring the menu for you, thena I go get the wine.' Giuseppe shot to the bar, picked up two menus and returned to first offer me one, which was accompanied by a slight bow, and then handed the second to Rex. 'Scusi, I fetch the wine now. Oh, one moment, how could I forget.'

He produced a cigarette lighter from his pocket and lit the candle which was set in the old wine bottle in the centre of the table. Once he'd departed, looking over the top of my menu, I whispered to Rex.

'It's a bit intense here, isn't it? Not like the Blue Bell.'

'Relax, enjoy the fuss. Haven't you been to an Italian restaurant before?'

'No. Are they all like this?'

'Not all of them. I suspect it's a bit of an act. Just go along with it.'

'I don't recognise anything on the menu. What do you recommend?'

'Okay, leave it to me. I'll order for you.'

I lay my menu on the table and leaned a little closer to Rex. 'If it's anything like Spanish food, I don't like too much garlic or dishes with lots of fish.'

Rex smiled at me and nodded. 'How was your holiday in Spain?'

'Very nice. I think I'll go again someday, only next time I go with a friend.'

'Anyone special?' Rex asked, eagerly.

'Holly is keen to go with me. By the way, I hear you two split up. What happened?'

Rex looked disappointed. 'Oh, this and that. It just didn't work out.'

'I thought you two really had a thing together?'

'You know how it is. She's a teacher and I have my job. I'm not allowed to talk about what I do and she was always going on about the kids at school. We simply drifted apart.'

'But she knows what you do for a living. Why wouldn't you talk to her about it; not the detail, of course, but generally?'

'It's not the same. Knowing is one thing; telling her about what I'm working on is an entirely different matter.'

'Well, maybe you just didn't try hard enough,' I responded, somewhat sharply.

Rex suddenly sat upright. 'What! What has my relationship with Holly got to do with you?'

'She's my closest friend. That's what it's got to do with me. It was through me that the two of you met. And, if that's going to be your attitude, you can eat your lunch on your own.' I picked up my napkin and threw it across the table at him. Snatching up my handbag, I marched towards the exit.

'April!' called Rex in a pleading voice.

'Signorina!' called the waiter. I flung open the restaurant door, turned right and began striding along Middle Street towards Exchange Street where I'd left my car. If Rex was going to come after me, he would be hot on my heels at any moment, so I ducked into a dress shop, going straight to the back of the store to hide behind a rail of dresses that were on an end-of-summer sale. Spotting Rex outside the shop window as he cast around looking for me, I picked up two dresses at random, taking them into the fitting room. To my horror, it was a communal changing room, as in the more modern shops, not one with small private changing rooms. On the opposite side of the changing area was a rather large woman wearing pink bloomers and a straining corset. She was pulling a lavender flowered dress over her head. A young shop assistant was hanging onto the hem of the dress, trying to ease it over the woman's lumps and bumps.

'I've changed my mind,' I told the shop assistant, 'I'll leave them here,' indicating the dresses hung on the wall of the changing room. Going back through to the shop, I looked out of the window, checking for any sign of Rex in the street outside. He was nowhere in sight but I knew he was still out there trying to find me. I suspected the first place he'd try to find me would be at my office, so that meant I couldn't get to my car. As I wondered what to do next, I caught sight of a black and yellow East Yorkshire bus coming along the street. I knew the bus route it would take would pass close to where I lived. Waiting the minute or two at the bus stop as I watched the bus slowly make its way through the traffic towards me, it felt as bad as waiting my turn to go in to see the dentist. I had nowhere to escape if Rex found me before the bus arrived. The last thing I wanted was a scene in public, outside the shops.

When the bus arrived, I nipped up to the top deck, followed by the conductor. As the bus pulled away from the kerb, ticket in hand, I stared through the window trying to spot Rex. As the bus reached the end of Middle Street, Rex was still nowhere in sight. I let out a sigh of relief. Eventually, the bus left the busy centre of Driffield, heading out of town. My thoughts returned to the restaurant. I couldn't believe it. I was behaving like a teenager, not a grown woman. Rex was right. I had no right to interfere in his relationships. Now, I would have to apologise to him. I hated the idea of having to do so, but it had to be done. I consoled myself by agreeing to telephone him when I got home. Suddenly, I found myself getting to my feet and depressing the button to signal that I wanted the bus to stop. By the time I'd reached the platform at the rear of the bus, it was slowing and pulling in towards the kerb. The bus had only taken me a couple of streets away from the town centre, so it was an easy walk back towards my office to telephone Rex.

The converted house in which I had my office and shared with three female companions was eerily quiet. My companions, who also ran their own businesses from the premises, didn't work on weekends, except Patsy. She gave music lessons on Saturday mornings. But it was Saturday afternoon now, and I had the house to myself. As I closed the front door, on the inside, I found a piece of paper stuck in the letterbox flap. It was from Rex. It simply read.

Sorry, will call you at home later.

Scrunching up the note, I felt worse than ever. It should be me apologising to Rex. Suspecting that he was no longer in Driffield trying to find me and had gone home. I raced out again, slamming the front door behind me and hurrying to my car. I figured that by the time I got home, Rex should have arrived at his home in Wetwang. Which meant, if I was quick, I could telephone him before he called me.

Driving home a little faster than I should have done, I parked the car on the drive and rushed into the house, hanging my handbag on the coat hook in the hall next to the telephone stand. Snatching up the receiver, I dialled Rex's home number. It rang three times before being answered.

'Rex, I'm sorry. Let me make it up to you,' I babbled down the speaker before he could apologise first.

There was a silent pause on the other end before a female voice said, 'he won't be a moment dear; he's just come in.' I could feel my neck and face glowing as I waited for Rex to come to the phone. I'd never be able to face his mother again. Before Rex took the phone from his mother, I heard him ask her who it was on the other end.

'She didn't give her name. The only words I could understand were Rex, sorry and make-up.'

Rex's voice came down the wire. 'Hello, Holly?'

I felt a stab of pain in my heart. His first thoughts were of Holly, not me. I almost choked. I waited a moment before I spoke.

'No, it's April.' Clearing my throat, I continued. 'I'm sorry, Rex. I behaved badly, storming out on you the way I did. I don't know what came over me. Please forgive me. Let me make it up to you.'

This time, the silent pause was on the other end of the line. Then he spoke.

'It's fine, April. There's no need to apologise. I know how much Holly means to you. I should have realised.'

'That's kind of you to say so, Rex, but I'm the one at fault, and I know it. You can buy me lunch another day, but not at the Italian restaurant. It'll be a long time before I can face up to going in there again.'

Rex laughed, 'Okay, April, anything you say.'

'I'm going round to my parent's house for Sunday lunch, tomorrow. If you like, I could tell Mummy you will be coming too. We could go through the list of archery club members together.'

'That sounds great; are you sure your parents won't object to me dropping in?'

'Mummy, won't mind. I'll call her and tell her you're coming. I'll see you there tomorrow at about twelve.' Putting down the telephone, I felt a whole lot better after smoothing things over with Rex.

Chapter Six

Sunday

As I steered my car up onto the drive at my parent's house, they both came out of the front door to greet me. It was one of those things my mother did which had irritated me when I lived at home, but now that I had my own place, I looked forward to it each time I visited them. As we walked into the house, Daddy led the way and Mummy, her arm linked through mine, told me about the great idea she'd had after speaking to me yesterday. She had invited Rex's parents to lunch as well.

'It's been such a long time since we've all got together for a chat. I thought it would be lovely to invite them too,' she said, full of enthusiasm.

I had an inward groan as I recalled my inane babble down the phone when Mrs Barker answered the telephone instead of Rex. This was going to be an embarrassing encounter if she'd recognised my voice. The Barkers hadn't arrived yet, so Mummy led me to the kitchen to help her finish preparing Sunday lunch. There wasn't much to do except pipe a swirl of whipped cream onto each of the trifles we were to have for dessert and then dry a few pans as Mummy washed them. As we worked, she told me about Mrs Makepeace at the Women's Institute and how Mrs Makepeace upsets everyone by being domineering. Apparently, she is good at giving advice but not at taking it from others. After that, Mummy told me about the neighbours. They had hired a professional painter and decorator to paint the outside of their house, and so Mummy had persuaded Daddy to do the same. She went on to say, Mr Jones, Mummy's favourite butcher on the High Street, had retired and sold his shop. I listened politely to all she had to say, adding a few 'oh really,' when needed and 'she didn't' with a 'how sad' in the right places when all I really wanted to do was speak to Daddy. I wanted to know the latest news on the forged fivers situation in Driffield. Finally, the sound of another car pulling onto the drive sent Mummy scurrying to the front door; the Barkers had arrived. I followed Mummy, hoping to take Rex to one side for a private chat, but Daddy beat me to him.

'Sheltie, Bernard, how nice to see you again, you to Rex; come through to the lounge; I'll make us a drink,' said Daddy.

Mummy gave Mrs Barker a welcome kiss on the cheek, before escorting her to the lounge. I followed behind like a lost lamb trying to keep up with the flock. By the time I arrived in the lounge, Daddy was at the drinks cabinet, bottle in hand, pouring sherry into six glasses arranged on a tray. I don't know why Daddy wanted Rex with him. Daddy knew Rex wouldn't be able to talk about his work, so the conversation would inevitably turn to banking and golf, and I knew Rex hated golf. Mummy was already deep in conversation with Mrs Barker. They were talking about their respective fundraising ideas for the Women's Institute. After a couple of minutes, Rex gave up standing with the two bank managers and came over to me.

'How is the investigation business going?'

'Slow,' I responded. 'But, I've had a thought that I'd like to share with you, but it will have to wait until we are alone; apart from that, I plan to start my investigations in earnest on Monday morning.'

The sound of a bell ringing in the kitchen silenced everyone in the lounge.

'April; come and help me serve up. Charles, you take our guests to the dining room and get them seated. I've got a nice leg of lamb for lunch.'

So, whilst I put the boiled carrots, peas, cauliflower and roasted potatoes into Mummy's best dinner tureens, she placed the leg of lamb on a carving plate and then made the gravy from the juices in the roasting tray. By the time I'd finished delivering the vegetables to the dining room, Mummy had finished the gravy. She carried the roast whilst I followed with the gravy boat. As I entered the dining room, I was struck with a feeling of absence. Looking around, I searched for what was missing, and then it occurred to me, Holly wasn't here. I suddenly felt very guilty about the girl who I'd brought to East Yorkshire from London. She was my friend, my pseudo-sister, as I called her. She had lived with us for a while. She had risked her life helping me with my last big case. How could I have forgotten her so easily? The guilt I felt eased a little when

I looked at Rex. She wouldn't have come, not with Rex being here, not after the two of them had broken up. Feeling better about her absence, but still determined to have a day out with her shopping and going to the cinema, I took my seat at the table. Inevitably, it was next to Rex. I don't know what Mummy was thinking; what did she want, Rex, to chat me up in front of everyone?

As soon as lunch was over, I made a suggestion.

'Mummy, why don't you take Mrs Barker for a stroll around the garden, while Daddy takes Mr Barker into the lounge for a whisky or two so they can continue their talk about golf? Rex and I will do the washing-up.'

As the sink filled with hot water and I donned a pair of mummies washing-up gloves, and Rex brought through the dirty dishes from the dining room.

'Okay, you've got rid of the grown-ups,' said Rex playfully. 'What's on your mind?'

'Mr Hood. He's an American. When I went to his house to interview his wife. She never mentioned that her husband was an American. I didn't make the connection when I saw the football trophies on the mantelpiece in his house. No one except the archery club owner had thought to mention that Mr Hood was an American. Don't you think that is a bit strange?'

'Why, what difference does it make?' shrugged Rex.

'Mrs Hood never mentioned it. When I was speaking to her, I didn't hear she didn't have an American accent. She is English, so it never occurred to me that Mr Hood might be anything other than English until Mr Bodkin at the archery club mentioned it.'

'So what? It doesn't change anything.'

'It does. It adds a whole new dimension to the puzzle. What was an American by the name of Robert Hood, who said he'd never heard of Robin Hood, doing taking up archery in England? Why did a dead American have a hundred pounds of forged fivers inside his writing desk? Who would want to kill an American accountant?'

'Well, I suppose, when you put it like that, it may seem a bit odd.' But don't go jumping to conclusions; it could all still be a coincidence.'

'I don't think so. I think Mr Hood was involved with the forgeries. He was probably part of the gang and his job was to smuggle the forged fivers to America and dispose of them over there by getting them changed into dollars. But, during an argument with another gang member, Mr Hood gets himself killed.'

'Well, it's possible. But I don't buy it. What about Mrs Hood? If you are right, it would mean that she was also involved in his criminal activity somehow, so why would she call the police in and then hire you as a private detective to find his killer? If she was involved in what her husband was up to, she'd want to keep it quiet.'

'You may be right, but what if calling me in to investigate his death is just a rouse to deflect attention away from her? The police don't seem to be very interested in Mr Hood's death. I wonder if they know he is an American?'

'I'm sure they do. You need to find more evidence proving that Mr Hood was involved in a crime before informing the police of your suspicions, and you've no evidence against Mrs Hood at all. If you accuse her of being involved in her husband's murder, she'll take you off the case and you'll lose access to a vital source of evidence.'

'I know that. I'm just bouncing ideas around so I can think them through. Anyway, I'll know more once I've interviewed some of Mr Hood's associates at the archery club and spoken to the landlord of this pub in Leconfield where Robert Hood went gambling.'

'I'll go with you to the pub; remember what happened last time you went into a pub on your own?'

'I don't need reminding, thank you; however, I was hoping you'd want to come with me.'

Just then, Mummy and Mrs Barker returned from their tour of the garden, so I ended my chat with Rex.

'Come to my office on Monday morning,' I instructed.

'My, you have got through that washing-up quickly. I'll have to invite you to Sunday lunch more often,' beamed Mummy.

'Thank you for the lunch, Mrs Showers. It was an excellent meal,' responded Rex.

Monday

Rex arrived shortly after nine, breaking up my usual morning cuppa with my office mates. Jennifer gave me her *Oh yes,* look as Rex entered my office. She'd met Rex before and knew we were friends. Rex helped himself to the chair in front of my desk, and I took my place. Removing the list of archery club members from my handbag, I placed it on my desk for us both to see.

'I want to interview all of them and visit the pub in Leconfield,' I said, thinking aloud.

'Well, at this time of day, the pub will be closed,' added Rex.

'It could be the best time to catch the landlord; he won't be busy with customers.'

'I still think it's a bit early in the day; he'll have been up late last night, clearing up after Last Orders was called.'

'Good. If he's tired, he's more likely to let something slip if he's got anything to hide. We already know Mr Hood was going there to play cards, so we can use illegal gambling as a lever against him.'

'True, but Robert Hood was taken there by someone from the archery club. I think we should find out who that was first and get some more insights as to what else goes on at the pub before we confront the landlord.'

'No, we go to the pub first and question the landlord. After we leave him, he'll be so mad at the person who he thinks has informed on him, that he'll call and threaten them. Then, when I interview the members of the archery club, the one who's the most rattled will be the one who took Mr Hood to the Leconfield pub.'

'Yes, I see your point.'

'But there is one problem; it's Monday morning. Everyone I want to interview from The Golden Shot will be at work. I'll have to interview most of them after they get home.'

'Yes, of course,' conceded Rex.

'After visiting the pub we can make a list of all the printing businesses in and around Driffield and then pay them a visit; there can't be too many. I found a footprint in Mr Hood's kitchen. The footprint was made by someone who had stood in spilt ink and with Mr Hood having a hundred pounds of forged fivers in his house, it suggests to me that he might have been the one visiting a printing business unless he has a printing machine at home.'

'What about interviewing Mrs Hood again?'.

'I will, later. Once I know more about what her husband has been up to. Come on, by the time we get to Leconfield, the landlord should be up and preparing the pub for opening at eleven.'

'Okay, you go tell one of your office friends that you're going out for a while. May I use your telephone? I need to phone work and let them know I won't be in until later. You don't mind closing the door, do you? You know I have to be discreet in my kind of work.'

'Sure, go ahead.' I closed my office door and left Rex to make his phone call. Popping across the hall, I stuck my head around Jennifer's door.

'I'll probably be out all day. If anyone calls me, will you take their phone number and tell them I'll call them later?'

'Sure thing, have fun,' said Jennifer, and winked at me. I smiled back, closing her office door. As I turned around, Rex came out of my office.

'All sorted at the BBC?' I asked cheekily.

Rex told anyone who asked and didn't know his real work, that he was a radio technician for the BBC as he'd been a radio technician and operator in the army.

He chuckled, 'Come on, let's get going.'

We arrived at the Black Bull public house in Leconfield to find a rundown brick building on the corner of Main Street and Arram Road. A place that was long overdue for a lick of paint and interior lighting that penetrated into the corners of the public bar, as the windows along the wall that sided onto Main Street had been bricked up. The front door was closed, but not locked, so we went in. The stench of stale beer and cigarette smoke clung to the dirty walls and amber-stained paintwork. If Rex hadn't been with me, I would have turned away from the place immediately. It was just before opening time and we were the only people in the pub.

'We're not open yet.' barked the large sweaty man behind the bar.

'I'm looking for the landlord,' I replied. He fixed me with his pale, watery blue eyes.

'Who's asking?'

Pulling a business card from my handbag, I placed it on the counter.

'My name is April Showers. I'm a private detective. You host card games here on a Tuesday night. I'd like to know the names of the players?'

'Don't know what you're talking about. There's no gambling on these premises on Tuesday nights or any other night.'

'So, you must be the landlord. Mr..?'

'You're the detective. Figure it out.'

Rex removed a key from his jacket pocket and ran it the length of the bar, gauging out a deep line of brown, beer-strained varnish. 'Oops, I'm sorry; I seemed to have had a little accident with your bar top.'

'Hoy!' exclaimed the man behind the bar as he moved forward to push Rex away. Rex was quicker, with his free hand; he grabbed the man by the shirt collar and slammed his head down onto the bar.

'My colleague asked you a question; now be a little more polite and answer her,' snarled Rex.

The man tried to push away from the bar, but Rex held him tight. 'Fox, Lenard Fox,' he spluttered. Rex released him and returned to my side. Surprised by Rex's sudden burst of aggression. I gave a little cough and prepared to ask my next question as the landlord readjusted his clothing.

'Mr Hood came here on Tuesday nights to play cards; who with?'

'I don't know anyone by the name of Mr Hood!' insisted Lenard Fox.

'Do you need reminding that you are required to answer the lady's questions truthfully, Mr Fox?' said Rex in a low, menacing tone. Lenard licked his lips nervously and cleared his throat.

'A few regulars do like to play cards on a Tuesday night. I know nothing about playing for money. They just use a quiet room at the back for a few friendly hands of cards.'

'I see. Tell me, who is in this so-called theoretical, friendly card game?'

'Just a couple of local lads, sometimes one or two from the airbase, Jack from Driffield, and just recently there's been a new guy. All I can tell you about him is that he's middle-aged and a Yank from the way he speaks.'

'An American. Do you get many Americans in here?'

'No.'

'Would you be so kind as to show me the room where they play cards?'

'It's just a storeroom.'

'Then you've nothing to hide or be afraid of,' interjected Rex. Reluctantly, Lenard led us to the back of the pub and unlocked a door. Inside, I saw the table and chairs set underneath the room's single light, and the stacked boxes of whisky along one wall.

'You're getting ready for the Christmas rush a little early, aren't you, Mr Fox?'

'I buy it when it's cheap. Is that all? Can I get back to the bar? I could have customers waiting.'

'Names and addresses of the card players!' demanded Rex.

'I don't have names and addresses,' pleaded Lenard.

'Names will do,' I intervened.

Back at the bar, Lenard jotted down the names of the card players on a notepad, removed the page and handed it to me.'

'Thank you, Mr Fox. I know where to find you should I need to speak to you again.' Rex and I left the pub and went back to his car.

Back in Driffield, I went to wash my hands after being in the grubby pub. Then, I joined Rex in my office. Together, we compared the list that Lenard the landlord had given me to the one from the Golden Shot club.

'Look,' I said to Rex. As I pointed at one name on the landlord's list. 'Jack Frisket, his name is also on the archery club list.'

Rex gave me a knowing smile before saying, 'well, we'd better go pay him a visit.' He got up quickly and started for the door.

'What's the rush?' I asked.

'Oh, no rush. I just thought you'd want to go now.'

'I fancy a sandwich and coffee before we go. Interviewing him may take some time and I don't think very well when I'm hungry.'

'Okay, where would you like to go?' asked Rex.

'I usually go to the cafe in Market Place.'

'Fine, let's go, my treat.'

I got to my feet and picked up my handbag. 'You're being very amenable. What are you after?'

'Nothing. I just thought you'd like a little help with this case; that's all.'

I stopped next to my desk and stared at Rex. 'What you really mean is; that I can't solve this case without your help!'

'No, I didn't mean it like that. I just wanted to be helpful. I got the landlord to talk to you, didn't I?'

'So you don't think I could have got him to tell me what I wanted to know without you acting like a thug? There are more ways than brute force to get a man to talk. A few kind words and a smile go a long way.'

'Isn't that how you got into that mess the last time I had to rescue you?'

'You smug, male chauvinist, pig. Get out! I don't need you! Go back to your cloak and dagger games and stay out of my business!' I chased him from my office, slamming the door behind him. As I sat and seethed in my chair, a few minutes later there was a tentative knock on the door.

'Go away!' I screamed at the unseen person. The door opened anyway and a hand holding a cup of tea appeared around it.

'Fancy a cuppa?' It was Jennifer's voice.

'Come in,' I relented. With a cup of tea in each hand and a packet of chocolate digestives under her arm, Jennifer entered and then pushed the door closed with her heel.

'I thought you might want to talk?' She placed the teas on my desk, sat down, opened the packet of biscuits and waited.

'He an arrogant, egotistical, so and so,' I blurted out.

'All men are; you should know that by now,' said Jennifer. 'Treat them like children and they're fine.'

'You're married. It's different.'

'Maybe, but men are men all the same,' said Jennifer.

'Well, you can keep them,' I told her, unable to hide the disappointment in my voice.

'Have a biscuit. The chocolate has melted a bit where I've been holding the packet under my arm, but they still taste okay. I find chocolate calms the nerves.'

I took a biscuit and snapped it in half and then quartered it.

'Rub your tongue over the chocolate until it melts. It tastes much stronger that way.' I did as Jennifer instructed. Breathing through my nose, I let out a sigh.

'See what I mean?' she continued.

'I can't just eat biscuits for lunch; come on, I'll buy you a sandwich at Rosie's in the market. Go get your coat.' So whilst Jennifer went to get her coat, I took the teacups through to the kitchen.

Over cheese and ham sandwiches, tea and an apple turnover, we talked about men, work, what was happening or not in our daily lives and our hopes for the future. It was one of those conversations I'd missed now that I lived alone. Walking back to the office, I decided that this coming weekend, I would spend at least some of it with a friend instead of working.

As Jennifer returned to work, I retrieved my car keys from my handbag and said 'see you later,' to her.

Jack Frisket's home address was not far away. His name being the only one that appeared on both lists, he had to be the best person to start with. If he was out, I'd talk to his wife, maybe get some background on him and learn where he worked. I arrived at his terraced house five minutes later to find two pints of milk on the doorstep and a newspaper half shoved through the letterbox. It didn't bode well for finding anyone at home, but I went through the motions of knocking on the door and waiting. I knocked again, harder this time. No one answered, but an elder neighbour came out. She looked shabby and unkempt; her hair held up in a bun, her slippers stained and worn; she looked as though she lived alone. She looked me up and down, sizing me up. 'He's out.'

'I'm trying to find him. Do you know when he'll be home?'

'He should be at work, but I ain't seen nor heard him for a couple of days.'

I took another look at the milk bottles and newspaper. 'Does he live alone?'

'Aye. You're after him, are you? Does he owe you money?'

'No, nothing like that. I just wanted to speak to him. Do you know where he works?'

'He's got a small printing works on East Gate North.'

'Thank you.' I remembered that was also where the Golden Shot club was, and that there was a printing business next to it. As I started the car, I watched the old lady toddle across to Jack Frisket's house, removed his newspaper from the letterbox, tuck it under her arm, and then pick up a milk bottle in each hand before returning to her own home.

Turning into the lane that led to the archery club, I found the printing works and wondered why I hadn't noticed it earlier, but hindsight can be an unforgiving mistress. Driving past the archery club; I stopped outside the printing business next door. A sign on the front read 'Speedy Printers,' in larger letters and below it in smaller print, it read. All your office, shop and business needs at great prices. The archery club and the printers were the only two businesses nestled behind the houses down this back lane. The lane continued beyond the printers a short way, providing a turning space for delivery trucks and vans to turn around after drop-offs or pickups from the two businesses. I used it to turn my car around, so it was pointing in the right direction when I left. Parked in the corner was a red van with Frisket's Printers – Driffield, painted on the side.

There were no lights on at the entrance, although the sign on the door read open. Inside, all was quiet. I'd expected to hear machinery and presses working, maybe even someone working in the reception area, but all was still. I felt the prickle of goosebumps on my arms and a shiver ran up my spine. For a moment, I considered leaving but told myself not to be stupid.

'Hello! Shop!' I got no response. I looked for a bell to ring or a buzzer to press, but there was none.

'HELLO! SHOP!'

Faced with the choice of leaving or exploring further, the tingles running up and down my spine urged me to go on. A door to the side of the customer counter looked as though it led into the back of the premises. It, too, was unlocked. Pushing the door open, I called again. No one replied and no sound of working machinery came from within. Taking small steps, I went through the door and down a short corridor. I could see a room containing machinery at the end of the corridor. This was the main entrance to the printing room. Reaching the end, I scanned the workplace. There was no one around.

'Hello,' I knew I was wasting my time calling out, but it seemed like the right thing to do. I waited, taking in the layout of the workplace before me. Machines dominated the area closest to me. To the right were stacks of shelves containing tins of various sizes, rolls and boxes of paper and all sorts of other stuff I didn't recognise.

Set in the back wall was a large roll-up door opened by a chain, with an empty space in front of it for loading and unloading deliveries. Close by was a forklift truck. Its two lifting forks were still raised to chest height. It looked strange and menacing, like a mechanical beast with its claws out, ready to strike.

Now I'd come this far, there seemed little point in not having a good look around. Working my way between the machines, there was no sign of work in progress. In fact, the place felt cool, as though no work had been done here for some time. Continuing on, I came to the first of the shelves. Walking up and down the aisles between the shelving, I gave the contents of the shelves a cursory look. Apart from finding a few empty spaces, the items stored there meant very little to me apart from those marked printer's ink, or the different-sized boxes and rolls of paper. However, I did find a variety of paper targets; the type used at archery ranges. It was another link to the club next door, but hardly incriminating evidence.

Making my way to the end of the row of what I assumed were various types of printing machines. I spotted scattered sheets of paper on the floor. As I went to investigate what had caused the mess, I stopped, frozen to the spot. A man lay unmoving on the concrete floor, a red stain beneath him, pooling to one side. I put my hand out to steady myself against one of the printers as my knees went weak. It took a moment to regain my senses. However, taking a deep breath, I moved a little closer. Bending down to check for signs of life, I stopped just before touching him. He was dead, I knew it. His chest was covered in blood, which had spread out from around two small holes in his front. The blood on the floor had pooled to the side of his body and had become thick and black as it dried. His skin had taken on a pale, wax-like texture. Straightening up, I took a step back from the body. This was a job for the police. I looked around for a telephone, but before I found one, I heard the door at the front entrance open and close, followed by a man's voice shouting, 'Hello.' Looking around frantically, I couldn't see anywhere to hide. If it was the killers returning, I'd have to pretend I hadn't found the body by getting further away from it. I'd pretend to be a customer looking for the owner. As I returned to the corridor, heart thumping, rehearsing my lines in my head, the door at the far end opened and Rex's familiar frame filled the space.

'Thank God, it's you.' My relief at seeing a friendly face was so intense, I almost ran to him and threw my arms around his neck. Our previous disagreement was suddenly no longer important.

'I guessed you'd find this place,' he said.

I took a deep breath. 'There's a body in the back; I think it's Jack Frisket. He looks like he's been dead for some time.'

'Show me.' Taking Rex back to the body, he bent down for a closer look. 'Yes. I suspect he's been here a couple of days. Have you moved him?' he asked.

'No.'

'Have you called the police?'

'Not yet. I was just about to do so when you came in.'

'Good, then there's time for us to search the place. Let me lock the front door so we're not disturbed.' Rex returned a few seconds later. 'Frisket isn't in any condition to complain about us looking around, so we'd better get started.'

'I've already searched the place. Apart from the drums of printer's ink and packets of paper, there's nothing here to show he was producing forged fivers.'

'In that case, we need to look for clues as to where he was printing the banknotes,' insisted Rex.

I relented. I knew there was nothing on the storage shelves to help, the machinery in here wasn't going to produce any clues, I needed to look and find something that wasn't right or was out of place, but knowing nothing about how a printer's workshop should look, I was a bit lost. Having never seen one before, I went to examine the forklift truck. Walking around it, I had to avoid the forks that had been left at chest height. As I looked at the truck, it seemed out of place, somehow. It was in the way where it had been left, making reaching the loading bay door awkward. Looking at the controls, I noted the key was still in the ignition and in the on position, the battery power indicator read zero. I called Rex over to have a look at it to confirm my thoughts.

Getting into the driver's seat, he switched the ignition off and on and moved some levers, but nothing happened.

'It's been used, and the ignition left on,' said Rex. 'That's why the battery is dead.' He stepped down from the truck and looked around before crossing to a spot in the corner. 'Look,' he pointed to a thick electrical cable left on the floor. 'This is the truck's parking and charging place. If Frisket had used the truck, he would have put it back in its place to recharge it?'

'That's because he didn't use it,' I said. 'The person who killed him must have used it.' Suddenly, things began to make sense.

'Jack Frisket must have had a falling out with his partners. They killed him and used the forklift truck to load everything they needed to make more forged fivers into a van or truck. Having done that, they left as quickly as possible, leaving the forklift truck switched on.'

I crossed to the loading bay door and pulled on the chain that opened it.

'Look, the door isn't locked. The killer just pulled the door closed from the outside and made his getaway.'

With the loading bay door open, more light came inside the printing room. Returning to where Frisket's body lay, I pointed to an open space on the floor.

'Look here.'

'There's nothing there,' said Rex.

I inhaled and let out a sigh, thinking, typical of a man. 'Look; can't you see it?' I said with more emphasis. 'The shape on the floor. There's a shadow in the dust left by the machine that once stood there, and these two scratches on the concrete floor. If you check the forklift truck, I bet those two scratches on the concrete are the same distance apart as the forks on the forklift truck. Whoever killed Jack Frisket took the printer that was standing here so they can print more banknotes. There are also spaces on the shelves over there. The killer has also taken the materials he'll need to make more forgeries. There's nothing left here for us to find. All the incriminating evidence, apart from the body, has been removed.'

'If they had transport, why didn't they take the body with them?' asked Rex.

'Because, if they were seen loading it into the van or stopped while transporting it, explaining away the equipment in the back of the van would be easy, but a dead body is a different matter. This place is surrounded by houses. Anyone looking out of a rear window could have seen a body being carried out of here, but they wouldn't think twice about equipment being moved out.'

'Why didn't the killer just reverse his van into the loading bay?' He could have loaded the body out of sight of any watching eyes.'

I thought for a moment. 'Because his van wasn't a van, it was a truck or lorry, too big to bring inside. That's also why the forks are at chest height; the bed of a lorry is higher from the ground than that of a van. The murderer we are looking for is someone who was driving a lorry or truck.'

Rex scratched his head as he thought about my theory.

'You could be right. It all fits the evidence we have here. But why did they kill Frisket?'

'I suspect he was either stealing a few notes for his own use and his partner or the gang boss found out, or he wanted a larger share of the profits and the murderer didn't like the idea.'

'Do you think the deaths of Hood and Frisket are connected?' asked Rex.

'Definitely; apart from the forged fivers, they both belonged to the same archer club, and they played cards together. They were probably partners.'

He gave the matter a few more seconds of thought. 'Now we have a good idea of what has happened here. You go next door to the archery club and ask them if they've seen or heard anything unusual happing here or if any large lorries have been coming and going. We must discover the whereabouts of the lorry and where it has taken the printing press. I'll stay here and telephone the police. I'll tell them about the body. When they arrive, I'll say I found it. That way, you won't have the police calling you in for questioning.'

'Thanks. I'll go now.'

*****

Later that same day, Rex reported back to Colonel Bempton at GCHQ Scarborough.

'Sir, Miss Showers is on the case. She is investigating the source of the forged banknotes and the death of Robert Hood, as you requested. I'm monitoring her progress from a distance and I'll keep you informed of any new evidence she uncovers.'

Chapter Seven

Thankful to be away from Speedy Printers and Jack Frisket's body, I made my way to the Golden Shot next door. Taking a deep breath before entering, I composed myself, deciding not to say anything to Angie about the dead body next door. Angie was at the reception desk. Giving her a friendly smile, I casually walked over to her.

'Hello again, busy?' I asked.

She eyed me suspiciously. 'Not really. Mondays are always slow. Is it Mr Bodkin you want to speak to?'

'Not especially. I just wanted to ask a couple of routine questions. You'll be able to help me. I've just been to Speedy Printers next door, but there doesn't seem to be anyone around. Have you seen the owner go out recently?'

'No. He sometimes comes in here at lunchtime to shoot a few arrows, but I haven't seen him for a couple of days,' said Angie.

'I suppose he's very busy. Does he get a lot of trade?'

'Quite a bit. I often see vans and trucks coming and going. Sometimes, the big ones block the lane, and then Mr Bodkin has to ask the drivers to move so our customers can get in or out.'

'Have you noticed anything unusual happening next door? People who you wouldn't normally see going into a printing shop. The wrong sort of vans or trucks pulling up outside.'

'Why, what's happened?'

'Oh nothing, I just came to talk to Mr Frisket, but he's not there, and I was wondering if you'd seen him go out with anyone, or if strangers had visited him? It's just that his van is still parked outside.'

'That old thing is always parked in the corner. He only uses it when he has to make a delivery. As for strangers, how would I know? There are always people coming and going from next door. Mr Bodkin knows Jack Frisket better than I do; you should speak to him.'

'Is he available?'

Angie looked at the clock on the wall. 'He's giving a private lesson at the moment, but he'll be finished in ten minutes if you want to wait.'

Whilst I waited, I took the time to look around the shop. As I was doing so, two men in RAF uniforms entered, bought a couple of items each, and then left.

'Is archery popular up at the RAF base?' I asked Angie.

'It seems to be getting that way. From what I've overheard from the guys who come here, there's an officer who's keen on archery and wants to set up a Driffield RAF team to compete with teams from other RAF bases.'

I pulled out the list of names and checked it. Two of the names had their addresses listed as RAF Driffield.

Right on cue, the archery instructor came through to the shop with a young student.

'Well done, Billy. See you same time next week,' he told the lad as he left.

'Miss Showers is here and would like to speak to you, Mr Bodkin,' announced Angie.

I stepped out from the corner of the shop where I had been waiting. I couldn't help but notice how Mr Bodkin's shoulders dropped when he saw me, and I wondered if he would cooperate with the interview.

'If you don't mind, Mr Bodkin, May I speak to you in private; it is important?'

He didn't answer immediately, as though deciding if he should. Then, he made a show of checking the time, 'I can give you five minutes.' He turned and walked towards the bar seating area. I followed him, and when he took a seat at a table, I sat opposite him.

'I'm sorry, but I may as well tell you now. You are going to find out soon anyway,' I said matter of factually, hoping to gain his confidence with my disclosure. 'I've just come from the Speedy Printers. Jack Frisket; he's dead. I found him a few minutes ago. My colleague is calling the police. They should be here soon, and I'm sure they'll want to speak to you.'

I watched his reactions to the news. Kevin Bodkin went pale at hearing another one of his students had died. His immediate response was to run his hands through his hair as he processed the sad news.

'What happened to him?'

'I can't be one hundred per cent sure, but it looks as though he was shot.'

'Shot - Why?'

'That's what I'm trying to find out. Have you heard anything like a gunshot coming from next door?'

'No.'

'Have you seen any strange comings and goings from next door in the past day or so?'

'No, there's always people coming and going. I don't keep track of who visits him. I have my own business to run.'

'Angie said you sometimes have problems with his customers parking out front and blocking access to this place and that you have to go out and ask them to move; is that true?'

'Yes, sometimes, but there's never been any trouble over it; they just move the truck or van further down the lane.'

'These vans and trucks? Are they always the same ones?'

'I don't think so. I don't see them all, but Jack Frisket does work or should I say, did do work for lots of small firms in this area. There's no telling where some of his customers come from. You should check his order book.'

His order book! The words hit me like a slap across the face. Why didn't I think of it?

'Thank you, Mr Bodkin, that will be all for now. I must get back to my colleague. He'll be wondering where I am.'

As soon as I stepped outside the archery club, I discovered two police cars and a black unmarked van had arrived. A police constable stood guard at the front door to Speedy Printers.

Steeling myself for the confrontation to come; I put on a confident face and marched towards the constable on guard at the door.

'Sorry Miss, you can't go in there,' asserted the constable as he stepped in front of the door to stop me from entering.

'It was me who found the body inside. I think the Inspector leading the investigation will want to speak to me, don't you?' Taken aback by my confession, the constable stepped aside without another word. Continuing to the print room, I spied Rex speaking to a plain-clothed man.

'This is Miss Showers, Inspector,' announced Rex as I approached.

The plain-clothed man turned to look at me. I recognised him as the Inspector who had interviewed me in my office. 'Good afternoon Inspector Longstreet.'

'Miss Showers. Mr Barker has been bringing me up to speed with your investigation. I must say, I'm disappointed that you didn't think to keep me informed of your findings.'

'I had nothing conclusive to tell you, Inspector. Mr Barker was with me when I found the body. He reported the discovery as required and I am here to give you a statement; therefore, I am complying with your requirements.'

The Inspector glanced up at Rex before replying. 'So it seems, Miss Showers. Mr Barker has given me all the details I need. I don't think I will need to bother you for a statement.'

'Why thank you, Inspector; that is very considerate of you.'

It was my turn to glance up at Rex and wonder what he had told the Police officer. Inspector Longstreet had let me off the hook too easily. Rex had obviously pulled rank on the policeman and reined in the Inspector's authority over the case. I got the suspicious feeling that Rex knew more about this case than he was letting on. But that would have to wait for now. I wanted Frisket's order book.

'Well, if that is all, I'll let you two get on with it. I think I will just have another look around whilst I wait for Rex.'

I slipped away, leaving them talking. As casually as I could, I looked for a desk or filing cabinet; Jack Frisket's order book would be close by. There was nothing in the print room resembling office space, so I made my way to the front of the premises. Behind the counter, I found a tall dark-green metal filing cabinet and chair set in front of a narrow table with a wire tray full of paperwork needing attention on it. With one eye on the door to the print room and the other scanning through anything that vaguely looked interesting, I went through all the documentation in the wire tray. There was nothing of interest, just orders and paid receipts from customers. Next, I started on the filing cabinet. The top drawer contained three box files crammed with more receipts, but they were all stamped; Paid. I tried the next drawer; it, too, contained various box files filled with assorted papers. How Frisket ran a business with this kind of administrative mess was beyond me. I couldn't find any sort of order to his paperwork. Finally, in the bottom drawer, I found a tin box, some books, and what looked like a broken child's toy made up of lots of wheels. Ignoring the tin box and the toy, I concentrated on his books, one of which was an accounts ledger; another was a list of suppliers, with telephone numbers and addresses, and the last one was a list of customers and their contact details. Placing them on the counter, I went back to the tin box. It contained keys of various shapes and sizes. However, there were two sets of identical keys, each bunch looped together with string. Snatching up one set of keys, I dropped them in my jacket pocket and replaced the tin box in the drawer. There wasn't time to go through the books I'd found, so I folded a newspaper around them and headed for the door. The constable standing outside spotted me with the large bundle of newspapers under my arm. He was about to say something when I beat him to it, by telling him the Inspector wanted him inside. As soon as his back was turned, I made a dash for my car. Driving out of the lane, I headed for home.

Dropping the books on the dining room table, I flicked through the accounts ledger, looking for any unusually large transfers of money. I checked back six months and found nothing that couldn't be explained away as normal transactions for a printing business. I had no further success with the list of suppliers or customers. Deflated by my lack of progress, I sat back to think. The police would be looking for these books, but I suspected that I would have about twenty-four hours to return them before they were missed and the police started asking where they were. If Jack Frisket kept any records of what he did with the forged five-pound notes, he must keep them in another book. One that he's kept hidden. I'd have to return to Speedy Printers tonight to replace the books and search for any secret place Frisket had hidden records of his illicit dealings.

The sound of the telephone ringing made me jump and my thoughts came back to the present.

'Driffield 2366.'

'Hello, April? Where did you get to?'

'Oh, sorry Rex; I suppose I should have come back and said something to you before I left Speedy Printers, but you and the Inspector seemed to have such a lot to talk about. I thought I'd go home as the Inspector didn't require a statement from me.'

'Shall I come to your house so we can talk?' asked Rex.

'No, not today. Stop by my office tomorrow if you like. I plan to re-interview Mrs Hood tomorrow.'

'Great. I'll be there.'

'Okay, Rex, see you tomorrow.'

I put the phone down and stared at it.

'What are you up to, Rex Barker?'

Still wondering about Rex, I went to the kitchen. I was ready for a cup of tea and something to eat. I still had a busy evening ahead of me. There was an interview or two to do before it got dark and then later, I had to break into Speedy Printers to replace the accounts books I'd taken. Then search the place again, looking for the paperwork that Frisket must have secreted away out of sight.

With tea and a sandwich in hand, I scanned the list of archery club members that were in Robert Hood's group. All of them had addresses next to their names, but not all of them were contactable by telephone. Terrance Nock, Danny Gold and Charlie Bowyer had no phone numbers attached to their addresses. I could understand why for Danny and Charlie, their address was listed as Barracks B, RAF Driffield and it was probable Terrance Nock didn't have a phone at home, which left me, Dr Pfeil and Andy Stringer. I telephoned both their numbers but got no answer. Looking through the list of names once again, I discovered Terrance Nock lived close to the Golden Shot and Speedy Printers. Deciding that it would be worth calling on him on my way to the print works and if he was at home, getting one interview out of the way. Killing two birds with one stone, as the saying goes. A quick visit to the bathroom and a change of clothes were in order. I chose a pair of black close-fitting slacks and a black roll-neck sweater, as well as my most comfortable and sensible shoes. A black jacket finished my outfit choice for the evening. Slipping a small torch into my jacket pocket before picking up Frisket's books and keys, I headed for my car.

There was nowhere to park outside Mr Nock's house. It was down a short avenue with no vehicle access, so I had to park my car further along the street. I felt a little uneasy in this neglected part of the town of rundown Victorian houses. Dusk was setting in. Some of the streetlights had come on. Walking beneath a dead one, and looking up, I noticed it had no bulb in its socket. Someone had stolen it. The tightly packed houses felt oppressive, and it was a relief to reach Mr Nock's address. I pressed the button of the doorbell, waited a few seconds and was about to leave when the door opened a little.

'Yes,' came the voice from the shadowed face inside the house.

'Mr. Nock? My name is April Showers. May I speak to you, please?' The door opened a little further, and I got my first look at the man behind the door.

He was probably in his late forties but looked older with his unkempt hair and stubbly chin. He was wearing a waistcoat over a collarless shirt; both looked grubby.

'What do you want?' asked Mr Nock.

'I'm sorry to bother you during the evening, but I'm investigating the deaths of two fellow students at the archery club you all attend. May I come in and ask you some questions?'

'Are you something to do with the police?'

'No, Mr Nock, I'm a private investigator. May I come in, please?'

'Who's died?'

'If you let me in, I'll be able to tell you all about it, Mr Nock.' He hesitated a moment, then opened the door wider.

Inside, the room was lit by a standard lamp in the corner, next to a fake leather armchair. A pile of crumpled and discarded newspapers rose from the floor below the lamp. There was a cup and saucer perched on one arm of the chair. Mr Nock crossed to the armchair and sat down.

'Pull up a chair and sit yourself down,' he instructed. The only other chair in the room was an old, wooden, straight-backed chair in front of a brown, drop-leaf table with barley-sugar twist legs. Turning the chair around to face Mr Nock, I sat down and removed my notebook from my handbag. Mr Nock looked at me expectantly, waiting for me to start. It was then that a thought occurred to me. *Should I be telling him about both the deaths associated with the archery club or just the one?* I cleared my throat. It had to be both.

'I'm sorry to inform you, Mr Nock, but Jack Frisket and Mr Hood have died.'

I waited a moment to let it sink in.

'With Speedy Printers being so close to your address, I was wondering if you knew Jack Frisket socially, away from the archery club, I mean?'

He didn't answer or react straight away. Slowly, he clasped his hands together until the whites of his knuckles appeared. Then I noted the slightest hint of a smile at the corners of his mouth.

'Oh dear, I am sorry to hear that.' There was no hint of sincerity in his voice. 'What happened?'

'I believe Mr Frisket was murdered? But Mr Hood may have died in a tragic accident.' Again, Mr Nock did not respond immediately.

'Would you like some tea?' He began to get up.

'No, thank you, I don't have very long. I have another appointment. How well did you know Mr Frisket and Mr Hood?' Mr Nock gave me a look of disappointment and returned to his seat.

'Not at all. I'd seen them at the archery club. However, they spent most of their time talking together and not mixing with the rest of us. Maybe if they'd spent more time practising and less time socialising, they'd have made better archers. I have my own bow and arrow set, you know.' He pointed to them in the corner of the room. I gave them a quick glance.

'Yes, Mr Nock; they look very nice. So you would say Mr Frisket and Mr Hood were very close?'

'How did Mr Frisket die?' asked Nock.

'That is what I'm trying to find out, Mr Nock.' I didn't want to tell him too much. 'You say they were close friends? Do you know what they talked about?'

'You believe Mr Hood killed him, don't you?'

'No, Mr Nock,' I answered emphatically.

'How did he die?'

'I don't know; that is what I'm trying to find out. When was the last time you saw Mr Frisket or Mr Hood?'

'Are you accusing me of their deaths, Miss Showers?'

'No, Mr Nock. I shall ask the same questions of everyone I interview.'

'I see. I'm sorry, Miss Showers, I don't think I can help you. I didn't know Mr Frisket or Mr Hood very well. Are you sure you wouldn't like some tea?'

'No, thank you, Mr Nock.' I was getting nowhere with him. I looked at my watch.

'I need to be getting along. There is someone else I must see this evening.' I put away my notebook and got up. 'Thank you for your time. Goodnight.'

Mr Nock followed me to the front door, which I opened without waiting for him to do it for me. As I stepped out into the street, I looked back at him. He was framed in the doorway with a faint glow from inside surrounding him.

'Please, come again; if you think of anything else, I can help you with,' he said as I walked smartly away. I didn't answer him, simply giving him a quick wave of acknowledgement. It was dark outside now and it didn't help my feeling of danger when I discovered that half the street lights weren't working. Deep dark stretches of shadow cosseted the pavement and doorways along the street. My car was parked in one such forbidding absence of light. A skinny mongrel stared at me as it crossed the street. Hurrying along, wanting to distance myself from the creepy Mr Nock. The lack of working street lights and the deep shadows intensified my feelings of danger around every corner. My car was only a few steps away now, so I let my pace slow to a more natural step. Releasing a sigh, my racing heart returned to a more normal rate. With a final look back over my shoulder to reassure myself that I wasn't being followed, I retrieved my car keys and opened the driver's door. Once safely inside, I wondered if I'd just had a lucky escape or if I was just overreacting to a socially inadequate man.

'Stupid girl, next time take someone with you to an interview,' I told my reflection in the rear-view mirror. Starting the car engine, my focus returned to my next task, a visit to Speedy Printers.

Turning into the lane that led to the archer club and printers, I drove into almost pitch darkness. There were no street lights down here. However, afraid my car headlights may attract attention, I switched them off, only leaving the sidelights on to illuminate my way. Driving tentatively forward, I reached the end of the lane and parked my car in the turning space. I turned off the car's sidelights but left the engine ticking over as I waited to see if I'd attracted anyone's attention. My eyes

126

adjusted to the dark. Finally, satisfied no one was going to come out to ask me what I was doing parking in the lane, I switched off the car engine, scooped up the books I'd borrowed from the printers earlier, and got out of the car. There was just enough ambient light from the windows of the surrounding houses for me to make out the dark shape of the building in the confines of the lane. A dog barked from someone's backyard; I froze. The barking stopped; I crept towards the front door of the printing works. With the books tucked under my left arm, I took out my torch, putting it in my left hand to hold and shine it on the front door, whilst with my right hand, I used the keys to unlock the front door.

Once inside, my footsteps sounded like drumbeats in the empty darkness. Even though I knew there was no one around, I crept behind the counter, replacing the accounts books back to where I had found them in the bottom drawer of the cabinet. Working my way through the cabinet drawers, looking for another book that contained Mr Frisket's illicit transactions, I came up frustrating empty-handed.

'Come on, girl, think. If you were Frisket, where would you hide a book that had to be easy to reach?' I muttered under my breath.

I was sure there must be one somewhere in this mess. Sitting in Jack Frisket's office chair, I cast around for a hiding place. I looked over, under and behind, everything in reach. The dark-green metal filing cabinet was the only thing I hadn't tried to move because of its size and weight. I'd searched the drawers twice and had not found a hidden book. Then the thought occurred to me, it may be taped to the underside of a drawer. Pulling out all the drawers, I found nothing. Then I removed the drawers to check the back of them; nothing. After that, I looked inside the empty shell of the cabinet. As my torch beam lit the interior, I noticed them. Two small bright steel bolts, held in place by nuts, high up on the inside of the cabinet, right at the back. There was something bolted to the outside rear of the filing cabinet. I needed the chair to stand on, but looking over the top of the cabinet, I spotted a small notebook sitting in a slim tin pocket attached to the back of the cabinet. Standing on my chair, I reached over and down the back of the cabinet to retrieve the book. As my fingers grasped it, I felt a wave of excitement tingle through my body. Returning to my seat, I opened the notebook at a random page and shone my torch on the contents. I was confronted with gibberish. The book was written in code. I let out a curse of frustration. It was time to go home taking my new find with me.

After making sure the front door of the printers was locked behind me. I hurried around the corner to my car. This time, I didn't need to be so careful about not making a noise; by the time anyone came out to see who was in the lane, I would be gone. With the engine running and with the lights on full beam, I exited the lane, speeding for home with the notebook on the seat beside me. I was home in less than ten minutes and feeling very pleased with myself as I cosseted my find. Heading straight to the kitchen, I put the kettle on and grabbed a packet of chocolate digestives from the cupboard. If I had a code to break, I needed some thinking food to do this with.

Sitting in my favourite armchair, with my legs curled up beneath me, tea and biscuits at the ready and pencil and paper on the arm of the chair, I opened the notebook. Looking through a few of its pages revealed that each page was written in the same way with four columns of evenly spaced letters and numbers, each row across the page a different set of characters, all except the top line, they were always the same sequence of letters and numbers. The top line had to be the column headings. So, starting with the simplest coding method I could think of, I began by substituting the letter A for each number 1 and B for each number 2 and so on. It didn't take long to realise this simple substitution code was not working. Jack Frisket was using something more sophisticated to encode his books. But it had to be something he could remember easily, as there wasn't a second code book with this one behind the cabinet to act as a decoding crib. Pouring myself a second cup of tea, I tried reversing my system by turning the alphabet back to front and substituting the letter Z for a number 1 and Y for a number 2. It still didn't work. After an hour of trying various permutations of letters and numbers, I was still getting nowhere with the code. Realising that breaking his code was going to take me far longer than I had thought, I suddenly felt exhausted. Maybe a fresh start in the morning would make the difference.

Tuesday
I awoke with a splitting headache and still feeling tired after an evening's unresolved code-breaking attempt. Pulling the bedclothes up under my chin, I rolled over to hide my face

from the morning light coming through the curtains. What I desired most of all right now was for someone to bring me a cup of tea in bed and the knowledge that I had a relaxing day ahead of me with a friend browsing the shops. Donning my dressing gown and slippers, the only way I was going to get a cup of tea was to make it myself. By half-past eight, I'd had two aspirin and two cups of tea. Feeling more like getting dressed and going to work, I picked up the coded notebook along with my notes on the code and slipped them into my handbag so as not to forget them. It was time to go upstairs to get washed and dressed. Twenty minutes later, I entered my office, followed by George, the postman.

'Morning April, how's tricks?'

'How do you always manage to be so cheerful in the morning, George?' I asked him as I hung up my jacket.

'Easy. Once I'm out on my rounds, I'm my own boss, and, so long as it's not raining and there are no nasty dogs guarding garden gates, what's not to like about my job? Fresh air, exercise, meeting people. Who could ask for more?' He dropped a handful of envelopes on my desk.

'Maybe you've got the best job in the world?' I suggested.

'You could be right, April. See you tomorrow.'

After dealing with the post, I placed the coded notebook on my desk along with the notes I'd made whilst attempting to break the code last night. Pencil in hand, I was just about to start work on the code again when I heard a man's voice out in the hall. Closing the notebook, I got up to close my office door when Rex came in. Promptly sitting down again, I placed the papers and the coded book into the top drawer of my desk.

'What was that?' asked Rex.

'Nothing much. It's just another case I'm working on. Anyway, what do you want?'

'I thought we could continue our investigation,' said Rex cheerfully.

'Our investigation? You mean my investigation. Don't you have work of your own to do, like hunting Russian spies, East German criminals and other undesirables?' I asked playfully.

'Not all the time. It's not like they're flooding into the country. Well, not this week anyway. I thought you were going to interview Mrs Hood again today? I could give her a call for you and see if she's in. We could go together.'

'No. Not today, Rex. I have other things to do.'

'Anything I can help you with?'

'Not really, just routine stuff.' I sat back in my chair and said nothing more. I just stared at him, waiting for him to make the next move. Finally, he gave in.

'I'll leave you to it, then. Let me know if there's anything I can do. I'll call later, maybe. We can go for a coffee or something?'

'Yes, Rex. I'll let you know. Bye.' Eager for him to leave, I didn't move until I was sure Rex had left the building. It was only then that I retrieved the coded book and my notes from the top drawer of my desk. Opening it, I began work. I studied the different permutations of substituting letters for numbers. But nothing worked. What made matters worse was Jack Frisket's messy handwriting. I didn't know if the letter 'z' was a 2 or if it was 'z' if I should be looking for the number twenty-six or if the number twenty-six was the two separate numbers representing the letters A and F. It was frustrating working with columns of numbers with no punctuation or sentence formation to resemble plain text. I was getting nowhere. After struggling with the problem for most of the morning, I gave up. Not being an expert code breaker, I had to admit it. I needed help. Only, there was no way I was going to ask Rex for help. The idea should have hit me earlier. But, I'd been so determined to do all the problem-solving myself that I'd completely forgotten about the one person who could help me, Annabelle; my friend and editor in the office upstairs. She must have edited lots of books for crime writers and learnt something about how fictional detectives deciphered secret codes. Coded book in hand, I raced for the stairs. With just the briefest of knocks on her door, I barged into her room, puffing from the exertion of taking the stairs two at a time.

'Annabelle, I need your help,' I blurted out as soon as I was through the door.

Annabelle, looking startled by the sudden intrusion, just sat staring at me, perplexed for a moment. Then she calmly removed her glasses and placed them on her desk.

'April, whatever is the matter?'

'I've got this coded book, but I don't know how to break the code. If I don't break the code, I won't be able to solve the case, and that's when I thought of you and knew you would know how to do it,' I said excitedly.

'What are you talking about? What code book?' asked Annabelle. I sat in the chair next to her desk and placed the coded book in front of her. I took a deep breath and let it out slowly before beginning my explanation.

'As you know, I'm working on a case that involves someone distributing forged five-pound notes. Well, I think I have found one of the forgers and where he has been printing the banknotes, but I can't prove it. However, I have found this book. I pointed to the one on the table, but it's in code. I've tried to decipher it, but I can't break it. That's when I thought of you. You must have edited a few books where one of the characters in the book has had to decipher a coded message, and then later in the book, the solution to the code is disclosed?'

'That's asking rather a lot of me, April. Do you know how many books I've edited over the years, and you expect me to remember details like that?' As Annabelle flicked through the pages of the coded book, I suddenly felt crushed and foolish. She was right. I'd got my hopes up under false pretences.

'What you need to do,' she continued, 'is visit the library. They'll have a book that will explain how to break codes like this.'

My hopes soared once again.

'Thank you. I'm sorry, I burst in on you, but I was so desperate to break this code, I didn't think of the obvious solution.'

I raced downstairs, locked the coded book in the top drawer of my desk, and grabbed my handbag and jacket. My next stop would be the library.

Chapter Eight

The library wasn't far away. It's located just behind Market Place, five minutes walk from my office, through the town centre. I didn't bother trying to find a book on cryptography myself; I didn't know in which section to look, so I went straight to the reception desk.

'Good morning. Can you help me, please? I'm looking for a book on cryptography. Would you direct me to the right section?' The woman looked at me over the rim of her glasses, clearly peeved at being distracted from sorting her index cards. 'I'm a writer,' I explained. 'I would like to know how secret codes work, so I can write about them correctly in my spy novel.'

The librarian slowly and carefully closed the index card drawer she was working through. Then came out from behind her desk.

'I would have thought someone of your age would be more interested in romance novels,' she said rudely.

I let the comment pass without rising to it. I needed her help far more than an argument. Instead, I consoled myself with the thought that she looked like the kind of woman romance had forgotten. She certainly dressed like it in her pre-war dowdy, dark green, two-piece outfit, and with her greying, mousy hair held up in a bun at the back of her head.

After leading me to a bookshelf, she left me alone to find the book I needed and flick through its pages. The first book I looked through started with simple substitution codes, the same as I'd been using, but quickly moved on to Caesar shift codes and then book codes. Reading on, I came across a code called the 'Jefferson disk' or, alternatively, the 'wheel cipher.' The book had a photograph of the device. To my surprise, it was very similar to what I thought was the child's toy I'd found in the bottom drawer of the filing cabinet at Speedy Printers.

The device had a single rod on which hung disks with letters or numbers printed around their rim. The book went on to explain that disc one represented the letter a, disc two the letter b, etc. The last ten wheels representing the numbers 0-9. All one had to do was set all the wheels in the correct order and you had the code to break the cipher. As the light of recognition grew brighter, I realised this would be an ideal coding device for a printer. To the unknowledgeable finder of such a device, it would not look out of place in a printer's workshop. Closing the book and leaving it on the table, I headed back to my office to make plans.

Seeing the photograph of the device in the book meant I had to return to the Speedy Printers to retrieve the 'Toy' from the bottom drawer. So, with another potentially late night ahead of me, I would have gone home to rest, only I had a busy day ahead of me. I still hadn't interviewed all the suspects. Andy Stringer, electrician and member of the archery club, was next on my list.

After a phone call to the Stringer home, I learnt from Mrs Stringer, that Andy Stringer worked for the Driffield All Electric Company and that they had been contracted to install the wiring into the houses being built on the new housing estate along Manorfield Road in Driffield.

A few minutes later, I parked my car at the entrance to Manorfield Road. The street was a mass of activity, with houses in various stages of completion. Workmen were coming and going in all directions. One look at the roads and the partially constructed paths prompted me to change into my wellington boots, which I kept in the boot of the car, having realised their necessity after my last big case. Suitably prepared, I went in search of the site foreman. I found him in a wooden shed/office at the entrance to the new estate. The door was open, though the foreman was nowhere in sight. I went inside. The place was a mess and smelled of old milk and stale cigarettes. The occupier was using a kitchen table as a desk and an old dining room chair to sit on. A large, white, half full of tea, a sandwich tin and an ashtray full of cigarette butts, occupied one corner of the table. In the opposite corner sat a telephone; the rest of the table was covered in an untidy mess of loose papers, pens and pencils of different colours. On one wall of the shed was a plan of the housing estate. On the opposite wall hung rows of clipboards holding papers.

'What you doing in there?' came a gruff voice from the door.

Spinning around, I smiled sweetly at the man in the doorway. 'I'm looking for the site foreman. Do you know where I can find him?'

'I'm the site manager. Who are you?'

I held out my hand in greeting and introduced myself, expecting him to respond likewise. 'April Showers, private detective.'

'Archie Carpenter. What do you want with one of my foremen?'

I retrieved my hand as he made no attempt to shake it. 'It's not one of your foremen I need. I'm actually looking for Andy Stringer. I've been told that he's an electrician working on this site.'

'That's right, I know Andy; he's a good worker. What's he done?'

'As yet, nothing that I know of, but he may have information that could help me solve one of my cases.'

'Well, he's too busy to stop work. Wait until he knocks off work tonight and talk to him then.'

'I wish I could, Mr Carpenter, but you see, I have to report back to the police about what he tells me. If I'm unable to talk to him, the police will have to come and take him away for questioning. You know what the police are like; they could keep him for hours, maybe all day. Whereas, I just need a few minutes of his time. Honestly, I won't disturb him for long.'

The site manager glared at me, knowing he was between a rock and a hard place, as he evaluated what I'd told him. I glanced at my watch.

'Oh, look at the time. I'll let the Inspector know Mr Stringer is too busy to talk to me right now.' I made to push past the site manager.

'Wait. He's in number eleven but I'm coming...' But, before he could finish speaking, another man came up.

'Archie, we've got a problem with the drains from twenty-four. They're not matching up with the main drain fittings. I need you to check we've got the right coupler before we lay the concrete for the path over the top of the pipes.'

The site manager looked from me to the man outside the hut and then back to me again.

'You can have five minutes with Andy Stringer. You'd better not be there after I've finished sorting this mess out.' He turned back to the man waiting outside. 'What the hell is going on? It's a simple job...' His voice trailed off as he followed the man to number twenty-four.

Free to find Andy Stringer, I set off up the left-hand side of the street. The house that I hoped would eventually be number eleven looked completed, apart from the mess of building materials in the garden. The front door was open, so I went inside and waited in the hall. I was greeted by two bare wires hanging through a hole in the hall ceiling, and three wires coming out of a hole in the wall just above the skirting board. My instinct was to wipe my feet, but there was no doormat and the floorboards were filthy, anyway. I didn't reckon that my muddy wellies were going to add much more dirt than was already there.

'Hello! Andy Stringer?' I called. The reply came from up the stairs. 'WHAT?'

I didn't answer; I just went up the stairs to find him. He was in the front bedroom, on his knees, attaching three wires to a wall socket. Standing in the doorway, I knocked on the doorframe to announce my arrival.

'Excuse me, Mr Stringer?' I took a couple of steps into the bedroom.

Without getting up or looking around to see who had arrived, he continued with his work. 'Yes.'

'My name is April Showers; I'm sorry to inform you this way but, I'm investigating the deaths of two men you may know.' He put down his screwdriver and turned to face me, getting to his feet as he did so, his face full of concern, ready for the bad news.

'It's Mr Robert Hood and Mr Jack Frisket. They were both members of the archery club that you attend. So, I would like to ask you some questions, if I may?' He looked at me blankly for a moment, and then he relaxed.

'Thank God for that. I thought you were going to tell me it was someone in the family or someone I cared about.'

'You mean you didn't get on with Mr Hood? And Mr Frisket?' I took out my notebook and pencil to make a note of Andy Stringer's response.

'Just a minute,' he replied, before passing me to stand at the door. He called out to someone else in the house.

'Hey Fred, you still down there?'

'What's up?' responded a distant voice.

'Up here a minute; a young lass is asking about two blokes from the archery club.' Moments later, I heard slow, heavy footsteps on the stairs. As Fred arrived, I couldn't stop my sharp intake of breath when I saw his face. His left side was badly scarred, and his left ear was just a shrivelled stump of what it should have been. His left eye had no eyelashes and the eyebrow above it was missing. Andy Stringer made the introduction, which, thankfully, gave me time to recompose my thoughts after the shock of seeing Fred.

'This is Fred, he's also a member of the Golden Shot.'

'Fred, this here is a private detective. She's come all the way out here to tell us about two blokes from the archery club. The lady says they're dead, Fred.'

'Which two blokes are you talking about?' asked Fred Button.

'Jack Frisket and Robert Hood,' I replied, realising this must be Fred Button, another person I needed to interview. As I continued to stare at Fred. Andy and Fred exchanged glances.

'We knew them, but not well,' said Andy.

'Yes. Jack's got that printing place next to the club. We don't know what business the Yank was in and don't care. We're not gonna lose any sleep over the death of that one, love. We hate Yanks, don't we Andy?'

'Yes, we do Fred.'

I looked from one to the other, confused by their rancour towards Americans. 'Why?'

'Well, just take a look at Fred; the Yanks did that to him.'

Andy then rolled up the sleeves of his shirt to reveal his scars. 'They're not as bad as Fred's,' said Andy, rolling down his sleeve again.

'We'll never forget who gave us these. Will we Andy?'

'You're telling me that the Americans did that to you?' I said, aghast at what I saw.

'Yes, love. You see, Fred and me was in the army together in North Africa. We got captured at Tobruk when Rommel made his big push. After that, we were sent to a prisoner-of-war camp in Italy, where we spent a year until Italy was invaded by the Allies. Rather than let all us prisons-of-war fall back into allied hands, the Germans put us on trains and moved us north. That's when it happened. American planes spotted our train. So they bombed and strafed it. We were in one of the wagons that got torn apart when a bomb exploded close by. Prisoners from some of the other damaged cattle trucks managed to get on top of the train and waved at the planes as they flew past, but the planes came back and bombed us again. They could see us all right; they knew we were unarmed. They could see us waving at them. The train had stopped on a bridge, but the Americans didn't care. They didn't stop killing us until they'd run out of bombs and bullets. Four hundred prisoners of war died that day, trapped in their wagons when the bridge collapsed. Fred and me was lucky, we'd got out onto the tracks and ran away from the train into the hills. We thought we were going to die, but we was found by some local Italians who treated our wounds. A few days later, a British artillery unit found us. They sent us to a first aid unit, and they arranged for us to be shipped back to a hospital in England. We've stayed together ever since. What pretty girl would look twice at us two now when they see us in this state? What makes it worse is when we hear the Yanks telling everyone that it was them that won the war. They make it sound like they did it all on their own. Why they want to stay in this country, I don't know, but I wish they'd go home and leave us alone.'

I could feel the lump in my throat tighten as Andy told his story.

'I'm sorry for what happened to you both, but it's my job to investigate the death of Mr Hood. I have to find the person who killed him and why.'

'Don't look to us for help, love; he's just one less murdering Yank to me,' answered Fred.

'If you don't speak to me, the police will come to find you. They will take you to the police station for questioning.'

'Ha. Do you think we are frightened of the police? What can they do to us that hasn't been done already? If you find the bloke who killed the Yank, tell us his name, and we'll buy him a pint. Now, if there's nowt else, lass, we've got work to do.' Frank was about to leave, but I hadn't finished with them yet.

'There is one more thing you can help me with. Have either of you been given a forged five-pound note?'

'Is that what the Yank was doing? Forging fiver's?' You reckon that the Yank and Jack Frisket were forging five-pound notes? sneered Andy Stringer.

'I don't know. That's just one of my avenues of enquiry. Have either of you received a forged five-pound note?' I repeated. Andy and Fred exchanged glances again.

'No, love,' replied Fred.

'What can you tell me about Jack Frisket?' I continued.

'Nothing more than we've told you already. He was mates with the Yank and he had the printing works next to the archery club. We didn't mix with them two, and we had no business with the print-works,' replied Andy.

'Thank you, gentlemen. I'll let you get back to work.' I retrieved a business card from my handbag and offered it to Andy. 'If either of you do receive a forged five-pound note, I'd be grateful if you'd let me know about it and where it came from.'

Andy Stringer took my card. 'Sure.'

'Thank you for your time. I know where to find you in case I have any more questions.' Leaving them in the bedroom, I left the house, heading back to my car. Pausing on the path outside the house with an uneasy feeling, I looked back over my shoulder and spotted Andy Stringer looking through the upstairs window at me. I knew it; there was something more between those two than they had let on. Neither of them had asked how Robert Hood or Jack Frisket had died. Next time, I interview them, I'll pay them a home visit; speaking to them separately may get them to open up and talk more freely. They both bore grudges against Americans and had a reason that might make them see Robert Hood as an easy target to take revenge upon. As I walked back to my car, I tried to imagine the agony Andy and Fred must have suffered from their burns. It made me shudder.

After changing back into my day shoes, I got into the driving seat. There were still two more people from the archery club to interview, Danny Gold and Charlie Bowyer, both airmen from RAF Driffield. I'd never been on an RAF base before and I wasn't sure what the correct procedure was for me to get admitted to the airfield so I could talk to airmen.

I didn't even have a telephone number to call so I could make an appointment. There was only one thing to do, a frontal assault. Driving out of Driffield, RAF Driffield was only a few minutes away. Pulling up to the front gate, two guards immediately stopped me.

'May I see your pass?' asked Guard One as his face filled the open driver's door window. Guard Two stood with his rifle to hand in front of the gate.

'I don't have a pass, I'm afraid.' I held up my business card. 'I'm a private detective. I'd like to interview two of your airmen, if I may?' I gave him the sweetest, most innocent smile I could manage.

'You can't come in without a pass,' snapped Guard One.

'How do I get a pass?'

Guard one was bored with the conversation already. 'From the adjutant, Miss. Move on, you're blocking the entrance.'

'I'm sorry to be a nuisance, officer, but how does one contact the Adjutant?'

'I'm not an officer and I suggest you use the telephone, Miss. Now, move on, please.'

'Be an absolute darling for me and give me his telephone number.' Red-faced, Guard One glowered in at the open car window, before glancing across to Guard two.

Lowering his voice, he said, 'Move your car to the kerb over there; I'll be back in a minute.' He stood back from the car and watched as I parked my car at the side of the road, close to the entrance. He was only gone a couple of minutes before returning with a telephone number written on a scrap of notepaper. He passed it through the open car window.

'Come back if you get permission from the adjutant. If he says yes, he'll leave your name at the gate so we know to let you in. If not, you'll have to find some other way to contact your boyfriend.'

'He's not my boyfriend.'

'If you say so. But you can't come in today!' He smartly about-faced and then marched back to his place at the gate.

I'd got what I'd wanted; now, it was time to go back to my office and telephone this adjutant fellow, and hopefully, convince him to let me into the airbase to interview my suspects.

'You say you are a private detective investigating a suspicious death? Surely, that is a job for the police, Miss Showers.'

'The police are not investigating this case because they think Mr Hood's death was an accident, sir. Mrs Hood hired me because she believes her husband was murdered.'

'I gather then, it's only Mrs Hood that thinks that way? Is that correct?'

'Yes, sir, but there is another death linked to Mr Hood's death that is very suspicious and the police are investigating that one.'

'Miss. Showers, if the police are investigating both cases, I see no need for you to be on the case. The police will get to the bottom and discover the guilty parties. When and if the police want to interview any of the airmen on this base, they know the correct channels to use and we will assist them in any way we can. But, until then, I see no reason for you to disrupt the routine of this airbase, especially as you have no evidence that any airman has done anything wrong. Good day, Miss Showers. I'm sorry I cannot help you any further.'

The telephone went dead, leaving me feeling frustrated at hitting the brick wall of military officialdom. I toyed with the idea of calling on Rex and asking for his help in getting access to the airbase, but this was my case and I didn't want to use him unless I had no choice. I was going to have to find Airman Danny Gold and Airman Charlie Bowyer the hard way. As members of the archery club, they must visit the range from time to time, so that would be the best place to find and talk to them. Five minutes later, after a chat with Angie at the archery range, I knew which days the airmen usually came in to practice their bowmanship. A quick look at the clock on my office wall reminded me time was getting on and that I had a job to do later tonight. It was time to go home, have something to eat, and get changed into more suitable clothes for sneaking around Speedy Printers in the dark.

I parked my car in the turning area at the end of the lane next to Speedy Printers. Remaining in the car, I waited a few minutes, just in case someone had spotted me and came out to see what I was doing down the lane this late at night.

Dressed all in black and with my heart beating like a drum, I closed my car door as quietly I as could and then locked it. With the spare key to the printers in one hand and a torch at the ready in the other, I let myself in through the front door, closing it behind me and dropping the latch. It was cold inside; the air smelt musty and full of solvent fumes. I knew what I was looking for. So, returning to the filing cabinet, I went to the bottom drawer to get the child's toy. Picking it up, I inspected it closely. As soon as my torch beam picked out the detail of what I was holding, I knew I'd found what I was looking for. It wasn't a toy at all; it was the coding device, but this wasn't the place or time to experiment with it. Closing the drawer, I left as quickly as I could.

Once home, I was so excited about my new find; I had to try using it right away. Setting the device down on the table, it looked almost identical to the same one in the book of cryptography I'd read at the library. The simple, home-built construction of this device had given it the look of a child's toy until given closer inspection. It was mounted on a wooden base. An A-frame of metal tubing stood at each end of the base. The A-frames were joined together at their apex by a rod on which thirty-six rotating discs, also made of wood, hung. Around the rim of each disc were the letters of the alphabet and the numbers 0-9 and each disc could rotate independently of its neighbour. When I had originally tried my substitution code method of breaking Jack Frisket's coded book, I hadn't considered that both letters and numbers were interchangeable in the book. Staring at the device for a moment, I rotated a couple of the discs with my finger. They spun around and around until friction brought them to a stop. However, I still needed to know in which order to set the wheels to enable me to decipher the book. Frisket could spell out any word, set of words or sentence of thirty-six characters on the wheels to give him the means to code his book, and I didn't know what they were. Picking up the coded book and opening it on a random page, I transferred the letters and numbers from the top line of the page to the wheels of the device, and then I examined the positions of the discs to see if they spelt out a recognisable word anywhere around their perimeter - nothing. I tried another set of characters, but again, nothing that made any sense. I spent the next two hours setting and resetting the wheels in different letter/number sequences, hoping that I could decode one set of characters from just one column in the book, but I got nowhere. Too tired to keep trying, I left the device and the coded book on the table and went to bed.

Wednesday
The following morning, I took the coding device and book to the office, hoping that working on them there, after a good night's sleep, might bring some results. Unfortunately, frustrated with my lack of progress, and after spending another two hours getting nowhere, I gave up. As I sat looking at all my scribbles and crossings out scattered across my desk, I knew of one person who could help me. Only, I didn't want to give in and ask Rex for help. So I decided to stop and have another go later. I had just put the book and the device in the bottom drawer of my desk when, as I closed the drawer, Jennifer stuck her head around my office door. 'Coming for a cup of tea and a chat? Annabelle has made chocolate buns!'

I looked at my watch. Was it eleven o'clock already?

'I'll be there in a second.' Rubbing my temples to ease the pain behind my eyes, I took a deep breath, then fished out two aspirin from a bottle in my handbag and went to join Jennifer and the others. After twenty minutes of chat, tea, two aspirin and a chocolate bun, my headache had gone. I volunteered to do the washing up whilst the others went back to their offices. The distraction did its job, whilst keeping my hands busy; I planned the next part of my investigation.

A simple phone call to Angie at the archery club gave me what I wanted; Airman Danny Gold and Airman Charlie Bowyer would be at the archery club tomorrow morning. Feeling pleased with the progress I'd made this morning, I went to visit Daddy at his bank and take him out to lunch. It was also a good excuse to ask him if he'd come across any more forged fivers. A light lunch of sandwiches and coffee at the Bell Hotel, with my favourite man in the world, was a rare treat since I'd left home to live on my own. After exchanging news about how each of us was getting along, and how Mummy was doing, I gave him a brief rundown on how far I'd got investigating Mr Hood's death and that I'd found a second body at the Speedy Printers.

'Are you sure you shouldn't just leave this case to the police to figure out?' said Daddy, concern for me written across his face.

'No, everything was fine. I had Rex with me. I suspect the two main culprits in all this are dead. My guess is Mr Frisket, who owned Speedy Printers, was printing the forgeries and Mr Hood was creaming a few off the top to spend locally. After an argument, Mr Hood killed Mr Frisket. Then later, by pure accident, Mr Hood falls downstairs at his home, dying of a broken neck. The rest of the gang panic and dispose of as much of the evidence as they can, so they can't be incriminated in the murder of Jack Frisket.'

I couldn't prove any of what I'd just told Daddy, but I had to reassure him I was okay and not in any danger. After checking the time, Daddy called a waiter over and paid for our lunch.

'Hey!' I said lightly. 'This was supposed to be my treat.'

Daddy gave a little laugh. 'We should do this more often. But, don't forget your mother, she misses you too.'

'I won't, I promise.'

Going our separate ways, I returned to the office with a spring in my step, ready for another go at figuring out how that coding device worked.

I'd no sooner got it on top of my desk, along with the coded book, when Jennifer came in and sat down.

'What's that?' She asked as soon as she spotted the strange device.

'It's a mechanism for writing secret codes. I was just about to try to figure out how it works.'

Jennifer held it up and looked at it carefully, spinning the wheels around and around. 'It looks a bit like a child's toy, doesn't it?'

'It's actually very sophisticated,' I said, a little indignantly.

'So you don't have a clue how it works, then?'

'No, not yet, but I'll figure it out. Why? Do you think you know how it works?'

'Oh, no, not me, you're the detective. What do you know about it?' she asked.

I explained how I thought the device was set up to create a secret set of letters and numbers which could then be used as a new alphabet.

'So you just need to spin the wheels into the correct alignment to break the code?' said Jennifer, picking up the device.

'Yes; but there are thousands of variations to choose from.'

'Do you think the wheels would always be set in the same position?' she asked, whilst turning two wheels into a new setting.

'I expect so. It would get too complicated if you used a different code each time you used the device. How would you remember which code was for which message?'

Jennifer carefully turned the device around in her hands, making sure she kept it upright and didn't disturb the wheels she had already set into position.

'Look at this.'

She placed the coding device on my desk. 'I've noticed it before, at home, after my husband has been working on the car. He'll leave faint, oily fingerprints on whatever he touches.' Jennifer showed me the black smudges on either side of the wheels, and, as she adjusted each wheel to line up the smudges, a row of letters and numbers came into alignment on top of the coding device.

Spinning the device around to face me, I could see what Jennifer had spotted and what I had missed. Opening the coded book on a random page, I grabbed a pencil and a sheet of paper and jotted down the sequence of letters and numbers on the device. Then, below the first line, I wrote the alphabet and the numbers zero to nine. Heart beating like a hammer striking an anvil and my hand shaking as it held the pencil, I matched the letters and numbers to the lines of nonsense in the coded book. As the first column released its secrets to me, it revealed a column of dates. The second column was the money total. The third column was a set of letters and the last column revealed a set of letters and numbers, none of which made sense to me. I rechecked the setting on the coding device, but it hadn't moved, so unless Jack Frisket was using a different code for these two columns in the book, I would have to discover what the new letters meant.

After spending the rest of the afternoon deciphering what I could from the coded book. I had made some significant progress, but I still only had half the information from the book that I needed, as it hadn't revealed anyone's name. But the book had revealed how much forged money had been printed and when. In the last two columns, I was less sure what the initials represented. One could be drop-off locations with the last set of initials being the recipients. I didn't need to total up the amounts in each column to realise many millions of pounds of forged five-pond notes had been printed. But, I didn't understand; why had so little of the forged money had been released into general circulation? Sitting back in my chair, I rubbed my tired eyes. I was ready for a cup of tea and wanted to go home, but now that I'd deciphered the book, I had to decide what I was going to do with the information and the book. If I handed it to the police, I'd be in trouble for withholding evidence, but on the other hand, I didn't need or want it any longer. Having given the matter a few minutes thought, I concluded that there was only one sensible thing I could do with it. I'd found it hidden at Speedy Printers, so I would have to return the book and the coding device to Speedy Printers. The police needed to find them in their own time. Just as I reached out to pick up the coding device, the smudges along each side seemed to leap out at me and my hand recoiled from it instantly.

'April. You idiot!' I exclaimed to myself. I took a deep breath and let it out slowly. Rising from my chair, I went through to the kitchen next door and brought back a cleaning cloth, spending the next fifteen minutes cleaning my fingerprints off the coding device and every page of the coded book. Pulling the sleeve of my cardigan down over my left hand, I scrapped the coding device and the book off my desk and into my shopping bag. The next time I touched them, I'd make sure I was wearing gloves. I put the papers containing my notes from the deciphered book in the bottom drawer of my desk. Picking up my shopping bag and handbag, I went home.

Chapter Nine

Feeling hungry, I looked through the pantry, shuffling tins and packets around. I wanted something to eat but couldn't decide what to have. I knew what the real problem was. It was the thought of returning to the Speedy Printers later that evening which was making me anxious. The more times I visited that place after dark, the more chance there was of being seen by someone from one of the houses that backed onto the lane, but I had no choice. I couldn't do it during the day, there were too many people around. Finally, giving in to the easy option, I made a pot of tea and grabbed a packet of Scottish-made shortbread. Returning to the living room, I switched on the wireless to listen to the Variety Playhouse and then settled in my armchair. Gentle music filled the living room; the glow of the hot coals in the fireplace warmed the room as dusk fell. Picking up the local newspaper, I read about what had been going on in Driffield and the local area.

I didn't remember falling asleep, only waking up to the sound of laughter coming from the wireless and the chill of a cold room. A pathetic little flame in the fireplace tried to hang on to life between two exhausted bits of ashen coal. My cup of tea had only been half drunk, and a single triangle of shortbread lay on its plate with a bite out of it. An icy shiver ran up and down my back as I rose from my chair. As the fog of sleep cleared from my head, I checked the clock on the sideboard, it was half-past twelve. It was far later than the time I'd intended to set off, but I had to return the coded book and device. Snatching up my shopping bag containing the book and device along with my torch, I headed for the front door.

It had been a poor summer, but tonight there was the thin slice of a crescent moon, and a sky full of bluish/white stars filling the heavens. With any luck, I'd be home again in half an hour and could go to bed and rest properly. I felt chilled as I set off. It didn't help, only having to make a short journey; the car engine wouldn't have time to warm the interior of my car.

Just as I entered the lane, as before, I turned off my car headlights and cautiously made my way toward the turn that would take me past the archery club. I'd only driven a few yards when I jumped on the brake pedal. In the moonlight, I could see the outline of a van at the far end of the lane, where it opened up to allow vehicles to turn around next to Speedy Printers. My car was still hidden in the shadows of the narrowness of the lane.

At first, all I could do was stare in disbelief at what I saw in front of me. It was only when I caught sight of light reflecting against the side of the van that I remembered to switch off my side lights. As I watched, two human shapes came out of Speedy Printers carrying boxes and then put them in the back of the van. I'd been lucky. The thieves had been in the building when I arrived and hadn't seen my car or its lights. My thoughts raced as I watched the thieves. Are these the forgers? It was more than likely they were, and they were collecting more supplies. It was also probable that it was these two who had killed Jack Frisket and maybe Robert Hood. As I sat in my car transfixed by the unfolding events, I wondered what I should do about it. They still hadn't seen or heard me yet, which meant the van's engine must be running and was drowning out the sound of my car engine as it ticked over. I couldn't risk getting any closer. I would be seen, and then I realised my car was blocking the exit to the lane. Oh God, as soon as the thieves tried to leave, they would see me. I had to move. The next time both men went inside the printers, I slipped my car into reverse gear and backed it out of the lane and onto the street as slowly and quietly as I could. Once I was out of the lane, I reversed down East North Gate; parked at the kerb and waited for the van to come out of the lane. Lights still off and the engine running, I waited for what seemed like hours.

'What are they doing?' I asked myself with another look at my watch. Only five minutes had passed since I'd parked up. My heart was thudding; I could feel the tension in the back of my neck increasing.

'Come on. I could have done the job quicker myself,' I said frustratingly, tapping on the steering wheel.

At last, the van emerged from the lane. It was dark green, but other than that, it was like lots of other Bedford vans used by businesses all over the country. To my horror, the van turned in my direction; they would see me. Throwing myself sideways, I dropped onto the passenger seat, hurting my ribs on the handbrake lever as I landed. I let out a little curse but waited until the van went past me before sitting up and rubbing my smarting ribs. As the van made its way along East North Gate, I switched on my lights, slipped the car into gear and set off to follow them. At the end of the street, the van turned right onto Windmill Hill and then onto Scarborough Road. To my left, trees lined the road and beyond them was farmland. To my right, there were semi-detached houses, flaunting enormous gardens. We were heading out of Driffield.

At this time of the night, we were the only two vehicles on the road. Keeping my distance, I followed the van, only getting closer if there was a risk of losing them at a road junction. On and on they drove until they reached the village of Langtoft. Shortly after entering the village, the van slowed and then turned onto Back Street. Expecting them to stop at any minute at a house or shed along the way, I hung back. But the van continued on, turning left onto Scarborough Road again, only heading back towards Driffield.

Suddenly, the van stopped in the middle of the street, and the two men jumped out and began running towards my car. Braking hard, I stopped the car. As I fumbled with the gear stick to put the car into reverse gear, I stalled the engine. A look out of the windscreen made me jump. The two men had almost reached me. Slamming my foot hard on the clutch pedal, I pulled the starter, revved the engine and slipped into reverse gear, backing the car along the road. I didn't have the confidence to drive quickly, so the two men were still gaining on me. I risked pushing harder on the accelerator. The car increased the distance between me and the two men. Just as I thought I was getting away, I lost control of the car when I hit the kerb. The car bounced and mounted the pavement. Then hit the gatepost at the entrance to a small farm. Jolted in my seat, I was otherwise unhurt. When I looked through the windscreen, the men who had been chasing me had stopped in the middle of the road, looking to see what I would do next. I knew that if I got out of the car and ran, they would grab me. Equally, if I stayed in the car, they would catch me. It was a flash of light that made me glance out of the door window. A light had come on at a bedroom window of the house next to me. Seconds later, more bedroom lights were switching on up and down the street. Curtains were swished aside, and a face appeared in windows. I looked back at the men standing in the street, then slammed my hand down on the car horn button and held it there. As I looked around, more bedroom lights were coming on and more faces were appearing in windows, wanting to know what all the noise was about. It was enough to scare the men off. Letting out a sigh of relief, I watched them run back to their van and drive away.

My car engine after it had stopped when I hit the gatepost and I got a shock when I restarted it. The noise the car made was loud and horrible. Even so, I put the car into first gear and tentatively put my foot on the accelerator. The racket from the back of the car increased. It sounded like I was driving a tank; and the way the car bumped up and down when I tried to drive it, made me think a tyre had burst. The roar from the engine each time I pressed on the accelerator was so alarming, and the sound of grating metal was so loud when I tried to move the car. Even I, with my limited knowledge of cars, knew that I wouldn't be driving home in this car tonight. I switched off the engine and got out to look at the damage just as the owners of the farm gate came out to see what was going on. The man was wearing a raincoat and wellington boots over his pyjamas. The woman was similarly dressed, but she was wearing a nightdress, as I could see her knees and the hem of the pink flowery material below her raincoat.

'What's happened?' demanded the man.

'I'm sorry, but I...' I tried to explain.

'What do you mean by making all that noise in the middle of the night? You, youngsters, have no respect. Look what you've done to my gate. You're gonna have to pay for the damage,' interjected the man.

'I'm sorry, but...'

'Look at this mess. You can't leave your car there. I need to get my tractor out in the morning. I've telephoned the police. You need locking up. Making all this noise and causing damage to other people's property,' continued the man.

'Stop it, stop it, you stupid old fool. Sod your gatepost. I could have been killed tonight, and all you can think about is your gatepost and a bit of noise.' The man flinched back in surprise.

'Well, I never! Language like that and coming from a slip of a lass. No respect for your elders, you youngsters. What's the world coming to?' he declared, shaking his head as though he had all the rights in the world on his side.

The woman, who I presumed to be his wife, took the man by the arm.

'Let the girl speak, Harold.'

'Well?' said Harold, sticking his chin in the air, waiting for my excuses.

'Two men were chasing me. I hit your gatepost whilst I was trying to escape. They drove off when you came out to see what was going on.'

Harold's mouth dropped open. I could read the shock and disbelief on his face.

'You poor thing,' declared his wife. 'Come inside. I'll put the kettle on. Harold's called the police, but it'll be a while before Albert gets here. He lives in Kilham. It's only four miles away, but Albert does nothing in a hurry. He's only got a push-bike. What's your name, lass? I'm Betty, you've met Harold. Take no notice of him, he's all mouth, but he's a hard worker.'

I smiled at the woman and let her take me by the arm to lead me through the damaged gate. She directed me to an open door at the back of the house from which a light was shining.

'My name is April. Thank you. I am feeling a bit shaky; a cup of tea would be most welcome.'

Settled at the kitchen table with a mug of sweet tea that was so large that I needed both hands to hold it to my lips. I explained who I was and what I'd been doing that evening.

'Good heavens, are there really people like that? I'm glad we don't live in a city. I couldn't cope with all that going on,' proclaimed Betty in all sincerity.

I smiled at the idea of Driffield being thought of as a city full of iniquity.

'It's not all bad,' I said in the market town's defence. I was about to continue my tale when there was a knock on the door. A second later it opened, and a policeman stepped inside. He looked at the three of us and then focused on Betty.

'Any more tea in the pot, Betty?'

He grabbed a chair, placed it close to me, and sat down.

'Now then, what's been happening? I've seen the car,' he asked casually.

I explained everything that had happened during that evening all over again, whilst he made notes in his little black book.

'I'll have to speak to my sergeant about this. He won't be happy about crooks from Driffield coming onto our patch. Did you get the van registration number?'

'Yes, it's BGS 592.'

'Good, we'll find out who the van belongs to and nick him. Get him to come down to the station and explain himself.'

The policeman looked pleased with himself. I expect they didn't get much crime out in the villages and this had been worth getting out of bed for. He placed his little black book back in his top pocket.

'Any more tea in the pot before I head back?' he asked Betty.

'No, it's gone cold, and we're off to bed and so should you,' instructed Betty.

After the policeman had left, Harold asked me. 'Is there anyone you need to telephone? Someone who would come and collect you?' I thought about it for a moment, but before I could answer, Betty interjected.

'It's late; leave it until the morning. There's nothing much anyone can do at this time. You can sleep on the settee tonight, love, and then call someone to come and help you in the morning. Look Harold; it's after two in the morning. You go to bed. You've got work soon. I'll get April a pillow and a blanket. You can tow her car into the yard tomorrow and she can telephone someone to come and pick her up. Is that alright with you, lass?'

'Thank you, Betty. That's most kind of you. I'm sorry to be such a bother to you both.'

'Think nothing of it, lass. It's the least we could do after all you've been through.'

Thursday

My telephone conversation with Daddy in the morning was a tense one. Asking him to come and get me and then having to explain what had happened was very difficult. Later, I had to go through it all again with Mummy. I had made Daddy late for work. I apologised repeatedly for the inconvenience I had caused him and the upset I had caused Mummy. They repeated their desire for me to abandon my detective agency, saying it was too dangerous. I avoided answering them on the matter.

Back in my office later that morning, tired, irritable and carless, I telephoned the local garage to arrange the recovery of my poor Morris. After that, I visited my insurance brokers to inform them about the accident. They told me I would have to wait until my car insurance company got an estimate on the repair bill before repairs could start. With no car, it was going to be difficult to carry on with my investigations. Loathed as I was to admit it, I needed Rex's help.

The walk back to my office was a lonely one. I was just about to telephone Rex when there was a knock on my office door. Standing at the entrance to my office were Inspector Longstreet and his side-kick, Sergeant Rivers. My spirits sank even further. They crossed the floor to my desk with no invitation to do so. Sitting down without so much as a 'Good Morning, Miss Showers, may we come in?' The Inspector's first words to me were.

'I hear you had a bit of a bump in your car last night.'

My immediate reaction was one of anger towards the police officers and relief that I'd left the coded book and the device at home after Daddy dropped me off at my house this morning.

'Come in, Inspector, will you take a seat?' I said sarcastically. 'My insurance company is dealing with my car and any repairs needed to the farm gate.'

'Yes, I know, Miss Showers. I've already checked. That is not why we are here. In your statement to the Kilham police officer, you said two men chased you. Why was that?'

'I was keeping watch on Speed Printers when I spotted a van parked outside the property. Two men were loading stuff into the back of it. When they drove off, I followed them.'

'Why didn't you telephone the police about what you saw?' asked Sergeant Rivers.

'Because you wouldn't have arrived in time to stop them, and they would have got away. Whilst I was following them, I was able to get the van's registration number. You already know all this. I told it all to the police officer last night. Why are you here instead of arresting those men?'

'Ah, yes, the registration number. You said you were following a green van?' The Inspector did his best to look thoughtful.

'That's correct.'

'How fast was it travelling, Miss Showers?'

'Why? Is that relevant?'

'Well, you see, Miss Showers, our records tell us that the vehicle you were following last night is the registration number of a steamroller belonging to Driffield Town Council Works Department. So I ask again. How fast was this steamroller travelling, Miss Showers?'

'Hilarious, Inspector. Obviously, the number plate of the van is a false one.'

'Or, in your panic, you misread it or you are making the story up to cover the real reason why you drove into that farm gate. Had you been drinking last night, Miss Showers?' suggested the Sergeant.

I didn't bother answering the idiot sidekick, but asked the Inspector, 'Why are you here, Inspector? You must have a copy of my statement?'

'Well, you see, I have a niggling little problem. A beat officer on patrol saw you reverse out of the lane and wait for the green van before you followed it. So you had plenty of time to call the police and tell us what was happening. Why were you at Speedy Printers so late at night? Any vehicle entering the lane that late at night would have been up to no good and be a prime suspect for investigation! Why were you there, Miss Showers?'

'I'm sorry, Inspector. Clearly, I am not very adept at undercover work. I simply made an amateurish mistake.' I smiled at him sweetly, hoping he'd buy the lie. Agonising seconds passed as he weighed up my answer.

'Leave this investigation alone, Miss Showers. If you interfere any further and get in my way, I will arrest you. Do I make myself clear?'

'Yes, Inspector.' I agreed, just to placate him.

After the Inspector had gone away, I pulled a notepad and pencil from the top drawer of my desk and jotted down what I'd learnt so far.

Clients Name   Mrs Hood

Victims Name   Mr Robert Hood

Victim

Possibly murdered, or could have died by accident at home.

American, working for a British firm of accountants.

British wife.

Had a hundred pounds of forged five-pound notes inside his desk at home. They are different from those currently in circulation.

He was a gambler at the Black Bull and a member of the Driffield Golden Shot Archery club.

Questions:-

Why didn't Mrs Hood tell me her husband was an American?

Why are his forged banknotes different to those in circulation, and why are there two different types of forgery?

Why did he only try to deposit one type of forgery at the bank when he had both types?

Where did the second set of forgeries come from, if not Jack Frisket?

Is there a second forgery gang in the area?

Did Hood meet Jack Frisket before joining the archery club?

Where does the gambling at The Black Bull in Leconfield fit in?

Did Hood kill Jack Frisket, or did Jack Frisket kill Robert Hood?

Why didn't the police spot that the one hundred pounds was forged money?

Speedy Printers is still being used to acquire printing materials. So the forged money is still being printed; where was the van heading before it forced me to stop?

Who are the men in the green van?

I sat back and looked over my notes, letting out a sigh. I had too many unanswered questions. It was all a giant jigsaw puzzle, but with no picture to help me fit the pieces together. I included more people I thought could be involved.

Kevin Bodkin - Archery club owner. He knew Jack Frisket and Robert Hood. He bought supplies from Jack Frisket's print shop.

Is he in the forgery business, and using the club to disperse the banknotes?

Or did Bodkin kill Jack Frisket for trying to use forged notes in his club?

Why would Bodkin Kill Robert Hood?

Doctor Pfeil – Still to be interviewed.

Terrance Nock – bin man. He's lonely and disliked Jack Frisket for stealing a potential friend. He's also short of money and lives close to Speedy Printers and the archery club.

Did he kill Frisket and Hood because of the insult of being excluded from their friendship?

A war hero left with mental problems. He came across as a bit strange when I interviewed him.

Andy Stringer - Electrician and Fred Button – Plumber. Both are close friends. Both were victims of the Americans during World War II. They both still harbour a deep grudge against Americans.

Is their dislike of Americans enough to make them take revenge on one man for their pain from years past?

Danny Gold – RAF   -   Still to be interviewed

Charlie Bowyer – RAF -   Still to be interviewed

I looked at my watch. If I was quick; I could get to the archery range just before the airmen usually arrived. Grabbing my handbag from the bottom drawer of my desk, I was just about to get up when the telephone rang. I hesitated; should I or shouldn't I?

'Hello, April Showers detective agency, April Showers speaking.'

'Miss Showers, my name is Dr Pfeil; I believe you are investigating the deaths of two members of the Golden Shot Archery Range. It just so happens I am a member of the club. Do you think I am in any danger?' His German accent was strong, taking me by surprise, but his English was good.

'Dr Pfeil, how good of you to call me. I suppose it was to be expected that word would soon get out about the deaths of Mr Hood and Mr Frisket. As you knew both men, I was hoping to arrange an interview with you; may I do so? When would it be convenient for me to come and see you?' I removed my notepad and a pencil from the top drawer of my desk.

'Oh, err; I hadn't expected that you would want to interview me. Is that really necessary?'

'I think it would be for the best, Dr Pfeil. It will be far easier and more convenient for you to tell me what you know about Mr Hood and Mr Frisket than the police. If the police haven't spoken to you yet, I am sure they soon will, and they will not wait for you to arrange an interview time or place; they will just turn up unannounced. You know what they are like.'

'What! The police come around here, to my home? But I hardly knew Mr Hood and Mr Frisket. I thought you were investigating the case.'

'I am Dr Pfeil, but I am not the police. However, they are conducting their own investigation into the deaths; and will want to interview everyone with any links to Mr Hood and Mr

Frisket. I'm sure you have nothing to worry about, but if I could come and see you, I may be able to reassure you about how the police work. Maybe even reassure them how cooperative you have been?' It was a cheap trick, using the doctor's German heritage against him to play on his fear of the police, but I needed a breakthrough in the case. I held my breath, hoping to get the answer I wanted.

'Very well, Miss Showers, I will speak to you.'

Arriving at his address, I paid the taxi driver and then turned around to get my first impression of Dr Pfeil's house. It was a bungalow; on Park Avenue, off Scarborough Road in Driffield. A smaller and more humble home than I had expected for a doctor. As I opened the garden gate, the front door to the house opened, and a middle-aged man wearing a dark jacket over grey trousers came out to peer at me through wire-rimmed glasses as I drew closer.

'Dr Pfeil, how nice to meet you,' I held out my hand in greeting, but he didn't accept it. He just stood aside so I could enter his house. He indicated toward the lounge.

'Please take a seat, Miss Showers.'

'Thank you for agreeing to see me, Dr Pfeil.' I took a seat in one of the armchairs in front of the fireplace. He took the other one.

The doctor got straight to the point. 'What is it you wish to know, Miss Showers?'

'Only what you know about Mr Hood and Mr Frisket.'

'Mr Hood was an American, Mr Frisket was English. They both went to the archery range that I do.'

'Is that it, Doctor? Didn't you try to socialise with them? That would be the normal thing to do between people who share an interest, wouldn't it?'

'I may have done given more time. As you can tell, Miss Showers, I am not English. I am German. I was captured after the allies landed in France and interned in a prisoner-of-war camp here, in England. After the war, I stayed here. I was a doctor in Germany before the war. So it didn't take me long to retrain here. Then your country created the National Health Service, which guaranteed me a job and income. I live quietly, seeking simple pastimes. I have few people who I can call friends, mostly colleagues at work, so I was hoping taking up archery would expand my social life.'

'But, did you ever get to know Mr Hood and Mr Frisket?'

'Not very much; Mr Hood was the quieter of the two. Mr Frisket talked too much for my liking. He liked to show off and boast about how good he was at archery. He would brag to everyone each time he scored a bulls-eye. He was very competitive and Mr Hood, being an American, encouraged him.'

'So you are saying you are not competitive?'

'I am; I just let what I achieve speak for me.'

'Do you still have family in Germany, Doctor?'

'A brother and a sister. What has that to do with the deaths of Mr Hood and Mr Frisket?'

'Nothing, I expect. I was just making conversation. Do you visit them?'

170

'I have done, once. It is difficult, you understand. They live in East Germany. Really, Miss Showers, why are they important to you?'

I could see he was getting anxious about where my questions were leading, so I changed the subject.

'They are not. What do you know about the printers next door to the archery range?'

'Nothing, should I?' He snapped back.

'Mr Frisket owned it. It was his body that was found.'

'Who by; the police?'

'No, me.'

'Ah, I understand now. You have a personal interest in your investigation. That changes things a little.'

'In which way?' I asked.

'The police must also consider you as a suspect for the murder. I can assure you, Miss Showers, that I know very little about Mr Hood and Mr Frisket. I would tell you more if I could, but I can't. I had nothing to do with their deaths. However, it is my duty as a doctor to assist you in any way I can.'

'Thank you, Doctor. I will leave you in peace. Don't worry about the British Police; they bark loudly, but on the whole, they are a good bunch.'

'Thank you, Miss Showers. Here, take my card; call me if you need me for anything else.'

'I will Doctor; thank you. Goodbye.' We shook hands as we parted and then put his business card in my handbag.

Chapter Ten

I'd no sooner settled into my office chair when Jennifer entered.

'I've done enough for today; fancy a cup of tea?' she asked cheerfully.

Having just got back from Dr Pfeil's house. I was parched, as well as foot sore.

'Yes, please, I'm all in. I don't think I'll do anything else today except go home to soak my feet. I'm missing my car already.'

With tea in hand and the biscuit tin between us, we settled at my desk.

'I've never wanted to learn to drive,' said Jennifer, sipping her tea. 'There are too many cars and lorry's on the road, all going in different directions; I don't know how you cope with it.'

'You get used to it.'

'What will you do without a car?' she asked.

'I'm not sure. I suppose I could hire one or I could ask Rex for help. But I'm reluctant to get Rex involved; he'll use it as an excuse to try to take over my investigation. But; on the other hand, his work connections could be very useful in helping me break through one or two official barriers.'

'Go on, call him. I like seeing him around the office; he's a bit of a hunk.' Jennifer giggled.

'You can't say things like that, you're married.'

'Well, it doesn't mean I can't appreciate a good-looking fellow when I see one.'

'The trouble is, he knows it, and coupled with that job of his, it makes him arrogant.'

'Go on, I'm sure you can tame the beast in him,' said Jennifer suggestively. We both burst out laughing.

'Right, that's enough.' I looked at my wristwatch. 'It's time for me to catch the bus home.'

Friday

As soon as I arrived at work, I was on the telephone with my insurance brokers, asking for an update on my car. They told me it was too early to get a response from my insurers and that I would have to wait a few more days. They said they would contact me by post with a decision about repairing or scrapping my car. Disappointed by the broker's answer, I dropped the telephone handset back onto its cradle, saying aloud, 'what do I do in the meantime?'

With the indifference of the insurance broker's to my plight at the back of my mind, I started work.

I didn't get the chance to interview the airmen; yesterday, so I needed to arrange a new date and time. If I couldn't get onto the airbase to see them, I'd ambush them at the archery range. It also occurred to me that I could also do with another chat with Mrs Hood. I had a nagging feeling that her explanation of the events leading to her husband's death didn't ring quite true. I also remembered what Dr Pfeil had said about helping me.

Last night, whilst I was in bed, I'd thought of a way he could help me. He was the perfect person to discover the exact cause of Mr Hood's death. Dr Pfeil would have legitimate access to Mr Hood's autopsy report, with no one asking him awkward questions, and a telephone call to Dr Pfeil confirmed his willingness to help me. He assured me he would call me back later in the day after he had read Robert Hood's medical report.

My next phone call was to Angie at the archery range. Angie told me that the airmen would be in on Saturday morning. Unfortunately, I'd arranged to visit Mummy and Daddy this Saturday morning, which meant I would have to catch the airmen as soon as they arrived at the archery range to interview them.

With most of my future arrangements made, I was only left with Mrs Hood to interview. She lived in the village of Little Driffield, only a few miles from my office. Ten minutes at most by taxi. So I dialled the number for Mrs Hood and prepared to arrange an appointment to visit her. After dialling her telephone number, I heard a couple of loud clicks on the line before the ringing tone came through. At first, I thought there might be a problem with the line, but the ringing tone continued, so I put the interference down to maintenance work being carried out on the line. Then Mrs Hood answered.

'Hood residence, Mrs Hood speaking.'

'Good morning, Mrs Hood. This is April Showers. I hope I haven't caught you at an inconvenient time, but I would like to come and see you, if I may? I would like to confirm a few details about your husband's case.'

However, before Mrs Hood could answer, I heard a man's voice in the background say 'Miss Thornwick, would you...' The hollow sound of an open telephone line suddenly changed to one of complete silence. A couple of seconds later, Mrs Hood's voice returned.

'Miss Showers; how very nice to hear from you. Do you have some news for me?'

'I'm sorry, Mrs Hood; if you have guests, I can call you back later on?'

'No, no; it's quite alright. It was just a neighbour calling me. They have gone now. How can I help you?'

'I was hoping to come and speak to you about your husband. I have a few more questions I would like to ask you?'

'Couldn't you ask me the questions over the telephone, Miss Showers?'

'I could, but I think it would be better if we met face to face on such a personnel matter as your husband's sudden death.'

'Yes, I suppose you are right. When were you thinking of coming?'

'I could be there in a few minutes if that is convenient for you?'

'Oh no, I'm sorry, Miss Showers. I have something to finish with my neighbour. Can we say in an hour? Better still, an hour and a half? How would eleven-thirty suit you?'

'Yes, that will be fine. I'll look forward to seeing you; goodbye.'

I put the telephone down with a feeling of unease. Who was the man's voice in the background? Was that her neighbour? Who is Miss Thornwick? And why did the telephone line sound so strange? I puzzled over it all for a moment, finally deciding that the man's voice was probably her neighbour and Miss Thornwick was someone else in the room with them. The strange sound over the telephone line could easily have been caused by a poor-quality telephone connection out of town to the village of Little Driffield.

Promptly at eleven-thirty, the taxi dropped me outside Mrs Hood's house in Little Driffield. She must have seen me arrive because the front door opened as my taxi drove away.

'Good morning, Miss Showers, please come in.' she said, pleasantly.

Again, I noted the lack of grief in Mrs Hood's demeanour, which seemed strange for someone so recently bereaved. But, I was here to discover who the house intruder and murderer of her husband was, not speculate over the quality of Mr and Mrs Hood's marriage. Even so, that may be an avenue of enquiry for later. Judging by the lack of grief she was showing, I had to consider her a suspect.

I sat on the sofa as I had done on my previous visit. I couldn't help noting the amount of dust which had accumulated on the coffee table in front of me. Mrs Hood took the armchair. In the seconds before we started speaking, I glanced around the room. Something was missing. The room wasn't quite right, or how it should be, but I couldn't place what was wrong with it.

'How may I help you, Miss Showers?' Mrs Hood brought my attention back to her.

'Please, won't you call me April?'

'If you wish? What is it would you like to ask me?'

'I've learnt that your husband was an American. You never mentioned that when I saw you last. How did you both meet?' There was a pause before she answered.

'He was a serviceman over here during the war. Is it important?'

'Maybe, if the person you say came to your house and killed him, knew your husband back during the war years.' Whilst Mrs Hood gave the matter some thought. I asked my next question.

'There is also the matter of the one hundred pounds you found in your husband's bureau and gave to me as a down payment towards my fee. I had them all checked at the bank; they are all forgeries. Where did you say your husband got them from? They could be the reason why your husband was murdered.'

'I don't believe I did say. In truth, I don't know where the money came from. I can only presume that he won it in a card game.'

'Yes, that was my guess as well. Though one hundred pounds is a lot of money to keep in a bureau and not in a safe or bank. Why do you think your husband didn't put the money in the bank?' Again, there was a pause before Mrs Hood answered.

'I don't know, Miss Showers. I can only assume he hadn't got around to it.'

'Is it possible that your husband knew that all the notes were forgeries, and that is why he didn't deposit them in his bank?'

'Are you accusing my husband of actually printing the banknotes, Miss Showers?'

'No, Mrs Hood. I'm just trying to establish if your husband knew the banknotes were forged ones. If he did. They may be the very reason why he was murdered. You see, your husband befriended a man by the name of Jack Frisket, who owned a printing business. Did he ever mention that name to you before he started gambling?'

'Not that I recall. Do you think he was the one who killed my husband?'

'I'm not sure; it's too early to tell yet.'

'But are you getting anywhere with the case, Miss Showers?'

'Yes, Mrs Hood, but I'm still in the very early stages of my investigation. I have lots of unanswered questions.'

I stood up as though ready to leave, spotted the trophies on the mantelpiece, and picked one up.

'Your husband played football, Mrs Hood. He must have been very fit?'

'Yes, he liked his soccer, though he stopped playing some years ago.'

As I replaced the trophy, I noted the circle in the dust where it had stood. That was it! Turning to face into the room, I looked at the walls and then all the surfaces; there were no photographs of Mr Hood in uniform or of Mr and Mrs Hood's marriage.

'Thank you, Mrs Hood, that will be all for now. I'll keep you up to date if I learn anything important. May I use your telephone to call for a taxi?'

'Yes, of course, help yourself.'

Crossing to the bureau, I picked up the telephone and dialled for a taxi. While there, I watched the number in the centre of the dialling disc spin around. It read Driffield 2366. My call was answered, and the taxi ordered. It would arrive in about ten minutes.

'Thank you, Mrs Hood. I won't detain you any longer. My taxi will be here soon. It's a nice day; I'll wait across the road by the duck pond.'

'If you are sure, April? There is a bench next to the pond if your taxi is later than expected.'

I stopped on the front doorstep, an afterthought occurring to me.

'There is one more thing I forgot to ask you. Have you seen a green van passing through the village? Registration BGS 592.' For the first time, I noted a change of expression on Mrs Hood's face at my questioning. It softened, as though she was actually pleased to hear the question.

'No; I haven't. Thank you, April. I will certainly keep a lookout for it.'

'Goodbye, Mrs Hood. I will call you if I have something new to report.'

'Goodbye, April, thank you for coming.'

Mrs Hood closed the front door, and I crossed the road to sit on a park bench opposite the village pond. I couldn't help looking back over my shoulder at the house. I had the uncanny feeling that things were not as they should be. Deep in thought, time passed quickly, and I didn't hear the taxi arrive until the driver pipped his car horn to attract my attention. As I crossed the grass to the taxi, I glanced across at the Hood house. A curtain twitched at a downstairs window. I was being watched. Getting into the back of the taxi, I instructed the driver to take me to Horsefair Lane, just across the main road from the pond, but to park out of sight of the Hood house. Once around the corner, I instructed the driver to stop and wait until I returned. He reminded me that the meter was still running, so I gave him a ten-shilling note with the promise of another when I returned. Cautiously making my way to the corner of the lane, I spied around a high hedge to get a better look at the Hood house. Mrs Hood was standing on the pavement outside the front door. A few seconds later, Rex pulled up in his distinctive car. Mrs Hood got in. As I watched Rex, I felt a rush of confusing emotions flush through me. I felt betrayed, used, lied to, and let down. Then, with a roar of his car's powerful engine, Rex drove off in the direction of Scarborough Road.

Returning to the taxi, I asked the driver to take me back to my office.

By the time the taxi dropped me off outside my office on Exchange Street, I was furious. I desperately wanted to telephone Rex and demand to know what was going on, and what was his connection to Mrs Hood. However, as I threw my handbag and coat on my desk and reached for the telephone, I hesitated. A new plan was coming to mind. As I couldn't trust what Rex told me and I couldn't trust anything Mrs Hood was saying. I was only left with what I had discovered. However, Robert Hood was dead, as was Jack Frisket, and I knew they were both linked to the forged five-pound notes.

My plan began to take shape. I had to keep Rex in the dark. There would be no more visits to Mrs Hood in Little Driffield. No more cooperating with the police. This case was suddenly very personal. I no longer considered Mrs Hood as a client and Rex a friend, though they were both clues as to what this case was all about.

I knew Rex was an MI5 operative, so it was a reasonably safe bet to think that Mrs Hood was one, too. Therefore, it's a reasonable assumption that Mr Hood is also connected to the security services. Was Robert Hood an agent who had gone bad or an agent who had been discovered by the enemy and then killed? Maybe he'd discovered who had been forging the five-pound notes, and that was why he was dead. I began pacing the floor whilst I thought through possible scenarios. A knock on the door stopped me in my tracks.

'Not now Jennifer, I'm busy!'

I took up pacing once again. The house had to belong to Robert Hood. The American football trophies on the mantelpiece had his name on them, and that was another point. Mrs Hood had referred to them as soccer trophies, but they weren't soccer trophies. The lack of family photos around the room only made sense if he wasn't married and lived alone. Which meant Mrs Hood was not Mrs Hood and was probably Miss Thornwick, the name I'd heard called out in the background whilst I was on the telephone to her. She must be an MI5 agent working with Rex. So, why has MI5 involved me in the case? I paced the floor some more. There had to be a link to the forgeries behind it all. Was Rex using me as bait to lure out Robert Hood's killers? He had to be. I'll never speak to him again. Just how low can a man go? No. There had to be more to it than that. If this was simply about forged five-pound notes, the regular police or Special Branch would be dealing with it. If Rex was interested in the forgeries, it had to be an international gang that was involved in the goings-on. Then a new thought occurred to me.

As Robert Hood was an American, were the forgers also printing American dollars as well as British pounds? That would explain why the American was involved. He must be an American law enforcement agent, investigating the forgeries for the US government, another reason why Rex was involved in the case. The American government would want to know what had happened to their man, so was Rex investigating Mr Hood's death on their behalf? That would make sense.

I stopped pacing up and down my office and sat down at my desk, feeling pleased with myself. I'd worked out what was going on and why everyone was involved with the case. My next step was to finish my interviews and work out who the crooks were. Two members of the Golden Shot Archery Club were dead. Both of them had connections to forged five-pound notes, but I now needed to know if any of the other members of the club were involved with the forgery business. And, if they were, who was likely to turn up dead next and warn them, and in return, hopefully, learn more about the murderer?

Danny Gold and Charlie Bowyer, the RAF men, would be at the club tomorrow; I had to make sure that I was there waiting for them.

Saturday

Up and ready in plenty of time to get to the Golden Shot Archery Club before it opened. It was my plan to catch Danny and Charlie as they came into the club, and before they started their archery practice, waylaying them for an interview. I'd use the informal approach with them. So as I stood in front of the fireplace in my living room, I had a quick check in the mirror; my hair and make-up were done, and I was wearing an attractive dress instead of my professional detective look. I looked like most other young modern women my age. By the time the two airmen had figured out that I'm more astute than they realised, they'd have told me all I wanted to know. A shoulder bag with matching shoes completed my outfit. The sound of the doorbell ringing announced my taxi.

Arriving at the archery club five minutes before it opened was perfect timing. Looking through the window, I could see Kevin Bodkin, the owner and instructor, inside at the reception desk. The door was locked, so by tapping on the window and using some friendly sign language, I indicated to Mr Bodkin that I'd like to talk to him.

'Thank you for letting me in, Mr Bodkin. I hate to be a nuisance, only I must speak to Danny Gold and Charlie Bowyer on an urgent matter. Those silly guards at RAF Driffield won't let me into the airbase to speak to them. I won't keep them long, and I promise not to disrupt what you are doing. I'll take them through to the lounge and buy them a drink.' He looked at his watch. I knew what he was doing; he was giving himself time to think before giving an answer.

'Please, Mr Bodkin, Kevin. It's really important.' I clasped his hands in mine and smiled at him sweetly.

'Okay; you can wait in the lounge and I'll send them through to you when they arrive.'

'Oh, no, please, I'd like to wait here to meet them. Just give me the nod when they arrive, unless they're in uniform, then I think I'll be able to spot them.' I didn't want Mr Bodkin warning them that a private detective wanted to speak to them.

Kevin Bodkin smiled at my self-deprecating quip.

'They never turn up in uniform. Don't worry, I'll let you know when they arrive,' he assured me.

I didn't have long to wait, thank goodness. I had already browsed the shelves in the shop on a previous visit to the archery range. The array of bits and pieces required to repair, enhance and decorate an archer's equipment was baffling, and most of it seemed somewhat pointless to me. As far as I was concerned, once you'd bought a bow and a few arrows, what more could you want?

As two men approached the shop door, Mr Bodkin called over to me.

'Here they come now.'

Crossing to the reception desk ready to intercept them before Mr Bodkin could, I tensed, waiting to pounce. This was probably going to be my only chance to interview them. As they entered, they spotted me immediately and paused in the doorway, looking me up and down.

'Hello, you must be the airmen from RAF Driffield?' I suggested cheerily.

'And, who might you be?' asked the taller and slightly older looking of the two as he grinned from ear to ear.

'My name is April. I'm a reporter for the local newspaper. We've heard about two local airmen taking up archery and I thought it might make a nice local interest piece for the paper. Come through to the lounge, we'll be able to chat more comfortably in there.' I spun on my heel, forcing the hem of my dress to flare out a little as I did so and headed towards the lounge. The airmen followed me like two hungry wolves on the scent of easy prey. Sitting on one of the comfortable, upholstered bench seats with my back to the wall, the guys selected wooden chairs on the opposite side of a round drinks table. Angie was behind the bar as we entered the lounge. As we sat down, she drifted over to us.

'Would you like a drink?' asked Angie.

'You can have what you like; within reason, I'm putting the cost of the drinks on my expenses account with the newspaper.'

'Bitter for us, thanks,' said the older one.

'I'll have an orange juice, please.' Angie returned to the bar to get the drinks.

'Right lads, tell me your names.'

'I'm Danny Gold.'

'And, I'm Charlie Bowyer.'

'Now tell me; what was it that attracted you both to archery as a sport?'

'The air force,' declared Charlie with a smile. 'The air force is keen to see recruits take up sports; I fancied doing something different. When I saw an advert for this place, I liked the idea. So, I asked permission to get an archery team organised with the view of starting competitions between our airbase and others in East Yorkshire, and, surprisingly, they agreed.'

'I suppose it must be very convenient having Speedy Printers next to the archery range? It's a handy place to get your competition leaflets printed.' was my next question.

'Not really. All our leaflet and poster printing is done on the RAF airbase,' replied Charlie.

'Oh, yes, of course, it would. I suppose you've heard about Mr Hood and Mr Frisket. It must be upsetting to hear about two members of this archery club being found dead?' The smiles dropped from Danny's and Charlie's faces. There was a pause as they thought about what to say until Danny responded.

'Yes, it was terrible news. We didn't know them well. We met them for the first time when we began taking lessons here.'

'So, you didn't socialise with them away from the club?'

'No. How could we? We are restricted to the airbase most of the time,' said Danny.

'Yes, I know, but you get time off; you're here now,' I declared. 'And, I imagine, the RAF gives you extra time off for archery lessons. After all, you are doing this for the benefit of your fellow airmen and the RAF?'

'Well... yes...' stammered Charlie, before Danny interjected.

'The RAF gives us two extra hours a week off our normal fitness training to practice archery on the airbase. Unfortunately, it's only when we get our weekly leave that we can come here, usually on Wednesdays.'

'But today is Saturday?'

'Yes. Well, we do get a weekend off every now and again,' interjected Charlie.

'That must make it difficult to get good enough to reach competition-level standards?'

'Not really, it's the same for everyone on the air base, so you see no one archer gets more of an advantage than another,' continued Danny.

'It doesn't sound as though the RAF is being all that helpful?' I suggested sympathetically. Whilst we were in the lounge, Terrance Nock, the road sweeper, came in and sat at a table two places away from us.

'No, you're wrong. The RAF is paying for our lessons and they've bought all the kit for the team we are going to set up at RAF Driffield. We just have to become more proficient ourselves so we can teach other airmen, of course,' insisted Charlie.

I crossed my legs, exposing my knees. The eyes of both airmen flashed to the exposed skin and, while they stared at my knees, I asked my next question.

'Did Jack Frisket or Robert Hood ever mention receiving a forged five-pound note?' Instantly, I had both men's full attention.

'Why would they do that?' asked Danny Gold.

'You must know forged fivers have been circulating around the shops of Driffield. I've checked with some of the shopkeepers. Have any found their way onto the airbase?'

'No,' insisted Danny. 'We would have heard. A notice would have been put up about it by the C.O.' Danny's eye's never left mine and silence fell across the table as the airmen waited for my next question.

Charlie broke the silence. 'I know Robert and Jack liked a small bet with each other during archer practice, and I once overheard them talking about a game of cards that they went to, somewhere. It wasn't in Driffield, it was somewhere else.'

I switched my attention to Charlie. 'Gambling men? Didn't you fancy joining in a game with them?'

'Mug's game,' said Danny, a hint of derision in his voice.

I kept up the gambling angle of my questioning. 'I heard they liked a game of cards at a pub in Leconfield. There's a rumour that some counterfeit five-pound notes exchanged hands there as well. The landlord of the pub wasn't best pleased about it, I can tell you.'

Charlie and Danny looked at each other. 'Thanks for the drinks, Miss. Charlie and me need to get some practice done before we run out of leave time.' Danny Gold stood up, giving Charlie a nudge to follow suit. I got to my feet with them.

'Thank you for your time?' I began following them out of the lounge, saying. 'Maybe we can talk again?' Neither man looked back. A comment from behind me stopped me from leaving.

'Up to no good; those two are. If you know what I mean.' The cryptic words in my ear made me jump and turn around sharpish to find Terrance Nock standing far too close to me for my liking.

'What do you mean by that?' I snapped.

'I couldn't help but overhear what you were talking about. It's just that I've seen them around when they should be at work. They get more time off that airbase than they said. Maybe they are on official business when I see them, as they're often in uniform. But, I don't expect they think that counts as time off the airbase.'

'Mr Nock, will you get to the point, I have work to do?'

'I expect the RAF does do all its own printing at the airfield, but RAF Driffield buys all its printing supplies from Speedy Printers next door. I've seen men turn up at that printer's in RAF Land Rovers to collect supplies. I also noticed that you didn't tell Danny and Charlie you are a private detective.' He stared at me, his face remaining expressionless.

'Take a seat, Mr Nock. Let me buy you a drink.' I signalled for Angie to come over and take our order.

'Yes?' asked Angie, somewhat curtly.

'I'll have a scotch, a double if you please,' requested Mr Nock.

'Orange juice for me, please Angie.' 'Very well, Mr Nock. What do you know?'

'RAF Land Rovers are easy to spot because of their markings. They turn up a couple of times a month. Usually with one or both of those two, occasionally, it's other airmen who collect printing materials.'

'Are you suggesting that Danny and Charlie knew Jack Frisket better than they were letting on?'

'I'm saying they knew Jack Frisket and about this archery club long before they joined here to start archery lessons.'

Mr Nock tapped the side of his nose with his finger and winked at me.

'Very well, tell me more.' Angie arrived with our drinks. Mr Nock picked up his glass and swallowed his scotch in one mouthful.

'I'll have another one of these if you don't mind.' I nodded at Angie.

'This had better be worth it, Mr Nock.'

'I'm a street cleaner, right? Invisible to most people. They think me and the job I do are beneath them. However, I see all sorts of things when I'm out and about with my broom. I have a routine. These streets I do on a Monday, those streets I do on a Tuesday and so on throughout the week. I get to know people's habits. People have routines; Mrs Bagshaw always does her weekly shopping on a Tuesday morning. Ralf Mortimer always goes for a pint at the Tiger on Friday lunchtime. Coopers, the butchers always get deliveries on Monday morning at eight o'clock...'

'Yes, yes, I get the picture.'

'Well, I live not far from here, as you know, and as I live on my own, I sometimes go for a walk of an evening. It helps pass the time; if you know what I mean.'

'And?'

'Well, sometimes, when I come down the lane outside here, I've seen a green van with two men loading it with boxes from the printers.'

'Who's van is it? Do you know?'

'No. It's always been too dark to see the faces of the men, but one time, in the light from an open door at the printers, I spotted Jack Frisket when he was loading stuff into his van late at night.'

'It's Frisket's printers, Mr Nock. There is nothing unusual or helpful in that news.'

'No, I know that. But what I mean is; the men who come with the green van. I know where they park the van during the day. I've seen it when I've been on my rounds.'

'Now you're talking, Mr Nock. Where is it?'

'What's it worth?'

I was taken aback by his question, although I quickly realised I should have been expecting it. He'd made my skin crawl the first time I'd met him, so his asking for money should not have come as a surprise.

'Mr Nock, I may be a private detective and not an official police officer, but I have to report all I discover to them. When I leave here, I shall go to the police and tell them that you know where a crucial piece of evidence is being hidden that is relevant to a crime they are interested in. Now, I can either tell the police how helpful you have been to me, or I will inform them that you have attempted to extort money from me in exchange for that evidence. Which would you prefer?'

'But I haven't asked for money. That's not what I meant at all.' He squirmed in his seat, looking nervous. 'I just thought that if I gave you some helpful information leading to the arrest of the criminals, there might be a reward and you might know what it is. I mean, if, as you say, these guys are involved in a serious crime, the police often offer a reward for helpful information leading to an arrest. I was just asking about that. I wasn't asking for anything from you.'

'I see; very well, Mr Nock, where is the green van?'

'It's parked on Skerne Road. Across the railway lines, just down from the malting houses. I suppose no one thinks it unusual to see a van parked outside a malting house, only I noticed it was the same one that I'd seen late one night at Speedy Printers.'

'Thank you, Mr Nock. I promise to let the police know how helpful you have been.' I left and rushed home to get changed. If I wanted to visit this van he was talking about, I would have to disguise myself a little and take on the appearance of a woman who worked at the malting warehouse.

After getting the bus home, I changed into slacks, a sweater, sensible shoes, a jacket and a headscarf. Then, I returned to town, getting off the bus at the railway station and making my way to Skerne Road on foot. The walk gave me time to go over what Mr Nock had told me, and I wondered what he was doing down a dark alley late at night. That was when I remembered all the bedroom windows which overlooked the archery range and the printers. My revulsion for the man increased.

As I crossed over the railway lines, the malting houses were just up ahead, and parked at the roadside was a van. It was green with the registration number BGS 592. The same van I had followed the other night. The same van out of which two men had jumped to threaten me in Langtoft. I stopped before I got too close to it. Crossing to the opposite side of the road, I walked past the van, giving it a sideways glance. There was no one sitting in the driver's seat. Walking on, up ahead, I spotted a large warehouse-type building. Once I'd reached it, I turned around and walked back. I'd found the van I was looking for, but not the men. I had a big decision to make; do I tell the police about the van and let them deal with it, or do I watch the van and wait for the men to come back to collect it?

Chapter Eleven

Sunday

I'd spent the entire weekend walking up and down Skerne Road, watching and waiting for the men to turn up, which they didn't. On Sunday afternoon, when the rain started, cold, tired, bored and hungry, I gave up and went home. Deeply disappointed with my wasted weekend, I decided that I had to find a more practical way of keeping an eye on the van.

Monday

Sat at my desk with a cup of coffee, ready to write up the notes I'd taken on Saturday; I was interrupted by George, the postman, with a handful of envelopes.

'Morning April; how's tricks?'

'Morning George, I'm busy, as usual.'

'Ah, you're on a murder case. Who's dead, and who are your suspects? I might know them. You know what us postmen are like; eyes and ears of the world,' he said eagerly, hovering close to my desk.

I closed my open file. 'Who said I was on a murder case?'

'You just did, by not denying it. Well?'

'It's none of your business, George. Where's my post?'

'Sorry, April. It's here; nothing exciting today. It all looks like bills, apart from this one; it's handwritten.'

I held out my hands to receive the letters, and George duly filled them with envelopes. 'Goodbye, George; see you tomorrow.'

'Bye, April. Have a nice day?'

'You too.'

Leaving all the other envelopes on one side, I selected the handwritten one. It was from Dr Pfeil. It was short and to the point, but it made interesting reading all the same. The doctor had found Mr Hood's autopsy report. The cause of death was a blow to the back of the head with a blunt instrument. Traces of oil had been found in his hair. As well as in and around the wound on the back of his head. Printing ink and dirt were found embedded in his forehead, further suggesting he was struck from behind whilst bending down. After which, he had fallen forward onto his face. However, the fall was not from a high enough height to break the skin on the victim's forehead. The autopsy results suggested he had been killed in an industrial setting. The date and time of death were recorded as Wednesday 5th between 10 am and 12noon. The date and time of death shown in the autopsy report were three days before Mrs Hood had called me in on the case. The medical report proved that Mr Hood had not died at home; but somewhere else. This was the evidence that I needed to show that I'd been lied to ever since I'd been brought in on the case. I dropped the letter on my desk and sat back in my chair to think. Why had Mrs Hood, if that was her real name, picked me to investigate the death of her husband? The police already knew Mr Hood had not died at home. So why were Sherlock Holmes and Dr Watson, the two rude detectives from the Driffield police, hounding me over the forgeries? There was clearly a connection between the deaths and the forgeries. I could only conclude that I was being used by someone to solve the two crimes. The only thing I had to figure out was by who and why? Was it the Driffield police? I'd embarrassed them before by solving cases they had struggled with. Were they using me to solve the case? So, at the final moment, they could step in and claim the credit? Or was it Rex and his shadowy colleagues from GCHQ and MI5 who were using me to unearth East German spies as they had done once before? I had seen him at Mr Hood's house. I felt hurt at the idea that Rex would use me in this fashion yet again.

Rationality kicked in. Rex couldn't be a willing participant in using me in this way. So, he had to be lurking close by, watching me. This was a green light for me to press on with the case. Embolden by the idea that Rex was hiding in the wings, ready to save me if things got tough.

I was sure that if I could discover the identities of the two men who used the green van. I would solve both cases. Only, standing on street corners or walking up and down Skerne Road every day waiting for someone to collect the van was impractical. I needed help. I needed a car. Something Terrance Nock had said to me came to mind. He had told me he was invisible, and he was right. I had done what he said other people do. I'd seen dustbin men, road repair men and road sweepers like Mr Nock doing their daily jobs and completely forgotten about them as soon as they were out of sight. He had a job that people turned a blind eye to. He was part of the ordinary. The day-to-day street furniture that we all expected to see and took for granted. Loathed as I was to admit it, he was right, and because of it, I needed him. He could watch the van for me and then let me know when and where he had seen it. I was happy with my new plan, however; I knew it would only work if I could convince Mr Nock to help me. I shivered at the thought of having to deal with the smelly, creepy little man again.

Distracting myself from thinking about Mr Nock, I picked up the next letter from my desk. It was from my insurance company. My little green Morris Minor had been scheduled for repair. Unfortunately, due to a heavy workload, it would be four weeks before my car was returned to me. 'I can't be without a car for four weeks,' I exclaimed, out aloud, slamming the letter down on my desk. Letting out a sigh of disbelief, I had to face the fact that I needed to hire a car. Remembering my visit to the garage on Middle Street and the cars in the showroom, I could kill two birds with one stone. The search for a replacement car and being able to ask Mike Bentley, the garage owner, if he'd received any more forged five-pound notes.

'Miss Showers. How nice to see you again, and so soon. Have you caught the forger?' Mike Bentley crossed the car showroom floor with his hand raised, ready to take mine; an instinctive reaction for any salesman. We shook hands.

'No, not yet, I'm sorry to say. Have you received any more forgeries?'

'No, thank goodness. I think word must have got out that I'm carefully checking all the banknotes I get.'

'That's good to hear. Though, the real reason for my visit is to hire a car. I'm temporarily without one. Do you have anything available?'

'It's not my line of business. You don't get many people wanting to hire a car in Driffield. Though I may be able to help you. A customer brought his car in to be repaired. Unfortunately for him, the bill was more than he could afford, so he told me to keep the car. It's an old pre-war Hillman Minx. Unfortunately, it's not the type of car I want customers to see in my showroom. You can use that if you like. How does five-pound a week sound?'

I thought about it for a minute. 'May I see it before I decide?'

'Sure, it's just out back. Follow me.' The salesman led me through a door at the rear of the showroom into a yard full of cars. 'It's the black one, just there.' He pointed to the car in the corner of the yard. The car looked very old-fashioned. It was long and had four doors. The headlights stood out on either side of the radiator grill like giant bulging eyes. It reminded me of a small hearse with its flat vertical windscreen, flat roof, and blunt rear.

'Are you sure you don't have anything else?'

198

'Sorry, Miss Showers, all the other cars you can see here either belong to customers and are in for repair or they are being cleaned up and got ready for selling.'

It was difficult not to look disappointed. 'Very well, Mr Bentley, I will take it.'

'You won't regret it, Miss Showers; it's a very comfortable ride, though a little heavy on the steering; you'll soon get the hang of it. I'll have it cleaned and filled with petrol for you. One of my lads will deliver it to your office as soon as it is ready.'

During lunch in a cafe, I resigned myself to the ordeal of driving around in the old Hillman Minx. After all, I'd only have to put up with the thing for four weeks. The time would soon pass.

With nothing urgent to do that afternoon, I sat at my desk waiting for the Hillman to arrive. It gave me time to think about the unpleasant Terrance Nock and how I should go about getting him to help me. Unfortunately, it meant another visit to his house, in the rundown part of town, as he didn't have a telephone. Only this time, I wanted to take someone with me, but who? In the past, I'd used my father, Rex, or Holly to chaperone me when visiting suspects. But, the trouble was, Rex was out of the picture because I didn't trust his motives. My father would learn too much about the work I do and try to stop my investigation, saying it was too dangerous for me. And as for Holly, she had been through enough on a previous caper to involve her. I resigned myself to going on my own, telling myself, what is the point of all those Judo lessons you've been taking if you still need someone to hold your hand when visiting a suspect?

'Mr Nock, I have a favour to ask of you!' He opened the front door wider and indicated for me to come in. As I entered the living room, I noticed how little it had changed. The mess and clutter I'd seen previously was still all there. This time, glancing up at the mantelpiece, I spotted a photograph of a young man in an army officer's uniform. Picking it up to look at it more closely, I asked.

'Your brother? I can see the likeness in you both.' Hoping to strike a friendly note with Mr Nock.

'No. The photograph is of me. It was taken in North Africa during the war, just before I was sent home. You said you had a favour to ask of me. Would you like tea?' He took the photograph from me and replaced it on the mantelpiece.

'Yes; if you are willing. No, thank you. When we spoke earlier, you said something interesting. You said you were invisible when you were at work. I need someone invisible.'

'I don't understand, Miss Showers?' Nock, put down the teapot he was holding and took the chair opposite me.

'I need some help to discover who is using that green van. I watched it for two days but no one came to collect it. That's when I thought of you. You said you sweep that street regularly, so I'd like you to watch the van for me. I'd like you to telephone me when you see the men take the van away or even if you notice the van missing. I have to establish a pattern of how often they use the van. As they always bring it back to the same spot. When I can predict their comings and goings, I will drive down there, park up nearby and watch for its return. That way, I'll learn who is using the van. I'll then follow them to their home address.'

'I see,' said Nock, leaning back in his chair to give the matter some thought.

'I will pay you for information received, Mr Nock. I don't want you to think that I'm trying to take advantage of your good nature.' Again, Nock took his time before answering.

If; I do as you ask. It will cause me a great deal of inconvenience, Miss Showers. To do the job properly, I will have to alter my routine and cleaning plan. I usually only go along Skerne Road once a week. For your plan to work, I would need to go up and down there two or three times a week, maybe more. Any less and it could be months before I notice the van has been moved.'

'Yes, I see what you mean. I didn't realise you only visited Skerne Road once a week.'

'Sometimes it's less than that. If I have to clean up after a big market day. Skerne Road is a low-priority road as far as the council is concerned.'

'Yes, I suppose it is. It's not the town centre, is it?' My idea now seemed foolish.

'So you see, to visit Skerne Road more frequently, I would have to ignore my regular round, and if the council got wind of that, they'd want to know what I was playing at.'

'As I have said, Mr Nock, I will pay you for your trouble. On the other hand, if the task is too arduous for you, I'll find another way of tracking the men.' I picked up my handbag, ready to leave.

'No. No. I'll do it, for the time being, at least,' said Mr Nock.

'Thank you. When can you start?'

'You haven't said how much you are willing to pay me yet?' Nock had a glint in his eye.

I paused, pretending to give the matter a lot of thought. I'd already decided that if I was too generous, it would encourage him to string out the task for as long as possible. So, I had to make him hungry for the reward.

'I'll pay you ten shillings per week just for watching for the men. But I will pay you five pounds when I get the message telling me they have arrived at the van. Seven pounds a week is about what you get paid by the council, isn't it?'

'Close enough, Miss Showers. Or may I say, April, now that we are partners?'

'We will keep our arrangement professional, Mr Nock. Can you start tomorrow?'

'Yes, Miss Showers. But when I telephone you, how will you get to Skerne Road in time to follow them?'

'Don't worry, Mr Nock, I have that problem in hand. I will post a letter to you each week containing a ten-shilling note until the job is done. Thank you for your time, Mr Nock. I need to be on my way.'

Walking into town after my visit to Mr Nock, I prepared to put the second part of my plan into action. At the hardware shop on Middle Street, I bought a carpenter's awl and then returned to my office. My timing couldn't have been better. Just as I was walking along Exchange Street, I saw my hire car arrive.

The driver got out. He hadn't spotted me and went into my agency. I followed, hot on his heels.

After the delivery driver had demonstrated all the different switches and controls of the car to me, he left me with the keys. Now, I figured, was as good a time as any to put part three of my plan into action.

Taking my seat behind the steering wheel of the Hillman Minx and closing the door, I made myself comfortable. My senses were filled with the smell of the newly polished leather seats, stale tobacco, and a hint of engine oil. After winding down the window, I inserted the key into the ignition and pulled on the starter knob. The engine burst into life and settled to a reassuring purr. Starting slowly at first, as the car was much larger than my old Morris Minor. I inched the car forward, cautiously gaining speed as I became more familiar with its handling.

Once I'd reached Skerne Road, I drove up to and parked behind the green van, using the bulk of the black Hillman to hide what I was about to do. Leaving the engine running, I pulled the carpenter awl from my bag and got out of the car. After checking to see that no one was watching me, I pushed the awl into the rear tyre of the green van. For a second or two, there was a loud hiss of escaping air. The green van tilted back slightly; the deflating tyre, losing pressure to flatten out on the road. After another look around to ensure the coast was clear, I got back in the Hillman and drove away.

The Hillman picked up speed as I drove along Skerne Road and out of Driffield. My face was hot and flushed, and my hands trembled a little; I smiled, triumphantly. It was payback time. Continuing along the road, passing through the village of Skerne, taking my hire car for a drive through the country felt like a good idea. Too excited to return to my office, I drove towards the coast, picking up the road to Bridlington. Freshly prepared coffee and ice cream came to mind, so I drove north.

At first, Bridlington seemed very quiet, but then I reminded myself it was a Monday and also out of season. Parking on the seafront, I strolled along the prom, breathing in the sea air and letting the wind blow through my hair. It was relaxing watching the seagulls skimming over the waves as the waves rolled onto the beach. A row of hardy fishermen lined the beach with their fishing rods. Other people were walking their dogs on the sand and a sightseeing boat sailed out of the harbour. My walk led me into the town centre and, before I knew it, I was standing in front of the Italian-style café. It was where only a few months ago, Natalie West had been the waitress. She was in prison now, along with all the others who had conspired to murder my aunt and benefactor. I spotted the owner behind the counter making coffee at the espresso machine. It was time to move on. Crossing the road, I entered an ice cream parlour, ordering a Knickerbocker Glory and a coffee. The coffee here wasn't anywhere near as good as the one I would have got in the Italian-style cafe across the road, but the Knickerbocker Glory ice cream lived up to its name. I took my time, enjoying the opportunity to indulge myself. The rush of excitement I'd felt after puncturing the tyre on the green van had warn-off, and I was left wondering what I should do next. There was nothing left to do except go back to my office and wait to hear from Mr Nock.

Back behind my desk, I couldn't concentrate on anything other than wishing the telephone would ring. I went through my plan of how to follow the van, repeatedly, thinking of all the ways it could go wrong. What if the men had finished with the green van and had now abandoned it? What happened if they wanted it during the night? They could fix the punctured tyre when Mr Nock wasn't there to see them and warn me. So should I start watching Speedy Printers at night, just in case the men returned when it was dark? I had a better idea. I'll go back to the van and do more damage to it. Enough to force the men to send it to a garage to be repaired? The idea grew in appeal. The only problem was, apart from crashing into it with another vehicle, I didn't know what to do to it.

There was a light knock on my office door before Jennifer came in.

'It's eleven o'clock. You look ready for a cup of tea and a biscuit or two,' said Jennifer with a smile.

With one last look at the telephone, I resigned myself to the fact that it wasn't going to ring in the next fifteen minutes.

I said, 'good idea.' And followed her through to the kitchen, leaving my office door wide open so I could hear if the telephone rang.

'What's the matter?' asked Jennifer.

'This job I'm on. It's driving me nuts.'

'The one about the dodgy fivers?'

'Yes. I believe two people have died because of them. I don't know who I can trust. Everyone I thought was on my side; tells me lies. I'm sure Rex is mixed up in it. I don't believe Mrs Hood is Mrs Hood. Mr Nock is Mr Creepy. All the other suspects seem to have something to hide, so are being unhelpful. The only thing I have been able to do is set a trap for the men who ran me off the road. And I'm having doubts about that plan because I've got to use Mr Creepy.'

'Um. I suppose it's a bit like making a cake.'

'What?' The comparison confused me.

'You know what I mean. You gather all your ingredients together, and then you mix them up. You find yourself up to your elbows in flour, sugar and butter. There's more mess on the table than in the mixing bowl. Then you pour the mixture into the baking tin and put it in the oven. You then spend the next three-quarters of an hour praying for a good result until it's time to take it out. You either end up with a big fluffy sponge or a flat biscuit stuck to the bottom of the cake tin.'

I laughed. 'That's a strange analogy.'

'Good. At least you've cheered up a bit. I was getting worried about you.'

I watched Jennifer pour tea into our cups, staring at the brown liquid as it drained from the spout of the teapot.

'That would do,' I exclaimed out loud.

'What would?'

'Tea, no, water. I could put water into the petrol tank, then they'd have to take the van to a garage to get it fixed.'

'Who and what are you talking about?' asked Jennifer, looking more confused than ever.

'I have had an idea of how to discover the identity of two men and where they live. I'm sure they hold the key to solving the mystery of the forged five-pound notes. Only, I don't know where to find them. So, I've just devised a plan to bring them into the open, but it has a lot of holes in it. But, thanks to you, I've had a brainwave. If I put water in the petrol tank of their van, they will have to take it to the garage to get it fixed. The garage is only open during the daytime, so that narrows down the times they can take it in. The garage on Middle Street is the only place in the area where they can take it to get it fixed. So, if I watch the garage, I find the men I'm looking for.'

'You're a genius, April.'

'Only if the plan works?'

'When are you going to do it?' asked Jennifer enthusiastically.

'Tonight.'

'Can I go with you?'

'Jennifer!'

'Well, why not? I could act as your lookout. And, besides, I never get to do anything exciting. Please, April. I'll do exactly what you tell me to do, and it'll be safer for you if we go together.'

I thought about it for a few seconds. 'What will your husband say when I come to collect you so late at night?'

'Um, I hadn't thought of that. I know, I'll telephone him and say you've invited me round to your house. I'll tell him it's your birthday or something and that I'll be home late.'

'You're mad; you know that, don't you?' But I felt a lot happier knowing that I would have a friend watching my back.

'However,' I continued. 'You mustn't breathe a word of what we are about to do to anyone, not now or ever. What we are going to do is a criminal act.'

At home that evening, I felt strange having someone else in the kitchen with me as I prepared dinner. Even when I invited Mummy and Daddy around for a meal, I'd completed all the preparation beforehand to show them that I was perfectly capable of living on my own. Somehow, this was different; this felt good. It was more intimate and cosy having Jennifer at my side while I boiled some potatoes and grilled a couple of lamb chops each. That's when it occurred to me. I'd lived in my new home for months and never thought to invite my work colleagues around for a housewarming party. I put the party on my 'things to do list' for when my current case was finished.

After dinner, I took Jennifer upstairs to change. She couldn't go out with me in her work clothes, so I lent her some of my casual clothes. All evening we talked about our work, her husband, what we liked to buy when we went shopping; anything but what we were about to do that evening until Jennifer looked at the clock.

'What time will we be setting off?' asked Jennifer.

'About eleven. It should be quiet enough by then.' I could see Jennifer was getting nervous, so I switched on the TV to act as a distraction. We watched a weekly drama about a girl who'd become pregnant and had run away from home. As soon as the show had finished, I switched off the TV, saying. 'Let's go.'

We sat in silence as I drove towards town. The tension in the car, palpable until Jennifer broke the silence. 'I feel like I'm going to a funeral, sitting in this car.'

'I sincerely hope not,' I snapped back. We both laughed. Jennifer's jibe at my car was just what we both needed to lift our anxiety about our mission.

I brought my car to a stop behind the green van. We both had a good look around before getting out. The road was deserted. Once out of the car, I looked down at the van's punctured tyre. No one had been to fix it. I removed the filler cap from the green van's petrol tank and Jennifer passed me the lemonade bottle full of water. It only took a few seconds to empty the entire contents of the bottle into the tank, but it felt like an eternity. I gave Jennifer the empty bottle, jammed the petrol cap back into place, and then shooed Jennifer back towards my car.

We drove away, heading along Skerne Road away from town as I had done earlier in the day. Out of sight of the van, we both let out a scream.

'Oh, my God, that was fun,' said Jennifer, bubbling with excitement. 'Can I come with you again when you do something like that?' She continued bouncing up and down in her seat. I didn't answer her; instead, I kept driving, turning back towards home at the next junction. All the way home, Jennifer never stopped talking; she had everything planned out. She would be Watson to my Sherlock Holmes. I didn't have the heart to burst her bubble. I let her enjoy the moment.

At home, she changed back into her work clothes, and I drove her home. I was tired. The long day had taken a lot out of me emotionally, so while Jennifer continued in her fit of excitement, I stayed silent. When I stopped my car outside her house, she paused before getting out.

'Thanks April. Just wait until tomorrow when I tell the other girls at the office about what we did tonight.'

I held onto her arm, preventing her from getting out of the car. 'Jennifer, I meant it. You can't tell anyone about what we did tonight. It was illegal. Also, if, by chance, those men learn who is responsible for what has happened to their van, they may take revenge on you, your husband and me. Remember, two people connected to this case have already been murdered. You cannot say a word to anyone about what we have done.'

Her expression became more sombre. 'Sorry, April. I won't say a word, I promise.'

Chapter Twelve

Tuesday

Jennifer was already at work by the time I arrived. She followed me into my office, closed the door, and came across to sit on the chair I kept for clients.

'I'm shattered. I didn't sleep a wink last night. How do you do this job and stay sane?' she said, looking very bleary-eyed.

'I don't know. I suppose you just get used to it. Believe me; it's not like this all the time. Most of my work is boring, routine stuff that barely pays the bills. If it wasn't for the inheritance that Aunt Violet left me and the rent I get from you, Patsy, and Annabelle renting offices in this house, I'd have to close up.' I dropped my handbag into the bottom drawer of my desk.

'Is there any tea?' I asked. We decamped to the kitchen.

'What did you tell your husband after I dropped you off at home?'

Jennifer ran her fingers through her hair, took a deep breath, and let it out slowly. 'I told him I helped you cook a meal, that we had a few drinks and chatted all evening.' She yawned and then rubbed her eyes.

'You should take the day off. Go home and get some sleep.'

'I can't; I've got too much work to do.' She yawned again and then took a sip of tea.

'Okay, then you'd better grab forty winks in your office. Come on.' I led Jennifer back to her office. 'Right, sit down and put your feet up here.' I turned her wastepaper bin upside-down and lifted her feet onto it. 'Now, lean back.' I laid her coat over her like a blanket. 'Close your eyes and get some sleep. I'll wake you in an hour.' Before leaving her office, I closed the curtains and lifted the telephone receiver off its cradle.

'Thanks, April,' said Jennifer, softly, as I left her office.

Having returned to my desk, I also wished I had the time to take forty winks, but it wasn't going to happen. I also had work I should be doing. The trouble was that I couldn't settle and put my mind to starting work. Having sabotaged the green van, I now impatiently waited for Mr Nock to telephone me. To tell me someone had come to collect it, but couldn't drive it away. After an hour of inactivity, I went to wake Jennifer. She was in the same position I had left her in, so instead of waking her, I went to make a cup of tea. With a fresh cup of tea in hand, I awoke Sleeping Beauty. It took her a few seconds to come around, but having a fresh cup of tea to hand made the difference.

'Oh, thanks, April; you're a lifesaver. I'm still tired, but my brain seems to be working again, though I'm not so sure about my back. These chairs are not designed for sleeping on.'

'Well, you could always buy a camp bed and put it in the corner of your office.' I said with a touch of laughter.

'Don't mock; it may come to that if I don't finish all this work in the next couple of days. So, I expect I'll be working overtime for the rest of this week.'

'You'll manage; I know you will. I don't have any typing for you to do, so I won't be adding to your workload until I make some progress with my current case.'

'How is it going?'

'Slowly. I need to give what we did last night time to work. With this case, I've sort of - put all my eggs in one basket, as they say. All I can do now is wait for things to happen.'

And, wait is what I had to do. With no other jobs to work on, I spent the next two anxious days twiddling my thumbs and reading the local newspaper. I was looking for reports about damage to vehicles on Skerne Road or any news about forged five-pound notes. I was tied to my office, waiting for the telephone to ring. Even the police had not been back to bother me. Never had I spent so much time with nothing to do and feeling so stressed. My world was focused on the telephone on my desk, wishing it to ring.

Thursday

I'd had a frustrating day yesterday, followed by a night of doubt and bad dreams. I arrived at work earlier than usual and I was on my second cup of tea as well as halfway through a packet of biscuits when George, the postman, arrived with my morning mail. He was his usual joyful self. However, I wasn't in the mood for his early morning witticisms and unfairly sent him away rather tersely instead of engaging him in our usual bit of banter. As he left my office, the telephone sprang to life.

Snatching up the receiver from its cradle, I held it to my ear.

'Yes!' I heard the pips on the other end of the line; the call was coming from a phone box.

'Miss Showers?' said the voice.

'Yes! Is that you, Mr Nock?'

'Yes, I'm in the phone box on Skerne road. The green van is being collected by a breakdown truck. The garage name on the truck is Middle Street Garage & Repairs, Driffield.'

'Well done, Mr Nock. You get back to your normal rounds. I'll take it from here. Call in at my office the next time you are passing, and I will pay you the rest of your fee. Thank you for all your help.'

Happy with the news I'd just been given, I slammed the phone down. My plan had worked. I was so elated. I felt as though I had won the jackpot on the football pools. Sitting back, I let the relief wash over me for a moment.

'Right, lass, you've got work to do.' I said out loud. Grabbing my bag and coat, I was quickly out of the door and on my way to the garage on Middle Street. Standing outside a shop not far from the garage, I waited for the breakdown truck to arrive with the green van. Eventually, it came slowly down the street with the green van on the back. Watching it intently, I was desperate to see if the owner was with the van. But my wait was in vain. As the breakdown truck drew closer, I was disappointed to see only the driver of the recovery truck in the cab. There was only one thing left for me to do. It was time to have a chat with Mike Bentley, the owner of the garage.

'Miss Showers, I didn't expect to see you again so soon. There's nothing wrong with the car you've hired, is there?'

'No. No. Mr Bentley, I am very satisfied with my hire car. However, there is one thing you can help me with. I've just seen your recovery truck take a green van into your yard. It just so happens that I am curious to know who it belongs to.'

Mr Bentley looked at me suspiciously before answering.

'Is it important? You see, it is not my normal practice to divulge my clients' details.'

'Nor I, Mr Bentley. Only I need the information. It's in connection to a crime that I'm investigating.'

'Still; I don't know, Miss Showers. If word got out that I just gave away customer names and addresses to anyone. It could ruin me.'

'I understand your concerns, Mr Bentley. But you see. The owner of that green van may be involved with the forged five-pound notes, which have been circulating around town lately.'

'I see what you mean, Miss Showers. The call about the van came in first thing this morning. I found the van key in an envelope when I arrived at work this morning. Someone must have put it through the door last night, along with the van's description, registration and address. A telephone call at eight o'clock this morning from a man calling himself Mr Smith confirmed the details. He told me he could not start the van, and that someone had punctured one of its tyres.' I noted the look of realisation spread across his face before he continued. 'I told him to phone back tomorrow, saying I would let him know what was wrong with it and how long it would be before it was fixed.'

'Did he give you his home address?'

'No. I've got his van. If he doesn't pay his repair bill, I'll keep his van. Then, I telephone the police myself. Once the police have established the van has been abandoned through an inability to pay the repair bill, it is mine. I'd be able to sell a van like that for more than the cost of the repairs to it.'

'I see. Just for your information, Mr Bentley. The van has false number plates on it. They were stolen off a council steamroller. Speaking of which, I'd be grateful if you would let me know when he plans to collect it. I would like to know who this Mr Smith is.'

'You're not going to cause a scene in my garage, are you, Miss Showers?'

'Of course not, Mr Bentley. I simply want to identify Mr Smith and then follow him to his home address. I've no intention of confronting him or even being seen by him. I'll be watching your garage from across the street.'

'Very well, Miss Showers. I will telephone you as soon as the owner tells me when he plans to collect the van. My mechanics will look at the van first thing tomorrow morning. After that, it depends if the repair means waiting for spare parts to arrive or if the job is a simple mechanical adjustment to get the van rolling again. Once I know how long the repair will take, I shall inform Mr Smith and your good self when it will be ready for collection.'

'Thank you, Mr Bentley. However, there is one more thing you can do for me. I'd like to borrow the key to the van: I'll bring it straight back after I get a copy made of it.'

'Make sure you do, Miss Showers.'

I left the garage feeling as though I should have told him I already knew what was wrong with the van as I had caused the problems, but I thought it better to hold that information back in case he let something slip to Mr Smith. I returned to my office. The van was my only genuine lead; all my other suspects had someone to give them an alibi or were helping me with my enquiries. That afternoon, I took the key to have a copy made. As soon as I got the chance, I was going to inspect the interior of that van.

Friday

Just before ten o'clock, I received a phone call from Mr Bentley at the garage. His mechanics had fixed the problems with the green van, and the owner had arranged to collect it on Saturday morning at nine o'clock.

Saturday

At eight o'clock, I was parked opposite the garage on Middle Street. I sat in my car, intently watching the garage, waiting for the green van to appear. However, Middle Street is the busy shopping street of Driffield and it was filling rapidly with shoppers, even at this early hour.

I had hoped to identify the owner of the green van as he arrived, but all seem quiet at the garage, apart from the occasional driver stopping for petrol. Then I saw it. The green van was pulling out of the rear garage yard onto a side street. The van owner must have entered the building through the yard at the rear of the premises. As the van was turning away from me, I didn't have time to see the driver's face. I started my car and indicated to pull out. But, by the time I had my car away from the kerb, the green van was turning left. I was about to lose sight of it.

Beeping impatiently at some pedestrians who were about to cross the road in front of me, I turned onto Albion Street, putting my foot down on the accelerator as I did so. This big old Hillman Minx wasn't as nippy as my little Morris Minor, but it picked up speed smoothly. As I drove around the bend in the road, I caught a glimpse of the green van just before it turned another corner onto Harper Street. Following it, I saw it turn left onto Wansford Road. Not wanting to be spotted, I hung back a little. A lesson I had learned the hard way when I'd previously followed the green van. After about half a mile, I saw it turn onto a rough side track, so I pulled into the kerb. It was impossible for me to follow it in my car without being noticed. So, there was nothing else I could do except follow the van on foot. I kept a pair of wellington boots in the boot of my car for such emergencies. During my last adventure, I had to cross a farmyard wet with mud and cow manure, ruining a good pair of shoes.

The track the van had used ran alongside a field containing grazing cattle. On the opposite right-hand side of the track was an allotment. Each plot of land with its own tool shed, and some had greenhouses. Keeping my attention on the track ahead of me just in case the green van returned, I hurried forward. Before long, the allotment ended. Then, after passing a high hedge, I found a cemetery with rows and rows of neatly laid-out gravestones. Distracted by the sight of the gravestones, I felt a shiver run down my spine. The memory of me as a small child, standing next to my parents, watching my little brother's coffin being lowered into the ground, came back to me. Ever since that day, I had never been able to visit a church or cemetery without being swamped with emotion and fear. I felt my knees weaken, so I put out a hand out to steady myself against the graveyard's metal fence. As I was recovering my composure, I looked up. In the distance, I saw someone walking toward me.

In desperation, I staggered into the graveyard, crossed a swath of grass and knelt by a grave. Fighting the effects of nausea, dizziness and the feeling as though the ground was about to open up and swallow me. I tried to make it look to anyone passing by that I was tending to the grave of a loved one. I heard footsteps on the track as the person walked past the graveyard. After waiting a couple of seconds, I then risked a glance over my shoulder and spotted Danny Gold going past the gate. Turning back to the grave, I inhaled deeply. The scent of grave flowers was heady and sweet. My stomach heaved, and before I knew what was happening, blackness took me away from my surroundings. I came to with a splitting headache. Unsteadily, I sat up. A bitterness filled my mouth. I wiped my mouth with the back of my hand, the memory of what had happened to me slowly returning. The acrid smell of vomit made me examine the splatter on my dress. Luckily for me, most of the contents of my stomach had gone over the grave. Embarrassed beyond belief and fearful that I had committed a terrible sin, I pushed back from the grave. Still dizzy, I staggered to my feet, longing to be away from the grave I had dishonoured. It was only then that I remembered Danny Gold. Spinning around, I looked for him. I was all alone. Making my way to the gate, I spotted him at the end of the track, just before it reached Scarborough Road. As I lent on the cemetery gatepost, I took a deep breath and then turned to look back along the track from where he had come. Rather than following Danny Gold, I chose to find the new hiding place for the green van.

The van was easy to find. It was at the end of the lane, inside a large wooden shed with no doors. The shed was on land belonging to Cemetery Lane Farm. Studying the farm and its outbuildings for a few minutes, I concluded that Danny Gold was renting the parking place for the van. It was a working farm and a safer location to leave the van than the on-street parking he'd been using on Skerne Road. But the new parking location led to another question. Was the farm or its owner connected in any way to the forging of five-pound notes? Or was Danny Gold using RAF Driffield as the location to print the forgeries?

After returning to my car, I drove home to change my dress. By the time I'd freshened up, it was almost lunchtime. As it was a Saturday, I knew Daddy would be at home and I wanted to speak to him before he went out shopping with my mother.

As usual, Mummy was on the front doorstep to greet me as I drove my car into their driveway. I don't know how she knew when I was turning up, but she did. She must have a sixth sense. As we met, she put her arms around me and gave me a big hug.

'Hello, Mummy, I thought we could have lunch together,' I said.

'You know it's always a pleasure to see you, April. But I suspect you have an ulterior motive behind this sudden need for lunch together.'

'Mummy, how could you even think of such a thing?' I put on my hurt feelings expression.

'All right. All right. I'll believe you, this time. Come through to the lounge and say hello to your father.'

'You haven't been home to see us for weeks; I was worried about you.'

'Don't exaggerate, Mummy. I was here just the other weekend.'

'Well, it feels like weeks. You know how much I miss having you at home.'

'I know Mummy, but I'm all grown up now. I can't have you looking after me all my life.'

'You don't know what it's like for me with just your father at home now. You wait until you're married and your children leave home, then you'll know what I mean. Speaking of which, have you seen Rex recently?'

'Rex and I are not speaking.'

'Oh, April, what have you done?'

'Me! It's not me. It's him.'

'Why? What's he done?'

'He treats me like a child, as though I don't know what I'm doing. He uses me. I will not be patronised by him or anyone else.'

'I'm sure he's just trying to help,' conceded Mummy. She left me with Daddy and went through to the kitchen.

'And to what do we owe the honour of this visit?' asked Daddy.

'Please, Daddy, don't be like Mummy.'

Daddy washed down his mouthful of a cheese sandwich with some tea before asking, 'Okay; what is it you want me to do for you?'

'Really, Daddy! You're the one person who can see right through me; yet doesn't treat me like a child. You are right. I need your help with my investigation. You won't like it, but it's for the good of the bank in the long run, and you will be helping the police solve a crime...'

'Yes. Yes.' He interjected. 'You've got me convinced, even though I know I will not like it. Tell me what you want.'

'I am pretty sure I know who is behind the five-pound note forgeries, only I don't have enough evidence to go to the police yet.'

'Who is it?'

'It's one of the men from the archery club, but I can't prove it yet.'

'You have to tell the police what you know.'

'I can't. I don't have the proof. And you know what the police are like. If I tell them who my suspect is, they will pay him a visit and frighten the man off with lots of questions. This man can't be working alone. So, if the police interview him, his pals will remove the money and any evidence of what they have been doing before the police arrive, and they will find nothing. Then all my work will have been for nothing.'

'I see. But you still haven't told me what you want me to do.'

'I need to know who owns the little farm at the back of the old cemetery.'

'For that kind of information, you need to apply to the Land Registry Office,' said Daddy.

'Yes, I know that, but I don't have the time to waste waiting for them to answer my query. I'm hoping that whoever owns the farm on Cemetery Lane; does his banking in Driffield and, as you are the manager of the biggest bank in town, the farmer probably banks with you.'

'It's a bit of a long shot to assume that, and even if the farmer does bank with us, I can't just give away his banking details. I'd lose my job,' insisted Daddy.

'Yes, I know. But, I don't want the man's banking details, though, I must admit, they may be useful. I just want his name so I can check him out.'

Mummy arrived with a tray loaded with more tea, sandwiches, and cake.

'I'll see what I can do,' said Daddy as Mummy put down the tray on the coffee table.

'What are you two plotting?' asked Mummy.

'Nothing, I was just asking Daddy for some advice. I miss our little chats.'

'That's nice, dear. We don't see enough of you, you know. And tomorrow, I'm doing your favourite for lunch, roast chicken.'

Which meant I was obligated into turning up for lunch. She knew what my answer would be.

'Lovely, but I have a couple of things to do first, so don't expect me to arrive as early as I usually do.'

Taking leave of my parents after numerous cups of tea and two pieces of cake. I returned home to spend the rest of the afternoon reading and relaxing. Tonight, when it was dark, I decided to return to Jack Frisket's printers for another look around.

Late that night, I left my car on the street and walked down the alley leading to the archery range and the printers. Using my duplicated key, I let myself in through the front door. It no longer felt strange being here after hours. I'd been here so many times now it all felt very familiar, even in the dark. Nothing had been disturbed in the outer office. Passing through to the printing area at the back, all seemed as it should. Until that is, I checked the storage shelves – more ink, paper, and chemicals had gone missing. As I stared at the emptying shelves, the realisation of what was happening struck me. The thieves weren't taking the stock for use at RAF

Driffield. They wouldn't be able to justify buying print supplies from a place that had closed down. They were getting their legitimate stock from elsewhere and stealing from here to get materials to print more banknotes. The few forged five-pound notes that had been in circulation around Driffield and Beverley had been a mistake, probably greed on the part of Robert hood or Jack Frisket. Now Hood and Frisket were dead; the casual spending of a few forged five-pound notes had dried up. However, the forgery business was still in full swing. The continual theft of stores proved it. Which could only mean one thing. That at some point in the future, a massive release of forged five-pound notes was planned. This was not about printing money for a get-rich-quick scheme - it was about destabilising the entire British economy. A shiver ran up my spine. I toyed with the idea of going straight to the police but then decided against it. I'd have to explain what I was doing here in the middle of the night with a key to the premises and why I hadn't reported my suspicions earlier. My next thought was to call Rex. He and his cloak-and-dagger friends would be able to deal with the forgers, but then, I'd miss out on any credit for all the work I'd put into solving the case. Rex would hush up the affair. No, I had to take this a bit further, to a point where I would get some credit for all my work. I had to prove that Danny Gold was involved in the forgery business. The murder of Jack Frisket and Robert Hood would be a bonus. Rex could take the credit for breaking up the rest of the forgery gang, as it would get hushed up and not publicised, anyway.

Sunday

A telephone call to the archery range at ten o'clock confirmed Danny Gold and Charlie Bowyer had not reserved a time for archery that day. So I made my way to the farm on Cemetery Lane, where the green van was now stored. It was still there. The two things combined could only mean that Danny Gold and his friend had not been given leave from RAF Driffield this weekend. Remembering my interview with Danny and Charlie at the archery club. Danny had said that they usually got every Wednesday off. Only, usually, did not mean always. I needed an assistant, someone to watch the print works at night – Mr Nock.

His house was close to the Speedy Printers, so I drove to his house and knocked on the door.

'Mr Nock, please forgive me for calling on you unexpectedly on a Sunday morning, but I need your help again.'

He looked at me with bleary eyes. 'You'd better come in, but I'll tell you now, I won't be able to change my rounds again; not like last time.'

He stepped aside to let me in. His living room stank of sweat, stale cigarette smoke and burnt toast. An empty side plate covered with crumbs balanced on the left arm of his armchair, and a half-finished mug of tea rested on the right arm. He picked up the tea and took a sip. 'Fancy one for yourself?'

'No. Thank you. I don't have much time.'

I took the seat opposite him and, before he could ask, I explained why I'd come to visit him.

'Mr Nock, you proved very capable the last time I asked for your help. Now I need your help again. I will pay you as before, only this time, it wouldn't mean changing your daily rounds at work.'

I paused before giving him the bad news. 'This time, I need you to be my night watchman.' I paused again to let the message seep into his still, sleepy head.

'Every night, from when it gets dark until midnight, I would like you to watch Speedy Printers and telephone me the minute anyone turns up. The job shouldn't last for more than a week, two at the most.' He studied me before taking another sip of tea.

'How much?'

'How does ten shillings a night sound?'

'A pound sounds better.'

'Mr Nock. I am not made of money. All I'm asking for is a couple of hours of work per night.'

'Yes, Miss Showers, but what happens if these murderers see me? I'm no spring chicken. They could murder me as well. You're asking me to put my life on the line for you.'

'Very well, Mr Nock. A pound per night, it is. Can you start tomorrow night?' He paused again before answering.

'Aye, but only until midnight. I have to be at work in the morning.'

Wednesday

It was just as it was getting dark when my home telephone rang. As soon as I picked up the handset, I heard the frantic voice of Mr Nock. He didn't wait for a response from my end of the telephone before he blurted out a series of statements.

'Miss Showers, the green van has turned up at the printers, and Danny Gold is driving it. You'd better get over here, fast. I'm not staying here in case he sees me. I'm going home.' The telephone line went dead as he slammed down the receiver at his end. I didn't even get a chance to thank him for his call. Not bothering to turn off the lights in my house, I grabbed my bag, jacket and car keys. I didn't even bother to change out of my work clothes, though I opted for a sensible pair of flat shoes.

Forcing the old Hillman Minx to go faster than it had done for years, I swerved it around corners and raced down streets more recklessly than I'd ever driven before. Within a few minutes, I was parked on the street near Speedy Printers, waiting for the green van to exit the lane which led to the print works and archer range.

I daren't get out of my car to check if the van was still down the lane in case Danny Gold spotted me. As I sat and waited, I could feel myself shaking with anticipation of what was to come.

Then, sooner than I had expected, the van appeared at the entrance to the lane. The urge to start my car and switch on the lights, ready to give chase, was intense. However, remembering how the driver of the green van had spotted me following him last time, I waited until the last second before starting my car's engine. Only after seeing the van take a left turn as it left the street, did I switch on my car's headlights and pull away from the kerb.

This time, I'll keep my distance following the van and only get closer to it if there was a risk of losing it. It soon became apparent that the green van was heading out towards Langtoft as it had previously when I followed it.

I switched off my car's headlights. Driving with sidelights only to reduce the risk of being seen by the driver of the green van. Halfway through Langtoft, the van turned sharply left onto Cottam Lane. Using the blind corner as cover, I raced up to the junction to gain ground. Switching off all my car's lights, I eased my car around the turn very slowly. The van had slowed down. Its twin red taillights acting as beacons for me to follow, tracing the twists and turns in the road ahead. After a quarter of a mile, the van turned right and disappeared. I drove past the spot where the van had turned off the road and saw that it was heading towards some farm buildings. Breaking hard, I stopped and then reversed my car back down the road, before driving through an open gate onto a track that ran across a field; I parked my car. Turning in my seat to look over my shoulder, I could see the black outline of farm buildings against a star-lit sky.

Retrieving my wellington boots and a torch from the boot of my car, I made my way to the place where the green van had left the Cottam Road. As I peered around the corner of a hedge, in the distance, I could see two figures unloading the van and transferring its contents into a building. Using the hedge as cover, I headed towards the back of the building, keeping out of sight of the two men. Needing the lights of the van to see by, the men hadn't turned off the lights of the green van or switched off its engine. Evidently, they were not planning on staying longer than they had to. By the time I'd got myself into a better position to see what was going on, Danny Gold and his partner were locking the door to the outbuilding.

'Right, job done,' said Danny. 'Let's get the van back to Driffield. Then we can be back to the airfield before midnight and our passes run out.' It was as they got in the van and out of the shadows that I recognised Charlie Bowyer as the second man.

The van turned around in the farmyard and then left. Stepping out from my hiding place, I shone my torch around to get a better look at where they were hiding their stolen printing materials. I found two other large, shed-like outbuildings, but they were in a very poor state of repair, with rotted timbers and missing corrugated sheets from their roofs. The one used for storage looked and smelt as though it had previously been used as a cattle shed. Choosing to check out the house first, I crossed the farmyard. As I walked around the outside of the farmhouse, I noted how it was all boarded up. The farm was deserted. A sign nailed to one of the boarded-up windows read 'For Sale.' Returning to the cattle shed used as a store, I stared at the building. I couldn't understand why anyone would bring their stuff here to store it. There was no sign of anywhere suitable to set up a printing press, especially one that prints money. There was no electricity supply to power the machinery. After checking the padlocked front doors of the shed, I realised there was no chance of me forcing the heavy-duty lock and chains and breaking in that way.

Dropping the padlock, I made my way around the outside of the shed. It, too, was in a poor state of repair, but better than the other two. At the back of the shed, close to a broken downpipe, I found a couple of rotted boards. One had split up the middle. I gave it a kick, and the crack extended further up the board. I gave it another kick, and a splinter of wood about an inch wide broke away. Inserting my fingers, I pulled at the rotten board. The rusted nails and rotten wood gave way without too much effort. With growing confidence, I worked on the hole until there was a gap large enough for me to squeeze through.

Inside, with the aid of my torch, I discovered more boxes of printing supplies than had been unloaded tonight. There were boxes filled with bottles of chemicals and inks. Large packets of paper were stacked on pallets. In the back corner opposite the hole I'd made in the wall, I found new empty wooden crates stencilled with the words, Gas Masks. I let out a low whistle. I already knew some forged banknotes had been printed, but if they were planning on filling the crates with counterfeit fivers, they would be printing millions of pounds worth of banknotes. As I continued searching around the shed, I wished I'd brought a notebook with me to list everything I had found. Then, to my horror, I heard a heavy-engined vehicle and a screech of brakes. I froze on the spot. As I looked toward the shed doors shining between the wooden boards, I could see the lights of another vehicle outside. A voice boomed through the darkness.

'Right, you two, get those doors open; we haven't got all night.'

Chapter Thirteen

At the sound of someone fumbling with the padlock on the shed doors, I darted towards the hole in the shed wall. Just as I was about to squeeze through, I heard the chain on the shed door drop away. There wasn't enough time left for me to make my escape before the doors opened. So I dived behind a stack of empty crates. The shed doors opened, and, in the light from the lorry's headlights, I could see three men standing in the entrance. All three were in RAF uniform; one was dressed as an officer.

'Take two boxes of chemicals, two of ink, all the packets of paper, and three empty crates, and don't forget their lids,' ordered the officer.

His companions began work. It took both men to lift each box of ink or chemicals and carry it to the back of the lorry. Each trip was scrutinised by the officer standing at the door. The men loading the lorry took their time with their precious cargo, careful not to drop any of it.

Fearing the men would find me when they came to collect the empty packing cases, I looked for an escape route. My opportunity came when all three men were distracted whilst loading the lorry with a heavy box. I sneaked back towards the hole in the wall on my hands and knees. It was now that I regretted not changing into slacks before dashing out of the house. I was still wearing the dress I'd been wearing earlier in the day. Small stones and pigeon mess which littered the dirty floor caked my hands, knees and dress in filth. I had to bite my lip to prevent myself from crying out each time a bit of grit cut into my bare knees or hands, but I crept on. Unfortunately, I had to stop before reaching my escape point. I had gone as far as I dare. I feared trying to go back through the hole in the wall would make too much noise and alert the men. So, slowly covering myself with discarded straw and feed sacks, I hoped the disguise would be enough to fool the casual eye in the darkness of the shed's interior. It didn't take long for the men to collect everything they needed. As soon as the shed doors were closed, I stood up, brushing a spider from my leg and cobwebs from my hair.

As I squeezed back through the hole into the cover of the night, I heard the tailgate of the lorry slam into place. As I reached the front corner of the shed, the airmen were aboard their lorry and had started its engine. I watched the lorry drive forward a little and then stop. It was manoeuvring to turn around. The driver was doing a three-point turn in the farmyard. This was my chance; it was now or never. Using the opportunity of the manoeuvring lorry to my advantage, I ran towards the open back of the lorry. It would make one more stop before clearing the yard and leaving the farm. The lorry stopped. I sprang up, leaping onto the lorry's tailgate and inserting my left foot into the toe step of the tailgate. As the lorry pulled away, I lifted my other leg over the top of the tailgate and landed on the floor of the lorry between two crates. After all this time of watching and waiting for a lead, I was determined to discover exactly where the forged banknotes were being printed.

To my surprise, the lorry journey didn't last long. I'd only just gotten myself settled when I felt the lorry swerve to the left and then stop. Voices from inside the lorry cab called to someone outside. After an exchange of words, we set off again. A peek out of the back of the lorry confirmed what I suspected. We had gone through a security gate. A sign above a well-lit brick building read RAF Cottam. I was surprised to learn that I was on an RAF base. How, I wondered, did the forgers hide what they were doing? As the lorry drove further into the military base, my mind raced frantically. What do I do now? I didn't even know that there was an RAF base at Cottam until I saw the name over the security gatehouse. A worrying thought occurred to me. Was this place a real RAF base or a fake one set up to fool the locals as part of the forgers' plans to print money without being discovered? Judging by the number of crates I'd seen in the shed, these men had to be printing enough banknotes to make setting up a fake airbase worth it. East Yorkshire was littered with RAF bases. No one would break into an RAF base or question what went on there. I looked out of the back of the lorry, hoping that it would soon slow down enough for me to jump out, but it didn't. Its speed increased as it followed a concrete road. After a couple of minutes, it finally slowed and then turned sharply left before stopping. The sudden manoeuvring of the lorry threw me off balance. As I lay on my back in the corner of the lorry, I heard the lorry cab doors open and then slammed closed. Then I heard the crunch of hobnailed boots on a hard surface as they marched along both sides of the lorry. I shuffled behind an empty crate. As I waited, I heard a voice call out.

'It's late. Get to bed. You can unload the lorry in the morning. Be back here at eight o'clock sharp. We've more printing to do, and not much time left before the deadline.'

The talking stopped. I listened to booted feet walking away, leaving me to wonder what I should do next. The mention of the deadline had me intrigued. Had I discovered them just in the nick of time to save the country from a flood of forged currency? I hoped so. Solving a case of this importance would establish me as a real private detective. But how was I going to prevent them from getting away with it? My first task was to get back to my car. Easier said than done, I thought. Getting out of the lorry was one thing, but making it off the base without being captured was going to be more difficult. Or should I go straight to RAF Cottam's commanding officer and report what is going on? They were hard choices. The C.O. may be the leader of this band of crooks for all I knew. With the military involved, Rex was the best person to approach with what I'd discovered. Getting to my feet and then making my way to the tailgate of the lorry, I pushed the tarpaulin cover aside and swung my leg over the tailgate to

236

climb down. I was just about to step down when a pair of powerful hands grabbed me by the waist and lifted me off the back of the lorry. As I let out a shriek of surprise, a hand was clasped over my mouth. As soon as my feet touched the ground, the person who had grabbed me spun me around. The man was in an RAF officer's uniform.

'Who do we have here – a stowaway?' He said sarcastically.

Stupidly, I tried to explain why I was in the back of the lorry thinking he was a real RAF officer, but he just laughed at me.

Really Miss, if you are going to hide from someone, next time, don't wear such strong-scented perfume. I caught a hint of it at the farm but thought I must be mistaken, or it was the residue from a girlfriend on one of the lad's uniforms. I take it you are not a girlfriend of one of my lads – no, of course, you are not. I smelt it again, only much stronger this time when I got out of the lorry just now. That was when I realised we must have a stowaway hiding in the back of the lorry. Who are you, and why are you here?'

From out of the darkness came Danny Gold.

'Her name is April Showers. She come into the Golden Shot one day and was asking me and Charlie questions about Jack Frisket's print shop and forged five-pound notes. She said she was a reporter for the Driffield rag.'

I pushed the officer's hand off my waist and took a step back. Danny Gold moved in closer. I thought it best to let them do all the talking. I was in enough trouble as it was without adding to it by giving away information about myself.

'What are we going to do with you? Miss Showers, newspaper reporter? Does your mother know you are out late?' I bristled at the insult but kept quiet.

'Kill her and then dump her body on the road. Make it look like a road accident,' insisted Danny Gold, taking me by the arms.

'No. As soon as anyone found her, there would be an investigation. Her editor would read her notes. If they contain names, and the police check them, the names will lead them straight here, to us. No. We keep her alive for now. She may come in useful. Keep her safe, at least until we are out of the country. Then, it won't matter what happens to her.'

'So what are we going to do with her?'

'Tie her up and lock her in the hangar. Don't forget to gag her. I don't want a passing security patrol to hear her calling out,' instructed the officer.

Using what the officer had said about not killing me because I was a reporter, I continued to play the role. He'd also answered another question. This was a real RAF airbase if it had security patrols.

'You won't get away with this. My absence will be noticed when I don't turn up for work tomorrow. My boss will phone me at home, and when he can't find me; I'll be reported missing. It won't take my editor long to find the notes I left, saying I was coming here looking for evidence of murder and forged banknotes.'

The officer looked down at me and smiled. 'Nice try, Miss Showers, but it won't wash. First of all, I suspect you followed us to the farm, which means you didn't know where we were going, or you wouldn't have needed to follow us. Secondly, you had to climb into the back of the truck to discover where we went next. Which means; you had no idea where you were going, so you couldn't have left a message for anyone telling them where you were going. You are alone, Miss Showers. However, on the off chance that someone does come looking for you. I will leave a message at the main gate saying that you turned up looking for a green van which you had lost track of and were sent away without being allowed admission to the airfield. Believe me, Miss Showers, if you give me any trouble, I will shoot you and explain your death as a tragic accident. I'll tell the police that you were trying to break through the wire fence onto the airfield and were shot by a security patrol when you didn't respond to a challenge. This is military property. You have no rights here. If you had, you would have gone through the proper channels, and an investigation would have been carried out by the Military Police. Therefore, you have no evidence pointing at us or this airfield, which is why you had to hide in the back of the lorry to find out where we were going.' 'Take her away.'

Danny Gold grabbed my arm and began shoving me towards the hangar next to the lorry.

'You won't get away with this!' I screeched feebly after the officer as he walked away.

'Keep quiet, or you'll get a slap!' instructed Danny Gold. His threatening words only added to my humiliation by the officer seeing through my bluff so easily and, I was terrified of Danny Gold as he rough-handled me into the darkness of the hangar. Overpowered, I had no option but to allow myself to be pushed further inside the hangar. From a table, Gold retrieved a length of rope and fastened my hands behind my back. He then tied me to a chair, after which I was gagged. Seemingly satisfied that I was going nowhere, he left. I was on my own, with no hope of the cavalry riding over the hill to save me. If I was going to get out of this mess in one piece, I either had to make a friend of one of them or pray that they would make a mistake and I could find a way to escape.

I waited until I was sure everyone had gone from outside of the hangar. When the only sound I could hear came from birds on the roof of the hangar. Their webbed feet paddled awkwardly back and forth on the corrugate roof in the darkness. I began my struggle against my bonds, but after a great deal of twisting and turning, I got nowhere. My wrists were sore and painful. My hope of escape died.

I spent a long, cold, uncomfortable night drifting in and out of sleep until Danny Gold arrived the following morning.

Chapter Fourteen

Thursday

'Good morning, Miss Showers. I hope you had an uncomfortable night?'

I felt dreadful. I had a numb bum from sitting in one position on a hard chair all night. My mouth was dry from the gag, and I desperately needed a pee. I mumbled at him through my gag, but he ignored me. I mumbled at him again, this time wriggling on my chair.

He turned to face me, 'what do you want?' I mumbled at a higher pitch and wriggled more frantically. Finally, he untied the gag.

'I need the toilet,' I said thickly, finding it hard to form my words because my mouth was so dry.

'Ah, yes. I imagine you do. There is a latrine outside. It's primitive and smelly; plumbing is limited this far out on the airfield. I will allow you to use it if you promise not to try to escape. It only has one door in and out and not much privacy. The men don't need it as there are no women personnel on this base. I will wait for you at the outer door. Do you agree with my terms?'

I nodded my head. Released from my chair, I gingerly stood up, feeling all my muscles complaining at the same time as blood flow returned to my limbs. He untied my hands and then led me by the arm, taking me to the door of the hangar.

The latrine was about twenty yards away. A grey-painted wooden thing not much bigger than a bus shelter. The walls stopped just above head height. Between the top of the walls and the roof, the structure was open to the elements. The sloping roof was supported by posts protruding up above the walls. There was also a gap at the base of the walls. I wondered for a moment if I could squeeze through the gap beneath the wall and make my escape, but the opening looked too small. As we approached the latrine, I tried to imagine the smell inside the primitive toilet and prepare for it. A cloud of flies circled beneath the roof on a thick, velvety, foulness of methane. I choked back a retch. There were two cubicles inside, and each one had a wooden board with a hole in it for a toilet seat. Cut-up squares of newspaper hung from a loop of string attached to the wall of each cubicle. The smell was as bad as I expected, but I was desperate to go after my long night on the chair. At least there was a bucket of cold water, soap, and paper towels for washing my hands afterwards. I made a mental note never to join the RAF. As soon as I came out again, Danny Gold re-tied my hands.

'May I have a drink and something to eat?' I asked politely before he replaced my gag. He hesitated, then said, 'you'll have to wait. I'll see what I can do for you a little later.'

242

Desperate to learn more about what they planned for the forged money, I asked.

'I don't see how you can get away with releasing so many forged banknotes into circulation. You look like you have crate loads of them?'

'We do, Miss Showers. But you are thinking on a too smaller scale. We have no intention of allowing all our money to be released just yet. Flying Officer Blenheim has other plans for it.'

'Blenheim – is that the officer's name?' Gold stared at me for a moment. I could see from the expression on his face that he was wondering if he'd just made a mistake or not. He didn't say anymore.

Taking me by the arm, I was forced back inside the hangar in a hasty manner, returned to my chair and tied to it. Danny Gold left. I heard the padlock on the hangar door lock and was then given a shake to ensure it was tight and secure. I was left on my own once again. In his haste to leave, he hadn't gagged me. I didn't know if he'd forgotten to replace it or if he thought it was unnecessary as the hangar I was enprisoned in stood isolated far from any other building.

There was enough natural light inside the hangar to see most of my surroundings. The inside was largely empty, except around the area where I sat. I could see five wooden crates, the same as the ones at the derelict farm, only these were sealed. In the corner, I spotted the missing printing press from Speedy Printers. It being here explained the dust shadow I found on the print room floor at Speedy Printers. Alongside the printing

243

press was some other equipment which I guessed was also part of the money-forging enterprise. On a large table below a frosted window sat wads of unwrapped printing paper, cut to size and ready for use. On a separate table, I saw containers of ink. But, frustratingly, I couldn't see anything that would help me escape from this chair, even if I could have reached it. Disillusioned by my search for tools to help me escape, I could only hope that someone would return soon and at least feed me and give me a drink.

As I recalled the events that had brought me here, I remembered the lorry outside. The one I'd seen the men loading last night, and had later brought me here. It still contained the extra printing materials they collected last night, so it stood to reason that Danny Gold and the others must be planning to print more banknotes and, I hoped, would return to continue their work sooner rather than later today. However, as the day wore on, my head began to ache along with the rest of my body. The hangar had been cold during the night, but now I could feel the temperature rising as the morning sun beat down on the large roof, heating the interior. The pain in my head intensified and my tongue swelled. It was getting hard to breathe and think in the stuffy air. Cramp grasped my calf muscles in a painful vice, making me cry out in pain. As the pain grew, I remembered an old trick that someone had told me. With the chair still tied to my body, I pushed down with my toes, forcing myself to stand in a crouch but stretching the muscles in the backs of my legs. The pain in my calves eased, but as the muscles stretched and relaxed, I lost my balance, toppling over. I watched the floor getting closer in slow motion. I felt helpless, not wanting to, but having to accept the inevitable as I crashed to the floor. There was a flash of intense light, pain, and then blackness as my face hit the floor.

When I regained consciousness, I was sitting upright again. The pain in my head returned instantly. Above the searing pain, I could hear people talking and the steady clanking rhythm of the machinery. I lifted my chin from my chest. With it, I felt my stomach rise. Despite the pain wishing it to stop, the impulse to empty my stomach won the fight. Luckily, because of the time that had gone by since I'd last eaten or drank anything, very little came up and splattered onto my front and down my chin. It was only then that I noticed I could only see out of one eye. I let out a cry of pain. A shadow passed in front of me, and a voice asked, 'what have you been up to, little lady?' I blinked the one eye I could see through, and my vision focused on the face of the RAF officer from last night. He took out his handkerchief and wiped away the vomit from my face, chin, and the few drips that had landed on the front of my dress.

'Water,' I uttered through thick lips. As he got up and walked away. I coughed; lightning bolts and stars seared through my head and across my face; dizziness made the room spin. I took a deep breath and closed my eye.

'Here, drink this,' I heard a voice say. I opened my good eye and focused on the mug of water held before my lips. I drank; slowly at first, but as my mouth absorbed the cool liquid, the instinct to gulp was overpowering. Forcing my head forward and opening my mouth further, I greedily wanted more.

'Steady, young lady, not so fast,' said the voice.

As the mug ran out of water, I finally looked up at the person holding it and saw the RAF officer.

'Thank you.'

'You've got a nasty cut above your left eye and lots of bruising down the side of your face. You look like you've been in a pub fight. Hopefully, you've learned a lesson and will sit still from now on. I'll get the first aid kit and clean you up.'

He returned a few moments later to put a green metal medical box on the floor next to my chair. Alongside the medical box, he placed a bowl of water. Lifting the lid on the box, he pulled out a wad of cotton wool, dipped it into the water and then very gently cleaned my face with it. I flinched as he touched the tender skin, but held still as the coolness of the water soothed away some of the hurt. After washing away the dried blood covering my left eye, I could open it a little. Finally, he reached the cut above my eye. Dropping the blood-stained cotton wool in the bowl, he removed a fresh cotton wad and a bottle from the box.

'This is going to sting a bit,' he said, as he dabbed the wound.

Instantly, I jerked away from his touch as the antiseptic set fire to my face.

'Sorry,' he said in a soft voice.

I stiffened at the pain, and he quickly finished what he was doing. Just as I thought he was all done, he removed a bandage from the box. I looked at him questioningly.

'Best keep it clean,' he said matter of factually.

'Does it matter? You're going to kill me anyway,' I said crossly.

'Oh, you are the pessimist,' he responded sarcastically.

As he dressed and bandaged the wound on my head, he continued to talk.

'We're nearly finished here, and then we'll be gone. Within a few weeks, the airfield will be closed down. Our job is to pack everything and move it out to other airfields that can use the equipment we have been storing here. The Ministry of Defence is selling off this airfield and putting all of us out to pasture. We, like this airfield, and many other servicemen in the country, are surplus to requirements these days. We will be jobless. So, with no future job prospects, we are creating our own pension fund, and then we'll disappear to the South of France or Spain or somewhere else nice and warm. Where the sun shines every day, and the girls are pretty. We'll live out the rest of our lives in the lap of luxury. However, you, my injured little dove, may come in useful as a bargaining chip if things don't go to plan. Besides, if we kill you now, should your body be found here, there is a chance it would lead the police to us. So you are going on a little holiday with the rest of us. You may even get to like us and want to stay with us,' he said wryly as he collected up the first aid box and bowl.

'What you mean is, get to like you.'

'We'll see,' he said over his shoulder as he walked away.

I couldn't believe the arrogance of the man. But at least I'd learnt he had no plans for killing me just yet.

'May I have something to eat?' I asked.

As he came back to me, he told me. 'Breakfast is over; the canteen is closed. I can't get you anything to eat until lunchtime, but I saved you a bacon sandwich.' He held out a plate holding thick slices of bread crammed with masses of bacon. 'Unfortunately, it has gone cold now.'

My stomach heaved at the sight of it.

'I'm sorry. I don't think I'm ready for anything that heavy, and besides, I would need the use of my hands to eat it.'

'True,' he replied flippantly. He put his hand in his jacket pocket. 'Maybe you'd prefer some of this?' He held up a bar of chocolate.

'Yes, please.' Something sweet to eat was exactly what I wanted.

He unwrapped the bar of chocolate and then broke off a row of squares. He put two in my mouth, and the third one, he ate. I let the chocolate settle on my tongue and then pushed it against the roof of my mouth. There was a sudden rush of flavour and sweetness as the chocolate melted on my tongue. I closed my eyes whilst my tongue played with the sweet delight in my mouth. As the chocolate dissolved, I wanted it to melt faster, to fill my mouth with its thick creamy texture of liquid sweetness. I swallowed once, twice, and then the chocolate was gone. I opened my eye and saw him watching me with a smile on his face.

'You seem to have enjoyed it.'

I felt my face burn with embarrassment. 'I'm hungry; what do you expect?' I snapped.

'Want some more?' he asked.

'No!' I did, but I didn't want to give him the satisfaction of watching me eat it. He shrugged his shoulders and turned away.

'What's your name?' I asked. He stopped and turned to face me. ·

'Flying Officer Blenheim,' he said smoothly, and then returned to his men at the printing press. I couldn't hear what they were saying over the noise of the machinery, so I watched them work. Pages of banknotes went from machine to machine. One press added colours to the paper, and the others printed words or numbers until the finished sheets were cut into the size of five-pound notes. They were then bundled up and stacked on another table. There they waited to be packed into the wooden crates. The men worked all through lunchtime, splitting into two shifts, taking it in turn to go and eat. When the second shift returned, Flying Officer Blenheim brought me a tray with a covered plate. I could smell the hot food above the powerful chemical vapours given off by the presses. Blenheim placed the tray on an empty crate and then pushed it towards me. Alongside the plate were a mug of tea and a spoon. He untied my hands and stood back.

'You must be ready for this. I'm sorry, there's no knife and fork. You'll have to make do with just a spoon. There's no point in taking risks with potential weapons, is there?'

I didn't answer him. After massaging my wrists, I lifted the lid from the plate to find a large portion of steak pie, mashed potatoes, peas, carrots, and gravy. At first, the portion size seemed enormous, but as I began to eat, my hunger took over, and I didn't stop until the plate was empty. I washed the meal down with half the mug of tea, leaving the rest.

Unfortunately, the pain in the side of my face flared up again after my meal. My facial muscles were still bruised and tender, rebelling against the act of eating. I touched the side of my face with my fingertips, gingerly discovering which areas were the most sensitive and searching for signs of damage to my skin. Finally, I found the bandage around my head and the injury it protected.

I looked up at Blenheim. 'Is it a bad cut?'

'Not as bad as it looked at first. I doubt it'll leave a scar, but I'm no doctor.'

'Are you able to get me some aspirin to help with the pain?'

'I'll see what I can do later,' was his reply. He held up the rope, so I put my hands behind my back, ready for him to tie me to my chair. After which, he cleared away my tray and rejoined his men. I spent the rest of the day fighting the need for sleep by watching the men printing the money. They all seemed to have their own jobs, and production was fast and efficient. Despite the noise, I could feel sleep trying to win me over. Just as I was about to give in to my body's increasing demands to sleep, the printers and other machines were switched off, and silence returned. In a reverse of activity, I was suddenly wide awake, only now I could overhear what the men were saying to each other.

Flying Officer Blenheim gathered his men before him.

'Tomorrow, I want you to load up the truck with all this machinery. Make sure you remove everything. I don't want anything left in here that can connect us with the printing of banknotes. Leftover printing ink, chemicals, the lot. It all has to go. Return it to the derelict farm. Bowyer, Gold and I will stay here and check and stack the crates and place them near the hangar doors, ready for when we leave. We only have one more day to go, so all evidence of what has been going on here must be removed, understood? Right, you all know what you must do tomorrow. Good work, lads. If you're quick, there's just enough time for you to get a brew in the canteen.'

'What about the girl?' asked Danny Gold.

'She'll be coming with us tomorrow. For tonight, though, she can stay where she is. I'll come back to check on her later and settle her in for the night. But that'll be after I've given my daily report to the Commanding Officer.'

Before they all left the building, Flying Officer Blenheim came over to me to replace my mouth gag.

'I won't be gone long. But when I return, I'll bring you back something to eat and drink,' he said.

'Please; one request before you go. When you come back, will you bring a blanket? It gets awfully cold in here at night?'

'I'll see what I can do?' He filled my mouth with the cloth and then tied it behind my head. Without saying another word, he left me, turned off the light, and locked the hangar door behind him.

I must have dozed off because I was suddenly awakened by a bright light. The hangar lights had been switched on, and Blenheim had returned. He placed a plate and cup on the empty crate he had used as a table for my lunchtime meal and pushed it in my direction. As the crate advanced towards my knees, Blenheim said, 'good evening.'

I couldn't respond, so waited until he untied my gag.

'I need the toilet.' I said insistently, desperately needing to go. Blenheim untied my hands and, keeping a firm grip on my arm, led me to the door and then to the latrine. Once outside, I noted the sun was down and that very soon, it would be dark. Blenheim loitered far closer to the latrine entrance than Gold had done. It felt intrusive and intimidating, but I had to go.

When I came out, he was waiting at the entrance. Blenheim grasped my arm once again. Anger was now taking over from my fear of what might happen to me.

'When are you going to let me go?' I demanded. He didn't answer. 'I need to wash properly.' I continued. He still didn't respond. 'I need to change my clothes; they stink.' I pulled up abruptly. He responded by tightening his grip on my arm and dragging me forward.

'You'll manage for one more day, then you'll be off my hands,' he replied.

It wasn't the response I was expecting.

'What did you mean by that?' I demanded.

He forced me forward, making me stumble and fall on the uneven ground. The rims of my wellingtons slapped around my calves as I forced myself to a sitting position. I wished that I'd never put the damned things on.

Angrily, I stared up at him. 'What are you going to do with me?' I demanded, not sure if I really wanted to know the answer.

'Think of it as a...' he paused, 'as a change of career opportunity.' He gave me an evil smile.

A shadow passed over me, taking away all my bravado. I didn't like the sound of what he'd said or the way he said it. What he had in mind scared me. He helped me to my feet, and I allowed myself to be directed back into the hangar. As we passed through the door, he picked up a thick woollen blanket and handed it to me, 'compliments of the house.'

His little quip did nothing to ease my feelings of apprehension.

My supper comprised a Spam fritter, chips and beans. They had gone cold whilst I'd been away. Despite my hunger, I didn't eat it, although I drank the mug of tea.

'Finished?' He asked, hovering with the rope in his hands. I nodded. Just before he was about to tie my gag into place, I made a request.

'Will you wrap me in the blanket and lay me down on the floor once you've tied me up? I'd rather you shoot me now than spend another night tied to that hard chair.'

I meant it. The pain in my back, arms and legs was becoming unbearable from being forced to remain in one position for long periods of time. He paused, giving the matter some thought.

'Please?' I begged.

He released me from the chair and untied my hands.

'Stand up.' I did as I was told. 'Hold out your hands!' He re-tied my hands in front of me and then wrapped the thick woollen blanket around me. With the rest of the rope, he tied the blanket to me. I felt like a half-prepared mummy from some horror film. He replaced my gag and then lay me down on the floor. He watched me for a few moments as I lay on my back, staring back at him. At least in this supine position, I'd be more comfortable and get a little more sleep.

Once he'd gone and the lights had been turned off, I tried wriggling and rolling about on the floor to loosen my bonds, but he must have been a regular boy scout in his younger days because none of the ropes slackened. I gave up trying to escape my cocoon as my body protested against my fight with the tight ropes. Lying on my back, I stared up into the darkness, wondering what he had meant by his 'change of career' comment. Trying to figure it out made me tired, and after two nights of little sleep, it wasn't long before I felt myself drifting off.

Suddenly, there was a roaring sound. I tried to cry out and sit up, only I couldn't do it. I was wide awake and frightened, wondering what on earth had made the great, rumbling roar in the dark. Gradually, as my senses rationalised the noise, I realised that what I had heard was an aeroplane landing close to the hangar. I listened to the sound of its engines getting further away and then stopping. I waited anxiously for someone to arrive, but no one did. All went quiet, and even though I tried to stay awake, I couldn't, and my eyes closed for the last time that night.

Chapter Fifteen

Friday

I awoke feeling stiff, but thanks to my blanket, I had remained warm all night, unlike the previous one. It was light outside, and I wondered what the time might be and when someone would arrive. All I knew for sure was today was the day that Flying Officer Blenheim and his crew of forgers had been working towards. Only, I was the fly in their ointment. I was the one who was putting their well-laid plans in jeopardy. I was the one they needed to dispose of; permanently. Blenheim had said I was in line for a career change and the thought of it worried me. His word inferred I was not to be killed, but what could be worse than that?

I began to struggle, hoping to loosen one of the loops of rope wrapped around me. I could feel them move, but not enough to make much difference to my situation. The exertion quickly made me breathless, and I had to give up. As I lay helpless, waiting for Blenheim to return for me. The fear of what he had in store for me loomed large in my mind. It gripped my heart in its vice and crush it till it hurt. I even cursed myself for taking up a career as a private detective. Tears burned my eyes and ran down my cheeks as I gave in to the unknown. After allowing my fear to ebb and escape with my tears, I clung to the one bit of hope I had in this horrible mess. The words - change of career. No matter what this change was, if I was alive, eventually, I would get a chance to make an escape, and that was all that mattered to me right now - a tiny glimmer of hope.

Hearing the hangar door open had me looking across to see who was coming in. It was Danny Gold with all the other men I'd seen yesterday. One of them opened the large hangar doors whilst others began dismantling the printing presses and other machinery, but Danny Gold came directly to me.

'I've been told to get you ready.'

'What do you mean? Told to get me ready. Ready for what?'

'We're leaving. F.O. Blenheim told you about it yesterday. The airfield is closing soon. So we have to transfer all the RAF equipment on this airfield to other airfields that need it.' Gold bent down and untied the rope holding me in my blanket cocoon.

'Where are we going?'

Gold let out a sigh. 'All the RAF equipment on the base is being shipped to other airfields around the country,' he repeated. 'This printing machinery will go back to the farm. The money is – well, you'll see, you are going with it on a little aeroplane ride.' His condescending smile as he spoke filled me with alarm.

256

'What! Where to? Why?'

'I don't know the details. Blenheim just said, we'll all get a bonus because of you. Come on, I've got to take you to the latrine and then feed you.'

When I returned to the hangar, Blenheim was waiting for me. He'd set up the empty crate as my table, and my chair was placed in front of it, ready for me. On the crate lay a tray with a plate of bacon, eggs and toast and, alongside the plate, a mug of tea.

'Good Morning, Miss Showers. I'm sure you're hungry. You may be pleased to learn that you are being moved today, so you'll need a filling breakfast. I suggest you tuck in. I don't know when you'll get the chance to eat again,' said Blenheim cheerfully.

'Where are you taking me?' I asked as I sat down. 'I can assure you I'm not getting on the plane I heard landing during the night.'

Blenheim shot a glance of annoyance at Gold. 'We'll cross that bridge when we come to it,' said the officer crossly. Half-starved after not eating yesterday's Spam, I tucked into the breakfast like a ravenous animal, washing it down with the over-sweet tea the RAF liked to serve.

'Now what happens?' I asked disdainfully.

'We wait,' announced Blenheim, staring at me.

'For what?' I asked, feeling worried.

'For the sleeping tablets, I crushed into your tea to take effect.'

I clutched at my stomach as though it might slow or prevent the effect of the drugs. I suddenly felt foolish for falling for his trick. The thought of being unconscious and at his mercy terrified me.

'I can't have you causing a stir and giving us away when we are so close to completing our mission. With any luck, we'll never meet again after you've fallen asleep. By Monday, it will all be over. We will all,' he opened his arms indicating all present, 'be on civvy street, and as free as birds; to come and go as we please, only, we'll all be rich. very rich,' he explained matter-of-factly.

I was confused. It was hard to comprehend the amount of danger I was in. Apart from being held a prisoner, I was being treated quite respectfully. However, it contrasted dramatically with the threat in Blenheim's words and manner. However, I didn't get long to ponder the dilemma. After a couple of minutes, I felt the first effects of the drug. Panic set in. I tried to stand, to run away, but Gold and Blenheim had stayed by my side, waiting for signs that the drug was taking effect. Putting their hands on my shoulders, they forced me back into my seat. I'd never taken sleeping tablets before, so I didn't know what to expect. Forced to accept the effect of the sleeping draft as it crept over me. I began to feel dizzy. I tried to fight off the desire to close my eyes by focusing on the other men working inside the hangar. As the sensation of dizziness grew stronger, I gripped the edge of my seat to steady myself, and then, just as I felt myself falling, everything went black. The last thing I remembered was hands grabbing me once again.

*****

'Quick! Catch her,' ordered Blenheim. To prevent April from falling off her chair, Blenheim and Gold forced April's unconscious body back into an upright position.

'I'll hold her, you tie her hands behind her back,' instructed Blenheim. Steadying April's body, Blenheim allowed her to lean against him whilst Gold gathered up her hands and secured them behind her back.

'Right, turn that crate over. I'll take her legs. You grab her under the arms,' ordered Blenheim. Before April was lifted from her chair, Blenheim removed her wellington boots.

'She won't need these anymore,' he said as he threw the boots aside.

Together, Blenheim and Gold lifted April into the crate, after which Gold nailed down the lid.

'Make sure all these crates are loaded on the plane together and each one is clearly labelled gas masks,' insisted Blenheim. 'When they arrive in Germany, they'll go straight into storage without being checked. No one wants gas masks these days. They're a *just in case of an emergency* item these days. I will be flying out to Frankfurt with the cargo. I made the excuse to the C.O. about this being the last cargo I would send anywhere for the RAF, and that I wanted to ensure it arrived at its destination correctly. He knew I was just after a final free ride to Frankfurt, but all he said was, 'Make sure you're back for Monday morning.'

'I wish I was going with you,' said Gold. 'I've never been overseas.'

'After I ensure the money and the girl are safely collected by our German friends, you'll have enough money to go anywhere in the world,' replied Blenheim reassuringly.

'How long before I get to see my money?' asked Gold.

'A few days. Our share of the money is being put into Swiss bank accounts for us. When I come back from Frankfurt, I'll have a letter for each of us containing our Swiss account numbers. When I informed our German friends about Miss Showers, they were very pleased and added a bonus.'

'What will they do with her?'

'I don't know, and I don't care, but I can guess. She's young and good-looking. They'll either put her to work in Frankfurt or sell her on.'

Over the course of the next two hours, the hangar was emptied, and the aeroplane loaded with its precious cargo.

'Wait here next to the plane,' Blenheim instructed Gold, 'and make sure no one messes with those crates. I'm going to have a word with the pilot. We should be taking off soon.'

Blenheim left Gold standing next to the Dakota aeroplane whilst he headed off toward the officers' mess.

Inside, drinking tea and reading the newspaper, he found the pilot and co-pilot of the Dakota.

'I've come to report that the aircraft is all loaded and is ready for your final check of the cargo before take-off,' said Blenheim confidently.

'Sit down, have a cup of tea; there's no rush,' suggested Flying Officer Stirling, the pilot.

'I thought you guy's had a schedule to keep,' said Blenheim, surprised at their lack of enthusiasm to get going.

'No can do, old chap. The weather has closed in over the channel. We've got to wait for the all-clear from the Met boys before we can go. Don't want to end up in the drink. That wouldn't do at all,' said Stirling flippantly. Blenheim, shocked by what he'd just been told, looked at the pilot as though he'd said something disparaging about his mother.

'Something amiss, old boy? You look a bit rattled,' continued the pilot.

'No, nothing. It's just that I've had my lads get the plane loaded in double-quick-time, and now you're not leaving. How long do you think the delay will be?' asked Blenheim, as he regained his composure.

'Hard to say, old bean. The storm front might pass through in an hour, or it may stick around for days. Just in case that happens, do you think you could put Reggie and me up for the night?'

Blenheim ignored the remark, his mind going into overdrive because of his live cargo. *What about Miss Showers? How long will she stay asleep? What will the Germans do to me if I'm late delivering the money? What happens if the flight is cancelled and the freight has to go by road and sea?* After assessing his options, he came to a decision.

'I'll arrange for your aircraft to be unloaded,' said Blenheim.

'No thanks, old bean. There's no need. Most likely, the front will pass through in an hour or two. There's no need to think about that just yet.'

His efforts frustrated once again, Blenheim finally snapped.

'I thought pilots were taught how to fly through bad weather?'

'Steady on, old chap. We are.' The pilot put down his newspaper to give Blenheim his full attention. 'We are also taught not to take unnecessary risks as well. That aircraft is fully loaded and heavy. In bad weather, it'll bounce about like a rubber ball. If it gets ice on the wings, it'll fall out of the sky like a brick. If we get struck by lightning, we could lose an engine or both engines and strong winds could blow us way off course. I decide if it is safe to fly or not unless overruled by a senior officer, and you are not my senior officer.' The pilot took a deep breath, picked up his newspaper and, just before settling to read it once again, he said to Blenheim. 'I'll get a weather update in an hour. I'll know more then.'

Blenheim, realising he was not going to be able to push the pilot any further without making him suspicious about his motives for a quick getaway, left the officers' mess.

Standing outside the entrance, he looked at his watch and began to calculate time and distance in his head. It was a four-hour flight to Frankfurt; so long as the plane left before two this afternoon, it would arrive while it was still light and not be delayed further. He looked up at the clear blue sky above his head and cursed. The weather was one of the few variables he'd been unable to account for in his original plan. Deciding to pre-empt the pilot, Blenheim marched to the airfield's operations room for a weather update.

Inside the operations room, Blenheim found a sergeant and a lance corporal. All the staff that was left in the once busy office at the heart of the RAF airfield. Both men stood to attention as he entered.

'At ease, men. I'd like a weather report for the English Channel, Sergeant. I've got an aircraft stuck on the field, and I'd like to get it away as quickly as possible. I understand the weather is bad over the channel. How is it looking?'

The sergeant left his desk and crossed to a wall covered in clipboards holding charts. Taking one down, he studied it for a moment and then crossed to Blenheim, handing the chart to the officer.

'It's not looking good for the next couple of hours, but these things tend to be out of date by the time they reach us.' The sergeant looked at the clock on the office wall. 'There's another update due to arrive from the met office in fifteen minutes. I could let you have a copy when it comes in.'

'Thank you, sergeant. Send it over to the officers' mess, would you? It's important.'

'Yes, sir.'

Blenheim returned to the officers' mess, ordered a coffee, and picked up a copy of the local newspaper. On the front page was a photograph of April Showers with the caption, 'Local female private detective, April Showers missing for two days.' The front page coverage went on to ask members of the public to keep a lookout for her before continuing to say how worried her parents and her friends are for her safety. The newspaper explained that no one had seen the missing detective since Wednesday last, or knew where she was. The newspaper also mentioned that the police were searching for a black Hillman Maxi car, hired by Miss Showers from a local garage, as finding the car may give a clue as to her whereabouts. Blenheim slammed the newspaper down onto the table, knocking over his coffee cup. Not stopping to pick it up, he strode from the officers' mess and headed for the fully loaded Dakota. Danny Gold was still keeping an eye on it.

Gold stood to attention and saluted as Blenheim approached.

'She's a bloody private detective,' declared Blenheim. 'And her bloody picture is all over the front of the newspaper.'

Gold let his arm drop to his side.

'What do we do?' Gold asked anxiously.

'I'm not sure. I'm still thinking about it. The newspaper says no one knows where she is. We can't take her off the plane, or the pilot will ask what we are doing. The only thing that may bring the police sniffing around here is if they find her car. It's a black Hillman Maxi. She couldn't have driven far in those wellington boots she was wearing, so her car must be close to the farm. Find it. Take it to the farm and lock it in the cattle shed out of sight. Report back to me when you return.'

'I'll need a chitty to get a car from the pool and a pass to leave the airfield,' Gold reminded Blenheim.

'Two more days, and I'll be free of this madhouse,' muttered Blenheim to himself. 'Come to my office. I'll fill out the forms for you.'

After sending Gold off on his mission to find April's car, Blenheim returned to the officers' mess to await the latest weather report. Taking a seat near the window, he stared up at the blue sky above East Yorkshire, wondering how the weather could be so perfect here and yet stormy over the English Channel. A steward asking him if he would like a drink distracted him from his thoughts.

'No, thank you.' The steward left him. Blenheim risked a glance at the Dakota pilot. The flying officer had laid down his newspaper and was chatting with his co-pilot. Blenheim wondered what they would do if they knew they had a passenger asleep in a crate on their aeroplane. His plans, so meticulously made after learning he was to be discharged from the air force sooner than he had anticipated, had accounted for every eventuality except being discovered by a female private investigator so late in their execution. He'd even successfully adapted his plans to cope with April's unexpected appearance on the airfield and arrange for her disposal to his advantage. But the weather, everyone was at the mercy of the English weather, and that was unfathomable.

Blenheim's attention peeked when the sergeant from the operations room entered the mess. He handed a piece of paper to the pilot and then came over to his seat.

'I'm sorry, sir, it looks like you are going to be delayed for at least another hour.' He handed Blenheim the weather report. 'The report does say the storms passing through the channel quicker than expected. Is there anything else, sir?'

'No. Just keep me up-to-date with the weather reports.' As soon as the sergeant's back was turned, Blenheim checked the time on his wristwatch. There was still enough time for one more weather report before the flight would have to be cancelled for today.

Another half-hour passed painfully slowly before the mess steward brought Blenheim a note. It was from Sergeant Gold and read, *missing goods located and returned to stores.* Blenheim let out a sigh of relief and then slipped the note into his pocket.

'Is the sergeant still waiting outside?' asked Blenheim.

'Yes, sir. Shall I fetch him in?'

'No. I will go out to speak to him.' As the mess steward departed, Blenheim headed for the door.

Outside, Blenheim indicated that Gold should follow him away from the officers' mess. When they were out of earshot of anyone entering or leaving the building, Blenheim stopped.

'Well done. Did anyone see you?'

'No,' replied Gold.

'But we do have a problem with the weather,' said Blenheim. 'There has been another delay to our departure due to bad weather over the channel. That woman will need to be taken off the plane unless it leaves soon; so get the lads ready to help with the unloading.'

Danny Gold looked shocked. 'You said those sleeping pills would keep her quiet.'

'Yes, they will. I just don't know for how long. They help my wife sleep through the night, but whether they are strong

266

enough to keep that private investigator asleep until the plane reaches Germany, I'm not so sure. I gave her three times the dose my wife takes, so she'll sleep for a while yet. But these weather delays are bothering me. I don't want her waking up halfway through the flight or just as we land in Germany. Just ensure all the lads are available to unload that plane tonight if there are any more delays to the flight.'

'What will you do with the pilot?' asked Gold.

'Don't worry about him. I'll keep him and the co-pilot entertained whilst you get April Showers off the plane.'

As Blenheim and Gold talked outside, the pilot of the Dakota left the officers' mess, heading in the direction of the control room. A few minutes later, he returned with a fresh sheet of paper in his hand. In the meantime, Blenheim had returned to the officers' mess and was sitting next to the window when the pilot walked in.

'Good news, Blenheim. We can get going. I've filed a new flight plan that will divert us around the last of those storms over the channel. It means we will be a little later than expected before arriving in Frankfurt, but at least we will get there today. You're not the only one in a hurry to get going. It's my wife's birthday today, and before I left Germany this morning, I promised to take her out tonight. So you see, I can't let her down, can I? Get your gear; we'll be taking off in fifteen minutes.'

'I'm all packed and ready to go. I'll be at the plane in five minutes; I just need to let my sergeant know that I'm leaving.'

As the pilot of the Dakota walked around the outside of his aeroplane doing his last-minute safety checks, his co-pilot was inside the aircraft doing the preliminary pre-flight checks when Blenheim returned with a small, soft suitcase.

'Stow it in the back,' instructed the pilot, 'and make sure it's securely tied down. It's likely to be a bit bumpy over the channel.'

After Blenheim placed his suitcase behind the cargo webbing in the back of the aircraft and tied it down, he checked the crate that encased April. No sound came from inside. Unable to resist the temptation, he wrapped on the side of the crate with his knuckles. All was silent. Reassured that his prisoner was still sleeping soundly, Blenheim joined the co-pilot in the cockpit.

'Pilot Officer Wellesley; welcome aboard sir. We rarely get passengers on these flights. You can sit in the navigator's seat. We don't need a navigator these days. Once the pilot has decided which route he wants to take, it's down to me to keep him on track.'

'Thank you,' answered Blenheim.

'There's no heating on the plane, so you'd better put on this flying jacket. It gets cold at five thousand feet.' The co-pilot left his passenger and returned to his pre-flight checks.

Blenheim took the jacket and put it on, then strapped himself into his seat. As he waited, he wondered about his hidden passenger in the crate. How would she respond to the cold while she was unconscious? He knew she was wearing a jacket, but it wasn't one made from a sheep's fleece. *Too late to worry about it now*, he told himself. The co-pilot returned.

'Excuse me, sir. There are a couple of flasks of hot chocolate up there,' he pointed to two thermos flasks strapped to a shelf, 'once we level off; if you get cold, help yourself.'

'Thank you..?'

'Reggie Wellesley, sir.'

'Thank you, Reggie. I may do that.'

Chapter Sixteen

The same Friday

The phone rang on Rex Barker's office desk at GCHQ Scarborough, distracting him from a pile of routine paperwork.

'Barker!' He announced enthusiastically down the phone line. He hoped the caller would have a problem that needed solving urgently, or at the very least, something more interesting for him to think about than routine reports. The voice on the other end of the line was that of Miss Thornwick, Colonel Bempton's secretary.

'The Colonel would like to see you,' was all she said before the line went dead. Miss Thornwick had delivered the Colonel's message bluntly and to the point in her usual efficient way.

Rex closed the files on his desk and locked them in his drawer. The Colonel was not a man to call you into his office for a cosy chat, which meant something serious had happened, and Rex Barker had been chosen for the job of resolving it, or he was in serious trouble.

When Rex entered Colonel Bempton's outer office, Miss Thornwick was busy at her typewriter. Rex had learned in his short time at GCHQ Scarborough that the formidable secretary did not want to be interrupted.

'You can go straight in,' she announced, much to Rex's surprise, as he was normally kept waiting. He knocked on the inner office door, which led to the colonel's sanctum, and entered.

'Ah, Barker, just the man. Take a seat.' The Colonel got straight to the point. 'Our American friends are getting impatient. They want to know who killed Robert Hood. My boss assured the Americans that we had everything under control, but he has had to give in to pressure from the Home Office. Consequently, the CIA chief in London has sent a Mr Lee Garrett up to help us find Hood's killers, and I've been instructed by my superiors to work with him. So drop whatever you are doing. I'm assigning you to the job. I don't care how you do it, but keep Garrett away from this station and keep his gun in his holster. You know what our American cousins are like. They still think it's the Wild West out there and that they can do as they please. Remind him this is England. We have standards to maintain. We do not go around re-enacting the shootout at the OK Corral. Get over to the Grand Scarborough Hotel. Garrett is waiting for you.'

'Yes, sir.'

'By the way. How is your lady detective getting on? I thought she would have had something to report by now. Are you sure she is up to the job?'

Rex wasn't ready for the question, as it had been the Colonel's idea to get her involved, not his. And since April had fallen out with him, he'd lost contact with her.

'I'll check in with her and get an update today, sir. Just as soon as I've welcomed Mr Garret to Scarborough. With the American joining the team, now may be the time to inform Miss Showers of the full extent of what she is investigating; it may speed things up a bit.'

'As you see fit, but keep American involvement to a minimum.'

'Yes, sir.'

Fifteen minutes later, Rex was parking his car outside the Grand Scarborough Hotel. After checking with the receptionist that Lee Garrett was in his room, Rex headed for the lift. Room 314 was at the end of the corridor. Unfortunately for Garret, it was not the end where the rooms had a sea view, but where the rooms overlooked the town centre. It also had a busy road running below his window.

Rex knocked on the bedroom door, hoping that he would like the CIA agent and they could work together. He'd never worked with an agent from another country before. So he was looking forward to seeing and hearing about how the CIA operated despite the Colonel's insistence that he kept the American away from GCHQ Scarborough. When the hotel room door flew open, Rex looked up into two big, bright blue eyes, a smile of sparkling white teeth and a chin that looked as though it had been chiselled from granite. The face was topped with a closely cropped crew cut of blonde hair.

272

'Good morning, Mr Garrett. My name is Rex Barker. I believe you are expecting me.'

'Hi. Come in. Come in. Take a seat. Would you like a coffee?' The mountain grabbed Rex's hand with a fist that would have put a grizzly bear's paw to shame and pumped his arm up and down.

'Thank you. Yes, please.' His ploy worked; Garrett let go of Rex's crushed digits to make him a coffee. Rex took the only seat in the room and counted his fingers to ensure they were all there and still working.

'How do you like your coffee, with cream and sugar?'

'Just cream, please. Is this your first visit to Britain?' asked Rex.

'Yes. This is my first European assignment. I'm fresh out of the marines after being in South Korea for a few years. I helped supervise an undercover operation over there and got some good intelligence out of North Korea about their missile program. So I was offered a job with the CIA.' He thrust a cup of coffee towards Rex.

As Rex sipped his coffee, he couldn't help wondering how a six-foot-six-inch blonde American could go undercover in North Korea. When the average height of a North Korean is five feet tall, and they all have dark hair. But decided the story could wait for another day.

'What have you been told about the case we are to work on?' asked Rex.

'Only that Robert Hood was one of our guys, and the Brits are having trouble finding the ones responsible for killing him.'

'We do have someone working on the case. In fact, I was planning on contacting her today for an update on the case,' responded Rex.

'Right,' Garrett sprang off the bed where he'd been sitting and headed for the door, 'let's get going.'

'Where are we going?' asked Garrett, as Rex started the engine of his Jaguar.

'To Driffield; it's a small town not far from here. We are going to speak to an old friend of mine. She's a private detective.'

'A woman and a private detective!' exclaimed Garrett. 'Back home, our ladies take care of the house and children.'

'I think you'll find that April Showers is not your typical woman. She's a bit more independent than most.'

'You mean, butch?'

'No, not at all. April just knows her own mind.'

'Ah, one of those types. Doesn't she mind MI5 using her to do their dirty work for them?'

'It's not like that. We Brits just don't like to make a big deal about these things. We keep our investigations low-key. The fewer people who know what we are doing, the better.'

'What you are saying is, she doesn't know who she is investigating or why?'

'No. It's not as bad as all that. April knows Robert Hood has been murdered, and that he has something to do with forging banknotes.'

'But he didn't, so why would she think that?'

'Well, to cover the real reason he was murdered; the tracking down of foreign agents in East Yorkshire. The Colonel thinks Mr Hood may have stumbled onto the forging racket by accident.'

'Do you get many foreign agents in East Yorkshire?'

'Oh yes. You see, East Yorkshire faces east towards Europe and beyond that is Russia. It also doesn't help when this part of the country is full of EX-WWII military bases, most of which have been reassigned after the last war. Their main purpose these days is monitoring what the Soviets are doing. We have several fast jet interceptor squadrons up and down the coast. Some ours, some yours. We listen to the Soviet radio broadcasts, we follow their ships, and we intercept their aircraft as they approach our coastline. We also have a series of defensive missile sights to protect'

'So, you think it's the Soviets who are printing British currency to undermine the British economy, and you don't want them to know that you know about it?'

'Something like that.'

'Why don't you arrest these agents?'

'Because we want to ensure we capture all of them. Which includes their contacts abroad and their equipment for printing forged banknotes.'

'And you think this lady private detective can do that for you?'

'Oh, yes. With a little help from me, and maybe with your assistance.'

Rex brought the car to a stop on Exchange Street in Driffield, and with Garrett in tow, they entered the converted house that April used as an office.

Rex gave a brief knock on her office door before entering. The room was empty. Rex crossed to April's desk, looking for a note, but didn't find one. Garrett followed Rex and Jennifer from across the hall, followed them both.

'Hello, Rex. April's out I afraid.' Jennifer was speaking to Rex, but her eyes were all over his companion. 'Who's your friend?'

'Lee Garrett, Ma'am. Pleased to meet you. Rex is just showing me around and we were wondering if Miss Showers was at home?'

'She doesn't live here,' laughed Jennifer. 'We don't get many American visitors. I could show you around if you like?' Jennifer continued, suggestively.

'That's a good idea,' suggested Rex. 'You could take him home for supper and introduce him to your husband.'

'Oh Rex, you know I'm only kidding. Why did you have to spoil the dream?'

'Sorry, Jen. Do you know where April is? I need to speak to her.'

'No, she's not been in for a couple of days. In fact, I was getting worried. Normally she tells me if she is going to go away, so I know I need to lock up.'

'When was the last time you saw or heard from her?' asked Rex.

'Wednesday; she left here at the normal time to go home.'

'Did she say anything about the case she is working on?'

'No; why?'

'Thanks, Jennifer. I'll check at her home. She may be feeling a bit under the weather and simply taken a few days off work.' Without saying more to Jennifer, Rex made for the door.

'Nice to have met you, Ma'am.' Garret followed Rex from the building.

As Rex dove towards April's house, Garret asked, 'do you think something is wrong?'

'I don't know. But Jennifer was right about one thing. April usually tells her when she is not going to be around, or she'll leave a note with a contact address and phone number on her desk; she's done neither.'

'Could she be ill?' asked Garrett.

'Not without letting someone know,' responded Rex.

'Then maybe..?' Garrett didn't finish the sentence.

'Oh, God, I hope not,' exclaimed Rex. 'Come on.'

Rex's car screeched to a halt outside April's house. 'Her car's missing,' said Rex.

'Yes, but look at the house. It's nearly midday, and all the house curtains are closed,' said Garrett. Rex and Garrett were out of the car in a flash.

'You check around the back of the house,' directed Rex. He entered the porch and pressed the doorbell. There was no response from anyone inside. After a few seconds, he pounded on the door but still got no answer.

Garrett joined Rex at the front door. 'There's no sign of a break-in at the back.'

Rex pulled out his wallet and retrieved a slim lock-picking tool. After a few seconds of fiddling with the Yale lock, the front door opened. Inside the house, the hall and living room lights were still on.

'You check down here; I'll go upstairs,' said Rex. The men separated and, in less than a minute, met up again in the living room.

'Anything?' asked Rex.

'Nothing,' answered Garrett.

'Search again more thoroughly. Look for any sign of a disturbance or something out of place,' demanded Rex. 'I'll do the same upstairs.'

Later, back in the living room, Rex asked, 'find anything.'

'No, but I spotted an empty peg on the coat rack,' answered Garrett.

'Me neither. The bed hasn't been slept in. It looks like she came home, switched the lights on, closed the curtains and made something to eat before going out again. Which means April left home after dark but planned to be home before morning,' said Rex. 'She hadn't planned on being out all night. That's why she left the lights on. That's why she didn't leave a note.'

Moving to the hall, Rex picked up the telephone and dialled the number for GCHQ.

'Rex Barker. Get onto the Post Office switchboard for Driffield. I want to know the telephone number and address of the last call received at the home of April Showers and the last number she dialled from her house.' He dropped the phone onto its cradle.

'We'll visit her father and find out what he knows.'

At the East Yorkshire Savings Bank on Middle Street, Driffield, Rex and Garrett marched up to the bank manager's office door. Rex knocked once and then entered, followed by Garrett. Mr Showers looked up, startled by the sudden and unexpected intrusion. It took a couple of seconds for him to recognise Rex. Even so, the intrusion bridled him until a feeling of foreboding clouded his thoughts.

'Rex, what's the meaning of this?' questioned Mr Showers, getting to his feet. Garrett closed the office door.

'I'm sorry to intrude on you like this, but it's important.' Rex hesitated for a moment. 'What do you know about the case April is working on?'

A look of alarm spread across the bank manager's face.

'What's happened to April?'

'Maybe nothing, but she hasn't been at work for a couple of days, and her car is missing. I was wondering if you knew where she might have gone?' Mr Showers stared at Garrett. 'I'm sorry. This is a work colleague; he's helping me out for a few days.'

'How do you do?' said Garrett cheerfully in a thick American accent as he stuck out his giant hand in welcome. The bank manager's jaw fell open as he took Garrett's hand.

'Where's April?' Mr Showers asked again.

'I don't know,' responded Rex as calmly as he could. 'Has she said anything to you or Mrs Showers about going away for a few days?'

279

'No.'

'Has anyone else asked you about your daughter?' asked Garrett.

'No.'

'What has she told you about the case she is working on?' asked Rex.

Mr Showers had gone pale and hesitated before answering. 'She said she was trying to find out who was responsible for the counterfeit five-pound notes.'

'Did she tell you about any leads she had made?' asked Rex.

'No. What has happened to April?' demanded Mr Showers.

'I don't know. She's not been at work for a couple of days and she is not at home. Her car is missing, so I suspect she has gone somewhere in search of the people she is looking for. You know how single-minded she gets when she gets a lead. She's probably followed the counterfeiters to another town and hasn't had a chance to phone home or the office to tell anyone.'

The expression on the bank manager's face was as readable as a book, but he said nothing.

'I expect she'll turn up in a day or so and explain everything,' suggested Rex.

Mr Showers, his composure regained. 'Find her Rex. Keep me informed of your progress. I want my daughter back. You mustn't say anything to April's mother about her going missing. You only speak to me.'

'I'm sorry we had to break in on you like this. I promise, I'll find her,' Rex reassured him.

Back in the car, Rex and Garrett drove off toward Driffield's Police station.

As Rex approached the desk, he removed his identity card and showed it to the police officer on the desk.

'I'd like to see Inspector Longstreet,' said Rex firmly.

'Yes, sir. I see if he's available,' said the constable.

'I don't care what he is doing, who he is with, or if he's in Outer Mongolia. You will find him and get him here!' The desk officer flinched as Rex leaned across the desk to make his demand. It was a nervous police constable's hand that lifted the telephone receiver and dialled a number.

'Inspector Longstreet, there are two gentlemen to see you at the front desk, sir.' He put the phone down. 'The Inspector is on his way. Would you like to wait in the interview room, sir?' The constable pointed to a door on the left. Without further comment, Rex and Garrett went into the room to await the Inspector.

'Good morning, or is it afternoon? Time passes so quickly in this job. How may I help you?' asked the Inspector, flippantly as he crossed to the interview table and sat down. Rex and Garrett remained standing.

'Please, take a seat,' said Longstreet, indicating to the chairs on the opposite side of the table. Rex and Garrett ignored his offer.

'April Showers is missing. What do you know about the case she is working on?' demanded Rex.

The Inspector hesitated for a moment whilst he gathered his thoughts.

'Who are you?' asked the Inspector.

Rex and Garrett produced their I.D. The Inspector sat up straight but didn't stand.

'She's looking for the source of the forged five-pound notes, and so are we. I told her to report any information she discovers to me.' The Inspector put on a confident face.

'When was this?' continued Rex, already knowing the answer.

'A few days ago, when I went to interview her.'

'That's not the whole truth, is it, Inspector?'

'What, what do you mean by that remark?' The Inspector's conciliatory smile dropped from his face.

'You threatened her. You told her to leave the case to you, or she would be arrested, didn't you? You didn't want her investigating a case that could put a feather in your cap, did you? Instead of working with her, you pushed her aside. And now, a vital witness to all these forgeries has gone missing. What are you going to do about it?'

'But she's just a slip of a lass, a woman. This case is real police work. She should…'

'You are an idiot. I want every officer in this station out looking for her right now. You do not stop until she is found. By the time I've finished speaking to the Chief Constable, you'll be lucky if you still have a job by the end of the week. I want a progress report from you every day. Do I make myself clear?'

By the time Rex had finished with him, Inspector Longstreet was on his feet, looking as though he'd just been probed with an electric cattle prod. 'Yes, sir.'

Remembering the Colonel's request to keep Garrett away from GCHQ Scarborough, Rex added. 'We are going back to Miss Showers' office to search through her files for clues. Until she is found, I intend to use it as my office in Driffield. If you learn anything, contact me there.'

Rex grabbed the door handle, threw the door open, and stormed out.

Back in the car, Rex hammered his fist on the steering wheel.

'I shouldn't have been so hard on the Inspector. Yes, he's an idiot for not knowing what April was doing, but April going missing is as much my fault as his. I was the one responsible for bringing her in on the case. I should have watched her more closely, but we had a silly disagreement. I thought she would need my help to solve this case, and she'd come to me when she discovered Robert Hood's murderers. I assumed that she would need me when it came to capturing the culprits. But now, it looks as though she's tried to do it on her own, and she is in trouble. We'd better go back to her office and search her files for clues as to where she may have gone. She must have a list of suspects.'

'I understand. Sometimes, it can be tough working with a partner,' offered Garrett.

'The trouble is, she's not my partner, not in an official sense. We've known each other for years. Unfortunately, over all those years, we've always had an on/off relationship. You see, she's headstrong, and she's a hard woman to pin down.' Rex slipped the car into gear and pulled away from the police station.

'Let's get back to her office.'

As Rex and Garrett stormed into April's office. Jennifer followed up behind them.

'Back so soon; have you discovered something?' asked Jennifer.

'Not yet; that's why we've come back. I'm hoping April has left a case file in her desk. I want to know who her suspects are,' said Rex.

'You mean; April is in trouble, don't you?'

'We don't know for sure,' interjected Garrett.

While Garrett was reassuring Jennifer, Rex picked the lock in the drawer on April's desk. Finding a file of papers, he opened it. After skimming through a couple of pages, Rex slammed the drawer shut.

'I've got what we need.' Rex held up the file.

'You could read through the file here if you like. I'm sure April wouldn't mind, and I could make you both a coffee?' suggested Jennifer as she smiled at Garrett.

'Thanks,' said Rex as he dropped into April's desk chair. He opened the file and passed half the papers across the desk to Garrett for him to read.

'Two coffees and some biscuits, if you've got any?' asked Rex.

'Sure thing,' replied Jennifer, giving a glance and a smile at Garrett before she left the office.

When Jennifer returned to April's office, she found Rex and Garrett engrossed in April's paperwork, separating pages into different piles of interest. She set the coffee on the desk and the plate of biscuits within reach of Garrett.

'Cookies, thank you, Ma'am,' said Garrett, selecting a chocolate-covered digestive.

'Here's something,' said Rex, without looking up from the page. 'April has been using a man called Terrance Nock to watch a green van. I think we'll pay Mr Nock a visit and have a word with him.'

Just as Rex was getting up from his seat, the telephone rang. Rex answered it.

'April Showers detective agency.' 'Yes, Inspector.' Rex picked up a pencil and wrote on one of the pages from April's file. 'Right; we'll get over there for a look ourselves.' Rex slammed the phone down.

'A sighting. April's car was reported to the police station in Kilham a couple of days ago. A farmer complained about finding a car in one of his fields. However, when the police went to investigate, the car had gone. The Kilham police didn't follow up on the sighting as the car had been moved. They didn't know at that point that the incident was anything more than an abandoned car. The only thing that alerted them to something being amiss was when they checked the car's registration number and found it was registered to a garage in

Driffield. The police informed the garage owner about the car and were informed that it had been leased to Miss April Showers. The Kilham police had dealt with an incident involving April a couple of weeks earlier when she crashed into a farm gate in Langtoft whilst following some suspects. And Langtoft is very close to the field where April's hire car was last seen.'

'Right,' said Garrett. 'What are we waiting for?'

Rex's Jaguar screeched to a halt at the entrance to the field where April's car had last been seen. Searching for clues, Rex and Garrett found tyre marks in the mud leading up to and beyond the field gate, confirming that a car had been driven into the field.

'We can presume that April drove the car into the field, but why here?' said Rex as he scoured the area around the gate.

'If she was looking for something,' volunteered Garrett.

'But, what?' snapped Rex, as he followed the tyre tracks to the field gate.

'Not what, but who? She was following someone; they stopped; April parked the car and followed them on foot, but in which direction?' Garrett scanned the horizon.

Rex climbed the gate and walked a few yards into the field, following the tyre tracks in the mud until they ran out.

'The car stopped here.' Rex peered at the ground and found a small shoe print.

'She got out.' Walking back towards the gate a couple of yards, he found more shoe prints mixed with small boot prints.

'She's changed from shoes to boots.' The boot prints led back towards the gate.

'She's on foot.' Rex re-climbed the gate and looked back across the field. There was nothing more to find back there.

'Let's walk up the road a bit and see if we can find what April was interested in,' suggested Garrett.

A hundred yards further on, Rex and Garrett came to the entrance to the abandoned farmhouse and buildings. They glanced at each other without saying a word. They both knew that they had found what they were looking for. A brief scout around the outside of the house showed it to be undisturbed. Next, they investigated the outbuildings, quickly discovering the only one that was padlocked.

'Wait a minute,' said Rex. 'I'll pick the lock.'

'Don't bother,' said Garrett, and before Rex could stop him, Garrett pulled out his black .45 automatic pistol and shot the padlock off the door.

'We don't do that kind of thing in this country,' said Rex.

Garrett shrugged his shoulders. 'It's quicker my way.' He grabbed hold of the broken door fastening and heaved the door open. The rear of April's hire car was the first thing that greeted them. With Garrett leading the way, gun at the ready, they entered the barn. Rex rushed to the side windows and peered inside. There was no sign of April, though her car keys were still in the ignition. Garrett moved to the boot and gingerly turned the handle and lifted the lid. All he found was a pair of April's shoes.

'You were right about her changing from shoes to boots,' he called to Rex, holding up her day shoes for Rex to see.

'I'd guess April was discovered whilst spying on the people she was following. It's the only explanation for why the car was parked in the field and then moved in here.'

Discovering nothing more of interest in the car, Rex and Garrett turned their attention to the rest of the building and the abandoned machinery, and the discarded printing supplies.

Rex turned to Garrett. 'There's nothing here. This is just a convenient dumping spot for all this equipment. There's no sign of any printing going on in here.'

'So, where were they printing the banknotes?' asked Garrett.

'It has to be somewhere close. Either in the village or there must be another house or farm nearby.'

'We should move on?' suggested Garrett.

'Not yet. We need to search the grounds outside for signs of April,' declared Rex. An icy shiver ran down his spine at the prospect of finding April's body in a shallow grave or hidden under farm refuse. Garrett nodded his agreement, and the pair split up. As they searched the grounds around the abandoned farm, an increasing roaring sound made Rex look up. He heard aeroplane engines getting closer. Seconds later, the aeroplane passed low over the farm. Rex watched the Dakota climbing into the sky. Staring at it for a moment, he remembered his time in Africa and all the times he had flown in an aeroplane similar to the one he was watching. As the plane moved away, Rex continued his search of the farm's grounds.

Later that afternoon, April's photograph appeared in the local newspaper, with a caption declaring that she was missing. Rex threw the paper to the floor, knowing he'd made another mistake; he should have told the police to keep the story from the press. How was he going to explain April's disappearance to her mother?

Chapter Seventeen

Friday Evening

It was getting dark outside the aeroplane as Flying officer Blenheim stared through the Dakota's small, rectangular window. Below, he could see the lights from farmhouses and villages scattered across the landscape. The bright, snaking headlights of traffic making their way along dark roads captivated him. He knew he was somewhere over Europe. He'd watched ships making their way up and down the coast of England as the plane flew over the English Channel, but that was hours ago. From his seat behind the flight deck bulkhead, he turned to look down the length of the Dakota's interior to the crate which held his female captive. How long would she stay asleep, he wondered, and would she survive the bitter cold in the unheated aircraft? With the delay to his take-off in England, he wished he'd given her a larger dose of sleeping tablets. Darkly, he considered if he would have been better off killing her when she was first discovered, but she was young and desirable. Killing a woman was not the same as killing a man. Especially if that man was an idiot like Jack

Frisket. Frisket had deserved to be killed. The fool had put all his plans for the future in jeopardy by creaming off some of the banknotes for himself and spending them around the local town. The other guy had been collateral damage. He'd been in the wrong place at the wrong time. Looking at his watch, he wondered how much longer it would be before they landed. Unclipping his seatbelt, Blenheim got to his feet just as the aircraft flew through a bit of turbulence. With a bump and a shudder, it threw him sideways into the cockpit bulkhead. Pain shot through his shoulder. He clenched his teeth to hold back a cry of discomfort. Regaining his balance on freezing stiff legs and feet, he held onto the sides of the cockpit door with both hands and shouted across to the co-pilot, his voice having to compete with the noise from the two roaring engines.

'How long before we land?'

The co-pilot held up the palm of his hand, showing five splayed fingers and shouted back, 'five minutes.' And then he pointed out through the front windscreen. In the distance, Blenheim could see the long line of runway lights way ahead of the aircraft. He nodded at the co-pilot and returned to his seat. Having just made himself comfortable again, he felt the aeroplane bounce as a whirring sound passed through the plane. Looking outside, he saw the wing flaps lower. Moments later, there was another shudder through the aircraft announcing the lowering of the undercarriage. Grasping the arms of his seat, Blenheim braced himself for the jolt that would come when the aeroplanes wheels struck the runway. There was a screech of rubber on tarmac. Everything in the plane bounced with the impact. After what seemed like an age, he felt the second bounce before the plane settled to a rolling rumble as it ran along the runway. Blenheim let out a sigh of relief. Slowly, the rear of the aircraft descended to the runway as the plane slowed. Blenheim impatiently waited for the aircraft to come to a halt and let him out.

The plane slowed, and after a couple of changes of direction, finally stopped. Blenheim unfastened his seatbelt and got to his feet. At the same time, the co-pilot came through from the cockpit and opened the crew door, dropping the crew ladder into its holding slot on the lip of the aircraft's entrance.

As Blenheim approached the door, overnight bag in hand, the co-pilot smiled at him and in a cheeky voice said.

'After you, sir,' the co-pilot indicated to the aeroplane's door. 'I hope you enjoyed your fight this evening and will fly with us again someday soon.'

Blenheim let out a little laugh.

'At last,' said Blenheim, under his breath, as his feet touched the runway, 'made it.'

He was in Germany with his precious cargo. Nothing was going to ruffle his feathers now. Nothing could stop him from achieving his final goal.

'The officers' mess is just next to the control room, sir.' The co-pilot pointed across the tarmac to a row of buildings.'

'Thank you, but I'm going to wait until the plane is unloaded. I have to check everything goes into the storage hangar. It'll be my final duty as an officer in the RAF before I become a civilian.' Before the co-pilot could answer, the Dakota pilot joined them, overhearing what had been said.

'Sorry, Blenheim, you can't. This is a busy airfield in a foreign country. For safety and security reasons, only official ground crew are allowed to unload aeroplane cargo. It could be a couple of hours before they get around to unloading this plane, as it is not scheduled for departure for another two days. The engines need a service. Anyway, I promised to introduce you to my wife on her birthday. All the British officers and their wives will be there. You'll have a great time.'

Blenheim looked Flying Officer Stirling in the eye and then looked back at the silent aeroplane, not knowing what to say.

'Come on,' instructed F.O. Stirling, as he lead the way to the control room to complete the flight's paperwork.

'Are you alright, sir?' the co-pilot asked, as Blenheim hesitated next to the plane.

'Yes. Sorry. I was miles away.' Blenheim followed the co-pilot and pilot to the control room with one last look over his shoulder.

Panicked by the unexpected turn of events, Blenheim tried to think of a solution. He cursed himself for bringing the female detective with him. He'd got greedy, and it was that which was messing up his plans. Had he killed her in England, the delay in unloading the cargo would have been a minor setback. Now she risked bringing months of work crashing down around his ears. With his brain working overtime to come up with a plan to get his cargo, it was only when the sergeant in the control room asked him to sign the flight register that his thoughts returned to the here and now.'

'You've been assigned room twelve in the officer's quarters, sir,' said the sergeant.

'Thank you, sergeant.'

'See you at the gym at nine o'clock. There's a small band lined up so we can dance and there'll be food and drink as well. It'll be better than stale sandwiches and lukewarm coffee,' said Stirling as he left the control room. Blenheim looked at his watch; he only had time for a shower and a change of shirt before he would have to attend the party.

As he showered, he formulated a plan on how to get April out of the crate and off the airfield. He'd go to the party, ensure he was seen, and then slip away to make his way back to the plane to check on his sleeping prisoner. If her crate was still in the aeroplane, he would free her and get his German partners to smuggle her off the airfield. If the crates had been moved to a storage hangar, he would find her and do the same thing. Blenheim dressed, and, facing the mirror, straightened his tie. Then, before leaving his room, he made a phone call to his German partners.

'Hello, Fritz? I've arrived. Meet me at the aeroplane with your truck in an hour. No, I can't. I have to show up at a birthday party first. I want people to see me at the party. It'll give me an alibi should I need one.' Dropping the phone on its cradle, he left his room and made his way to the birthday party.

The sound of popular music coming from the base gym wasn't difficult to miss. Blenheim entered through the main doors and then turned left to enter a large sports hall already containing a large number of people. A small band played in the corner, and a few couples danced in the centre of the floor. Along the far wall and below the windows stood a row of tables covered with a variety of party dishes and bottled drinks.

'Blenheim!' called a voice from his right. Turning to see who was shouting his name, he spotted Flying Officer Stirling coming toward him with a beautiful lady on his arm.

'Glad you could make it. I wasn't sure if the long flight hadn't tired you out. May I introduce the birthday girl, my wife Barbara?'

'Happy birthday, it is a pleasure to meet you. I'm honoured your husband invited me.'

'Thank you..?'

'David. Call me David. I don't suppose there's any need to be formal tonight,' said Blenheim, shaking Barbara by the hand.

'Great, I'm Mike,' said Stirling, 'and you've already met Reggie, my co-pilot. Come over and get something to eat and drink. You must be starving,' encouraged Mike Stirling. Blenheim didn't hesitate as he followed his host to the buffet.

'I'll be cutting the birthday cake later, but in the meantime, help yourself to whatever takes your fancy,' instructed Barbara.

The arrival of more people caught Barbara's eye. Taking her husband's arm, she apologised to Blenheim for leaving him so soon and led her husband across the floor to greet the new guests. Blenheim helped himself to sandwiches and sausage rolls. Mike Stirling had been right about him being hungry, now the flight was over, and he'd relaxed a little, food had been on his mind ever since getting out of the shower. As Blenheim refuelled from the buffet, his thoughts turned to his prisoner encased in her crate. He reassured himself that if she hadn't woken up by now and raised the alarm, there was a good chance the drug he had given her was still working. Soon, it wouldn't matter. She would be off his hands along with the crates of forged five-pound notes. He dreamt of living the rest of his life in luxury on the sunny Andalusian coast of Spain.

*****

However, whilst Blenheim was taking his shower, the Dakota was being unloaded by the RAF airfield ground crew. Each crate was swiftly unloaded through the cargo door of the plane by a forklift truck and then transferred to a cargo trolley before being driven away to a cargo hangar. Unloading only took twenty minutes. It was the last job of the day for the ground crew, and the sooner they finished the job, the sooner they could go off duty. The forklift truck followed the tractor towing the cargo trolleys to the hangar and hastily unloaded the crates. There was no need for care to be taken as most of the crates were labelled 'Gas Masks.'

*****

Sensing a heavy jolt, I awoke slowly with a thumping headache, freezing cold and very stiff. In my confusion, I could hear vehicle noises, men shouting, and lots of bagging, and then suddenly it all stopped. My first instinct was to stretch my legs, but when my feet hit something solid, they recoiled. I opened my eyes. Where the Hell was I? Next, I tried to move my hands and arms, but I couldn't. My brain was fogged, the restrictions confounding and frightening me, and then my memories came flooding back. I remembered Blenheim saying he had drugged me before I felt myself drifting away. It was dark, and I'd never felt so cold in all my life. The pain that came with it was excruciating. My body trembled, it was hard to think of anything else but the cold.

I tried to stretch my legs again. My feet quickly found the obstruction from before. This time, instead of recoiling, I pushed. My body slid over the straw bedding on which I was lying, and my head hit another obstacle. Shuffling about, I soon discovered I was in a box. It seemed to take forever, but gradually my dulled brain began to function and allow me to take stock of my situation. Apart from the cold and being trapped in a box, it was pitch black. I had no way of telling if I was still in the hangar at RAF Cottam or had been taken somewhere else? Faint, faraway sounds penetrated my new world but were too unclear to make any sense of. I guessed I was alone.

The voice in my head screamed, 'get out of the box.' So I fought against the ropes that bound my hands and feet, but I couldn't loosen them. So, I brought my knees up to my chest and pushed down with my arms, forcing the rope which was around my wrists to pass over my bottom and then my heels. I winced at the pain as the rope tightened and dragged at the skin around my wrist. I almost panicked when I got my wrists stuck over my feet when passing my hands over them. But, with a teeth-clenching final pull, I dragged my hands free and around to my front. The exertions had warmed me up a little, but my muscles screamed for rest. Dragging the gag from my mouth eased my breathing, and I finally felt as though I was making progress. Then, using my teeth, I pulled at the knot that tied my hands, and as soon as that fell away, I freed my ankles. Though I was lying on a thick bed of straw, the box I was in was lined with thick cardboard. Feeling around the interior of my prison, I found the edge of the cardboard lining and pulled. It tore easily, revealing the wooden battens of a crate. I recognised the prison that held me. I had light now. Not much, but enough to see the outline of other box shapes around me. I was in a hangar, but where?

I pushed at the lid of my box, but it didn't budge. I tried the walls one after the other, but they were all nailed down. I toyed with the idea of calling for help but decided that was a bad idea. I didn't know if my shouts would bring friend or foe. My escape had to be my own doing. In frustration, I kicked my heels against the wall of the crate and heard a crack. I tried again and then again, harder and harder. I heard splintering wood before feeling pain shooting through my bare heels after they impacted against the wooden side of the crate. As each plank of my crate broke, I pulled and pushed at it with my hands, enlarging the hole. Finally, I broke off enough wooden boards to make a hole large enough for me to crawl through.

After releasing myself from my prison, I stood up. Pain shot up the backs of my legs as my heels took my weight, and I instinctively let out a cry. Leaning against the crate, I rested a moment. However, I steeled myself for what was to come.

Trying to walk was incredibly painful and slow work, but unless I planned on staying where I was, I had to be brave and put up with it. With one small step at a time, I made my way toward an exit next to the main hangar door. This hangar was larger, better organised, and filled with more crates than the one I had been held in before. I wondered where I'd been transported to and what I would find once I was outside. One painful step after another, and with plenty of pauses to rest my damaged feet, I made it to the door. Turning the lever on the deadlock, I pulled the door open, and the night air rushed in. With it came the smell of aviation fuel and the sounds of the night. Tentatively, I stuck my head around the door and looked around. Opposite my hangar was another of the same size. I was in a whole row of hangars, all exactly the same. I definitely wasn't at RAF Cottam. I turned left, using the wall of the hangar as support. The ground was covered in concrete. At the end of the rows of hangars, I could see more buildings with lights. In the distance, an occasional vehicle crossed my view. Walking grew more and more painful as stone chips aggravated the pain in my tender bare feet. If I was to stand any chance of getting away from here, I needed shoes. Just as I reached the corner of my hangar, I spotted two bright headlights in the distance coming towards me. In a panic, I looked about for a place to hide. The road between the two rows of hangars was too wide to cross before the vehicle would arrive. My only hope was to follow the outer wall of the hangar into the dark and hope to find somewhere to hide between the hangars.

Unfortunately, the ground between the hangars was even rougher than that out front. I stifled a cry of pain as, in my haste to hide, the stones cut into my feet. Then, out of the darkness, I found a metal box attached to the wall of the hangar. Across the front of it, in big red letters, was the word 'FIRE.' Dropping behind it and pulling my knees up to my chest, I prayed I was sufficiently hidden from view. As I rubbed my feet, I felt the warm stickiness of blood between my fingers. My heart broke, and tears flowed as I crouched and shivered in the darkness, waiting to be discovered. The arrival of the bright lights turned out to be a truck which stopped outside my hangar. I heard the slamming of a truck door, and someone shout.

'The side door is open.'

More voices followed. I heard the hangar doors open. Then muffled voices came from inside the hangar. Trembling, terrified and praying, I pushed myself as far back against the wall of the hangar as I could. A moment later, from out front of the hangar, I heard Blenheim's raised voice. 'Where the hell could she have got to?'

Another heavily accented voice demanded. 'Forget her. Help get the crates loaded and let's get out of here.'

The sound of a forklift truck moving backwards and forwards followed, and within a few minutes, I heard the hangar door being closed. The truck did a u-turn outside the hangar and was gone, but not before I'd got its registration number. FF J 10. Listening intently for the slightest sound, I waited until I was sure the coast was clear. Then, using the wall of the hangar as an aid, I pushed myself to my feet and headed back to the front of the hangars, where the road was smoother. Slowly and with frequent stops, I made my way to the end of the row of hangars. As I looked about, I could see that I was on an enormous airfield. Across the other side of the airfield, I could see lines of aeroplanes illuminated by lights from more hangars and other buildings. Fearful of whom I might meet in that direction. I turned left again.

As I moved away from my rows of hangars, to my right was a cluster of low buildings. They reminded me of the living quarters I'd seen on the RAF base at Driffield. To the left of the living quarters were what looked like office buildings, and further on, there was a large building with music coming out of its open windows. I returned my attention to what I guessed were the living quarters and then back to the building from which the music blared and made a connection. If there was a dance on tonight, most base personnel would be there. The accommodation blocks and married quarters would be empty. There would be no better place or time to find somewhere to get some shoes and discover a way off the airfield.

It took me some time, but eventually, I made it across the airfield to a group of small houses. In front of me stood rows of pre-fabricated bungalows. I only had a hundred yards of grass to cross before reaching the first of them and then asking for help. It was a desperate thing to attempt but driven on by the pain in my feet and the need to escape, I was ready to try anything. I'd staggered halfway across the grass when, from the shadows, a figure appeared and looked to be crossing my path. I stopped, my heart thumping; had they seen me? I couldn't believe it; after escaping from the crate and all the effort in getting this far, I was about to be discovered at the last minute. The other finger stopped; they had seen me. I had no choice, so I hobbled on, keeping my eye on the stranger. After a few steps, the figure came out of the shadows; it was a woman. She seemed to be staggering almost as much as I was. As we drew closer, she stopped again. Held herself erect and called out, 'you too?'

I didn't know how to respond, so said nothing. The other woman changed direction and came toward me. It was when she arrived I understood why she was staggering. She was drunk.

'Have you been to the dance?' I asked her.

'Yep. We don't get many of those in this God-forsaken, boring place.'

'Where's your husband?' I asked.

'Still at the dance. You know what officers are like; have to put on a show; do the right thing. That's why he packed me off home. I'd only had a couple of drinks and wanted a dance, a bit of fun. But, oh no, not in from of the C.O. I was embarrassing him. So I'm confined to barracks,' she slurred.

I let out a sigh of relief. 'Which one of these is yours?' I asked.

'That one.' She pointed to number three. 'Do you want to come in for a drink? I hate drinking on my own. You're new here, aren't you? I don't remember seeing you here before.'

'Yes, I'm still trying to find my way around.' Together, we staggered to her bungalow. Once inside, we flopped onto the sofa, both of us relieved to sit down. She stared at my blooded feet. Where are your shoes? She asked.

'I've lost them,' I said.

She let out a little laugh. 'It's been a long time since I've been that drunk.' She giggled. 'What do you want to drink?' she asked, staggering to her feet.

'I could do with a brandy if you've got one.'

'Coming right up, my dear. By the way, what's your name? If we are going to be friends, I've got to know your name.'

'April - April Smith.'

'I'm Carol. How–do–you–do?' She thrust the drink into my hand. 'Bottoms up.' She emptied her glass in one swallow. I sipped at mine as she filled her glass for a second time. 'Come on, drink up. Your husband won't be home for hours.'

I forced my brandy down and gave a cough.

'I bet you feel better already,' she said, filling my glass again. She moved across the room and sat in an armchair opposite me. 'We've only been married eighteen months, and this is our first overseas posting together. I'd never left England before...'

I stopped listening to her as the realisation of what she had just said hit me hard. 'Overseas posting! Where was I?' Then I remembered the foreign-sounding voice at the hangar.

'What's the local town like?' I asked, interrupting her from telling me all about her marriage problems.

'Brilliant. Frankfurt is loads of fun on a night out. There are masses of bars and clubs to go to. You'd be amazed at how quick they are rebuilding the place.'

By the time I'd finished drinking my second glass of brandy, I could feel the effects of the alcohol. Carol had just knocked back her forth and was slumping sideways in her armchair with her eyes closed. Desperate for something to eat, I went into the tiny kitchen and made a sandwich from some tinned SPAM. After that, I took a shower, stole some fresh clothes from her bedroom, putting my soiled ones into the rubbish bin out the back. I found a pair of tennis shoes in her wardrobe and tried them on. Like the rest of Carol's clothes, they were a size too big for me, but I was grateful for them all the same. Before I left the bungalow, I rifled through her handbag and took her purse and base pass. I didn't want to, and I knew she would be in loads of trouble for losing them, but my need was greater than hers. I placed a note on the kitchen table.

Sorry about taking your clothes and purse and everything. I hope to make it up to you someday. April.

Feeling a lot more comfortable, I left Carol asleep in the chair.

The rest, the shower, the fresh clothes and the tennis shoes all played their part in reviving me and easing some of the pain in my feet, but I still found them tender to walk on. I wouldn't get far without transport. Following the road through the married quarters, I eventually discovered the main gate to the airfield. I knew from trying to get into RAF Driffield that I would be challenged if I went anywhere near the gate. I had no choice if I wanted to escape. With Carol's pass in hand, I approached the gate. The sentry stepped forward, and I presented the base pass. He gave it a cursory glance and stepped back. Sucking up the pain in my feet, I walked through the gate as normally as I could. Across the road from the main gate, I spotted a bus stop. So I joined two other women waiting there. Standing apart from them so as not to risk being drawn into a conversation, I waited for the bus. Each time a vehicle went past, I turned away from the road, not wanting to be seen in case one of the passengers was Blenheim, and he recognised me. After a long wait, the bus arrived. I listened to what the other women said to the bus conductor and said the thing, 'Frankfurt Central.' I gave her a five Deutsche mark note. She glared back at me for a moment before returning four and a half Deutsche marks in change along with the bus ticket. The bus ride seemed to take forever as I had no watch to tell the time by, and I had no idea how far it was to Frankfurt Central. I assumed that my destination would be the bus station in the centre of Frankfurt and that I would recognise it when I arrived. The women I'd followed onto the bus sat in separate seats, so I guessed they didn't know each other. Alternating between looking out of the bus window and watching the women for signs they were getting ready to leave the bus helped pass the time.

As the bus entered the town suburbs, I saw the remains of derelict buildings and open spaces where buildings had once stood. The further into town we went, the more new construction I saw, and the fewer empty plots of land. The bus crossed over a bridge which spanned a large river, then another bridge which spanned railway lines. The bus turned right and began running through busy streets with shops and houses on either side of the road. Further on, the buildings turned into larger shops, bars, restaurants, and hotels. The traffic increased. More people got on the bus until finally, it pulled into a large bus station next to the railway station. It was when everyone got off the bus, and I followed. Even though it was dark and late, people were rushing about. Some were heading to other bus stops, and some went towards the railway station. I looked around, confused. Where should I go? I approached a young woman with suitcases who was seated on a bench.

'Excuse me; I am looking for the police station.' The woman looked at me with an expression of confusion. 'Police Station!' I repeated. She shook her head and looked away. I walked a little further and stopped an older woman walking toward me. 'Excuse me; I'm looking for the police station.'

'Polizei?' she replied.

'Yes, yes. Polizei.' I responded. She pointed towards the railway station.

I smiled and nodded my head, 'thank you.' I waved her goodbye and crossed from the bus station to the railway station. It didn't take long for me to find a uniformed officer. He was dressed more like a member of the army than a policeman. As I limped towards him, he spotted my approach and waited.

'Polizei,' I said as I stopped in front of him. He nodded. 'I-need-help.' I said slowly.

He looked down at me and shrugged his shoulders. 'Lady lost?' he said in a thick German accent.

'No. I need help,'

'What help?'

I didn't speak German, and I guessed his English wasn't up to the complicated explanation I wanted to share with him, so I held out my wrists as though they were handcuffed together.

'Help me!'

He looked at me as though I was mad. 'What help?' he repeated.

I didn't answer him. I just shook my hands in a gesture of wanting to be handcuffed and stared at him. He didn't bother putting me in handcuffs but signalled for me to follow him. So I did. He led me to a column on which hung a box marked POLIZEI. Opening the door on the front, he picked up a telephone handset and then pressed a large red button. After a momentary pause, a conversation started with the person on the other end of the line, and then the police officer hung up.

'We stay here.' He gestured with his finger to the ground, and he waited with me. A few minutes later, two more police officers arrived, one of them female.

'What seems to be the trouble?' asked the new male officer in very good English.

'I've been kidnapped and escaped. I need you to take me to the police station, so I can telephone home.'

'Kidnapped? Who by? Why?' asked the new male officer.

'I cannot say. First, I need to speak to one of your senior police officers.' A conversation I didn't understand ensued between all three police officers.

'Are you lost? Is someone chasing you?' asked the new police officer.

'No, yes. I need to make a phone call to England.'

Another conversation started.

While the three of them talked amongst themselves, in the frustration of the moment, I lost my temper and shouted, 'will you take me to the police station or not?'

'Okay, Okay,' said the new police officer. He then said something in German to the police officer who had made the phone call before turning and walking away. The first officer who had made the phone call acknowledged what the English-speaking officer had said and then walked off in the opposite direction, leaving me alone with the female officer. The female officer tapped my arm and then indicated for me to follow the English-speaking officer. Wondering what was going to happen next, I did as instructed. The English-speaking officer was heading towards the exit of the railway station. The female officer stayed by my side. She could see I was having difficulty walking but didn't offer to assist me. Still, I was in the hands of the police. My spirits rose a little as I began to feel safe for the first time in days.

Outside the railway station, I saw a police car parked at the kerbside, the male officer standing next to the open rear door. I got inside, and the female officer joined me in the back seat.

Chapter Eighteen

As the police car sped past the end of the railway station, I noticed we were heading back towards the bridges I'd come over on the bus.

'Where are we going?' I got no reply.

As we continued along the road. I recognised more places that I'd passed as I came into town. I was being driven back towards the airfield. Terrified, I turned to the female police officer.

'Where are we going?' I screamed. She said nothing, her face remaining enigmatically expressionless. It suddenly occurred to me they must think that I am a drunken member of the British armed forces, and they were taking me back to the airfield from which I had escaped. Panic set in.

'Police station!' I shouted. 'I want to go to the police station. Let me out!'

I made a grab for the car door handle, but it wouldn't open. The next thing I felt was something hard thrust into my back and the female police officer shouting, 'Halt!'

I stopped struggling and slowly sat back in my seat, then looked down and to my left. The female police officer had her gun pointing at my middle.

'Police station; ja, we are going to the police station,' yelled the police officer, driving the car.

Moments later, after crossing bridges, the police car turned right instead of left and then pulled up outside a building at the junction of two major roads into the city. I spotted more police cars parked down a side street. I let out a sigh of relief. Turning to the female officer who still had her gun pointing at me, I did the only thing I could think of at that moment; I smiled at her and nodded.

'Thank you,' I said softly. 'I'm sorry to have frightened you.' She didn't respond. The driver got out and opened the police car's rear door for me.

Inside the police station, I was led to an office and given a chair next to a desk.

'Wait here,' instructed the driver of the police car. The female officer stood beside me. At least she had put her gun away. The female officer never smiled. She reminded me of my Aunt Violet, short and rotund, only I never got to see aunt Violet in a German uniform. The thought of my aunt dressed as a German police officer made me smile. It would have suited her personality. Then, the vision of her lying dead across the hotel dining table sprang to mind, and my heart sank, taking my amused smile with it.

Looking around the large office, most of it was unlit, and the majority of the desks were vacant. I'd lost track of time. I only knew it was still dark outside. The wait seemed to go on forever; even my female guard looked bored as she stood beside me. I pointed to a chair. She looked at what I was pointing at and shook her head. After a while, a man in civilian dress arrived. The new man looked as though he'd been dragged out of bed. His hair was a mess, and he hadn't had time for a shave. After speaking to the police officers who had brought me to the police station, the female officer and the driver left me and went to sit at a desk across the room.

'My name is Inspector Everhart. What is your name, and why did you want to be arrested and brought to this police station?'

His English was clear and perfect, with only a hint of an accent.

'My name is April Showers. I'm a private detective from Driffield in East Yorkshire, England. I was investigating a gang of counterfeiters when I was discovered and kidnapped. For a while, they held me as their prisoner on an airfield in England. After a couple of days, they drugged me. When I woke up, I found myself in a crate. I managed to escape. But I discovered I was in Germany, not England. Getting arrested seemed like the best way of being brought to safety.'

Inspector Everhart studied me for a moment. 'Can you prove any of what you say?'

I thought about my response before answering.

'No. By the time you get permission to enter the British airbase, any evidence that I was there or that the counterfeit banknotes existed will have been removed.'

'Then, what do you want me to do?' asked the Inspector. 'Is there someone you can contact to corroborate your story?'

My mind raced through all the names of the people who had helped me discover the identities of the forgers, but only one stood out as to be of any real help.

'Rex Barker.'

'And, who is Rex Barker?' asked the Inspector. I suddenly felt awkward; did I have the right to tell the Inspector that Rex was an MI5 agent?'

'He works for the British government, a kind of police officer,' I responded hesitantly.

'Do you have his telephone number?'

I couldn't remember his work number, but I could remember his home telephone number. I looked across the office towards the windows to confirm it was still dark outside.

'What time is it?'

The Inspector looked at his wristwatch. 'Three-thirty.'

Rex would be at home. 'Yes, I know his telephone number.'

The Inspector picked up the telephone. 'What is it?'

Inspector Everhart dialled the numbers as I called them out. After a few seconds, he passed the telephone receiver to me. As I held it to my ear, I could hear the ringing tone as the call waited to be answered. There was a click, and then a sleepy but familiar voice on the other end of the line answered, 'Rex Barker.'

'Rex, it's me, April. I'm in trouble. I'm in a police station in Frankfurt, Germany. I know who the counterfeiters are.

Yes, I do. It's a long story. I'm sorry. Will you come and get me?' I looked across the desk. 'His name is Inspector Everhart.'

As instructed by Rex, I gave the telephone to the Inspector. While the Inspector listened to Rex, he made some notes.

'I understand.

'Yes, sir. Leave it with me; I'll make sure she is kept safe.' He passed the telephone back to me. I listened to the instructions that Rex gave me.

'Thank you, Rex. I'll do as you say.'

While I was on the telephone with Rex, Inspector Everhart spoke to the two waiting officers, after which they left.

I put down the telephone and asked for a pencil and some paper to write down the names of the people I knew who were involved with the counterfeiting operation, along with the registration number of the truck I'd seen taking the money away from the airfield. While I was doing this, the police Inspector was using the telephone again. When I'd finished writing, I passed the paper and pencil back to the Inspector. He ended his telephone call and looked at the sheet of paper.

'Thank you. I'll get some men onto this immediately. In the meantime, I have arranged for you to be taken to a hotel. A female police officer will accompany you and stay with you.'

I hoped it wouldn't be my Aunt Violet look-alike from the police car. However, when the female police officer turned up, she looked closer to my own age, except she was tall, blond, and slim. She was in casual but smart civilian dress. She held out her hand as she approached.

'Hello, Miss Showers, my name is Sergeant Eva Zimmermann. It's my job to look after you while you are a guest of the Frankfurt police.'

'Call me April, please.' I shook hands with her.

'Take her to the City Hotel. I will call them and have a room made ready for you,' interjected the Inspector.

A police car dropped Eva and me on the doorstep of a hotel, which was located not far from the city centre, on Westend Strasse. There was nothing fancy about the place. It looked like the type of cheap hotel travelling businessmen or short-stay visitors would use: polished wooden floors, functional pine furniture, and no lift to the upper floors. Eva checked us in with the night porter and then led the way to our room. We were given a twin-bedded room at the back of the hotel, on the third floor. As I closed the curtains, the view from the window was of the car park. After closing the curtains, I turned and looked at Eva. She had an overnight bag with her, which she dropped on the bed closest to the bedroom door.

'I am here to help you,' she said. 'I am not your prison guard. But all the same, I suggest you don't go out without me; you may get lost or worse still, your kidnappers may spot you. Inspector Everhart will contact the British airfield commander, explain what has happened, and request a visit to the airfield. Unfortunately, the British C.O. may say no unless the Inspector has proof that a crime has been committed by British personnel from the base, which he does not.'

'All I want to do right now is go to bed. I'm exhausted. Do you know what time it is?'

Eva looked at her wristwatch. 'Five-thirty. You get some sleep. I'll read my book until the rest of the hotel wakes up, and I can go down and get some coffee and rolls for us. Here, I took the liberty of bringing you one of my nighties and a clean pair of pants.' She delved into her overnight bag and brought out the clothes. 'They're nothing fancy, but it means you can undress for bed.'

'Thank you, that's very thoughtful of you. I have some money.' I blushed at the thought of how I had obtained it. 'Maybe we can go clothes shopping when I wake up?'

'Good idea. We'll be able to get to know each other a little better while we're out together.'

Eva retrieved a book from her bag, kicked off her shoes and lay on the bed. I took my borrowed clothes into the bathroom to wash and change. By the time I came out of the bathroom, Eva was asleep with her book lying open on the bed. There was nothing else to do but do the same. As I snuggled below the blankets, it felt like heaven compared to the crate or the hard chair. Falling asleep was easy.

Saturday Afternoon

As I awoke, I could feel my body aching. Even so, until I opened my eyes, it felt like I was waking up in my own bed and that everything which had transpired over the last few days had been a nightmare. Only I remembered it all too well. I looked across to the other bed and saw Eva, book in hand, reading.

She greeted me with, 'Hello, sleepyhead. How do you feel?'

'Like I've been kidnapped and locked in a wooden crate. What time is it?'

'Two o'clock.'

'Which day?'

'It's still Saturday. I'm sorry I fell asleep, only I had a late night on Friday. When I got called back to the police station to help you, I'd only had a few hours of sleep.'

'Let me get dressed, and then we'll go out to buy me some new clothes. I don't feel like anything to eat or drink just yet. Do you know when Rex will get here?'

'No, not yet. I telephoned Inspector Everhart earlier. He told me Mr Barker was flying out today but did not give a time for his arrival. However, he did tell me that the Commanding Officer of the airfield had received orders to assist the Inspector with all his enquiries and offer the Inspector any help he required.'

'Well, there's nothing much that I can do to help him right now, so we'd better do that shopping, I mentioned. But first, I need to arrange a wire money transfer from home. Which means I'm going to have to ask my father to help with that. At least I'll be able to reassure him I'm safe and will be home soon.'

When Eva and I got back to the hotel, the receptionist told us someone was waiting for me in the lounge.

'Stay here,' ordered Eva. 'I will see who it is.'

My first thoughts were that Blenheim, or one of his gang, had found me. Fear of being trapped in the crate once again returned. With my arms still full of shopping bags, I wanted to drop them and run or just hide behind the reception desk. But instead, I found myself frozen to the spot, my mind spinning, unable to think properly and just watching other hotel guests passing me by in slow motion. I felt sick with fear. Then Eva returned. I was just on the point of fainting when she asked me if I was feeling okay. A moment later, Rex's familiar face came into view, and my fear turned to relief.

'Hello, April.'

I was still feeling shaky; it must have shown because a moment later, Rex was at my side, relieving me of my bags. He and Eva then led me to the hotel lounge, Eva sitting at my side. I felt embarrassed and stupid and said so to Eva, while Rex went to the bar to get me a brandy.

'Don't worry. It's normal to feel like this. You've suffered a terrible ordeal over the past few days,' Eva reassured me, as she held my hand.

Rex arrived and thrust a glass towards me. 'Drink it quick. It'll perk you up.'

I didn't feel like being perked up. I just wanted to run away and hide in the corner, but I did as I was told. The brown liquid burned my throat as I swallowed. I coughed, set the glass down, covered my mouth, and coughed again. The effects of the cheap brandy cleared my head.

Thank you, Rex. It's nice to see you. I guess I'm still feeling tired. You got here quicker than I expected.'

'Yes. The boss pulled a few strings with the RAF. He got them to put on a special flight for me.'

'I suppose, now you're here, April will not need me anymore?' suggested Eva.

'Not so fast. I hope you don't mind, but I've had a word with Inspector Everhart. He has agreed for you to stay with April whilst we are in Germany. I'm going to be a bit busy until we get this case settled.'

'Sure. That is fine with me,' responded Eva enthusiastically. 'But I will have to go home and get some more clothes. I thought April would be going home today.'

I let out an inward sigh of relief at the thought of Eva staying with me. I liked her. However, I didn't want to be left alone with Rex, no matter how much I owed him for coming to my rescue.

'That's Okay. Get what you need for another couple of days' stay. Your Inspector has provided me with a car and a driver. They are outside now, waiting for us.'

'Why? Where are we going?' I demanded, suddenly alert once again.

'The airfield to start with,' said Rex, as he got to his feet. 'Are you feeling up to it?'

'But what about all my new clothes?' I exclaimed. Rex gathered them up. Eva and I followed him to the reception desk.

'Have these taken up to Miss Showers' room!' he dictated to the receptionist. 'Are we all ready?' he asked us.

While we were in the car, Rex asked me to tell him about everything that had happened to me since I'd gone missing last Wednesday. Time passed quickly; and before I knew it, we had arrived at the gates to the British section of Frankfurt airfield. Rex showed his I.D. to the gate guard, and the barrier was lifted. As our car drove towards the main building, two men in officers' uniforms came out and got into a Land Rover with RAF markings. The Land Rover pulled away from the building and drove ahead of us. Rex instructed our driver to follow it. A few minutes later, both cars stopped outside a row of hangars. One hangar had a guard posted at its door. It was my hangar.

Everyone got out, and while one of the RAF officers from the Land Rover went to speak to the guard on the hangar door, the other one came over to speak to Rex. He held out his hand in greeting.

'Hello, my name is Squadron Leader Blackburn; head of base security. I have a team inside opening every crate in the hangar, checking its contents and searching for anything that might lead us to where the forged banknotes might have been taken, sir.'

'Good, though I don't expect you will find anything. Miss Showers has already informed me that she saw a truck remove the crates containing the money. I'm hoping to find more evidence at RAF Cottam. Miss Showers gave all the names she knew to the German police, along with the registration of the truck they used, and they forwarded them to me. The German police are tracing the vehicle. Some of the men I am looking for are RAF personnel. Their files are being sent to me by wire. My people in England will interview the families of those named on the list to discover what they know,' Rex responded.

'It's going to take time to dispose of that amount of hard cash. If the German police can find the truck, there's a good chance they'll find the forged banknotes as well,' suggested S.L. Blackburn.

'I wouldn't count on it, Squadron Leader. They wouldn't have printed five crate-loads of banknotes if they didn't have the means of disposing of them quickly,' I interjected.

'Where do you think they would take them, Squadron Leader?' asked Rex.

'I don't know; you'd better ask the German police.'

The Squadron Leader turned to face me. 'You must be Miss Showers. Please, let me apologise on behalf of the RAF for the way some of our personnel have treated you.'

'Thank you, Squadron Leader. I intend to make those men pay for it.'

'But surely, Miss Showers, this operation is now in the hands of the British Secret Service,' said the Squadron Leader.

'That may be so, but the Secret Service hasn't caught the forgers yet, and the RAF has allowed these men to operate under the noses of their commanding officers for months, Squadron Leader.' The squadron leader cleared his throat and looked a little uncomfortable at the remark.

Rex chuckled, his face breaking into a sarcastic smile. 'You'd be making a serious mistake to underestimate Miss Showers, Squadron Leader. April is a very capable woman. May we have a look around inside?'

'Yes, sir. Follow me.'

We spent the next few minutes inside the hangar. Four airmen were systematically opening and examining the rest of the crates in the hangar. The crate I'd been smuggled out of England in was still there. It looked larger from the outside than it had when I was inside it. The sight of it sent a shiver down my spine.

When we returned to the police car, the driver informed Rex that the truck used to transport the forged banknotes had been found abandoned on the city outskirts. However, after being thoroughly searched by the police, a matchbook had been found inside the cab. The matchbook cover had the name of a club on it: Die Rosa Dame.

'Do you know how to get to this club, Sergeant?'

'Yes, sir,' replied the driver of the police car. 'Inspector Everhart has a team watching the premises right now.'

'Take us there,' demanded Rex. We all piled back into the police car and set off.

We drove back towards Frankfurt and into the city centre before heading down towards the riverfront and along the Untermainkai, the main road alongside the river. The police car slowed, the driver bringing the car to a stop. He turned in his seat to speak to Rex.

'We are in the older part of the city. The Rasa Dame club is just a little further up the road. I think it would be better for you to walk the rest of the way. I don't think the Inspector would like a police car parked outside the club.'

'Stay here. I'm going to get a closer look,' said Rex.

I wasn't going to let him get away with that. This was still my case to solve, even if I did need Rex's help.

'Not on your life. I'm coming to.'

'And so am I,' insisted Eva. 'My orders are to stay with April.'

Rex tried to protest, but he was outgunned and so reluctantly gave in. However, before getting out of the police car, Rex checked the pistol he had hidden beneath his jacket. Seeing what Rex was doing, Eva opened her handbag and checked her gun. I looked on, astonished at the pair of them. It had never occurred to me that Eva had been armed all the time we had been together.

'We don't know if the people or the banknotes are in this club, so don't ask any direct questions until we are sure and can call for backup.'

Eva and the driver of the police car exchanged glances; Rex picked up on it.

'What's wrong?' He asked.

'These sorts of clubs don't usually open until late into the evening. They are the kind of club men frequent for a good time with the girls that work there; if you understand my meaning,' said the driver.

'That's more reason to go in now. If we wait until tonight, the place will be full of people. They'll have moved the money before that happens. We need to get in there now.' insisted Rex. 'We may never get another chance to capture the money and the crooks. Give me the radio.' 'Inspector Everhart,' Rex waited for a response.

Then a voice over the car speaker answered. 'Go ahead.'

'Rex Barker here. I'm just down the road from the Rosa Dame club with Sergeant Zimmermann, Miss Showers, and our driver. I want to raid the club now. While there is a chance that the money is still inside the club. Do you have enough men with you to back us up?' There was a pause.

'With respect, Mr Barker, we don't even know if the money or the men we want are in there,' responded the Inspector.

'Then we need to find out,' snapped back Rex. 'When our police car pulls up outside the club, come and join us.' Rex handed the microphone back to the driver and indicated for him to drive on. Moments later, we stopped outside the club. Another police car screeched to a halt in front of our car, and police officers from across the street came running towards the club. All of a sudden, the street was full of police officers. Rex got out of the car saying, 'wait here until I send for you.'

I was about to protest at being excluded, but he slammed the car door.

'He can't do that to me. This is my case,' I complained.

As all the police officers entered the club. I got out of the police car, and Eva followed me. While waiting for Rex to return, I looked up at the front of the club and spotted two men exit from the top floor onto a fire escape. Eva noticed them, too. Instead of coming down to street level via the fire escape, they crossed to the roof of the building next door.

'Come on, we'll follow them.' I didn't wait for an answer from Eva. She was under orders to stay with me, and I knew she would. The building next door was separated from the club by a narrow alley. The fire escape connected the two buildings at roof level only. The second building extended to the corner of a side street. As Eva and I rounded the corner of the second building onto the street, we found its entrance. Pushing through the polished oak and glass doors, we faced stairs leading to the upper floors. Two bags of cement powder were stacked in the corner of the lobby. The door to my left was missing, and I could see inside the room. It was a mess. Building materials were scattered across the floor. Now I knew why the men had come across to this building; it was empty. With me leading the way, Eva followed as we rushed up the stairs to intercept the escaping men.

'Slow down, April,' called Eva. 'They may be armed.'

I reached the first floor and stopped to wait for Eva, who already had her gun in her hand as she came to stand next to me.

'I'll go first,' she insisted. Eva led the way, but more cautiously this time, as we made our way to the second floor. We were halfway there when we heard running feet on the stairs above us. We stopped. The sound of running footsteps continued to get louder and closer. Eva readied her gun.

As the two men came into view, one behind the other, I screamed, 'it's them!'

'Halt,' demanded Eva, her gun raised towards the men. They stopped partway down the stairs, and we all glared at each other. I recognised Flying Officer Blenheim, though I didn't know the second man.

'Good afternoon, Miss Showers. Fancy meeting you here,' declared Blenheim. He was behind the man I didn't know.

'Hands up,' instructed Eva. The stranger complied, whereas Blenheim stepped sideways, using the man in front as cover. Suddenly, there was a loud bang. Eva fell backwards, tumbling down the stairs to the first floor. Her gun slid across the polished floor into the corner. I ignored Blenheim and went to the aid of Eva. Blood stained the front of her jacket.

As I turned back to look at Blenheim, he was coming towards me with his gun levelled.

'Well, well, well. What are we going to do with you?' said Blenheim sarcastically.

The second man spoke to Blenheim in German. They exchanged a few words.

'He wants me to shoot you, Miss Showers. What do you think? Should I?'

I didn't give him the pleasure of an answer. I just waited for the bullet. It was strange. I didn't feel scared. I just felt guilty that my parents would never see me again.

'It's a pity I had to shoot your friend. I could have sold both of you.'

Blenheim's companion spoke to him again. Blenheim looked at his watch. 'It is time to go, Miss Showers. You go first. Stop when you get to the ground floor.'

I wanted to stay with Eva, but Blenheim urged me on. As we descended the stairs, the German man continued to raise his voice to Blenheim, who seemed happy to ignore him. Once we were back in the lobby, Blenheim ordered me to stop. Moments later, through the glass panels in the front doors, I saw a car pull up at the kerb. The German man went first. Once he'd reached the car, he held the rear door open.

'You go first, Miss Showers. Remember, I have a gun.' He slipped it into his jacket pocket with his hand still holding onto it. As I moved towards the door, he stepped closer to me. I pushed the left side door open but kept hold of it. As I stepped outside, I flung it closed behind me in Blenheim's face. There was an ear shattering bang followed by the sound of breaking glass, but I was away and running as fast as I could back around the corner, screaming for help. As I rounded the corner, I spotted a policeman standing next to one of the police cars.

'HELP! HELP!' I screamed. Another shot rang out from behind me. The policeman responded by drawing his own weapon and firing back. I was trapped in their crossfire. Stopping for a second, I ducked into the narrow alley between the two buildings. The police officer fired one more shot before I heard screeching tyres as a car sped away. The shooting stopped. I came out of the alley at a run, heading back to check on Eva. As I rounded the corner, Blenheim's rescue car was heading away from me.

Entering the building, I spotted the broken door glass and splintered wood. Running up the stairs, Eva was still lying in a pool of her own blood. She moaned. She was still alive. 'Thank God,' I exclaimed. She was badly hurt. I didn't know what to do, so I stroked her face, saying, 'I'm sorry,' over and over to her and repeating help is on its way. But it was only when the police officer who shot at Blenheim turned up that Eva received any real help. He pulled a handkerchief from his pocket and told me to press it hard to the wound in her shoulder.

'Stay like that. Don't move,' he instructed. 'I'm going to call for an ambulance.'

Whilst the police officer was away, I continued to speak to Eva even though she was unconscious. She'd been shot trying to protect me. She was like this because of me. Full of guilt, I vowed to give up the detective business if only God would let

Eva live. The sound of sirens getting closer and then screeching tyres on the street filled me with hope for Eva. A clamber of noise from downstairs followed. Someone was calling my name.

'I'm up here. Eva's hurt!'

Rex, followed by two more police officers and men in medical uniforms, appeared at the top of the stairs. The police officers continued on up the stairs. The medics took Eva away, and Rex began demanding answers to questions. I ignored him and went to sit on the floor in the corner of the stairwell. The questioning stopped as I stared blankly ahead of me. I was too full of guilt to answer him. So Rex went downstairs. Left alone, my right hand slowly reached down to my side to retrieve Eva's pistol from where it had fallen and from where I'd been shielding it from Rex's view.

Chapter Nineteen

Back in my hotel room, I sat on my bed, staring at the bed opposite, thinking of Eva. Inspector Everhart had informed me that Eva would be out of action for a long time whilst she convalesced. However, she would make a full recovery, thank goodness. In the short time I'd known Eva, I had come to think of her as a friend. And it was with the memory of seeing her lying on the floor bleeding fresh in my mind that I examined Eva's gun, familiarising myself with it. There was nothing I wanted more than to bring Blenheim to justice for her callous shooting on the stairs. The gun was small and black, heavier than I'd expected it to be. It didn't matter, just so long as it was deadly enough for what I wanted. I'd seen how Eva ejected the bullet clip when we were in the police car waiting to go into the nightclub. I ejected the gun's clip; it was full. Sliding the clip back inside the pistol grip made a satisfying click as it locked into place. The switch on the side of the gun was set to green, safety on. Letting it rest in my hand, I wrapped my fingers around the grip and placed my forefinger on the trigger. I pointed the gun at the wall. This was going to be easier than I thought.

Suddenly, startled by a knock on the door, I pushed the gun under my pillow, out of sight.

'Come in.' I called. Rex entered.

'How are you feeling?' He asked sympathetically.

'A bit shell-shocked,' I responded.

'It's good news about Eva, and we found all the crates of forgeries… thanks to you.' He added, almost as an afterthought.

'But Blenheim got away,' I responded bitterly.

'Yes, but we got the German members of the smuggling gang. We'll get Blenheim. With no friends or money, he won't get far.'

A glimmer of hope and the nucleus of an idea tumbled around at the back of my mind. 'What is going to happen next?' I asked.

'The counterfeit money will be burned, and the prisoners will be put on trial. The club will be closed down.'

'Even the girls who just worked at the club? What about them?'

'Prostitution is not a crime in Germany in the same way it is in Britain. The girls will be questioned by the police, and then set free.'

'May I watch when the police interview the girls from the club?'

'That's not up to me. But I can have a word with the Inspector and ask him to let you sit in on an interview.'

'Thank you. I'd like to know what makes the women do that kind of work.'

'Drugs mostly. They are all heroin addicts. They become prostitutes to pay for their drugs and the club owners exploit their need for money and drugs. It's a vicious circle.'

'I see. Thank God Driffield isn't like Frankfurt.'

'Is there anything you need?' asked Rex.

'No. Thanks. I just want a little time on my own to recover from this afternoon.'

'Yes, of course. I'll be in my room if you need me. Tomorrow we can go home.'

I didn't respond to his announcement about going home. I was still growing an idea at the back of my mind. Rex left my room, and I waited until I heard his bedroom door close before getting off the bed. I picked up my new handbag and retrieved Eva's pistol from under my pillow, dropping it into my bag. I crept to my bedroom door and opened it as quietly as I could, doing the same as I closed it behind me. At the hotel reception, I asked them to call me a taxi.

After getting in the taxi, I gave the driver my destination.

'I want to go to the Untermainkai,' I told the taxi driver. 'I want you to take me to a club where I can meet some ladies.'

The taxi driver leered at me, but I didn't care. He knew where I wanted to go.

As we drove along the Untermainkai, he slowed the car for me to view the clubs.

'Which one do you want?' he asked as we cruised past a few neon-lit shabby looking clubs.

330

'This is my first time in Frankfurt; I don't want to take too many risks.'

'I know the one. It's a little more expensive than the rest, but they don't ask questions, and they respect their customers.'

'That'll do,' I said, hopefully.

A little further up the road, the taxi pulled to the kerb and stopped. Remaining in my seat, I had a sudden attack of cold feet.

'Here we are, lady. This is the place.'

'I want you to wait here until I return. I thrust fifty Deutschmarks at him. There'll be fifty more when I return.'

'Lady, for that kind of money, I'll wait here all night for you.'

I flashed him a smile and got out. Taking a deep breath, I marched up to the door and went inside. At a desk, a large man in a black bow tie and suit raised his eyebrows as I approached. A sign behind him read ten Deutschmarks. I paid him, and in return, he gave me a ticket. Passing through another door, I entered the inner part of the club. A bar stocked with bottles lined one wall. Against the opposite wall was a low stage. Scantily clad dancers performed evocatively to the music. I found a booth and took a seat. A woman dressed in a French maid's outfit came over and asked me if I would like a drink.

'Brandy, please.'

'Are you waiting for someone?' She asked before leaving.

'No.'

'Ticket, please. Your first drink in on the house,' she informed me in a seductive tone.

When she returned, and as she was setting down my drink.
I asked the question.

'How do I get to meet one of the girls?'

She smiled back at me sweetly. 'Is this your first time?'

'Yes.'

'I know just who you want. I'll send her over to you.'

The waitress winked at me as she walked away. I took a
giant gulp of brandy. I'd just finished the brandy when a pretty
young woman came up and sat next to me. Her clothing was
cheap but smart.

'Hello. My name is Heidi. You like the company of other
ladies, yes?' She asked in a heavy German accent.

'Would you like a drink?' I asked her. I felt like I needed
another one.

'If you like. I'll have what you have.'

I ordered two more glasses of brandy from the French-
Maid-dressed waitress.

Heidi put her hand on my knee and cosied up close.

'Is there somewhere private we can go?' I asked in a
stuttering voice. The drinks arrived.

Heidi stood up. 'Follow me.' She led me across the club
floor to a door close to the stage. On the other side of the door,
we were away from the public part of the club. We were in a
corridor lined with doors. She opened one, and we both went
inside. The room contained a large bed, a washstand with a
stack of towels next to it, and a chair. A soft glow from a rose-
tinted bulb was the only light. Music from the club was being
piped through a small speaker in the corner of the room.

'It will be two-hundred Deutschmarks.' Heidi announced bluntly.

I removed the money from my purse and sat on the chair. Heidi looked at me, confused by my selection of the chair, and then she smiled at me.

'Don't worry. It's normal. I'm like you too,' she tried to reassure me as she drew closer.

'No. Stop. You don't understand.' But Heidi kept coming closer. So I stood up and backed away. 'I don't want sex. I want heroin.'

Heidi stopped dead in her tracks, the smile dropping from her face.

'What are you playing at?' she demanded.

'I'm sorry. I didn't know what else to do. I just want some heroin.'

Heidi relaxed a little as she saw how nervous I was. 'What makes you think you can get it here?'

'A friend told me.'

'Which friend?'

'One at the Rosa Dame, but the club has been raided, and I can't get what I want from there anymore.'

Heidi looked me up and down, weighing me up as she thought about what I'd said. 'How much do you want?'

'Enough to get me through tonight and tomorrow.' I had no idea how much that would be in amount or cash. I only hoped I still had enough money left in my purse to pay for it.

'It'll cost you another two-hundred Deutschmarks.'

I removed the money from my purse and placed it on the washstand.

'Wait here.' Heidi left the room. I did a quick check of how much money I had left. I calculated that if I could get out of here without spending any more money, I'd just have enough left to pay the taxi driver the extra I'd promised him. A couple of minutes later, Heidi came back and placed a packet on the washstand.

'Are you sure this is all you want? You've already paid for your time with me,' she said as she glided closer to me.

I was getting more than nervous now, to the point of being scared of what might happen next. Snatching up the packet, I edged towards the door, saying. 'No. Thank you. I have what I need. I have to go.'

I left the room and marched back towards the public part of the club. I walked smartly across the dance floor and was almost running by the time I reached the street. Thankfully, the taxi was still outside waiting for me.

Back at my hotel, I went straight to the bar on the ground floor and ordered a brandy. My hands trembled, and my knees were shaking as I picked up the glass, drinking it quickly. I took a deep breath and ordered a second. As the barman set it on the bar top, a familiar voice came from behind me.

'I was wondering where you had got to. I'd go easy on those, Inspector Everhart has agreed to you sitting in on one or two interviews this evening. Would you like to have dinner with me?' asked Rex.

I put down my drink and looked around. Suddenly, all my fears seem to evaporate, and I started to laugh.

'What's funny?' asked Rex with a hurt expression.

'Nothing; you wouldn't understand. Yes, please. But shouldn't we be going to the police station for the interviews?'

'There's no rush. The Inspector will be questioning the girls later this evening. After they start feeling the effects of heroin deprivation. It makes them more talkative. The more the girls cooperate and talk, the sooner they are let out to get their next fix.'

'Where are we going?'

'I've been told there's a nice, family-run place just around the corner on Wilhelm-Strasse. Do you fancy trying some local cuisine?'

'Sure. I'm suddenly very hungry.'

Fifteen minutes later, we were outside the Meyer Restaurant and café. It was a single-story brick building with a large window. The name of the restaurant was written in large gold gothic letters across the centre of the glass pane. Through the window, I could see tables illuminated with candles. The place was small and cosy looking, somewhere to relax, talk and take your time.

'It looks lovely Rex, let's go in.'

As soon as we entered, a man in a white open-necked shirt and wearing a crisp white apron that dropped from his waist to his ankles approached us and bowed.

'Willkommen Mien Herr, Fraulein, ein tisch fur zwei personen?'

'I'm sorry,' said Rex. We are English and our German is very poor. Do you speak English?'

'Oh, yes, sir. I was a prisoner of war in your country. I learnt to speak English very well. You would like a table for two?'

'Yes, please,' answered Rex.

'Please, come this way.' We were shown to a table halfway down the restaurant where net curtains separated the tables. It looked private, somewhere where a couple could speak privately and not be overlooked. Rex held my chair for me as I took my seat.

'May I fetch you something to drink while you browse the menu?' He placed two white cards on the table. Rex took his seat on the opposite side of the table.

'A bottle of your best Riesling, please.'

'Certainly sir, I won't be a moment.'

Leaning across the table to Rex, I whispered. 'I like the feel of this place. I hope the food is just as good.'

'It came highly recommended by one of our German police liaison chaps.'

The waiter returned with the wine wrapped in a pristine white cloth. He showed the wine label to Rex and then re-wrapped the wine bottle. The wine has been chilled, sir. Keep it wrapped in the cloth and it will help keep it chilled for longer. He poured Rex a taster.

Rex sipped the wine. 'This is an excellent wine Mr…'

'Meyer, sir. I am the owner. My wife does the cooking.'

'Thank you, Mr Meyer. Are all your wines this good?'

'I try, sir. But it is difficult still. I am just a small restaurant compared to the size of the many new hotels they are building in the city. My little restaurant is not important to the big vineyards anymore. Have you decided what you would like to eat?'

'I don't know what to choose. This is my first time in Germany. What would you recommend?' I asked.

'For you, good lady, I recommend the Kartoffelsuppe. It is Mama's best soup, and to follow Hamburger Labskaus.'

'What about for me?' asked Rex. 'I don't fancy soup, how about something else?'

For you, sir, the Swabian Raviolis Rostzwiebeln, followed by the Schweinshaxe mit sauerkraut. And for you both to finish the evening, Kirschdessert mit Sahne. It is my personal favourite of all Mama's dishes.'

'We will leave ourselves in your excellent hands, Mr Meyer,' said Rex.

During our meal, Rex and I talked about home, friends, and family. Not once did we bring work or forged five-pound notes into the conversation. Mr Meyer came and went like a ghost, collecting our empty dishes and delivering the next course. We finished the wine and drank schnapps whilst eating our cherry dessert. It was one of the most romantic evenings I had ever spent. In fact, as I finished my cherry dessert, I realised it was my first truly romantic evening. I felt giddy and alive. Rex was with me, and I felt safe. We felt right together.

Rex looked at his watch. 'It's time to go, I'm afraid.'

I didn't want to leave the restaurant. I would have been happy to sit there all night listening to Rex tell me about his time in Kenya. We said goodbye to Mr Mayer and complemented his wife's cooking, promising to return one day. Then, arm in arm, Rex walked me to the police station.

When Rex and I arrived at the central police station, my nervousness returned. As I got out of the car and looked up at the building, I remembered that I still had Eva's pistol and now a packet of heroin in my handbag with no idea of how to explain them away if we were searched before going into the interviews. Rex strode confidently up to the door and opened it for me, then led the way to the reception desk. He showed his I.D. to the officer and asked to be let through to see Inspector Everhart. The police officer didn't hesitate and opened the door to the inner police station immediately.

'The Inspector is waiting for you in the interview room, sir,' said the police officer.

'Thank you,' said Rex as he put away his I.D.

'I thought this place would be full of policemen and criminals,' I said to Rex as we walked along a deserted corridor.

'That's the offices at the rear entrance. These rooms are where the office staff and detectives work during the day.'

After passing along another corridor, we came to two doors, one marked Interviewraum Eins, and another one marked Interviewraum Zwei. 'These are the interview rooms the nightclub girls are being questioned in. Inspector Everhart is in room one. You go in that one; I'll go into room two. We can compare notes later,' suggested Rex.

I knocked on the door and went in. Inspector Everhart was sitting at a table alongside a female police officer. One of the nightclub girls, wearing handcuffs, sat opposite them.

'Good evening, Miss Showers. I will be conducting the interviews in German, so unless you understand our language, I don't know what you expect to learn. However, you are welcome to stay as long as you like,' said the Inspector.

'Thank you for this opportunity to act as an observer, Inspector. I will do my best to follow what is happening.' A chair had been placed in the corner of the room for me.

The Inspector refaced the nightclub girl and continued to question her. Though I did not understand the words spoken, body language is a universal language. The more the Inspector raised his voice, the more the girl retreated from him and failed to answer his questions. The girl from the club looked frightened, possibly more of her employers than the Inspector, as no doubt the girl had been arrested before. Rex had already explained to me that the girls would be questioned, and then sometime later tonight, they would be set free. I couldn't understand why the Inspector bothered to question them at all. There was no real incentive for them to assist him with his enquiries. The worst that could happen to them was to lose a night's earnings from the men they would have serviced. One by one, a series of girls passed through the interview room, each one saying very little. Each girl was browbeaten into silence under the Inspector's relentless interrogation technique. As the last girl left the room, the Inspector came to me.

'Did you understand anything of what went on?'

'No, just that the girls told you nothing of value. You frightened them too much.'

'It's all I can do. If the police arrested every girl working as a prostitute, we would have to build a prison on every street corner across Germany. There is very little proper work in Germany. What there is, goes to the men first. These girls have no education. There is little else they can do. We are rebuilding our economy, but it will take time to create proper work opportunities for girls like these.' His words made me wonder how many women in Britain were suffering the same fate. I'd found it hard to find a worthwhile job before becoming a detective.

'What are you going to do with them now?' I asked.

'Throw them out on the street. I've done my job. It's time for me to go home to my wife and get some sleep.'

With that, the Inspector walked away. Rex hadn't come out of the second interview room yet, so I was left on my own in the corridor. When I heard raised voices from the end of the corridor, I turned around to see what was happening. A female police officer was escorting a group of women towards the stairs. Two of the women I recognised as being interviewed by the Inspector. I got the flash of an idea and wanted to tell Rex about it, but I hesitated as I approached the interview room he was using. If Rex joined me, I would never get the girls to talk candidly to me. This job had to be done woman to woman. It was now or never. 'I'm sorry Rex,' I said to the closed door.'

I followed the women as they were led outside and set free. Once they were away from the police station, it was a long walk back to the Rasa Dame club.

'Excuse me,' I called as I trotted to catch up with them. 'Do any of you speak English?'

One of them stopped, turned, and waited for me. 'What do you want?' She asked as I drew closer.

'Thank you for stopping. I'd like to speak to you, if I may? I was kidnapped by the men who delivered those crates of English money to your club. They wanted to sell me to your boss so he could put me to work with you and the other girls, but I managed to escape.'

'So!' she said indignantly. She was about to follow her friends when I asked.

'Is there somewhere where we can talk; in private? I can make it worth your while.'

She looked at me, trying to make up her mind.

'Please, I'm not a police officer. Anything you say will stay strictly between the two of us. It won't take long.' I blurted in desperation.

She turned her head to look toward the other women she had been released with. They had continued to walk on without her and were well ahead of us now, taking no notice of the one who had stayed behind to talk to me.

'There is an all-night café across the road. We can go there.' She walked off in the direction of the café. I looked back over my shoulder to check for Rex. There was no sign of him, so I followed the woman.

'Two coffees please,' I ordered at the counter. 'Would you like anything to eat?' I asked the prostitute. The woman spoke to the café owner in German before leading me to a table.

The coffee arrived first with the bill. I paid for it, and the man went away to finish our order.

'What do you want?' she asked.

'Information,' I responded in a low voice.

'So you do work for the police?' She stood up.

'No. No. Please, let me explain.' Hesitantly, she sat down again.

'All I want is the man who brought me to Germany. The counterfeit money has been recovered, so the British police will lose interest in the case now, and the man responsible for kidnapping me will escape. I want him arrested. I want to take him back to England to stand trial for what he's done to me.'

A look of recognition crossed the woman's face. I didn't expand on the fact that things hadn't gone that badly for me, but I was under no illusion that they would have done.

'I need to know where he is hiding.' She shrugged her shoulders.

'What is in it for me?' she asked.

I reached into my handbag and slipped the packet of heroin across the table to her. She snatched it up, dropping her hands into her lap to examine it. The man from behind the counter returned with a large hotdog with various toppings. The woman remained still, hiding what was in her hands. Once the café owner had gone, she looked me in the eye.

'Do you have more of this?'

'No.'

'It's not enough,' she replied indignantly.

'I can pay you,' I said, sensing I was winning her over.

'How much?'

'Two-hundred Deutschmarks.'

'Five.'

I hesitated. 'I can only pay you five hundred if you are willing to wait until Monday. I need to get more money from the bank. You can have two hundred now, the rest on Monday.' I removed the last of my money from my purse, holding it at the ready.

'How do I know I can trust you?' she asked slowly.

'You don't. However, I'm trusting you to give me the information I need in return for this.' I turned my hand over to show the German banknotes. As she reached for them, I pulled my hand back. 'Where is he?' I asked firmly.

She sat back in her chair, looked across at the counter, and saw that the café owner was preoccupied. The man had his back turned towards us, so she slipped the packet of heroin inside the front of her dress.

'Where can I find you?' she asked.

'The Westend Strasse hotel.'

She hesitated once again, still trying to make up her mind about telling me more. Finally, she leaned in closer, and I did the same. In a whisper so low I could barely hear what she was saying, she gave me the information I needed.

'Out of the city. Along the river. Close to the Rumpenheimer Schloss, there is a house with a pier which juts out into the river. The owner of the house rents out rooms; no questions asked. New girls are taken there to be broken in before they are brought to the club. Your man may be there.'

I dropped the two-hundred Deutschmarks on the table. 'Meet me at the hotel on Monday morning, and I'll give you the rest of your money.'

I left the café and walked back to my hotel. There was one big problem with my plan. I'd run out of money and had no idea how to get more before the banks opened on Monday, and by then, Blenheim would be long gone. I cursed my over-abundant optimism to get revenge at any cost. This was Frankfurt, not Driffield. I should have known better than to make plans I couldn't stick to. I had no choice. I was going to have to bring Rex in on my plan, no matter how much it irked me to do so.

As I entered the hotel lobby, it was almost midnight. The bar was closing and the night porter was behind the reception desk.

'Good evening, Miss Showers. I trust you have had a pleasant evening? Would you like your key or a nightcap?' he asked.

'Interesting would be a better way of describing it. Has Mr Barker returned yet?'

'No. Not yet. Do you want to leave him a message?'

'No. Not really. I will see him in the morning. What I really need right now is an all-night bank. I've no money left. So I'll just have my key, please.'

'If you are short of cash, Miss Showers, the hotel can provide you with what you need,' replied the night porter, as though it were the most common thing in the world.

'What, right now?' I asked, totally surprised.

'Yes, Miss Showers. Mr Barker deposited a letter of credit with us from the main bank in Frankfurt. All you have to do is sign a receipt, and we can give you as much as you need, within reason, of course. The hotel doesn't hold as much money as a bank does.'

I looked at the man, unable to believe what I was hearing.

'Is there something wrong, Miss Showers?'

'No. No. Everything is fine. Could you let me have a thousand Deutschmarks, right now?'

'I don't have access to the safe, but I do have the key to the cashbox. I'll see how much is in there.' He lifted the black steel box onto the table at the back of the reception area and counted the banknotes inside.

'I can let you have seven hundred if that's okay?'

'Thank you; that will do.' I signed the receipt thanking Rex and the British Secret Service.

'Will you call me a taxi? There's someone I must visit before we leave Frankfurt. Ask the driver to wait; I'm just going up to my room to change first.'

I told the taxi driver to take me to the Rumpenheimer Schloss. I'd changed my clothes for something more practical: flat shoes, slacks, a sweater and a tight-fitting jacket with pockets. A handbag would just get in the way tonight. As the taxi sped through the night, I wondered if I should have left a message for Rex. But it was too late to turn back now and risk losing track of Blenheim. I'd explain everything to Rex in the morning.

The taxi dropped me at the entrance to the drive of the Rumpenheimer Schloss. However, I hadn't expected it to be a grand house with formal gardens. It looked like a fairy Disney castle with its pointed towers and gatehouse.

Passing the grand house and standing at a road junction, I had a choice of turning left or right. Ahead of me I watched slow-moving lights float by beyond a row of trees. I'd found the river. I turned right. The other direction led towards a small group of village houses. The direction took me past in front of the grand house and on into the darkness alongside the river.

Turning up the collar on my jacket and once past the grand house, the road turned into a single-width, country lane below a dike which held back the river. Climbing a set of concrete steps to the top of the dike, I got a better look at the river. It shimmered, black and cold, and smelt of oil and filth. The lights from enormous passing river barges rippled over the river's surface. The sound of the barges' engines rumbled from somewhere deep inside the dark, shadowy watery beasts as they glided by. Staring in amazement at this never-ending flow of barge traffic, I wondered what each vessel carried and where it was going.

Getting back to my mission, I continued on, this time staying on top of the wide riverbank. I'd decided it would be easier to locate the house I was searching for by finding the jetty that jutted out into the river.

It wasn't long before I spotted a row of red lights running out from the bank over the river and hovering above the black water. As I drew closer, the single row of red lights turned into two rows of red lights, and I could see the black outline of a jetty highlighted within the crimson halo of brightness. A small boat with a covered front cockpit was tethered to steps alongside the jetty. Reaching the Jetty, I followed a path down the embankment, across the road and to a house surrounded by a high hedge of dense conifer trees. Wooden gates blocked the drive, keeping what went inside the grounds private. There was no obvious alternative access to the house.

I walked around the outside of the hedge, looking for a weak spot to let me penetrate the house's outer defences. At a rear corner of the garden, a section of the conifer boundary had turned brown and died. It was dry and brittle. The lower branches of the conifers had lost all of their lush green foliage. The branches were easy to snap and break away, making it possible to push them aside so I could get through to the garden. A hundred yards away stood a three-story house in an untidy garden. Light from a room on the ground floor illuminated a patio. French windows stood ajar, and music drifted across the lawn.

Staying in the deep shadow of the hedge, I crept along the edge of the garden towards the house. Once I'd drawn level with the back of the house, I crossed to a dark corner and then made my way to where light spilt out over the patio. Heart beating fast, I listen for voices. I couldn't hear anyone speaking inside the house. The music of an American dance band coming from a wireless made it difficult to know if someone inside was speaking or not. The music stopped, a clipped German voice from the wireless made an announcement, and then a piece of classical music started. It was interrupted by static, followed by short bursts of different types of music. Someone was trying to tune in the wireless set to a different radio station in search of more popular music. The radio went dead. A man with a German accent asked someone else if they would like a last drink before they went to bed.

'Another whisky, please.' The sentence was too short for me to be sure who the speaker was, but his accent was English, not German. The sharp tinkle of glasses clashing together carried through the open doors into the night. Removing Eva's pistol from my pocket, I flicked off the safety switch and marched onto the patio and through the open doors. Blenheim was sitting in an armchair by the fireplace; another, older man was at a cabinet set against the far wall, pouring drinks from a decanter into two glass tumblers.

'Don't move.' I demanded, my gun pointing at the ready. The man pouring the drinks stopped what he was doing. Blenheim's hands gripped the arms of the armchair. Both men's heads snapped around to see where the voice had come from. I took another step into the room and then sidestepped around a table.

'Join Blenheim by the fire,' I instructed the older man with the drinks. With the decanter in one hand and a glass in the other, he slowly edged towards the fireplace. My eyes flicked from the older man to Blenheim as he spoke.

'Well, Miss Showers. I never expected to see you again. Though I have to say, it is a pleasure.'

The sparkle of something flashing towards me made me turn my head and lean sideways as an object hurtled past my face. Losing my balance, I stumble backwards. Both men lunged toward me. I felt the gun jerk in my hand as it fired off a shot. As I continued to fall, I pulled the trigger twice more. The shots were deafening. I didn't know if I was pointing at either of the men, but it made them duck for cover. The small of my back landed against a piece of furniture and stopped me from falling to the floor. I put my left hand down to steady myself, and my right hand with the gun came back to point in the fireplace's direction. Blenheim and the older man rose from the floor unscathed.

'What do you propose to do now, Miss Showers? Shoot us both; because that is what you are going to have to do? You don't think for one minute that we are going to let you arrest us or let you escape this house alive, do you?' announced Blenheim, brushing the creases from the front of his uniform.

I fired another shot into the top of the table that stood between us. Both men flinched back as splinters from the table shot up toward them. Blenheim recovered first and gave a sneering smile.

'Oops, you appear to have killed the table, Miss Showers. How many bullets do you have left? Do you know?'

'Enough,' I snapped back. 'Put your hands up and sit next to the fireplace.'

Both men complied with my instructions.

'Have you thought everything through, Miss Showers? Come, join us in a farewell drink?' continued Blenheim in his condescending manner.

'Telephone for the police,' I replied.

'Good luck with that. The telephone is in the hall. Should I go or my friend Peter? What do you expect us both to do? Sit here nicely while you telephone them?'

I looked around for an idea. Spotting the cord that held the patio door curtains back, I sidestepped back to where I entered the room. Blenheim jumped to his feet as I reach for the cord with my left hand. I fired another shot, this time into the chair where he had been sitting. It stopped him from advancing.

'That's another one you've used up.' He returned to his seat. I tossed the curtain cord to the older man.

'Tie his hands behind his back,' I ordered.

'Nein,' he snapped back at me.

'Oh, dear. He said no. The ball is now in your court, Miss Showers,' interjected Blenheim. 'I hope you are keeping count of how many shots you've fired.' He continued. 'Do you have the mettle to shoot us, Miss Showers? Have you enough bullets left to stop both of us? Tell me, Miss Showers. Do you know what it is like to shoot a person - dead? End their hopes and dreams for the future; deprive their loved ones of saying a last, fond farewell to their mother, father, wife or brother?'

'I know you do... or do you?' I responded, playing Blenheim at his own game. 'Eva, the woman you shot on the stairs: she will live. Were you trying to kill her, or did you lose your nerve at the last minute and hesitate, and that is the real reason she is still alive?'

'You will never know, Miss Showers, but remember; I did shoot her.'

Whilst I was distracted by Blenheim's equivocal dubiety, the older man lunged at me. Seeing him suddenly move from the corner of my eye, I fired in his direction. He screamed in pain, falling to the floor. As I stared at the man on the floor, Blenheim followed up with a lunge of his own. I fired; the bullet must have missed him because the next thing I knew, he was on top of me, trying to knock the gun from my hand. I lifted my left leg, brought it around between us, and then forced it against his neck, pushing him backwards and sideways. He fell heavily, hitting his head against the corner of his armchair. It was enough to daze him and allow me to recover my control and push the muzzle of the gun up under his chin.

'I can't miss at this range. Do you fancy finding out how many bullets I've got left now?' Moments later, I was surrounded by uniformed men, all of them shouting at the tops of their voices and pointing guns.

Chapter Twenty

Sunday

It was gone noon when I awoke in my hotel room. I had been troubled by nightmares and still felt tired as well as grumpy and strained. The memories of the previous evening tumbled confusingly through my mind as I tried to piece together everything that had happened. I gave up. I'd think about it later. Suddenly feeling hot and stuffy, I pushed back the blankets and took a deep breath. I needed a cup of tea. Proper tea, made the English way. The kind my mother made. I let out a sigh. How was I going to explain all this to her? I imagined the look I was going to get from Daddy. I was going to have to spend the next six months having Sunday lunch with them so they could keep a check on what I was doing. I let out another sigh. Come to think of it, that didn't sound too bad, for now anyway. Staring up at the ceiling, I wondered if Rex was out of bed yet. He'd stayed at the police station questioning Blenheim and his friend whilst I was driven back here.

Swinging my feet around to the floor, I sat on the edge of the bed, the need for a cup of tea getting me up. After a shower (there wasn't enough space in the small bathroom for a bath), I dressed and went down to the hotel bar; lunch was just finishing in the restaurant.

'Tea, with milk,' I sat on the barstool waiting for it to arrive. A tray containing a cup and saucer, a milk jug, a sugar bowl, and a tiny teapot were deposited in front of me. What's wrong with a proper-sized teapot? My mind screamed at the barmaid.

'Thank you; put it on my bill, please.'

I poured the almost clear hot water into my cup, stopped and then looked inside the teapot to check if there was any tea in it at all. A single tea bag floated on the surface. I gave it a poke with the teaspoon to encourage it to do its duty, but it stood up to my brutality and refused to give in. I filled my cup and added a little drizzle of milk. It tasted like hot water with milk. So, I gave in and ordered coffee.

As I looked around for a sign of Rex, the hotel receptionist came over and handed me a slip of paper. 'A message for you from Mr Barker,' she said and then walked away.

Reading the note, it simply said, *Be ready to leave by 5pm. See you later. Rex.* I screwed up the note and put it in the teapot. 'That'll teach you,' I scolded the teapot.

With time on my hands to use up, I visited Eva at the hospital. She was still in bed but looking a lot brighter than the last time I'd seen her.

'How is the investigation going?' she asked after we had exchanged greetings. I couldn't stop myself from smiling.

'That well,' she let out a little titter of laughter at my excitement.

'You already know the counterfeit money was recovered from the nightclub. Well, I got Rex to ask Inspector Everhart for permission to sit in on the interviews with the women that worked at the club. As you can imagine, the Inspector intimidated the hell out of them and they told him nothing of importance. So I followed them after they were released from the police station and managed, with a bit of bribery, to get one of the women to tell me where the gang's safe house was located. That's when I went to investigate it. After getting into the garden at the back of the house, I got close enough to hear Blenheim and another man talking in the living room. As the patio doors were open, I stepped through and arrested them.'

'And they just let you? They didn't try to escape?' said Eva, sarcastically.

'Well, I did have your gun. I picked it up from the stairwell after you were shot.'

'Good, I'm pleased you found it. I'll be questioned about what happened to my gun when I get out of here. Do the police have it?'

'Yes. Though I haven't told you what happened next. I had the attention of Blenheim and his friend, but no way of calling the police or Rex to come and help me. Blenheim started talking to me; trying to frighten me; to convince me I wouldn't succeed in arresting him. I'm afraid to say he did plant some doubts in my mind as to whether or not I could do it or not. Anyway, Blenheim and his friend made the mistake of tackling me too early. Shots were fired; the owner of the house was shot, and Blenheim managed to wrestle me to the ground. Only, I've been taking Judo lessons back in England. I'm not very good yet, but I was able to surprise Blenheim and threw him off balance just enough for me to regain the advantage. That's when Rex and the police broke into the house.'

When Rex didn't find me at the hotel he'd returned from the police station, he asked the night porter if he'd seen me. The porter told Rex about the taxi. The taxi firm told Rex the address I'd asked to be taken to, and the taxi driver said he'd seen me turn right at the river. After that, it was just a matter of searching the area where the taxi had dropped me off. It helped Rex to find me when I started shooting. With the patio doors open and it being late at night, the sound of the shots carried over a wide area. Rex and the police followed the sound of the shots to the house.'

'You were lucky. What would have happened if Rex hadn't followed you? You'd be dead.'

'Maybe. But I know Rex; we've known each other for a long time. We worked together on another case a few months ago. He likes to look after me. The trouble with Rex is that he's arrogant. If he wasn't such a so-and-so he'd be quite adorable. You see, Rex likes to be in charge all the time, and that infuriates me. I'm not like other women who want a husband and children, not yet anyway. I want to see the world; do things my way; be free.'

'What happened to the man you shot?'

'Oh, him.' I paused before continuing. Thinking back to what Blenheim had said; he was right. I'd never shot anyone or anything before, and I didn't know if I'd be able to do it again, not deliberately and coldly shoot anyone.

'He's here in this hospital. The bullet hit him in the head. The doctors don't know if he will live or not, or even if he'll be able to talk if he does recover.' The image of the older man lying in a hospital bed, fighting for his life, came to mind. Even though I'd been fighting for my life, I still felt guilty for what I'd done to him. Silence fell between us for a moment.

'As a police officer, it's the challenge I face every day,' Eva interjected into the silence. 'You did the right thing. He would have killed you if he could. Just keep telling yourself; it was you or him.'

A nurse arrived and began to check on Eva.

'I'd better go. Thank you for looking after me.'

'I wish you luck with all your dreams for the future. Remember me when you get home, and if you ever come back to Frankfurt, look me up.'

'You can count on it,' I said cheerfully.

Back at the hotel, I was packing the small suitcase I'd bought for taking home my new clothes when I found the clothes and RAF base pass I'd borrowed from Carol at the British airfield. Setting them aside, I finished packing my own clothes. There was a knock on the bedroom door.

'Come in.'

'All packed and ready to go?' asked Rex enthusiastically.

'Yes.' I closed the lid on my suitcase and locked it. 'Would you be a dear and carry that for me?' Rex willingly obliged whilst I picked up Carol's clothes to take downstairs.

'What are you going to do with them?' asked Rex.

'I'm going to ask the hotel to send them back to Carol at RAF Frankfurt; her name is on her pass.'

'Better not, security and all that. An RAF base pass is worth a lot of money on the black market. We'll drop them off at her home ourselves; we'll be flying home from RAF Frankfurt.'

When we dropped off Carol's clothes, base pass and the money I'd taken, it was an embarrassing exchange. I felt bad for taking them, but Carol barely remembered me and thought that she'd lost the pass and money somewhere on the airbase while she was drunk. She hadn't even noticed the clothes had gone missing from her wardrobe.

It had been a whirlwind two and a half days in Frankfurt. I was exhausted and pleased to be going home. The aeroplane we flew home in was smaller and more comfortable than I had expected. Rex explained that it was used by RAF VIPS and British diplomats on trips to Europe. He tried to make conversation, but I'd closed my eyes and with the gentle movement of the aeroplane and my general fatigue, I was whisked away to Neverland.

Rex woke me up just before the plane landed at RAF Driffield. When I looked out of the window, it was dark. It was also cold, but at least I was home.

'I don't have a key to get into the house,' I exclaimed.

'Don't worry, I had your father leave his copy of your front door key under the plant pot next to the door.'

'I don't have a plant pot next to my front door,' I replied, somewhat confused.

'You do now,' laughed Rex.

It was only now that I really missed them, my handbag and all the personal things that were in it. My car keys, my perfume, the handkerchief aunt Violet had given me with her initials on it. All the little items that made the bag mine.

Rex drove me home, and we found Daddy's key under a potted geranium. Before Rex said 'Goodnight,' he said he would call on me in the morning. His Colonel had requested a meeting with us both. I wondered what he would be like. Then I remembered my parents. I bet the conversation with the Colonel wouldn't be as hard as the one I was going to have to have with my parents. Leaving my case in the hall, late as it was, I telephoned my parents to let them know I was safely back in England and that I would pay them a visit the following afternoon.

Rex knocked on my front door at nine o'clock the following morning. I was ready for him. I'd had a good night's sleep and had awoken at my usual time for a workday. I stepped outside. The sky was overcast and the day cool. Rex had the hood up on his Jaguar, and I was eager to get in and sit in its soft leather seat. I didn't wait for Rex to open the door for me. Some of that formality was now behind us, after Frankfurt. Rex pulled away from my house, leaving a shower of pebbles in his wake as he gunned the car down the road, and I got to feel the thrill of the car's acceleration forcing me back into my seat.

'Thank you.' I said out of the blue.

'For what?'

'You know; for what happened in Frankfurt.' I felt irked at having to explain myself. I looked at him as he drove; he was carrying a big smug smile. Inwardly, I cursed myself for feeding his ego and remained silent for the rest of the journey.

At GCHQ Scarborough, Rex directed me to an office close to the entrance of the main building. It was sparsely decorated with only a few military paintings hung on the walls. A polished table with a few chairs around it stood on a carpet that had seen better days, and a long sideboard was set beneath the windows on which stood trays with cups and saucers, etc.

'Take a seat,' said Rex. 'I'll let the Colonel know you're here.' He picked up a telephone and dialled a number. 'Miss Showers is in room one.' He put the phone down. 'The Colonel won't be long.' Rex took the seat next to mine. He didn't speak but looked at his hands as he twiddled his thumbs. It was the first time that I had seen Rex show any sign of nervousness.

When the Colonel arrived, Rex got to his feet. The Colonel waved for him to sit down as he moved around to the head of the table. A woman in an RAF sergeant's uniform followed him into the room, sitting next to him. I didn't recognise her at first, but then it hit me. She was Mrs Hood. I glared at Rex. He picked up on my recognition of her.

'Later,' he whispered to me.

'Good morning, Miss Showers; it is a pleasure to meet you at last. Rex has told me a lot about you.'

I gave Rex another steely stare, wondering what he'd been saying about me.

'Thank you, Colonel. I take it you want to hear my side of the story and all about what happened in Frankfurt.'

'Yes, please, Miss Showers, if you wouldn't mind. Rex has provided me with a report on the case. However, it would be useful to hear about what happened from your perspective.'

I spent the next two hours going over everything of importance that had happened to me since I received the first forged five-pound note in Driffield. Ending my explanation with Rex and the German police arriving at the house on the outskirts of Frankfurt.

'Thank you, Miss Showers. I knew I was right to get Rex to bring you in on this case. You know, Rex didn't want you involved,' said the Colonel. 'Miss Thornwick, if you please?'

I shot Rex another questioning look as Miss Thornwick rose and left the room. Why had the Colonel wanted me involved and why hadn't Rex wanted to bring me in on the case?

'May I ask a question, Colonel?'

'Certainly, Miss Showers, fire away.'

'Why did you involve me in your case? Surely you have enough personnel to do your work for you?'

'Yes, we do. But, you see, there are times when it is more expedient to keep a low profile and watch others do the work. They tackle things differently from the way we operate. You disarm people with your charm and have a habit of flushing out people we may miss in our hurry to get the job done.'

'Does that make me a spy as well?'

'No, Miss Showers. It makes you a friend.'

'Do you normally let your friends get kidnapped during a case?'

'All friendships have their highs and lows. You were simply moving along with the case quicker than we anticipated.'

'When did you first know I'd gone missing?'

'A farmer complained to the police about your car in his field. The police traced the car to its owner, and he told them that he had leased it to you. The police were under orders to report everything involving you to Rex. After we checked at your office, home and with your parents and no one had seen you, we knew you were in trouble. The car disappeared with still no sightings of you. That's when we searched your house and your office. We interviewed everyone you'd spoken to and, apart from telling us what we already knew; they weren't a lot of help. It wasn't until we received your telephone call from Frankfurt that things started to fall into place. Once we were on the trail of the counterfeit money, the Home Office, the Foreign Office and the Treasury authorised me to use whatever resources I needed to recover the money and arrest the people involved.'

'But why did they send English five-pound notes to Germany?' I asked.

'The East Germans run several businesses in West Germany that border on the unlawful. They planned on using those businesses to launder some of the cash. The rest would be used by their agents here in Britain and in West Germany. Possibly to get their agents to visit all the banks in Germany and exchange the forged English banknotes for Deutschmarks, flooding the West German banks with counterfeit money. Most German bank tellers wouldn't be able to spot a forged fiver. When the forgeries were discovered, the German banks would complain to the Bank of England. Then, when the news of the counterfeit five-pound notes hit the international newspapers, there would be a run on the pound and the British economy would be ruined just at a time when it is recovering from the war. It would set back British redevelopment years. But, thanks to you... well, I don't need to say more.'

'But what happens if someone else tries to do the same thing, Colonel?'

'It no longer matters, Miss Showers. The current version of the five-pound note is to be phased out and replaced with a new design next year.'

Miss Thornwick returned, followed by two men in white jackets carrying trays of tea and sandwiches.

'A little light refreshment before you go, Miss Showers,' continued the Colonel.

'Do I get paid for my services to Queen and country, Colonel?'

The question seemed to catch the Colonel off guard.

'Let me see. There is the matter of your hotel bill in Frankfurt. The expenses you drew at the hotel. These all have to be accounted for. The government is not made of money,' said the Colonel.

'Colonel; I've just saved the country from bankruptcy. Surely some recompense for my work is justifiable?'

'Very well, Miss Showers. I will speak to the minister about it.'

After lunch, Rex drove me to my parent's house.

'Would you like me to go in with you?' He asked.

'No, thank you. This is something I need to do on my own. I'll see you later, maybe.'

I'd no sooner finished speaking when my parents appeared at the front door of the house.

'I'd better go,' I continued.

'Give me a ring when you have a day free; we'll go somewhere nice,' said Rex as I got out of the car. I didn't answer him; I just closed the car door and walked away. All my attention was on my mother and the tears rolling down her cheeks.

As Mummy encased me in a bear hug, I could feel her body trembling.

'I'm sorry, Mummy.' I heard Rex drive away.

Inside the house, I explained what had happened to me over the past few days. Only, I left out all the bits that included GCHQ, MI5, being kidnapped and shooting someone. I told her I had been hot on the heels of the counterfeiting gang and following them to Frankfurt without having the time to let her know what I was doing. Mummy seemed to buy the story, but I could read the doubts and questions on Daddy's face.

'Daddy, let's have lunch together one day this week, just like we used to do?'

He relaxed. 'I can make Wednesday?' he replied.

'That's settled then.' 'Come on Mummy, you haven't put the kettle on yet and I'm dying for a cup of tea. Have you any cake? I'll tell you what; you sit here with Daddy and I'll make the tea.'

We spent the rest of the day talking; mostly me apologising and reassuring them I wouldn't do anything so foolish and dangerous again. But being in my parent's house reminded me of someone who was missing; it was Holly. She was going to be the next person I visited. I needed a friendly face to share a jolly day out with.

Now you can buy any of these books directly from Steven.

Prices and availability subject to change without notice.